I0831377

The Eighth Master is a work of fiction. All events, names, characters, places, and businesses (except as noted below), are the creation of the author and are used fictitiously. Any resemblance to actual persons, living or dead, or actual incidents is coincidental.

Vaux le Vicomte is located in Maincy, France and is open to the public.

Sir Bannister Fletcher's 19th Edition (1987) of *A History of Architecture,* was published by Butterworths, London, United Kingdom and is out of print.

The author acknowledges (in no particular order) the trademark status and trademark owners of the following wordmarks mentioned in this work of fiction:

Google® is a registered trademark/workmark of Google, Incorporated
Wikipedia® is a registered wordmark of Wikimedia Foundation
Gmail® is a registered trademark of Google, Incorporated
Hertz® is a registered trademark of Hertz Equipment Rental Corporation
The Saint Regis™ San Francisco is a member of Starwood Hotels & Resorts
The Grand San Francisco Hyatt® is a Hyatt Corporation Hotel
Ferrari® is a registered trademark of Ferrari S.p.A. Esercizio Fabbriche Automobili E Corse
Mercedes-Benz® is a registered trademark of Daimler AG
BMW® is a registered trademark of Bayerische Motoren Werke AG
Porsche® is a registered trademark of Dr. Ing. h.c. F. Porsche AG
Lego® is a registered trademark of the Lego Group
Fortune® is a registered trademark of TIME, Incorporated
Forbes® is a registered trademark of Forbes Media LLC
Bloomberg® is a registered trademark of Bloomberg Finance, LLP
CNBC® is a registered trademark of NBCUniversal Media, LLC
Safeway® is a registered trademark of Safeway, Incorporated
Uber is a trademark in dispute between Uber Promotions and Uber Technologies
Sotheby's® is a registered trademark of Sotheby's
NASDAQ® is a trademark of NASDAQ OMX Group, Inc
Wharton® is a trademark of The Trustees of the University of Pennsylvania
tripadvisor® is a registered trademark of TripAdvisor LLC
Skype® is a trademark of Microsoft Corporation
K-Mart® is a trademark of Sears Brands LLC
Lloyd's® is a registered trademark of the Society of Lloyd's

The good quotes come from a great website. Check it out: *Brainyquotes.com.* The others speak for themselves.

Library of Congress Control Number: 2019914251

Illustrations created by Baumberger Studio, Portland, Oregon

ISBN: 978-0-578-57622-6

For Bjne

«»«»«»

Do not wait for tomorrow.

«»«»«»

To those that read, thank you.

«»«»«»

And with apologies to Thelonious Monk . . .

"Talking about music is like dancing about architecture.
In my case it's the other way around, but it's mostly what I do."
-- JD Rutherford

Pasadena, California

The Eighth Master

A Novel

«»«»«»

JD Rutherford

"Never talk to a client about architecture. Talk to him about his children. That is simply good politics. He will not understand what you have to say about architecture most of the time."

-- Ludwig Mies van der Rohe

Chapter One

Thick, damp fog enveloped the woods on the eastern slope of Howell Mountain. Gnarled trunks of moss-covered trees disappeared into the gloomy mist of the late afternoon, their leaf canopies creating ghostly shapes that hovered with vague menace over large granite boulders and manzanita shrubs.

A dark SUV rolled to a nearly silent stop in a deserted parking lot on the edge of the forested recreation area of Las Posadas State Forest. The four occupants of the vehicle emerged, closing the doors silently. They peered in all directions into the quiet, grey mist looking for anyone else in the area that might have observed their arrival.

On a sunny day the parking lot would have been full of cars, having been abandoned by their occupants for the trails that wound through the forested hillside. But in the fog, with evening nearing, the lot was empty. One of the vehicle's former occupants, dressed in bright, tight fitting riding gear of the sort that cycling enthusiasts wear to reduce wind drag, removed a mountain bike from a rack attached to the rear bumper of the vehicle. He then opened the rear hatch and the other three individuals each removed a duffle bag. Two were dressed completely in black clothing, while the third wore camouflaged fatigues. They performed a quick radio check and then three of the group moved silently up the path leading into the park, leaving the fourth to shift his weight standing guard by the vehicle in his biking attire.

Within moments, the group was out of sight. They walked silently for about a kilometer up the main path, before splitting up at a fork in the trail. The two wearing black continued up the trail for another 500 meters, while the third veered off almost immediately disappearing into the brush.

Fifteen minutes later, the man in the camo gear dropped to his knees in a large patch of tall grass. He had donned a hat covered in dried grass, making him nearly disappear to anyone who might have been watching. He then removed camouflaged netting from his duffle bag, draping it over his back and legs. Covered, he was indistinguishable from the grass that surrounded him. He lay on his stomach in the grass and peered through a pair of high powered binoculars, scanning a road down slope of his position.

The hillside and the downward slope were enveloped in a murky fog. The eerie shape of a large oak tree loomed up out of the greyness at his left at about 500 meters. Rows of grape vines curved away from his position following the contour of the slope, and were quickly swallowed in the gloom. His task was made more difficult owing to the lack of visibility. The road he was watching was barely visible through mist shrouded tree trunks and leaf canopies marking its edge.

"Unit one in position," he said softly into a microphone attached to head gear and a radio in his vest.

He waited for several minutes before getting a response.

"Unit three in position," came the whispered response.

It was less than a minute later when he heard the final member of the team check in.

"Unit two in position."

With his binoculars, he scanned the road until headlights of an approaching vehicle caught his eye.

"Traffic," he said into his radio. He watched for a moment. "Negative ID."

It grew darker and then seemed to grow colder. An hour passed with several more negative sightings.

"Traffic," he said again finally.

He watched the vehicle intently as it slowed and turned onto a dirt road below where he lay that led to a closed gate. A figure emerged from the car and was illuminated in the vehicle's headlights as the person unlocked and opened the gate.

"Target in sight . . . alone."

"Unit two. Copy."

"Unit three. Copy."

"Target in sight," came the response a few moments later from unit two.

The car with its solitary occupant drove slowly up the hill and came to a stop in a large open area. The engine and headlights were shut off. A man got out of the car and looked around the silent surroundings. Deciding that he was alone, he walked to the front of the car and opened the trunk and removed a package.

"Package moving," came the radio response from unit two.

"I see it," came the reply from unit three.

«»«»«»

Everyone seems to have an opinion about architecture. What is good; what is outrageous; what is a waste; and definitely, what is ugly.

As an architect, Neil Thornton met people on an almost daily basis who felt free to share with him their critique of the built environment and sometimes, his own work. He often wondered how many scientists or surgeons experienced anything remotely similar. The subjective nature of "art" is no doubt something that separated his experience with a public that is largely architecturally illiterate from the experience of other professions.

So he was not surprised on a bright October morning to find himself engaged in idle conversation about the state of the architectural profession and "lame ass architects" with a "gentleman" he had just met. Thankfully, David Johnsson was not his client and the monstrosity he was building was not one of his projects. As Neil's architectural practice was regional and centered in a small community north of San Francisco, the likelihood that he might have been involved with this project was more than a remote possibility. Not that he would have minded having a huge commission such as this one, it was just that this project was in such poor taste.

They had agreed to meet at the construction site of David Johnsson's emerging estate.

"I'm sorry to change the subject, but what time did you say the project superintendent planned to get here?" Neil asked.

The man had been sharing his disdain for architects and had moved on to regaling Neil with a very emphatic and opinionated dissertation about what was wrong with the local planning and building safety department. As one might expect, anything that stood in his way or required him to change his plans or spend additional money was beyond problematic.

"He was supposed to be here already," he huffed. He glanced back down the long and rutted dirt road that would one day lead from the edge of his property, up the hill, to the point where they were standing.

"Do you have a key to the gate? We could go on in and poke around," Neil suggested hopefully.

David Johnsson didn't hesitate. "Of course I do!" he barked. "He'll find us."

The construction site was situated at the top of the slope above a country road that skirted one edge of his property. Structural framing was silhouetted against a deep blue sky. Tall stands of pine were set back from the building site on either side, leaving room for formal gardens that had yet to be constructed.

The house, if it could be called that as its emerging mass more closely resembled something the size of a hotel, was being constructed on a site that had been graded in the midst of recently planted vineyards. The view down into the valley on this fine day was impressive to say the least.

They had both parked next to a locked gate in a temporary construction fence that surrounded the construction site. Neil's old, faded BMW was juxtaposed against a very clean, very shiny, and very, very expensive 1964 Scuderia Ferrari 275 Le Mans. When Neil had arrived, the gate down by the road was open, and he had driven up the hill to a dirt lot on the south side of the area that would be a formal forecourt. The concrete walls and exposed concrete deck of an underground parking structure had been fenced off inside the construction perimeter. The entrance to an underground car park disappeared on the left, outside the perimeter of the fence. A pile of construction materials had been stacked in front of the gaping hole to discourage entering the dark opening, but clearly, would not deter entry.

When Neil turned off his car, David was still in his car talking on his mobile phone and gesturing very emphatically. Neil checked e-mail on his phone and waited for David to conclude his conversation. When it seemed like he had ended the call, Neil got out of his automobile, only to realize David had taken or placed another call. So he walked up to the gate and peeked through the fence.

The entire area had been graded prior to construction, but was now bumpy and rutted. Weeds were encroaching from the edges. Piles of construction materials were scattered on top of the concrete deck that would eventually be finished to be the forecourt. Other piles of materials and debris were located around the building and up against the fence. Piles is probably too kind a word. "Mounds" would be a more apt description. Wind had scattered loose construction debris across the area and up against the fence. It was a most untidy scene.

Though the construction site was a mess, a partially constructed building of im pressive proportions rose from the clutter. The steel structure and exterior metal framing were in place. The roof sheathing was progressing, but was unfinished. Probably 20 percent of the rigid exterior insulation panels were in place starting on the south end. A couple of rolls of water proofing membrane had been installed, but were tearing free and flapping in the wind. A portion of the exterior wall had been mocked-up with the finish stone cladding that would presumably cover the entire façade one day. Beyond that, there was very little else in the way of exterior cladding to be seen. However, through the open exterior framing, a dense forest of interior studs merged into a shiny metallic mass. Several pallets of cementitious board had been placed through a temporary opening in the exterior wall on the first floor, but it didn't look from a distance like much of it had started to be put in place.

Upon turning back towards their parked vehicles, Neil was presented with a dramatic view down a gentle slope, framed by distant pines and oaks, to the valley beyond.

This was Neil's first time to meet David Johnsson, but his reputation had preceded him. He knew David was a "retired" hedge fund manager from New York that had taken a liking to wine country and planned to create a winery with some of his reputed wealth. New arrivals to the valley wanting to jump into the wine business were typically greeted with some skepticism by the long-term locals that had generations of experience growing grapes and wealth. Those that came to the area with new-found wealth, intent on early retirement to engage in the romantic pursuit of crafting fine wine, were eventually absorbed into the mix, if they had enough money to play the game at a high level.

David Johnsson did not seem to lack anything in the area of financial resources. Nor did he lack in vision, persistence, confidence, or expensive attorneys. He had made incredible progress in what was normally a very slow process. He had barged ahead repeatedly, challenging anyone and anything that stood in his way with layers of consultants, paid experts, piles of reports, and a lot of bluster and frequent threats of endless litigation. Charm and finesse, however, were constantly in short supply. While he had achieved much in a short time, he had also left a wide path of destruction in his wake and more than a few people who hoped to witness a catastrophic failure of some sort. The ultimate payback would, of course, be a shoddy label. Anyone with enough money can plant grape vines, build a crushing room and a cellar, and eventually bottle some "wine". But fine wine, that was more elusive. Even assholes could manage to do it, if they had enough money to buy the right grapes. And many assumed correctly that David was that kind of asshole. But still they hoped that some Karmic force would reestablish equilibrium and dispense the needed comeuppance.

The project had not yet earned the title of winery, but he was making progress. As with all controversial projects, David Johnsson had achieved a high degree of visibility. Everyone seemed to know about his project. The local press provided regular updates and, though he threatened to sue each time it happened, photographs from a drone and even close-up photos by someone trespassing on the property found their way on-line and into print. So Neil was not unfamiliar with him or his project, but had not been involved, and given the anger about David's aggressive approach to achieving his goals, Neil was fine with that.

David Johnsson had purchased a beautiful 854 acre parcel on the east side of the Silverado Trail. The property was reached from a side road that wound its way up the hill, cutting through acres and acres of vineyards, tree covered glens, and grass land strewn with massive, California live oak trees. An unpretentious metal gate, in a rustic fence, dating to the 1940's, was all that kept anyone with an interest from entering the property that straddled the ridge affording views of Lake Berryessa to the east, and the Napa Valley and the small town of St. Helena to the west. The construction project had been approved two years previously, after a combined four and a half years of planning, design, and securing entitlements. Getting a new winery approved is no small feat and a costly undertaking. The forest had been cleared, stumps removed, perimeter fences put in place, a reservoir built, irrigation systems installed and vines had been planted. David had the wealth and ego to aggressively pursue the process with the right consultants and, in time, he had won the needed approvals to start construction with some important restrictions that he was not pleased with. People with money, in Neil's experience, don't like being told "no". And David Johnsson was in a hurry. Six and a half years was well past the end of his patience.

The morning that David had called him, Neil had been sitting in his office wondering how he was going to pay his mortgage, without dipping further into his savings. Shelley, Neil's part-time assistant, had taken the call and had put David on hold briefly as she checked with Neil to see if he wanted to take the call. In typical receptionist mode, she had asked David what his call related to and if Mr. Thornton was expecting the call.

"No. But I will make it worth his time," David had said. Shelley needed no further encouragement to forward the call. Every now and then she managed to keep a sales representative or a broker from charging through the gate and getting to Neil, but if a caller sounded like a possible client, she always put them through.

David had immediately asked if Neil could come by his "winery" for a quick look, explaining that it was under construction and that he was not satisfied with the direction things seemed to be going.

Shelley could hear Neil's side of the conversation and was aware, along with everyone else in the Valley, of the "big project on the hill". So while Neil worked out the details with David, she googled him to see if he was really all that.

She was immediately bombarded with articles from Forbes, Bloomberg, CNBC, Fortune and a host of other outlets each with their own little bit of trivia about David Johnsson. Almost none of them had anything to do with this "house." They all were speculation on the next moves of his hedge fund, what charity he was supporting, what art he was buying, where he was seen vacationing and the like.

Shelley had been a finance major in college so the piece on his purchase of a Michelangelo Merisi da Caravaggio did not mean that much to her, except for the reference to the purchase price. She clicked on the article and scanned it quickly. He had purchased the piece at a Sotheby's auction in New York the previous spring, setting a new record for a piece by Caravaggio. She was impressed by the price, if nothing else.

She could hear Neil ask David about his relationship with his architect, as it is an old school no-no to encroach on another architect's relationship with a client. David seemed to have informed Neil that he had fired them.

That told Neil something, and it wasn't good.

"They were worse than incompetent!" David had blurted out over the phone, "They were French! I thought these guys were better than they turned out."

"I had this buddy at Cranston. He built a house in the south of France a couple of years ago. I saw it and liked it. So I figured the firm he used could do this. I flew to Paris twice and they sent a small army of people out here four years ago. But I haven't seen them out here again, so I booted them. The design is okay, I guess. But I want them to be here when I need them and when I ask about getting out here, I just get the run around." Maybe their reticence to flying all the way to California had something to do with his dismissive attitude, Neil thought.

Neil didn't know what "Cranston" was, but assumed it was some investment house on Wall Street. It was unusual that an architect would not be highly motivated to be engaged in observing the construction of a significant commission. Indeed, an architect's professional liability insurance in the United States basically required it. Maybe it was different in France, but someone in the firm had to have been licensed in California, or else they had to have partnered with a California architect. There was probably more to their reticence than he was letting on, but it wasn't necessarily relevant, so Neil didn't ask.

The firm David hired was located in Paris and making periodic trips to California would get expensive in a hurry. But for projects of this scale, the owner would routinely reimburse travel expenses. Neil knew an architect that was flown halfway across the country in their client's private jet for weekly meetings during the construction of their 34,000 square foot weekend "cabin". This, of course, followed frequent hunting and fishing expeditions planned to coincide with trips to personally source individual timbers from the client's private forest preserve.

If you have enough wealth, things that seem daunting to most people become trivial details. So distance and cost were not likely relevant to this situation. Neither was the fact that it was a "French" firm.

Neil asked what stage of construction the project had achieved, and David said that was part of the problem. The contractor was claiming he was well past 50% complete and submitting invoices for payment that seemed over the top. So he wanted Neil to come out and take a look and give him his opinion. He said he needed to find someone to review the work before he sued the contractor, so he had called Neil. He wanted Neil to write a report that would allow him to "sue the contractor's ass into bankruptcy." It looked like a good fight was directly ahead of David and that he relished the prospect of putting another roadblock behind him and in its proper place.

Neil told David he would only be able to include the facts as he observed them and that project completion was not an exact science. David didn't seem pleased with Neil's answer, but he let it go.

When Neil asked who was handling construction issues on David's behalf, David said he was. Neil asked him if he had some previous construction experience and got an earful. David didn't really have any experience, but he was well-financed. He wasn't the only one with an attitude. Neil just kept his to himself.

Neil probably should have walked away right there, as his instinct was yelling at him to do, but business at his practice had been a little slow and he was between projects. He tried to wiggle off the hook by rather lamely complimenting David on his experience and telling him that he didn't think he needed his input. Something about Neil's response seemed to galvanize David's resolve to retain him.

"Look. This won't take much time, and I'll make it worth your while."

"All right," Neil responded, "but in cases like this I work hourly. I need a small retainer in advance to cover our first meeting." He had learned the hard way that when he did not know the client, and something about the job seemed like it was going to be high-maintenance, he needed to ask for money up front. If the potential client paid it, fine. If not, their refusal affirmed his desire to walk away. More often than not they went elsewhere, and that is why he drove a used BMW instead of a new one.

David asked how much Neil needed, and was told his hourly rate was $200 and that he needed a cashier's check for $1,000. David laughed and said, "Sure, sure."

When Neil hung up the phone Shelley gave out a little hoot. "Woo-hoo! Sounds like we got something good!" she called from her office.

"Maybe," was Neil's less than enthusiastic response. "Or else it's a goose chase for another needy client that wants some free advice, but doesn't want to pay for it. I don't need that type of client at the moment."

"Are you going to do it?" Shelley asked.

"Of course," Neil said with a tinge of self-loathing. Architects joke that they are the second oldest profession and less well compensated than the first. In his case he thought the term "slut" might be more appropriate. Which meant he mostly gave it away.

"So what does he want? I just looked him up. He seems to be fabulously wealthy," she said.

"Oh, he's loaded all right," Neil said. "That's what makes what he's going to pay me a joke, based on the jam he thinks he's in. But I'll see what he needs. It might turn into something bigger."

David sent the check to Neil the next day via a local courier service. In retrospect, Neil should have asked for many thousands more.

«»«»«»

So here Neil was, the following Tuesday, waiting for David's contractor to show up and walk them through the building. It had been a beautiful summer and early fall. The rhythm of the Valley was slowing as the harvest was winding down. The tourists were gone. The weather had changed with a few cool foggy days, but the chill and drizzle of winter had not yet arrived. It was the window between seasons when there was a sense of relief that the harvest was in, most of the first crush was complete and everyone could breathe a little easier and slow down.

David finally got off the phone and began regaling Neil with his philosophy of life (money) and wine making and women and architecture.

It was at this point that Neil asked if David had a key and could they go ahead and enter the building.

There was no one there except for the pigeons that occasionally flew in and out of the many openings of the building's exterior.

When Neil asked where the construction crews were, David said that because he had not paid the contractor's last pay application, the contractor had stopped work and that his attorneys were spooling up for a fight. Neither of these bits of information were really surprising. When Neil asked how long the project had been stopped, David said it had been about 3 weeks.

Neil didn't tell him it looked as though the project had been abandoned for significantly longer than just three weeks.

Before they entered the site, Neil asked for, and David produced, a large roll of construction drawings for the building. It was a full-size set and included 447 sheets. Neil set the drawings on the hood of his car with an audible "humph." Large sets of full-size drawings get heavy, and this set was heavy. He removed several over-sized rubber bands and unrolled the set. He noted immediately that it had been stamped and signed by a licensed California architect, but judging from the name, he might have been local, or based in Paris. The architect's name on the stamp appeared to be François Pierre Beauchamp. The only address and phone number listed was for a firm located in Paris.

He flipped through the initial architectural sheets. The set was labeled "Volume 1A". The title sheet included a nice rendering of a French chateau that looked vaguely familiar and indicated that a Volume 1B covered additional engineering disciplines, while a second volume covered a separate winery building, and a third volume covered a natatorium and several support structures.

With the set opened like a book, it covered the entire hood of Neil's car with the edges of each end hanging over opposing fenders. Neil had seen renderings of the building in the local paper, but he had not really paid too much attention. He tended to favor high modernism, rather than most forms of neoclassicism and so had not really found the project to be of interest other than for its size and the controversy it was generating. Now, as he looked at the set, no matter what his personal opinion about the style of the design, he could not help but be impressed with the scale of the project.

Architectural drawings are typically arranged by design discipline starting with civil engineering sheets, then architectural sheets, structural sheets, and so on. In this case, having been produced in France in a style that paid homage to a neoclassical design sensibility popular in the 17th century, the set had been drawn with additional flourishes, notation in hand lettered French calligraphy, and metric dimensions. As a result, the drawings had an artistic flair that matched the design.

Turning past the introductory sheets that included a list of all the consultants, including contact information, a sheet index, and other information to assist the builder in understanding the organization of the set, Neil flipped to the overall site plan that showed the entire estate, with the chateau situated in the center of the property on the ridge of the hill. Formal gardens, in the French tradition, were shown on the sides and rear of the chateau, while the front of the house was reserved for a large entry court and fountains. What had once supported carriages and footmen, was now intended for automobiles and chauffeurs. The formal organization of the layout was intended to bring order and symmetry to the natural chaos of the undeveloped site. View corridors were to be cleared through the existing stands of pine creating views to the valley or terminating in architectural follies in line with the orientation of the chateau. Areas where grapes were to be planted (and in fact had already been planted) were shown with hatched lines filling irregular shapes that seemed to take advantage of what appeared to be preexisting clearings on the wooded site.

The plans called for the planting of a large number of mature oak trees along both sides of the entry drive. Neil had arrived at the construction site by driving up a dirt road that appeared to follow the path of the eventual road that was shown on the plans. He remembered seeing the oaks, so they appeared to have already been planted, although their care after planting was suspect.

When Neil had peeked through the fence while David was on the phone, he had not noticed the planting of anything around the chateau. Landscaping would typically be left to the end of the process to ensure that it was not damaged during construction, so that was to be expected. The plan also showed a very formal double set of stairs and a cascading fountain that spilled down from the chateau on the east side of the ridge and terminated in an circular water element. At the midpoint of the stairs, there was a large central landing. To the north, a significant building identified as a natatorium was to be situated along the eastern slope. An elegant formal walkway from the plaza headed north to the pool building, while another headed south to the winery building that was to be built an equal distance to the south. None of this was visible from Neil's location standing in front of his car peering down at the drawings.

Moving beyond the civil engineering sheets, Neil turned to the architectural floor plans where the impressive scale of the chateau became obvious. While the dimensions were in metric and the tabular data was captioned in French, he understood the plans to indicate that the building was approximately 2,500 square meters or almost 27,000 square feet on the main floor. The sheet title was *Piano Nobile,* or "noble floor." He didn't speak French, but knew this was the main floor. It was laid out following the classical principle of axial symmetry and balance. In this case it was an east-west axis. Once a guest arrived at the entry forecourt or *Avant-Cour*, they would access the chateau by climbing terraced stairs to a monumental arched entry loggia with engaged Doric pilasters supporting a pediment with entablature and statuary. To each side of the portico, identical wings created balance and symmetry. Beyond the loggia, lay a vestibule as wide and deep as the loggia. It led to the main salon, but was bisected by a five meter wide interior corridor that extended through the interior of the chateau from north

Figure 1 - View of East Façade

Figure 2 - West Perspective View

Legend

1. *West Portico*
2. *Vestibule*
3. *Hallway*
4. *Salon*
5. *East Portico*
6. *Dining Room*
7. *Service Area/Elevator*
8. *Breakfast Room*
9. *North Portico*
10. *Tea Room*
11. *Ladies Lounge*
12. *Ladies Toilets*
13. *Vestibule/Private Elevator*
14. *Map Room*
15. *Library*
16. *South Portico*
17. *Billiards Room*
18. *Cigar / Card Room*
19. *Men's Toilets*
20. *Stairs*
21. *Elevator*
22. *Mechanical/Electrical*

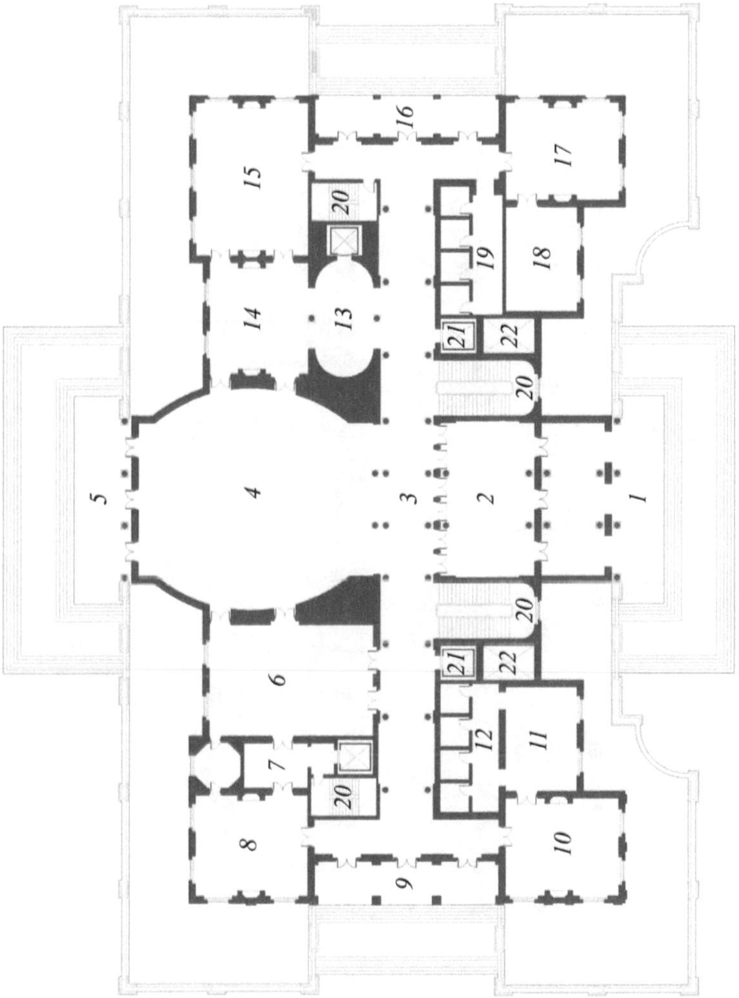

Figure 3 - Piano Nobile

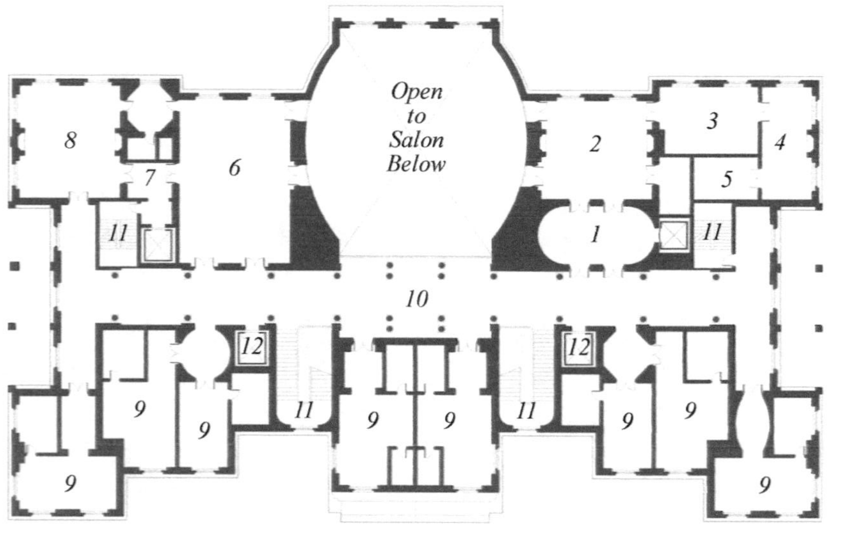

Legend

1. *Vestibule to Master Suite*
2. *Private Sitting Room*
3. *Master Bedroom*
4. *Master Bath*
5. *Closet*
6. *Family Sitting Room*
7. *Service Area/Elevator*
8. *Family Breakfast Room*
9. *Guest Suite*
10. *Hallway*
11. *Stairs*
12. *Elevator*

Figure 4 - Residential Floor Plan

Legend

1. *Hallway*
2. *Staff Quarters*
3. *Storage*
4. *Stair Access to Cupola*
5. *Mechanical*
6. *Stairs*
7. *Elevator*

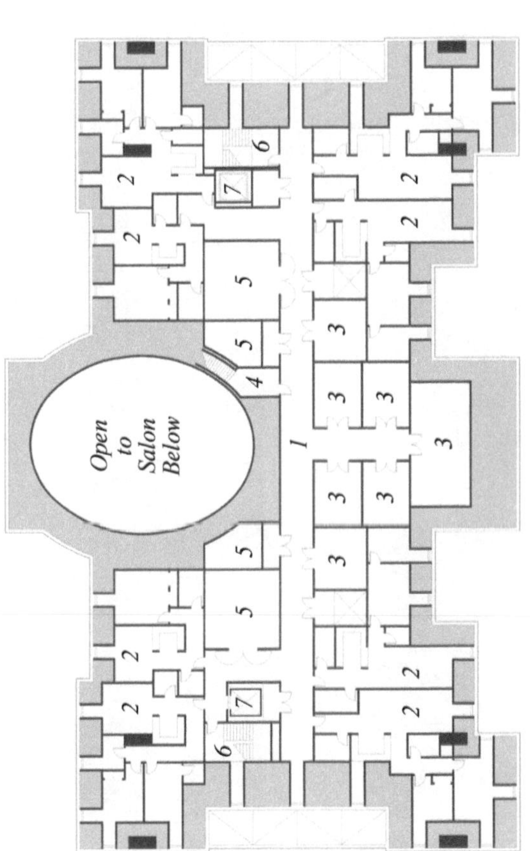

Figure 5 - Staff Residential Floor Plan

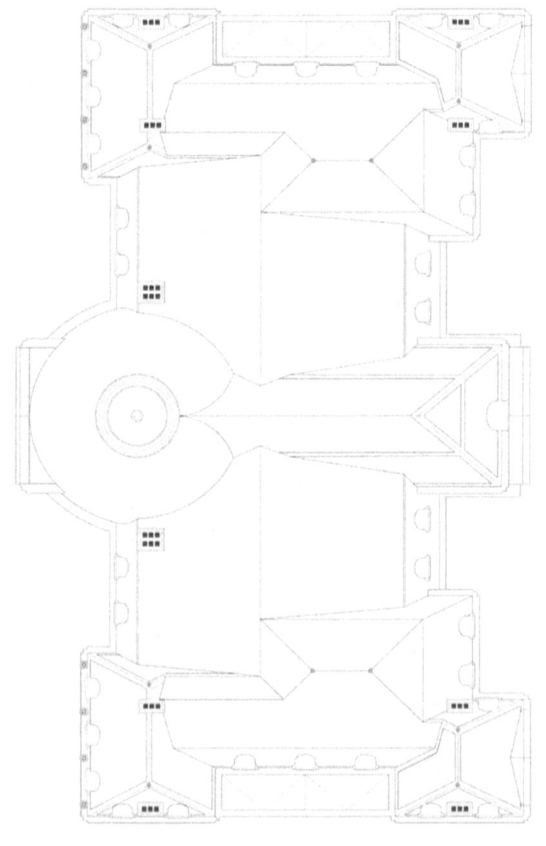

Figure 6 - Roof Plan

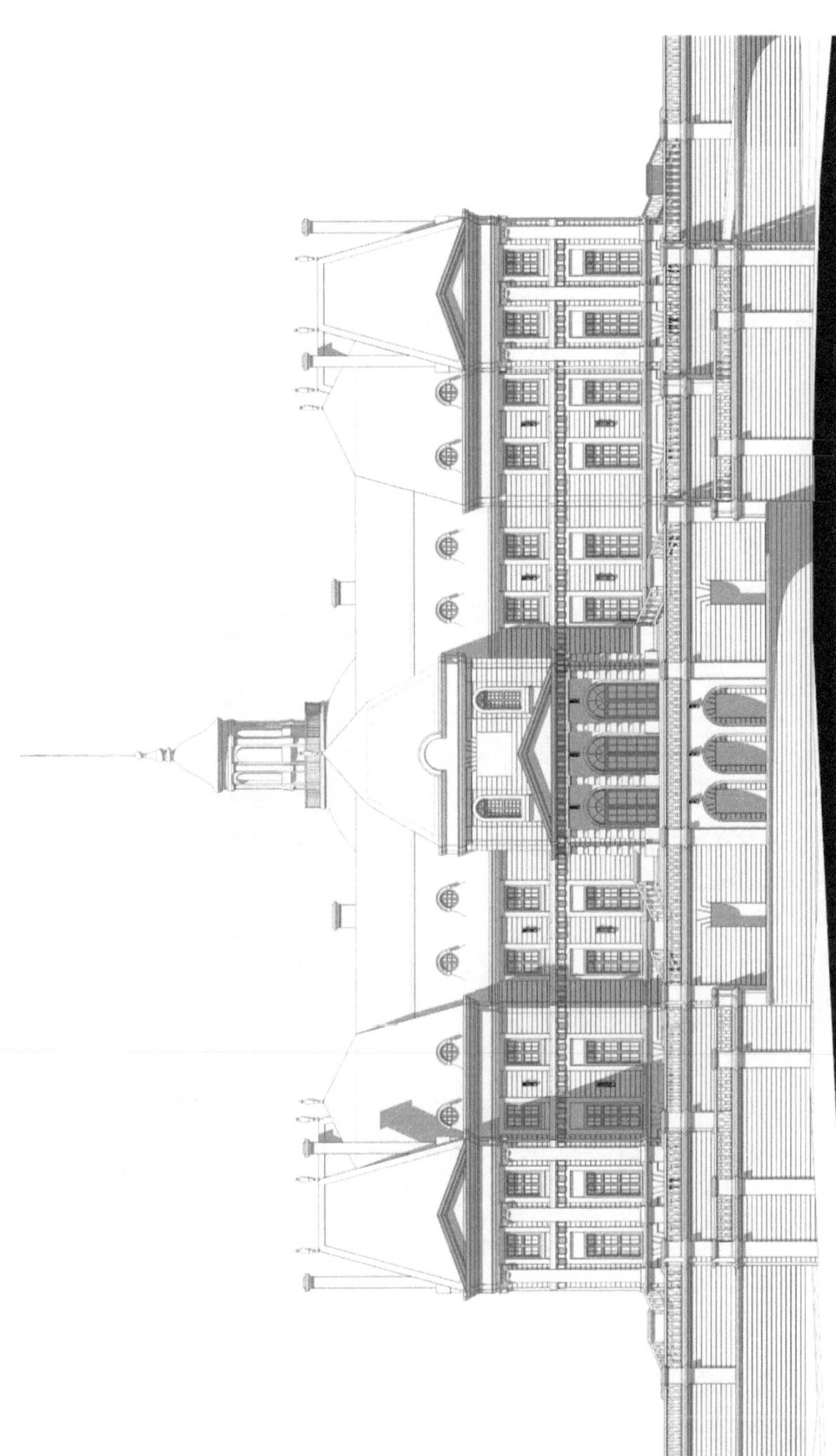

Figure 7 - West Elevation

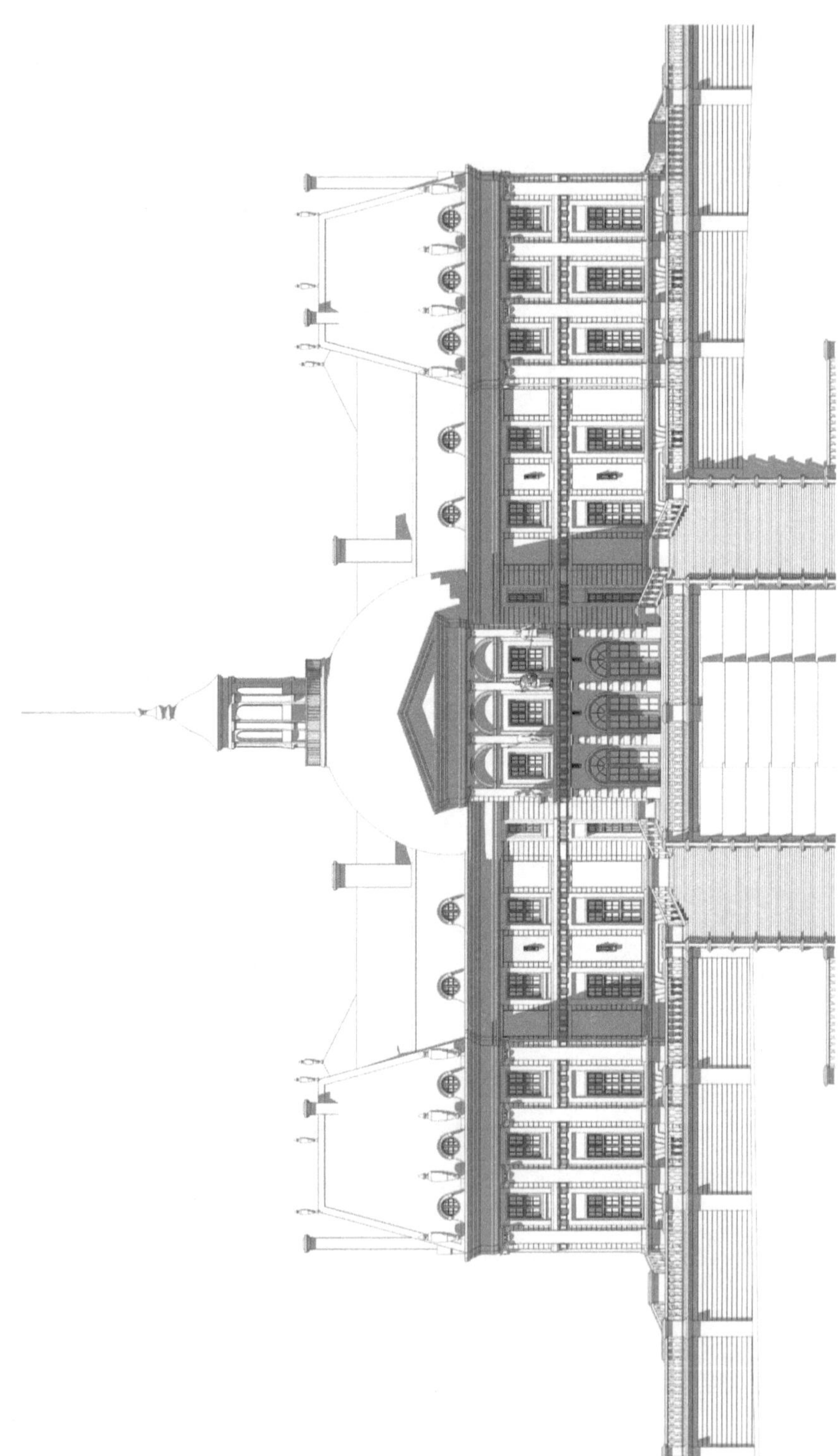

Figure 8 - East Elevation

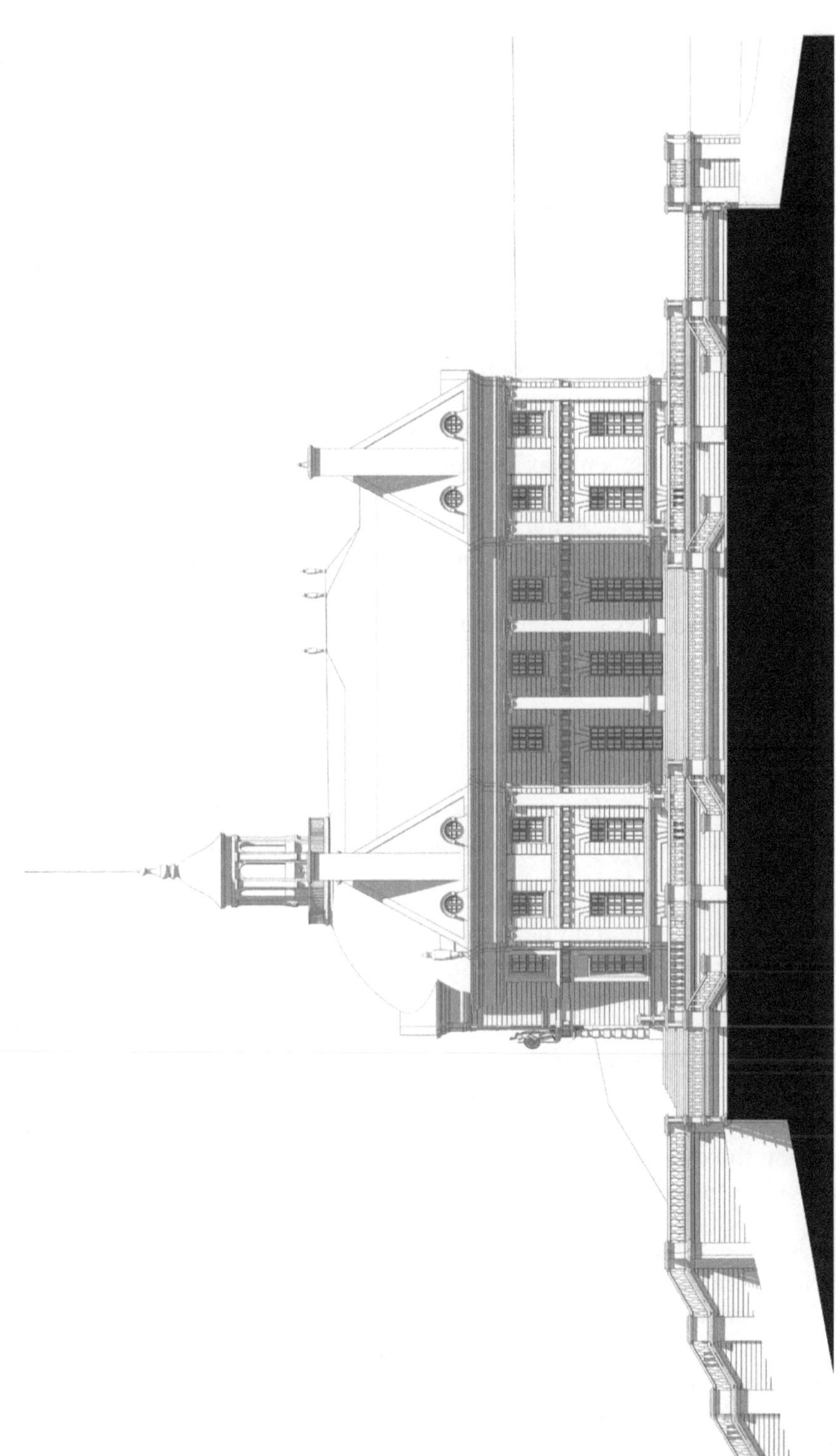

Figure 9 - North Elevation (South Elevation Similar/Reversed)

to south, terminating on each end in high windows and shallow loggia framing views of the gardens beyond.

The main salon was the show stopper space of the whole chateau. It was elliptical in plan and was covered by an elliptical dome. The salon looked east down another series of terraced stairs to a large patio, then down over the cascading stairs and fountains to a large circular pool partway down the side of the hill. Hidden from view from the top of the hill was a grotto on the up-hill side of the pool.

Adjacent to the salon on the southeast was a map room with doors leading to a large library. On the northeast side, there was a formal dining room and a smaller breakfast room. Both of these rooms were accessible by a service stair and elevator, for staff. The kitchen was located in the basement beneath the dining room.

The area of the chateau on the southwest of the main corridor supported monumental stairs, additional elevators, and both a men's billiard room and toilets. A mirrored set of stairs, elevators, women's lounge, powder room and toilets were situated in the northwest quadrant of the floor.

The floor-to-floor height of the ground floor was eight meters or about 24 feet.

The second floor housed family and guest suites, a private sitting room and a private breakfast room. The floor-to-floor height of the second floor was six meters or about eighteen feet. Owing to the exaggerated massing of the roof, the chateau would eventually support staff sleeping quarters in a fully improved attic.

Beneath the *piano nobile*, the first basement level contained the kitchen, a theater, a number of other entertainment spaces, such as a full-immersion, large-screen video gaming suite, and an indoor squash court, in addition to more toilets and shower and locker rooms.

The second basement connected to the sub-grade structured parking that extended beneath the entry court. A significant portion of the floor plan on this level was blank except for the words *"ne fait pas partie du contrat"*. The lowest level of the basement, the third sub-basement, was the barrel room. It was connected to the winery via a tunnel.

After looking at the set, Neil was impressed. It was big and gaudy, but seemed to be historically faithful to the style it was emulating. He was not a big fan of copying dead styles, but he had to give grudging admiration when it was done well. From the looks of the set, David had the money and intent to do it right. There must have been 160 or so sheets of just interior elevations and decorative detailing in the set, which was way more than one would expect from a more contemporary design.

The resurrection of historicist styles from the architectural graveyard of bygone cultures and value systems is considered vulgar and terribly unsophisticated by the reigning architectural intelligentsia. Neil got that. In architectural school they talked a lot about whether projects warranted being described as "Architecture" or "architecture". It was more than a mild put down to have your studio project described as small "a" architecture. If you subscribe to any of the several "serious" monthly architectural magazines focused on the profession, you would never see a project like David Johnsson's published or receiving awards or recognition. Those in the know would sneer and hold it up to derision as the folly of a wealthy fool with no taste. Neil had to admit that he fell into that camp. With all the money in the world, why recreate a 350-year old idea of elegance, modernity, luxury, not to mention *beauty*, *commodity* or *delight*, when you could create something of this time that captures current values, and the current sense of civilization's place in the universe?

Every architect has an inner muse. Some of them seem to be dead, or perhaps suffer from arrested development, but they speak through the designs of their host. At some point in every architect's career, they come to the realization that their god-like design abilities are limited by several factors beyond their control. The first and most important is gravity. Architects can do some "unnatural" things with modern materials and construction techniques, but they still haven't figured out how to get past gravity. The next thing that limits, or challenges, architects is materials technology. Construction technology has come a long way since the pyramids (big stacks of large stones) with respect to the materials architects have in their kit of tools. Looking back at the entire history of architecture, you can clearly see the point in each period where the architectural practitioners of a particular "style" hit the wall based on the limitations of the materials they had at their disposal. All they could typically do at that point was start to embellish the decorative motifs of the style, rather than push the boundaries of the technology. The Pharaohs didn't have the advantage of cement, and thus concrete. The Greeks didn't have the arch. The Romans had cement and the arch, but lacked steel. Current society has steel, but lacks taste or sophistication - except in small disjointed segments. Instead of describing the history of architecture as the evolution of style alone, it really must be thought of as the evolution of style based on advances in material science and a basic understanding of physics.

Another critical driver of architectural form is the energy paradigm of the time in which it was created. The initial impetus for creating architecture was the need of humans to seek protection from the elements. Humans could have stayed in caves, but caves were not always ideally located, among other drawbacks. If protecting ourselves from the elements is what drove the enclosing of space, then both excessive heat and excessive cold are important considerations. Ready access to affordable sources of energy to heat or cool a building have always been a driving design consideration. Most people don't think of it today, but a building without windows is as dark as a cave, and potentially just as problematic with respect to removing smoke or dealing with leaks in awkward locations at inopportune times. In fact, the majority of buildings in the West were dependent on basic wood fueled "fire" for warmth until sometime in the 18th or 19th century. So as advanced as some might think civilization is, in some respects, it is but a little distance removed from millennia of human experience.

All these design drivers are centered on human physiological imperatives. We can't see in the dark so we need windows. We can't seem to pass through solid materials, so we need doors. If we get too cold we freeze. If we get too hot we die. We need protection from predators and our enemies when we are asleep so we need locks on the windows and doors. Most of these factors are immutable and seemingly unchanging. Others have evolved at the edges over time. Neil's personal belief was that the profession would not see the next great shift in architectural styles until there was a breakthrough in the current energy model (or the current one collapses), or there is some new material technology that impacts our ability to resist gravity by spanning greater distances with less weight.

Whether any of these things factored into David Johnsson's decision to employ a 350-year old aesthetic is doubtful. Wealth and power have their own motivations. New money quite often seeks to wrap itself in the language and accoutrements of old money. Old money just wants to be preserved, undiluted.

To Neil, great architecture is the perfect fusion of art and science. When it is brilliant it combines the highest and best impulses of both. At its worst it is all of one and none of the other. But what was this thing that David Johnsson was gestating and coaxing into existence? Was it art? Old art perhaps. Was it wrong that he liked it? Was it science? Was there something amazingly technical about the materials or methods used to construct it?

No. It was going to be big and it is always hard to argue with that. It was going to have quality finishes imported from Europe. It was going to be Romantic in the true sense of the word. It was going to be safe, in the sense that is wasn't going to offend anyone's sense of style because it had already been tried. So more than anything, it was a missed opportunity. That is what made it disappointing to someone like Neil.

«»«»«»

Neil closed the set. David had been standing nearby looking over his shoulder as he reviewed the set, probably trying to gauge his reaction. "Well," he said, "what do you think?"

Neil turned and looked at David. "This is going to set a new standard for the Valley, I think." David beamed and nodded. It was just what he wanted to hear. The insult did not register.

"Do you recognize it?" David asked.

"It looks familiar," Neil said, "but I am not an expert in classical French architecture. In architecture school we got a broad survey of all the periods and all the styles, but there is so much history that it was a pretty cursory review."

Neil could tell that David liked having one up on his "expert".

"This is sort of a copy of Vaux le Vicomte," he said. "It was the precursor to Versailles."

"Well, at least I knew it was French!" Neil laughed. "I'll have to look it up when I get back to the office."

He asked David what his project budget was. David said it was a lot, but that the number was confidential. Neil told him that he thought the chateau was well over a hundred million if what he saw in the drawings was built with the implied quality. With the other buildings, equipment, the tunnel, road work, landscaping, and planting of the vineyards, he guessed David must be looking at double that, easily. Throw in soft costs, and he was probably pushing $300 million. With furnishings, who knew? The artwork alone could run into several hundred million if David was going to do it right. David just smiled.

"Okay. Don't tell me. I don't need to know," Neil said with a laugh.

Neil also asked if David had drawings for the winery and natatorium and if he could review those as well. David said he did, but that they were back at the hotel. He said he would send them to Neil later. Neil asked if they were going to be built under the same construction contract as the chateau.

"The winery is basically complete. They started on it first and kept it going, thank goodness. We just brought in our first harvest. But at the rate things are going, I don't think I will have them finish the house or the rest of it," David replied. "These guys promised to deliver everything early. They told me I would be so impressed with their quality. Told me all about their excellent reputation and it was all a load of crap!" He spat out the last words.

Neil nodded, but said nothing. There was probably no point continuing with a contractor that you were fighting with. Once the love, or trust, is gone it is difficult to keep going.

"Well, let's go take a look," Neil said. He was not going to lug the set around the site during their walk, so he left it covering the hood of his car.

David unlocked the gate and they walked across the dirt yard and concrete deck of the underground parking structure that had yet to be buried. It had been built utilizing a cut and cover technique that is considerably faster and less expensive than tunneling.

The steps from the forecourt to the entry loggia had not been constructed yet, so they climbed up a set of portable metal stairs and into the shaded, cool and slightly damp interior space of the *piano nobile,* through a gaping hole in the wall that would one day be sheathed in stone. Light from the far side of the house filtered through the interior framing. The main floor of the chateau was clearly intended to infer upon its owner instant gentrification.

They walked through the loggia and into the vestibule. Light from the double height salon flooded the vestibule through the rough metal framing of three arches. The interior metal framing and fire proofing for the stair shafts was in place, but the stair's stringers and treads were absent, leaving a dark hole that disappeared into the darkened levels below. The landing where the stairs reached the main floor was taped off with construction warning tape. The floor where they stood was covered with construction debris, in addition to pigeon droppings. There was a fine dust covering everything. In some places it was thick enough, and damp enough, to almost constitute mud. Construction lights had been strung overhead, but were not on. There were no tools in sight, but several wooden saw horses remained where left, supporting some uncut metal studs. Scaffolding on castors stood against the south wall. Metal trimmings from cut studs had been swept into a pile that had not been removed. In addition to the construction debris, the pile contained empty water bottles, coffee cups, and a soda can or two.

Neil hated a dirty construction site. It's the contractor's responsibility and prerogative to determine how and when to clean the construction, but for as long as he had been visiting construction sites on behalf of his clients, it had always been one of his pet peeves. He would probably get an argument from some of the contractors he knew, but he believed a clean construction site resulted in a better build. Once the debris from one sub-contractor was left strewn around the building or site, the next sub-contractor did not feel the need to clean up after themselves and pretty soon it piled up. It was just sloppy.

Neil pointed to the stair landing. "You're going to get cited for that when the inspector drops by. That's an unsafe condition," he said.

"Already happened," David grunted.

"And . . .?" he asked.

"And what?" David replied rather curtly.

"What did the contractor do to fix it?"

"Nothing."

"Humph." Neil opened a note pad and scribbled some notes. He also took a few photos of the room and the landing in particular. "It's still your responsibility," he said. "If anyone gets in here and gets hurt, or dies, the liability is on you."

"That's why I have lawyers," David said, as if daring anyone to try to sue him.

They moved on through the arched openings that would eventually be stone-clad piers leading into the salon. The rolled steel beams of the dome soared high overhead. Neil guessed it was at least 60 feet to the underside of the steel roof decking. Large arched windows framed views to the east.

This room would be the formal center of the social life of the building. The underside of the metal roof diaphragm could be seen through the structural framing. Plumbing lines for the fire sprinklers had been roughed in. Pigeons had begun to call the cavernous space home and had left their mark on the floor. The project had definitely been stopped for more than three weeks.

"Shock and awe," David said.

"I'm sorry," Neil said. "What? I was thinking about size of this room. It's massive. What is it, about 3,000 square feet?"

"Yeah. Shock and awe. This whole place is going to knock people on their backsides. I don't mess around. This is how you do it," he said.

"Do what?" Neil asked.

"Life. You mark the spot where you want to go, and then go there. This is the spot I wanted. This is the house I wanted. It's all part of the plan."

Without thinking, Neil said dryly, "You sound very focused."

"I know something about making money and being rich," David said. "When I decide to spend some of what I've made, I don't hesitate."

"What if someone or something gets in the way?" Neil asked. "You know, like the county design review process?" Neil chuckled. He knew this had to have been a fight.

David looked disdainfully at Neil. "Nothing gets in the way or stays in the way if you are committed. I have a philosophy. I decided at an early point in my life that nothing was going to keep me from achieving my goals. So far nothing has.

I set out to go to Harvard. I did. I set out to marry the hottest chick in my freshman class. I did. I set out to be successful on Wall Street and I was. I decided I was going to retire early. I'm still in my 50's." He looked quite pleased with himself and then a pained expression crossed his face.

"Wow. That's great," Neil said it without a trace of irony or sarcasm. He meant it, too. There were probably a whole bunch of casualties along the way that weren't quite so excited about David's success, but clearly he had achieved his goals.

"Well, as an average Joe, it all looks pretty crazy from where I am." Neil walked away to the far side of the room to emphasize his retreat on the subject.

"So, who is selecting finishes and fixtures at this point?" he called back over his shoulder. "If you fired your architect, someone has to step up and make a lot of decisions as this gets finished."

"I am," came the quick response.

Neil nodded. "I thought maybe your wife would be involved."

"Not that . . ." David caught himself as if there were more to say, but just left it there. "I have an assistant. She deals with a lot of the minutia."

They walked through more metal framing into what would be the formal dining room. It had been left in much the same state as what they had seen so far on their tour. A stack of metal studs filled the center of the space in the approximate location of a future monumental dining table.

"This is the formal dining room," David said.

"It's big. You married? Kids?" Neil asked. Asking about a client's family was usually safe territory, Neil thought.

David looked at Neil, weighing whether he needed this information and whether he wanted to go there.

"Twice. No kids," he said.

"Sorry. Not really any of my business." Neil turned away and walked further into the room. "It's just that this is going to be an impressive room. Great for family gatherings."

Neil walked through an opening into the breakfast room. The rough masonry for a large fireplace was in place. It was framed by a pair of tall openings on either side that looked north. The fireplace's finishes were missing, but the masonry fire box and chimney had been constructed and were waiting for the rest of the construction to catch up before being completed. The floor-to-floor height was easily 24 or 25 feet.

"This is going to be nice. The view is incredible. Where does your property end?"

Direct sunlight streamed into the space from the east. The openings in the walls where windows would one day be located framed views that looked down over vineyards that had been planted on the eastern slope of the property. Lake Berryessa glistened in the distance. The hills of the valley were a golden brown and dotted with oaks. To the south, the nearly completed winery was situated next to an already lush lawn. There was no drought on this estate. The lawn served as a connector back to an un-built stair and cascading fountain that was to descend from the house to a large ornamental pool. The lawn was flanked on each side by two rows of perfectly matching oak trees. Neil estimated they had spent at least fifteen years in a nursery. A walkway of decomposed granite lay beneath each row of trees connecting the winery to the future cascading stairs. A service road wound up from below and ended on the south side of the winery at a production yard that was hidden from view by the massing of the building. Where the house promised to be large and refined, the winery was rustic and evocative of an old and well established French wine estate. Neil could see from a glance that it had indeed cost a small fortune to construct. All the open space that was not being improved as gardens, was planted in row after row of young grape vines running in undulating ribbons of leaves that paralleled the terrain. Golden-yellow leaves, with an occasional hint of green, still clung to the vines.

The property curved to the north, judging by the extent of the vineyard that was visible from their current vantage point. Neil could see a graded pad surrounded by grapes and only a dirt scar where another lawn would be planted. He guessed that this was the future site of the natatorium.

David walked up beside Neil and pointed. "On the south, the property ends over beyond that stand of pine. I wanted to clear all the way to the property line for more vines and to get an even better view, but the bureaucrats at the county wouldn't let me. You can't see the property line on the east, because it's down in the valley. Then on the north, here," he waved his left hand in a northerly direction," it's five or six hundred yards up into those trees. Beyond that it's state forest, so I'll never have anyone clearing the trees or building close on that side."

"Wow," Neil said again. "I keep saying that! But this is a huge parcel you have. Amazing."

David liked that. "Yeah, well, like I said. If you are going to do something, go big."

They found a set of partially constructed stairs that led up to the second floor. It was adjacent to another shaft for a future staff service elevator. Again, the shaft was open with no protective barricade. They climbed to the second floor. It was in largely the same condition as the ground floor. Electrical rough-ins had begun in the south wing. Plumbing lines had been roughed-in in both wings. Duct work was in place in the plenum space, but had not been dropped or extended to the lower floors. There were to be four elevators; a private elevator for family use, two for guests, and one for house staff. It turned out all the shafts were open and protected by nothing but a piece of yellow tape across the opening. Neil guessed that the shafts must descend 60 or 70 feet to the barrel room below.

"You need to get the contractor to provide the proper barrier for all the shafts," Neil said. "If anyone falls down here, or at the stairs, you are going to get sued. I know you said you already told them, but if they are not responsive, you need to get someone else out here to do it. The contractor won't particularly like that, but any unsafe conditions open you up to being sued if anyone gets hurt. Even if it's one of the contractor's guys. You've got the deep pockets so they'll sue you. Since I've been out here, their attorney would try to sue me, too. So I will include my observation of the unsafe conditions in my report."

"I've got a locked gate and no trespassing signs," he grumped.

"Won't matter," Neil replied. David knew Neil was right and dropped it.

They walked through the rest of the second floor, but didn't climb up into the attic. Nor did they go down into any of the basement levels since they didn't know how to turn on the lights. It seemed dumb to Neil in retrospect to have not brought a flashlight, but that is the way it is with site visits. You never know what you need until it's too late.

As they walked back down the stairs to the ground floor Neil was curious about the cellar. "How many bottles will the cellar hold?" Neil asked.

"You mean barrels. There's a tunnel from the winery building to the cellar. It's already in. We'll bring the wine in barrels from the crushing room to the cellar where it will age. I had the architect make it big enough to hold about 12,000 barrels, plus accommodate a huge area for dinners and parties. There will be a big professional kitchen. It's going to be great."

Neil looked at David. He seemed tired with the recitation of these details. "You are doing it right," Neil said. "I hope you will invite me back when it's done."

David gave Neil a thin smile. "You bet!" he said. "The full tour will only set you back 50 bucks!" He laughed knowing that was more than the other wineries were charging.

Neil kept scribbling notes and taking photographs as they walked back through the chateau. “Are you really going to give tours and charge for them?” he asked.

“Oh, hell no!” he snorted! “I don’t need that hassle. People think I am doing this for the money or something. They don’t have a clue. This is going to be a very private place. Only my friends and family will ever be invited.”

From the sound of it, he didn’t have many of either.

When they reached the yard in front of the house, David asked, “So what do you think?” Just then, a large pickup truck pulled into the yard through the open gate in a cloud of dust.

“Here we go,” David muttered.

The truck stopped near where the two other cars were parked and a tall, muscular man with a deep tan who Neil guessed to be in his mid to late thirties stepped out of the cab. He glanced over in their direction and Neil gathered from the glance that he was not entirely pleased to see a stranger with David. Neil recognized the company name on the truck, but not the occupant.

“Morning,” he said cautiously, as he approached.

David said, “We’ve already been through.”

Neil stuck out his hand, “Neil Thornton,” he said. The contractor shook it and gave his name as Craig Stevens. Neil waited to see what David would say. This was his meeting and his contractor, so Neil didn’t see the need to go much further with his self-introduction.

“This is my new architect,” David said. Craig nodded as if this news was expected. He looked at Neil and asked with open skepticism, “You going to get me paid?”

Neil just loved being in the middle of a fight, especially when it really wasn’t his fight – at least not yet.

“Well, I appreciate Mr. Johnsson’s vote of confidence, but I am not technically his architect. I agreed to come take a look at the project.”

Neil typically found it better to engage in a little flattery at times like this, so he said to them both and yet to neither of them specifically, “This is really an amazing project. I’m sure everyone is looking forward to the day it’s completed.”

They both nodded as if he had been addressing them.

"David. If it's okay, I may need to come back and take some additional photos. I'll bring a flashlight and check out the lower levels."

David tossed Neil a key ring with a couple of keys on it. "Just mail them to me with the report," he said. "And don't sue me if you fall down one of those elevator shafts," he laughed.

"Okay," Neil said. "I was going to e-mail the report, but I can mail a hard copy if you prefer. I'm sure we'll be talking again in the next several days. Craig, it was a pleasure meeting you. There are several safety issues that you need to address. I understand the inspector has brought them to your attention, so you don't need me piling on, but you must address them as soon as you can," he said somewhat apologetically.

Craig said nothing.

With that Neil extricated himself from the situation by walking back to his car. As he reached the gate, he could hear raised voices. He didn't look back. He rolled up the drawings, put them in his trunk, got in his car and drove slowly back down the rutted dirt road to the entry gate.

"Not many architects have the luxury to reject significant things."

-- Rem Koolhaas

Chapter Two

When he got back to the office, the first thing Neil did was to go hunting for his Sir Bannister Fletcher. Shelley heard him as he entered and asked how it had gone from her office without actually getting up to greet Neil.

"It's big," Neil called back to her as he rummaged through his books. "Really big. Not that close to being done. But when it is, it will be something, if for no other reason than nothing has been built like it in North America in maybe a hundred years."

"Wow. Sounds amazing," Shelley said. The office was small enough that they could communicate without actually being in the same room by just speaking rather loudly.

"It's not amazing yet, but if he does it right, it will be."

He didn't remember the real name of the book he was looking for, but Sir Bannister Fletcher is what he had always called it. He found it on a book shelf in the dining room where he kept his "historical" reference books. He didn't really have much of a filing system for his architectural books. He had a few hundred, but knew his collection pretty well and mostly knew each book by its spine or cover. Sir Bannister Fletcher's *A History of Architecture* was about four inches thick and still had its paper dust sleeve.

It was a compendium, first published in 1896, of all the notable buildings from ancient times to the present. Although, the "present" in his edition, which was the 17th, stopped back in his architectural school days when he had purchased the book.

He tried to find the chateau David had referenced by sight, by flipping through the pages to the period that he thought would contain examples of high Baroque French chateau design. He didn't find it that way and had to resort to the index, only he could not remember what David had said the name was. He finally looked under chateau and found the correct section. He scanned all the images, but none of them seemed correct. So he hunkered down and read all the entries, eventually finding it. *Vaux le Vicomte.* That was it. There was a brief write-up, but still no image. He returned to his desk and googled the term. Under images, he was rewarded with hundreds of search returns for the chateau. Once he saw it he remembered it as having been an important piece of architecture. But he honestly could not remember anything about it beyond that the owner had been a member of the French court and had spent a kingly sum to build it.

Neil read the Wikipedia entry:

> *"Vaux le Vicomte was commissioned in 1657 by Nicholas Fouquet, the Superintendent of Finance to Louie XIV. He assembled a team of eminent designers, including the architect Le Vue, Le Brun an interior designer, and Le Nôtre a landscape designer. It was their first collaboration and was heralded in its day as a great success.*
>
> *The estate was constructed between 1658 and 1661 and was so large, it displaced three existing villages. Upon completion of the chateau, it is said that 18,000 people were necessary to keep it functioning. Most of these people came from the local villages that had been relocated to make way for the estate.*
>
> *In 1661, Fouquet threw a lavish fête, at the request of Louis XIV, to introduce the royal court to his new residence. Apparently the king had heard about the extravagance of the chateau and wanted to see it in person. The party was a huge success, featuring a play by Moliere, a feast, and lavish fireworks. The only problem seems to be it had more of everything than Louis XIV's own palace and was rumored to have cost over 16 million livre.*
>
> *The king stripped Fouquet of his title that very night and replaced him with Jean-Baptiste Colbert, who happened to be the one whispering in the king's ear that Fouquet had misappropriated royal funds to build the chateau. The new Minister of Finance promptly arrested Fouquet for embezzlement and threw him in accommodations that left much to be desired.*
>
> *Louie XIV either took or purchased most of the chateau's tapestries, furniture, and statuary, removing them to his own palace. He then hired Messiers Le Vue, Le Brun, and Le Nôtre to design a new royal palace large enough to safely avoid being upstaged again. The result being the Palace at Versailles.*
>
> *After his conviction, Fouquet ended up dying in prison, while his wife and sons were exiled from the property."*

You could glean a moral lesson from this tale: that flamboyance does not pay.

However, the resemblance between Vaux le Vicomte and what David was building was obvious and he seemed to not care about the perils associated with conspicuous flamboyance.

While not an exact replica, the design certainly paid homage to the original in many respects. Perhaps the most obvious difference was in the siting of the two chateaus. Vaux le Vicomte was located on a relatively flat site, compared to David's ridge top. The original had a moat and was surrounded by massive gardens. David's gardens were smaller and his property was covered in grapes, but his views could be argued to be as impressive as the original's, however different.

The layout of the original chateau was driven by the needs and tastes of its time. The vestibule and salon had originally not been enclosed, bisecting the *corps-longis*, or main building, into two almost identical halves. The *piano-nobile* had been divided between rooms on the west half of the floor that were reserved for the king himself, should he choose to visit, while the identical spaces on the east were reserved for Fouquet and his family, thus the matching pairs of stairs. This was apparently a departure from established chateau layouts of the time that included a single, monumental curved stair in the vestibule.

David had dispensed with the moat, which would have been problematic on a sloped site. But he replaced it with fountains on each side of the forecourt that gave a nod to the original. And whereas the original layout was along a north-south axis, his layout, for obvious reasons related to topography and views, was along an east-west axis.

The photos of Vaux le Vicomte depicted rich, lavishly appointed rooms. Highly detailed and ornate wood paneling lined nearly every room. The floors were covered in intricate patterns of multi-colored, polished stone. The windows were huge (no electricity) and were covered with heavy draperies. The ceilings were carved and painted in the highest expression of the craftsmanship of the time. It was high drama and high cost. No surface was left un-ornamented or unadorned. From his brief review of the drawings that morning, the interiors of David's replica would be equally ornate.

Shelley came into his office and looked over his shoulder at the images on the screen.

"Oh my god! Is that it?" she asked in disbelief.

"No. This is the real thing. It's called Vaux le Vicomte. It's like 350 years old and is outside Paris. This guy, David Johnsson, is building a sort of replica. It's not exact, naturally. But it shares more than just a passing resemblance."

Neil got up from his desk walked to the door. "I'll be right back," he said. "He loaned me a set of the drawings and I left them in the car." Shelley sat down in his chair and began to scroll through the images.

Neil disappeared for a minute or two, then returned with the largest set of drawings Shelley had ever seen. In the time that Shelley had worked for Neil he had never worked on anything as large as David Johnsson's project, so she had never really considered how large a set of drawings for a big building might be.

When rolled up, the set was as thick as a good sized tree trunk. Neil was huffing a little as he brought the set into the office and lowered it with a heavy thud on a drafting table. He tossed the keys David had given him on his desk and unrolled the set.

"What are those?" Shelley asked, nodding toward the keys.

"He gave me some keys so I can go back and take a closer look. We didn't bring flashlights and it was too dark to walk through the lower levels."

Neil flipped to the site plan and began to fill Shelley in on his morning's outing.

"So he has a big parcel of land a little southeast of town on this ridge." He gestured to the site plan and flipped the page to the floor plan. "The winery is done and the structural framing on the chateau is up." He was talking to himself as Shelley didn't really care that much about architectural details.

Shelley was an interesting person. She was 28 and an avid cyclist and rock climber. She had been working for Neil for about 18 months and so far, she had been a good fit. She had not needed a full-time job, and he couldn't afford her full-time anyway. She also had a part-time job at a winery working as a wine docent - which was a fancy way of saying she gave tours through the winery and then hosted the wine tasting and sales experience after the tour. Both jobs offered her flexible hours, which she liked because it allowed her to hit the Valley and mountain roads on her bike when she wanted to - which was almost daily. She had a degree in finance that was largely wasted working for him, but the accounting classes she had taken came in handy as she managed Neil's books. She was smart and energetic and a total self-starter. She was just the sort of multitalented person he needed in a small office to help keep all the plates spinning. When there were plates spinning, that is.

What Shelley thought was interesting and Neil thought was interesting about the project was miles apart. Even though she did not have an architectural background, she did have an aesthetic sensibility that was supportive of the creative process that Neil tried to foster on each project. She stared at the drawings intently and listened to him blather on about how much of the framing had been erected and where the electrical room was going to go and all the safety violations. Shelley had taken French in high school and could read most of the captions and annotations. When she did ask a question or two Neil thought she was very astute in her observations, when in fact, she was just reading what would have been obvious to anyone who knew a little French.

Later that afternoon, Neil started to write up his field notes and observations, including copies of the photos he had taken. From what he saw at the site, the construction of the chateau was probably about thirty percent complete. But the project was so massive that it was difficult to say if, in total, it was 50 percent complete. Guessing the level of completeness is more of an art than science as there are multiple ways to measure construction progress. Neil needed to see the rest of the set and tour the lower levels. David's assertion that the contractor was representing that the project was 50 percent complete may or may not have been accurate. He had not sent Neil any previous pay applications from the contractor or the contractor's schedule of values or any other project related paperwork, and given that Neil had just seen the drawings that morning for the first time, he really could not get very specific. There may have been unforeseen site related costs that the contractor was seeking to recoup that had taken the total invoicing past 50 percent of the contracted value of the project. This seemed likely given the amount of excavation for the cellar and tunnel, but without all the paperwork and considerably more time to study the drawings, a rough guess was going to be the best Neil could do.

Even with the plans that Neil had and the photos he had taken, he decided he needed to go back for a follow-up visit. But there was not enough daylight left by the time he decided he needed to go back for some additional sleuthing.

«»«»«»

Over the next couple of days, Neil was busy with some other issues, so he was not able to make his way back to David's property until Friday morning.

The gate was closed when he arrived. The weather had turned cold and cloudy and seemed to be threatening to rain. He got out of his car and fumbled with the keys David had given him as he approached the gate. It took him a moment to realize that while the gate was closed and the chain was hanging as if it were locked, it wasn't. He removed the chain and swung the gate open. Entering someone else's property had always seemed a little weird to him if they were not there. He felt somehow as if someone were watching, even though he had not seen any other cars on the road and it was a peaceful quiet morning. Except for the birds chirping away in the trees that lined the road, Neil seemed to be alone.

After opening the gate, he drove through and closed it again. He decided to lock it, too. Probably an unnecessary precaution, but when he was on someone else's property, he tended to act very cautiously. Nothing had ever gone wrong, but that did not stop him from experiencing the concern that it might. If he left the gate open and some kids got in and either vandalized the place, or got hurt, it didn't take much for Neil to imagine that David would probably turn his stable of pit bull attorneys on him.

Neil drove up the hill, just as before, and parked in basically the same place. He was surprised to see a pick-up truck belonging to the general contractor parked outside the construction fence. The logo of the company was emblazoned on the door. It looked like the same truck that he had seen the contractor driving the other day, but one white Ford 250 looks just like another. He exited his car and didn't bother to lock it. He may have been paranoid, but he wasn't that paranoid. He slipped one of his business cards under the driver's side windshield wiper of the truck. At least whoever was there would know who else was on site.

The gate in the construction fence was ajar, so he slipped easily into the construction site. He was carrying a clipboard with some small printouts of the floor plans. He had used his camera to take photos of several key floor plan sheets and had printed them out on his office copier. He didn't have a scanner in his office large enough to scan full size sheets and disassembling the set would have been a hassle. So he planned to make do with the small printouts. He also had his flashlight this time and was wearing a hard hat and a safety vest. Although there was no one there to enforce work site safety, it was good practice, but it also lent him an air of being "official."

After donning his vest and hard hat, Neil took his time exploring. This time around he did not make a bee-line into the building. He walked the entire length and width of the top of the underground parking structure, looking over the edges to see if waterproofing had been applied. He looked for conduit trenches that had not been completed, or exposed re-bar, or spalling concrete, or whatever happened to jump out at him as being unusual or incomplete. He took lots of notes and photos.

Eventually he was satisfied that he had seen everything of interest in that area and then walked around the full perimeter of the exterior of the chateau.

The first basement level of the chateau was actually built at an elevation that placed the floor plate about five or six feet above the surrounding grade on the uphill side. The west, or downhill side, was fully exposed at present, but would eventually be mostly covered with the grand, terraced stairs leading to the loggia. This placed the *piano nobile* on the second floor. This was typical of designs from that time. It served several purposes, including allowing access for servants from the floor below which was typically a service floor. It also elevated the main floor enhancing the views and status of its occupants. And it elevated the entire building, enhancing the profile of the structure when approaching and when viewed from afar.

Neil didn't bother to climb back up the temporary construction stairs to the *piano nobile*. Instead, he entered the structure from on opening beneath the loggia on the south side of the building. The walls of the first basement level were constructed of poured-in-place concrete. There were openings for windows, but they were much smaller than the openings for windows on the upper levels. As a result the interior was much darker. Instead of a structural steel frame, the structure of this floor was composed of concrete columns and shear walls. The layout was essentially the same as the floors above, having been based on classical design principles, but the concrete structure made this a design decision rather than a structural one. Metal stud framing was beginning to be put in place, furring out the concrete walls to their design thicknesses. Rough electrical was starting to be put in place. Fire sprinkler lines were in place. Ducts had been hung for the HVAC system. Progress was clearly being made before everything came to a halt.

As he moved into the interior of the floor, it got darker and darker until it was essentially pitch black. It was also quiet and tomb like. The space beneath the lounges and toilets above appeared to be designed to serve a similar purpose on this floor. Having separate men's and women's lounges is a very antiquated idea in this day and age, but in the context of a historicist design might actually heighten the sense of being in an old building. The future space for racquet ball, or was it squash, was just a large void. The area beneath the salon had a sloped floor and would make a very elegant and sizeable private theater. The space under the loggia was designated for a future bar, but was nothing more than a dark cavern storing stacks of construction materials. Neil found the location of the kitchen. It was huge, but entirely unfinished. It had a depressed slab that had filled with an inch or two of water. He didn't venture in but shined his light into the room. The light reflected off the water casting reflected rays onto the far walls from the glass-like surface of the water.

Nearby, he located the service stairs he and David had used to climb to the second floor on his previous visit and walked down to the second sub-basement level. There were no windows in this level as it was entirely below grade. It was completely dark and Neil decided he needed to look at the small plan he had brought along to familiarize himself with the layout.

This level included the parking structure in addition to the floor area under the upper floors of the chateau. As with the floor plates above, the floor area was about 27,000 square feet. The sub-grade parking added an additional 50,000 square feet or more and was laid out in a typical configuration that allowed cars to be driven and parked between columns.

The plan he had of this floor showed the same long interior corridor running in a north-south direction the entire length of the floor and appeared to be located directly beneath the corridors on each of the levels above. The spaces between the corridor and the parking area appeared to be laid out as service areas for staff associated with garage functions. The plan showed two service bays with lifts. There was an oil changing bay with a ladder to the area where a service technician would stand to have access to the underside of a car while changing oil. There was an office with an adjacent chauffeur's lounge and toilet. There was a separate toilet and shower/locker room, a car washing bay, a detailing bay, and parts inventory bay. Basically it was like a service department at a small auto dealer.

On his initial review of the drawings Neil had noticed that the space on the east side of the building was shown as blank space. He cast the beam of his flashlight from side to side as he walked south along the central corridor. It was not clear what was on the other side of the corridor wall. The wall appeared to be poured-in-place concrete. There were no doors or penetrations visible on the east side, but a couple of openings for future doors on the west side to the garage office. The stairs were enclosed on this level so there were openings at the landings. He had walked nearly the full length of the hall when he stopped again to review the small floor plan he had printed in his office.

The resolution of the image was not great and it was a fraction of the size of the original drawing. Architectural drawings are not meant to be reviewed at this scale, so there was limited technical information to be gleaned from the image. His intent for bothering to print the floor plan was just to have an image of the entire floor so that he could orient himself to the plan or make notes, if needed. Now as he found the correct print and shined his flashlight on the page, he was hoping to understand what was behind the wall.

The plans indicated that the undefined space extended west on the south end of the building to abut the parking garage. It appeared there was a roll-up door in the wall between the garage and the unfinished space.

He walked to the south end of the corridor where it ended at an open void where a future stair would be built. He was able to find his way through what he guessed would be a parts room and an adjacent service bay. He entered the garage and turned to his left and was surprised to find an actual steel roll-up door. Beside the door, he was even more surprised to find what appeared to be some sort of biometric security reader and a key pad. It looked like a thumb print scanner. A little red light glowed on the device. He touched the key pad and it was instantly backlit in a dim red light. He put his thumb on the darkened glass of the scanner. It beeped, but nothing else seemed to happen. He leaned down and grasped the lip on the bottom edge of the door and gave it a heave. It was locked.

"Duh," he thought.

David had given him a key ring with four keys on it. Thus far, he had only used two. No telling what the other two were for. As Neil stood there in the dark, he shined the flashlight down on the keys in his hand. Three of the keys were standard Schlage keys. The fourth was a sturdier key with a round head and a much more complicated tooth pattern.

As he stood there wondering if one of these keys might unlock the door, there was suddenly a loud metallic clanging sound behind him as if someone had dropped a heavy piece of metal. It reverberated through the quiet, still space for what seemed like a long time. To say he was startled would be an understatement. He whirled around and pointed the light into the cavernous garage in the direction of the sound. He then moved the light slowly to the left and right. Nothing. The hair on the back of his neck tingled. He listened carefully. In the silence, he thought he heard footsteps, or was it voices? Or was it just his imagination?

He tried to calm himself down by telling himself that either something that was left leaning against a wall or was otherwise left in a precarious position had finally fallen over or perhaps the contractor had returned to properly barricade the elevator and stair shafts.

After what seemed like several minutes of not hearing anything, he decided to check out the rest of the garage. He pointed his flashlight deep into the center of the garage. The closest columns were brightly illuminated, but as the light passed them, it seemed to be swallowed by the darkness, failing to reach very far into the garage before being overwhelmed by the gloom. At the far west corners, dim, shadowed light filtered into the garage from the vehicle entry/exit ramps that he had seen from the exterior. The light did not penetrate very far into the garage, leaving what lay between these openings and where he stood essentially pitch black. The location and pattern of the columns was barely discernible as they fell into complete darkness. He turned away from the dark void of the main space and poked his head into a couple of the auto bays, which were empty, save for stored construction materials. When he turned to peer into the last bay he was startled as a shapeless figure bolted toward him, knocking him down. Neil dropped his clipboard and the flashlight, which rolled away from him, while his hard hat bounced off the concrete and into the darkness. As he sat stunned on the concrete floor of the parking garage, he heard the footsteps of someone running. He rolled over and grabbed the flashlight, pointing it in the direction of the sound, but did not see anything. As he peered into the darkness, he saw the light momentarily change as a shadow interrupted and then disappeared into the glow of the northwestern vehicle ramp.

Neil was not feeling particularly brave, but as the person was running from him, he got to his feet, grabbed his clipboard and hard hat and sprinted after whomever it was. By the time he emerged breathless from the garage and into the bright daylight, there was no one to be seen. The day was still bright although fog was rolling in. The birds were oblivious to any danger he had felt.

As he caught his breath and calmed down from the adrenaline rush he had just experienced, he decided he had seen enough dark spaces for one day and would, perhaps, insist that David have the contractor turn the construction power on the next time. But that little red light on the scanner indicated there was already power in the building. What it was protecting was anyone's guess.

He realized as he walked to his car that the contractor's truck was gone. As he climbed into his car, he noticed that the glove box was open and everything in it was spilled onto the seat or the floor. The visors were both down and his car registration was missing. Damn it!

He immediately regretted not locking his doors. Getting your car broken into imposes a very unsettling feeling of being violated. It is also a very helpless feeling. Not only had he been bum-rushed in the dark, but his car had been ransacked. He was furious. So he decided he would call it quits for the day, if this was the best it had to offer.

He got out his cell phone to call Shelley to tell her that he would not be returning to the office, and then remembered she had asked for the day off, but that was nothing new. She often cut out early or took time off. She was probably out on a long ride through the valley. He could describe a parcel of land along just about any country lane throughout the valley and she basically knew the area. At least once a month, she would head out with friends and ride to some distant location that he might have thought twice about driving to, given the distance, and she would be there and back before lunch.

While Neil thought that Shelley's obsession with cycling bordered on the extreme, one of the things Neil lived for was taking long jogs through the valley. He decided this is what he needed to calm his nerves, so he returned to his place, donned his running clothes and shoes and set out for some time alone to process the morning's events.

The afternoon offered yet another change in the weather, with broken clouds and blue skies. The temperature remained cool, but Neil liked to run in cool weather. The views of the vineyards in the golden sunlight of the early fall erased the stress and left him feeling invigorated.

«»«»«»

The following week Neil worked a bit on the report for David. He didn't have any other active projects and could have finished it quickly, but he was curious about what lay behind the walls on the floor where the drawings were blank. He thought he might puzzle it through with enough time and perhaps another visit to the site. But after his last visit, he was in no hurry to go back. He was also pre-occupied with his own house which he was building himself on the side. He had been working on it through the summer in the mornings before it got too hot, or he ran out of money. It would have been faster to just hire someone to build it for him, but he didn't have the money for one thing, and he was designing it on the fly, for another. With an occasional paying job, and the sporadic nature of getting an inspector to sign-off on his progress, the going was slow.

Sometime in the middle of the week, he was in the office working on a 3-D model of his house on his computer when Shelley came huffing and puffing into the office as if she had sprinted the last mile or so. She parked her bike in her office, dropping her helmet and a backpack on the floor, and headed to the basement to shower off the sweat and grime of what must have been another long ride. He had not expected to see her that day as she had not been scheduled to work, and he was so engrossed in his modeling that he was startled when she burst through the front door with a casual, but winded, "Hey," for a greeting.

When she emerged back upstairs after her shower, she looked a little more put together. Her hair was wet and pulled back into a limp ponytail. She had thrown on a pair of jeans and a T-shirt and was carrying a sports bag with her damp riding gear.

"Another long ride, huh?" Neil asked without looking up, stating what seemed obvious.

"Yeah," she said.

"Where'd you go today?" he asked, as if it mattered, or he would even know.

"I rode up to Middletown and then down through Pope Valley and back over the hill by Lake Hennessey," she said.

Neil looked up from his monitor and over toward her office. She was bending down fiddling with her bike.

"Sounds like a long ride," he said.

"Oh, not really," she said. "But it's a good workout with two significant climbs."

"Is something wrong with your bike?" Neil asked, seeing that she continued to fuss with her gears.

"Yeah. I'm not sure what the problem is, but it was acting up on me as I came down the hill. I couldn't change gears for the last several miles. Luckily it was flat," she said.

Neil knew little about bike gearing so had nothing to offer.

"Are you busy?" she asked.

"Not really," he responded. "Why?"

"Would you mind dropping me by my place? I think I'll leave the bike here for now and try to fix it tomorrow."

"Let me save this file, and I'll grab my keys and we can get out of here," he said.

She waited patiently for the minute or so while he shut his computer off. It was nearly dark as they walked to his car. A layer of low cloud hung over the Valley as they drove from his office to where she lived. On their way, they were temporarily slowed by the passing of several emergency fire vehicles with lights and sirens blaring.

St. Helena is a small, sleepy little place without much excitement, except on holiday weekends or during most of the summer. Then it is transformed by an influx of tourists. The town is only about 5 square miles and is still predominately residential and agrarian in nature. There is a quaint downtown along the highway, all three blocks of it, that is remarkable for its well-preserved facades that date back to the mid-nineteenth century. There are a couple of famous wineries located on the main drag and all in all, it is not a bad place to stay if you are considering a visit to California's wine country. But there is never much going on and the sidewalks roll-up a little early in the evenings. That is the way most of the locals like it. But when anyone called 911 it seemed to get the entire local fire department to turn out, if nothing else because of sheer boredom. But this time it looked like there might be something to all the noise and confusion as both Neil and Shelley could see a plume of black smoke rising above a distant row of trees that bordered the Napa River.

"Looks like something's burning," Neil said with a hint of excitement in his voice. "Wanna check it out?"

"Not really," she said. "If you don't mind, I'd rather you just drop me off."

They were almost to her place, so Neil didn't insist. He dropped her off and then drove over to see what was going on. The fire and smoke had been extinguished by the time he eased past the emergency vehicles blocking most of the road.

"What was it with firemen that they always had to park their trucks in a manner to block traffic?" he wondered.

One of the volunteer fire team was directing traffic in full fire gear. At least it was bright yellow and easy to see, since he too, was standing in the middle of the road.

As Neil slowly drove past the emergency vehicles and over a narrow bridge he could see the burned out remains of an SUV with a bike rack on the rear bumper sitting in the middle of the Napa River. The river in the early fall was not very deep and the water barely made it to the bottom of the vehicle. The windows were all blown out and the upper portion of the vehicle was a sooty, charred frame. He couldn't tell if anyone had been inside or not, but a paramedic was standing nearby with her arms folded across her chest chatting with one of the firemen, neither of them displaying any sense of urgency. So Neil assumed all the excitement was over and headed back down the Silverado Trail, finding a less congested way back to town.

«»«»«»

On Monday morning next, Neil was sitting in his office sipping coffee while reading the morning news on the internet. His "office" implies a more formal an arrangement than it really was. Several years back, on the advice of his accountant, he had purchased an old bungalow near the center of town. It was zoned for both residential and/or office use, so he rented the second floor out to an accountant, and set up shop on the first floor. There had been times when he had retained the services of several employees, but he was between jobs and had let everyone go except Shelley. The house had a lived-in feel and smell to it; old wood that had absorbed the scent of years of coffee being percolated each morning combined with the odor of the endless succession of Sunday chicken dinners, maybe the hint of a cigar or two and pipe tobacco mixed in for good measure. The yard contained a large old oak, probably over a century old, and deep green grass. Mature shrubs hugged the house around the edges, hiding the house in places, but letting light in through the old double-hung windows. The house had been owned by an elderly woman who had bought it with her husband after World War II and raised her family there. She outlived her husband by 34 years and had lived in the house until shortly before her death. Her kids had all moved away, and after her passing they put it up for sale. Neil had left it largely as he found it, both because in its original condition it had been lovingly cared for and because he didn't have the cash to do much to it.

At any rate, he was in what had once been the living room, enjoying a cup of coffee while reading the morning news. Sunlight was streaming in through the windows. It was a peaceful morning. The excitement of the previous Friday had largely faded. Then the phone rang. Usually, that was a good thing. It might mean some business was in the offing. Neil answered the phone as Shelley did not typically arrive until at least 10:00 a.m. The male voice on the other end of the phone asked to speak with "Neil Thornton."

"Speaking," he said.

"This is Detective Andrews with the St. Helena police department. Do you have a moment?" he asked.

"Sure," Neil said. He didn't know if his voice belied the unusual feeling he had at the moment. He could not remember ever being called by a detective from the local police department or any police department, for that matter. He sat up in his chair and put his coffee mug down.

"I don't know if you remember me," the detective said, "but I play softball in the city league on the police department's team. I think you used to play on a team with a bunch of engineers."

"That's right," Neil said. "You have a good memory. We weren't very good." Neil did not immediately remember the detective.

"Is that why you stopped playing?" the detective asked.

Neil relaxed as the initial shock of being called by the police faded.

"The guys I played with didn't enjoy losing. There was one guy, I don't remember his name. Anyway he was the one who put the team together. When we kept losing he lost interest and it sort of fell apart," Neil said. "Do you still play?"

"Oh, yeah. Somebody has to beat the guys from the fire department."

They both laughed at that.

"As I recall, they were pretty full of themselves," Neil said.

"That is putting it mildly. They are good, but we manage to beat them once in a while."

The detective paused.

"Listen, the reason I called is that I am wondering if you know David Johnsson?" the detective asked.

"Do I know Mr. Johnsson?" Neil asked. "Yes. I met him the week before last."

"Have you spoken to him recently?" he asked.

“What’s today, Monday? I met him at his project site Tuesday before last. But I have not spoken to him since then. Why?” Neil asked.

“Would you have some time this morning to come down to my office?” Detective Andrews asked.

“Yeah, I guess,” Neil replied. “What’s going on?”

“I’ll fill you in when you get here. Do you know where the station is?” he asked.

“Of course,” Neil replied. “I’ll come right down.”

Neil hung up the phone with a strange knot growing in his stomach. Strange. It was all strange. He walked to the door leading to the stairs to the second floor.

“Judy? You up there?” he bellowed up the stairs.

“What’s up?” came the reply.

“Could you tell Shelley that I am going to be out for an hour or so if she comes into the office in the next few minutes?” he continued. “I’m running out for an errand. I’ll be back later. Need anything?”

“No,” was the distant reply.

Neil walked the four blocks through a mostly residential neighborhood to the police station and asked for Detective Andrews.

The municipal building that houses the police department is typical of the sort of building built in the early 1960’s to serve the public in a small community. It was designed with very durable materials with minimal adornment. St. Helena can trace its history back to the 1880’s and has a rich and eclectic inventory of Victorian structures. In more recent times, buildings have been constructed in an attempt to be evocative of some romantic notion associated with the wine growing nature of the region; some more successfully than others. But the municipal building was designed and built in a period between the city’s quaint past and its rediscovered romantic commercial appeal.

Neil recognized Detective Andrews immediately. He was a large, African American man with an imposing presence. Neil guessed he was about 30. He was bald, but as this seemed to be popular amongst men of a certain age, it would have been hard to tell if he was completely bald or had just shaved off whatever he had left for convenience and effect. Neil was of average height and build, but the detective must have been at least 6’-6” and looked like he could have been a linebacker.

The detective entered the public waiting room from a side door and greeted Neil from behind the counter. Neil made a valiant attempt to give the detective a firm handshake, but even so he about crushed Neil's hand.

"Thanks for coming down on such short notice," he said.

"Not a problem," Neil replied. "So what's up?"

"If you have a few minutes I wanted to asked you several more questions about Mr. Johnsson."

"Okay."

"My office is back here." He motioned for Neil to join him behind the counter as he moved back through the door to the office area hidden from public view.

Not having spent any time in a police station, Neil found it a rather odd sensation being led into the heart of the office. It was probably a symptom of having watched too many crime shows on television. Did he need a lawyer? No one looked up from whatever they were doing, so Neil seemed to slip somewhat anonymously into the detective's office. The detective gestured for Neil to sit down in a chair crammed between the wall and the front of his desk. He collapsed into a large, well-worn leather chair and stared at Neil thoughtfully before saying anything.

"Again, I want to thank you for coming in," he said. He paused, as if thinking carefully about the order of the questions he was about to ask Neil.

His office was mostly beige. Beige walls. Beige carpet. Beige desk. The ceiling was tiled with glue up acoustical tiles. The kind popular in the 1960's, and still available today, with little holes poked through in a seemingly random pattern. There was a single ceiling-mounted 2x4 fluorescent light fixture with a surprisingly clean plastic diffuser. His walls were adorned with an outdated map of the city, and a framed photo of the detective shaking hands with the "Terminator." The top of his desk peeked out from beneath a blizzard of papers. It was a wood grain laminate. Neil judged it to be an attempt to replicate the look of walnut. It was something that only an architect would notice.

"How long did you say you have known Mr. Johnsson?"

"I wouldn't say that I really know him. I think you know that I am an architect." He paused, waiting for a reaction, but received none. "He called me a few weeks ago and wanted my professional opinion about a matter relating to his construction project. It's pretty common to get calls out of the blue from people who are seeking my opinion or advice or are considering hiring me for a project," Neil said.

Neil assumed the detective knew what he was referring to when he referenced David Johnsson's "construction project." It seemed like everyone in the community knew. As an architect Neil may have had a skewed sense of what people knew in terms of local projects, but David's development plans had stirred up a lot of dust. Or at least Neil thought so. At any rate, the detective gave no indication that he did or did not know what Neil was referring to, so he continued.

"So he called me about three weeks ago and we met the week before last at the site of his new house and winery. We did a quick site visit. I'm working on my report, but haven't finished it yet."

The detective was taking notes and looked up as Neil paused.

"I still don't understand why you are interested in how I know Mr. Johnsson. Is he in trouble? Is he okay?"

Detective Andrews put his pen down and leaned back in his chair. He looked at Neil for several moments without saying anything and Neil had the distinct impression the detective was trying to decide if he believed him or if he could trust him.

"So the last communication you had in person with Mr. Johnsson was on the Tuesday before last?"

"Yes."

Again there was a long pause as he looked at Neil and thought about what he had just said.

"Was he supposed to call you about your report? Were you going to meet him and go over it?" he asked.

"No, I was going to mail it to him," Neil replied.

The detective, still leaning back in his chair, thought about what Neil had told him and perhaps what he suspected Neil had not told him and probably several different scenarios that had Neil guilty as sin and a couple more in which Neil was as innocent as a new born babe.

"Did you go back to the construction site?" he asked.

"I went back Friday morning that same week," Neil replied. "Kind of strange."

"Oh, yeah? Why?" the detective asked without looking up.

"Well, I went back because Mr. Johnsson and I had not been able to tour the lower floors because the construction power was off. So I went back with a flashlight and poked around," Neil paused.

"That doesn't sound strange," the detective interjected.

"When I got back to my car, someone had broken in and rifled through my stuff. Actually, I hadn't locked it, but I was parked behind a locked gate and I didn't think anyone was around so I didn't bother locking it," Neil said.

"And . . . ," he gestured for Neil to keep talking.

"And I noticed that my car registration was missing," he said.

"Anything else?" The detective furrowed his brow.

"I don't think so. They went through the glove box and dumped everything on the seat and the floor, but I don't keep anything in there except work gloves, maps, and the owner's manual."

"That is strange. Anything else happen that was strange while you were there?" he asked.

"Well, two things. When I got there, there was a truck parked outside the construction fence belonging to the general contractor. It was gone when I got back to my car."

The detective nodded, but said nothing.

Neil continued. "The other thing is something I probably wouldn't have brought up, because it makes me sound paranoid. When I was down in the garage . . . ," Neil stopped, realizing the detective wouldn't have any context for what or where the garage was.

"The project has a large subterranean garage," Neil explained. "It was dead silent and pitch black except for my flashlight and I heard a loud sound of heavy metal hitting something hard. It kind of startled me. But I assumed it was just a piece of steel that fell over. After I calmed down a bit, I was checking one of the auto bays, and someone jumped out of the darkness and knocked me to the floor."

"Scared the hell out of me," Neil said continuing. "I think I saw them running out of the garage up one of the vehicle ramps. I ran after them, but when I got above ground, no one was there. Then I went to my car and found someone had been in it." Neil waited for the detective to absorb what he had just said and to respond.

Detective Andrews sat for a couple of seconds still looking at the paperwork on his desk before looking up.

"That's a strange story," he said. "I think I would have been a little freaked out."

"I was," Neil said.

"But you didn't see anyone else other than that while you were there? Have you met anyone else in his organization?" The detective was doodling on the margins of a sketch pad.

"No. I didn't see anyone. Mr. Johnsson told me he had an assistant, but no, I have not met them."

"Her name is Lydia and she was also his girlfriend," he said.

"Oh, okay. I guess that makes sense," Neil replied.

The detective looked up abruptly. "Why?"

"Well, he said he had been married twice. I got the impression that he was recently divorced. That's all."

"Her name is Lydia Mankovich. She may have started out as an assistant, but she seems to have been promoted."

He kept referring to David in the past tense. Neil was beginning to wonder if David was dead. He didn't really want to ask, but couldn't help himself.

"Look. This is all rather odd," Neil said. "I've never been interviewed in a police station before and you keep referring to Mr. Johnsson in the past tense. Is he okay?"

"That is what we are trying to find out. He hasn't been heard from or seen in about a week. Ms. Mankovich called in a missing persons report. I'm just checking all the leads to the people that saw him last and apparently you are one of them," he said. "Do you have anything else to add that might be useful?"

Neil thought for a moment before speaking. "I keep my client's information confidential as a general rule. But in this case, I guess I can tell you the reason I was asked to visit his construction project. It may not have anything to do with anything, but it might prove useful to your investigation."

The detective looked up as Neil continued, "He is in a dispute with the general contractor. He hadn't paid them, so they stopped his job. When that happens, neither party is typically happy. Delays typically cost everyone money." Neil paused again before continuing.

"The only other person that I know had contact with him at the same time I did was the GC's site superintendent. We were supposed to walk through the project together, but he was late. So Mr. Johnsson and I walked it by ourselves. As I was leaving, a guy in a company truck showed up. It looked identical to the one I saw on Friday, but that doesn't necessarily mean he was there. His name was Craig something."

"You don't remember his last name?" the detective asked.

Neil shook his head "no".

"I could find it. I think he may have given me his card, but I'm not recalling his last name off the top of my head."

"Okay. Well I guess that is sort of an obvious place to start," the detective said. "We have interviewed Ms. Mankovich. She did not have much to add. She did say that he had received some ugly e-mail from people that didn't like his project. I haven't seen them yet, but they probably don't rise to the level of death threats, but we'll have to wait and see."

"Is there anything else I can do to assist you?" Neil asked.

"Not at the moment." The detective stood up and Neil quickly followed.

"Could you send me the contractor's name?" the Detective asked.

"Sure."

"You know how to find your way out of here?" he asked Neil.

"Yeah," Neil replied. He was glad to be getting out of there. He had done nothing wrong, but was somewhat shaken by the idea that a client of his might be dead or even might have been murdered.

Neil turned back as he left the office. "Are you sure he didn't just take off for Hawaii or something without telling anyone?" he asked.

"I'm not sure of anything and that is as reasonable a possibility as anything else at this point, except you'd think he would have taken his girlfriend. Wouldn't you?" the detective asked.

"I guess. If she was his girlfriend," Neil replied.

"You said you had not met her."

Neil nodded.

“From all indications, it would appear she was more than an assistant.” His phone rang and he sat down. “If I need you, I will call you,” he said before answering his phone.

“Of course,” Neil replied.

The detective nodded as he picked up the phone and Neil exited his office. “Andrews here.” The detective paused listening to the voice on the other end of the call. “It was a Hertz rental out of SFO?” He paused again listening to additional details. “I got it. Let me know if you find anything else. Thanks.”

"If you were a son of mine, I wouldn't want you to be an architect, because it's a tough way to be in the world."

-- Peter Eisenman

Chapter Three

By the time Neil returned to the office after his "chat" with Detective Andrews, Shelley had arrived. In addition to helping him with administrative tasks, she also pitched in with other chores, like cleaning the office where his interest and motivation left something to be desired. She was in the kitchen cleaning out the refrigerator without being asked. Her proactive work ethic ensured Neil would never let her go.

"Hey!" she yelled from the kitchen. "Where ya been? You should go out more often, whenever you do someone always calls."

Neil picked up the half empty coffee mug off his desk as he walked into the kitchen. He dumped it in the sink and poured a fresh cup.

"I'm not taking any new clients. Tell them all to drop dead!" he said.

She had no way of getting the gallows humor associated with the response, but she knew as an architect that he was always open to finding new clients and so he had to be joking.

"Right. Well I'll tell you what. This refrigerator is not going to clean itself, so maybe you should rethink that," she dead panned, "because the person doing the cleaning needs to get paid."

"So, wait. Let me guess. Someone wants to build a winery and is looking for a great local architect for the job." That was the standing joke – kind of like the one that always ends with "when I win the lottery."

She stuck her head around the refrigerator door and gave Neil an odd look.

"Do you already know about it?" she asked.

"What? Someone really called about a winery project? Nobody ever calls about winery projects," he said.

"That's not true. You just had that winery thing a couple of weeks ago. I think you are on a roll or something. Maybe word is finally getting around. Or maybe that guy is telling his friends or something. What did you say his name is?"

Neil made a face and thought about what she had just said.

"His name *was* David Johnsson and he *may* be dead or something. I was just down getting grilled about what I knew about him at the police station."

"What?! Shut. Up."

She struggled to her feet, tossed her sponge in the sink and shut the refrigerator door. When she cleaned she was really thorough and had been on her hands and knees cleaning the back of the lowest vegetable drawer.

"What are you talking about?" she asked. "Are you serious?"

"What are you talking about? Are you serious?" he said throwing her surprise back at her as he left the kitchen with his cup of coffee.

"Yeah. But tell me what happened," she said following him.

"I don't know what happened. I got a call this morning before you got here from a detective. 'Detective Andrews,'" he said, lowering his voice to it huskiest register. Neil put the detective's name in finger quotes.

"He asked me all about how I knew this guy and then finally told me he was missing. That's about it."

"Wow. That's kind of weird and creepy."

"It was a strange feeling walking into a police station to get questioned. I kind of wondered if I needed a lawyer or something."

"So where do you think this guy is?" she asked.

"How would I know? I met him once and he's gone. He's probably in Tahiti or something. They say he has his own jet so he could be anywhere. The person that reported him missing was his girlfriend. Maybe he just found a new girlfriend. He's rich."

"I know. Why do you think I wanted to know what was going on?" She brushed her hair back with an exaggerated flourish.

"You may have missed your chance."

"Damn you!"

"Damn me?! You can't blame me," he said with a laugh heading to his desk. "So what about this new project?" Neil's interest in talking about a missing rich guy he did not know was not as strong as his interest in getting more work.

"A guy called and said he was thinking about building a winery estate and heard you were a good architect" she said loudly as she walked back to the kitchen. "He said he checked out our website and gave us a call."

Neil sat at his desk and put his coffee down. "Where's his number? he asked as he rummaged through the papers on his desk. "Never mind."

Shelley had placed a phone note with a name and number on his computer key-pad. Neil sat down and picked up the phone and dialed the number. The name was Karl Stroughmann. The area code was not local. The number rang twice and a man answered the phone.

"This is Neil Thornton. I'm returning a call from Karl Stroughmann," he said.

"Ah, Mr. Thornton. This is excellent timing! I'm just coming to see you in your office. Are you there?"

"Yes I am," he said in surprise.

"Good. I'm coming up the walk."

Neil glanced out the front window and sure enough, a man in his late 30's or early 40's was heading toward the front door.

"Okay. See you in a second." Neil hung up the phone and headed to the door. The man was practically there as Neil threw the door open.

"Good morning," he said, as Neil extended his hand.

They shook hands and Neil invited him into the office. Neil must have seemed a little surprised. In addition to being surprised to be talking to someone on the phone as they walked into his office, he was generally surprised to be having a potential client walking into his office unannounced. In fact he could not remember it ever having happened before. The typical process was for the client to call or e-mail and then for Neil to return the call or e-mail and then for them to meet for lunch at an expensive restaurant or their club.

"Would you like coffee or something?" Neil asked.

"No. I'm good. Thanks." Karl Stroughmann had stepped through the open doorway and stood surveying the office.

Neil had left everything in the house pretty much as it had been when he bought it. It was an old house built in 1908 as a parsonage. The adjacent church had been torn down and replaced with several other houses in the late 1930's. The street was now one of the older, more gentrified streets in town with large trees and lots of shade. As Neil's staff was never very large, he managed to park the couple of employee cars in the driveway and on the street, when needed. As he had no staff at the present, other than Shelley, there were no cars in the driveway at all, save Neil's. Shelley typically rode her bike and Judy, his tenant, lived around the corner and usually walked unless it was raining.

The house itself was characterized by its deep porches. It was a two story house with a full basement. Almost no one builds a house with a basement in California, but the early transplants from the east coast seemed to think they needed a basement, so many of the really old houses have them. The house had a wide front door that led into a small, wood paneled foyer with a coffered ceiling. The original brass fixtures throughout the house somehow managed to survive, as had most of the finishes, including tiled fireplace surrounds and wallpaper. From the foyer, the house was organized around a central stair leading to bedrooms upstairs and what were service areas in the basement. Judy had her pick of the rooms upstairs, though all of them had essentially been converted into offices. She was his only tenant at the moment, but they came and went and the extra rent really helped during lean times. The house originally had a large, screened sleeping porch upstairs, but this was enclosed with large windows. This was where Judy was ensconced. She loved all the light. Neil used the basement as overflow space and for storage, when it was used at all.

Shelley had a small office off the foyer in what was once the parson's study. It had a large window overlooking the front yard and a smaller window on the side of the house facing a small gurgling brook that ran along the property line. The other wall had a fireplace which she used frequently during the winter. She said she only put up with Neil because he let her come and go as she pleased and because she liked her office. Her bike was in its normal place, parked between her desk and the fire place.

Neil's office was in what was the living room. It was a reasonably sized space with a fireplace in the center of the wall facing the foyer. Part of the room was set up as a seating area, the other half supported his desk and drafting board. He didn't really use the drafting board much anymore, but couldn't seem to get rid of it. That may be in part due to the fact that it was a convenient layout surface, or more truthfully, a place to stack paperwork that he had difficulty dealing with. The entire wall adjacent to his desk was original floor-to-ceiling French doors. He had some light gauzy curtains hung to control the light, so it was a nice bright working environment. The ceiling in the living room was also coffered and all the floors and stairs squeaked. He didn't mind the squeaks as he thought they were a natural artifact of the building's age and added character.

The dining room could support four workstations and was lined with his library of architectural books.

The kitchen had a small breakfast nook, besides being a functioning kitchen. There was a pantry. And off the kitchen, there was a utility room and an adjoining toilet. All in all, it had everything he needed for an office. He should probably have kicked Judy out and moved in upstairs, but it was good to get away from the office and he was in the middle of building his own house – but that was a whole other story.

As Karl Stroughmann looked around the foyer, Neil had the distinct sense that his practice and qualifications were being assessed as if his guest's decision to hire him might be influenced by what he did or did not see.

"Why don't we sit in my office," Neil suggested gesturing toward the living room.

They walked in and sat down. There were architectural books on the coffee table along with recent issues of several architectural magazines. Neil had placed study models on the end tables and lining the window sill. There were some fragment models and construction artifacts strewn about. He had placed a large site model on the mantel leaning against the wall. It sat where one would normally expect to see a large painting or mirror and reached nearly to the ceiling. It probably wasn't safe there, but once it had landed, it had never been moved.

"I like your space," he said. "It's what I would expect to see in a small rural architect's office."

"Ouch! Have you visited a lot of architect's offices?" Neil asked.

"A few," came his immediate reply. "But that wasn't meant as a dig. I was just trying to get a sense of what you do."

"Perception is reality," Neil replied. "But this is it," he said, waving a hand around the room. "The questions is, what are you looking for and can I be of any assistance?"

The man chuckled, "Exactly. That's what I am trying to figure out."

"So my receptionist said you are looking for an architect to design a winery."

"That's right," he said. "Have you ever designed one?"

"No, but as you might suspect, I have been through more than a few and have been asked that question countless times – if that makes me qualified."

Mr. Stroughmann considered that for a moment and then asked, "So you are here in the middle of wine country. Why haven't you ever designed a winery?"

"Well, it's pretty straightforward. The folks who come here with the money to build a winery from scratch usually have their pet architect all lined up before they get here. Sometimes they are in tow. The truth is, architecture has become so competitive that it's difficult to get significant commissions if you don't have a very high profile or a large portfolio of similar projects. As you mentioned, I am a small, rural architect. My portfolio is almost all local projects for the local community. Few of the people who live here own a winery and not that many are built. It's a complicated process to get the entitlements and permits. And," Neil paused here for effect, "for some reason, people in New York and Chicago have never heard of me."

He laughed. "Okay. Fair enough."

"So let me ask you, if you have the money for a winery and aren't from around here, where's your architect? And how did you find me?"

"You may not be aware of the fact that you have a reputation outside the region," he said, "but you do. I'm out here on business in San Francisco and decided to take a side trip. Being this close to the Napa Valley, I figured I might as well rent a car and drive up here. Since I'm checking out the area I thought I might check out a local architect while I'm at it."

Neil doubted that he had a reputation that extended beyond the Napa Valley. In fact, most days he doubted it extended to the end of the block. Even if what Karl Stroughmann said might have been true, Neil couldn't really wrap his brain around the idea that this man, a potential client, had just walked into his office out of the blue looking for an architect. But hey, it could be possible, so Neil wasn't going to send his guest away. That would not make sense either.

"Who can argue with that," Neil said. "Where are you from and how long are you going to be here?"

"Well, you were close. I am from Long Island which most people not from the New York area think is like being from New York. I've been here since Friday. I spent the weekend with two different realtors getting the same grand tour of the area and what's available. They basically told me all the same things, so that lines up with what I already know. I feel good about that. So today, I thought I would check out local architects. So far you seem like the most likely guy to work with."

"That's always good to hear," Neil said. "Who else have you checked out?"

There were exactly eleven architects in the area, if you included St. Helena and Calistoga. Four of them worked for his main competitor. They did mostly schools, but were well connected and would chase anything that moved. Three of the others were sole practitioners and did mostly hand-to-mouth residential projects. Two were retired, one of those being his good friend whose practice he had inherited. The other person worked for the City in the building department. And then there was Neil.

"Pretty much everyone," was Karl Stroughmann's response.

"Well. I always like to beat the competition," Neil said, knowing that none of these were really the competition when it came to being selected for a winery. That competition was in Santa Rosa or the Bay Area or in the clutches of some other client.

"So let's talk about your project. What are you hoping to do and when?"

"I've been following the progress of David Johnsson's development. It seems to me that what he is doing is something along the lines of what I want to do," he said. "Have you heard of him? One of the realtors told me they thought you had been working for him on his project."

"Gosh. You have to give me the name of that realtor," Neil said. "I need to take them to lunch or something. And yes, I have heard of him, but no I have not had anything to do with his project. But like everyone else, you can't escape the gossip and what not. He is such a force of nature that he attracts a lot of attention."

Neil paused.

That was interesting. As far as Neil knew he had not mentioned to anyone that he had been engaged by David Johnsson. Shelley knew, but that was probably it. But word tended to get around in a small community.

"I don't want to insult you or anything, but do you have his kind of money? His accomplishments have been well funded to date. It's true that a smaller project would probably not receive as much scrutiny or be as difficult to entitle, but certainly his money solved a lot of his issues."

"I think I have what I need, but I don't have what he has."

"So how big a winery are you planning and is it for fun or as a business venture?" Neil asked.

Karl Stroughmann did not look like he was old enough to retire, but then what does that look like? If you have enough wealth, retirement is a relative term. He appeared to Neil to be about his own age, only in a lot better shape. He was well built and looked like he could have killed Neil with his eyes closed, one arm behind his back, all with just his other thumb. His hair was cut close and of an indeterminate color. It was either blond or maybe brown but going grey. He was tan and lean. Neil guessed that he was over six feet tall. His dress was casual, but not sloppy. He seemed more coiffed than your average man.

"I want to create an award-winning wine and my plan is to either buy acreage with mature grapes on it, or to clear land and plant them, or both. I am open as to the size, but I think I need to secure at least fifty to one hundred acres. For me it's about the appellation and the grape variety. I don't care about the condition of the winery itself. I can do whatever is needed to get that into shape. I do want to build my own house, though."

"Are you going to market the wine?" Neil asked. This was his way of asking again if this was a business proposition or an avocation. And that was only important because people who built buildings for an investment always had pesky little things like internal rates of return and the like to guide their decision making, while those that built for love, tended to not be as worried about whether their return on equity was front and center all the time. And that created room for the creation of art.

"If I make enough to sell, fine. But I just want to make a great wine."

"Well. Wine has captivated the human imagination for millennia. If I can be of assistance I would certainly welcome the opportunity. Do you have any questions for me?" Neil asked.

"I was hoping that you had some winery design experience and maybe some drawings so that we could discuss my plans in the context of your experience. That is why I mentioned David Johnsson's project. I hear it is really amazing and if you had worked on it and happened to have a set of the drawings, that would be helpful."

Even though Neil owned the drawings and designs he produced, he would not typically show them to a prospective client without the blessing of the client who hired him or at least until the project was old enough that no one would care. It would also depend on the type of project and his agreement with the client. Additionally, it had been his experience that when a client was in the throes of a construction project on a proprietary design, they wanted to maintain their privacy. And when they didn't, it was better to let them decide how much to reveal and to whom. That was especially true regarding their project's cost.

As it was, Neil did have a set of drawings for David Johnsson's "house," but not the rest of the project including the winery and natatorium. He had signed a contract for the consulting and it contained a confidentiality clause, of course. It was David Johnsson.

Neil thought carefully about what he said next.

"Mr. Stroughmann, I may not need to clarify this point with you, but I want to go back to the issue of Mr. Johnsson. You asked if I had worked on his project and I said I had not. That is technically true. I have nothing to do with his project. However, he did retain me recently to review some construction related issues on his behalf. As you might expect, Mr. Johnsson values his privacy and included a confidentiality clause in our contract for my services. So I can't really say anything more about that. Additionally, while I do have some of his drawings, I can't share them with you without Mr. Johnsson's permission."

Karl Stroughmann was listening intently and nodded. Neil didn't think there was any point in telling him he had some of the drawings, but not all the drawings. Regardless, he could not show him what he had.

"It's not a problem. I just find it helps to go to school on other people's nickel when you can," Stroughmann said.

He looked around the room. The set of drawings that David Johnsson had given Neil was still laid out on his drafting table.

"I am leaving to head home later this afternoon," he said. He stood and extended his hand. "I know how to reach you. I'll decide what I want to do over the next several months and perhaps I'll give you a call," he said.

Neil stood too and shook his hand. "Thanks for stopping by," he said. "It was a pleasure meeting you and regardless of how you choose to proceed, I wish you the best. But before you leave, let me get you one of my cards." Neil retrieved one from his desk and handed it to him as they walked to the door.

"Have a great trip, and don't hesitate to drop by again – for advice or a second opinion the next time you are out here."

With that the man left and Neil returned to his desk. Shelley came out of the kitchen. The house wasn't that large and she had basically been able to hear the entire conversation.

"I thought that went well. I think he will call you back when he gets serious," she said.

"You're dreaming," Neil said. "But that is why I like having you around. I need a glass-is-more-than-half-full person to keep me optimistic."

She gave him a look and returned to the kitchen.

Something about Karl Stroughmann didn't add up for Neil. He had the vaguely disturbing feeling that he had just been probed by someone with an ulterior motive. There was just enough truth to what the man had said that it might be true, but just enough that didn't ring true that it probably wasn't. Only time would tell.

"Your life will be no better than the plans you make and the action you take. You are the architect and builder of your own life, fortune, destiny."

-- Alfred A. Montapert

Chapter Four

David Reginald Johnsson had in fact been born with a number of impediments that should have kept him from ever achieving the great financial success for which he had become famous. His father and mother were high school sweethearts from a small town in Wisconsin. It was the kind of rural town that had a small main street and one stop light and everybody knew everybody else. The economy ebbed and flowed with the price of corn and life was centered on the rhythm of planting and harvest time. To say that there was not much to do would be an overstatement. In fact, it was so dead, that being bored counted as an activity. For kids, there was nothing to do, except the obvious. His dad had an old pickup truck that he could drive and he had enough pocket money from working on his family farm to buy gas and beer.

Gas and beer probably abetted nature as it took its natural course. A senior year pregnancy was almost inevitable. His mom dropped out and gave birth just after his dad graduated. They moved in with his parents. She got a job as a waitress in the local café while he continued to work as a farm hand.

She didn't plan to fall for an older guy on the local volunteer fire department. It just happened. He came in for breakfast a couple of times a week and the casual flirting progressed to an active fling. She was young and pretty; two things that brought her attention from the men she served.

Her second pregnancy resulted in the early termination, not of the pregnancy, but of her marriage. She moved out, with David, and rented a room with an older couple. Her wages were not enough to cover her expenses, and it did not take long before she was drowning financially. Her fireman beau was not the marrying type, but he was willing to help financially in return for the physical benefits their acquaintance provided. It did not take long before her reputation attracted other men willing to provide financial help to such a "pretty young thing." One man led to the next and before long she was widely recognized and ostracized for her reputation as the local prostitute.

The older couple decided they could not have her as a tenant, given the circumstances. She moved out and packed her two boys and meager worldly possessions into her old car and drove to Minneapolis-St. Paul to try to get away from her reputation and make a new start. But that can be a tricky thing when you are low on cash and have two extra mouths to feed. She found a low-rent apartment in the low-rent part of town. She looked diligently for work while her meager savings lasted. But when her cushion ran out, she found herself on a street corner hoping to make a little money to pay the rent and keep the lights on.

Alcohol had remained a constant. Eventually, drugs entered the equation and that sped up the end. David's mother slipped further and further into a self-destructive cycle of addiction. She went in and out of jail a couple of times. By the time David was five he had spent a year living in his mother's car. Days were spent hanging out around the car playing on the curb or wherever they happened to be parked. The winter was the worst. David's brother, Keith, was only three. Their mother would bundle them up in the back seat and leave them with a little flashlight and a bit of food to fend for themselves while she worked her corner. She would return sometime the following morning. If she was sober, they would eat a hot breakfast at a local diner. If she had been abusing, they were lucky if she managed to find a local convenience store to buy a breakfast of junk food. Every now and then, she made enough to get a room at a flea-bitten motel. David liked staying in motels. They were warm and had TV's.

One day, his mother left at her normal time and never returned. As luck would have it, and it probably was just luck, David's mom had left him with his brother in a motel room. They were found two days later when the motel manager checked their room because their mother had not paid her bill. He called the police. The police called family protective services and David and his brother entered the "system."

Both boys were too young to know what was going on and why. They asked repeatedly, for months, about "mamma". The first home they went to, they were kept together. David did not remember much from this time. They were moved through several homes over the next several years. Each time, their stay was shorter than the last. None of this made sense to him. Being handed from stranger to stranger with lots of hugs and kisses and promises. The experience was more difficult for his brother. The lack of permanence and turmoil every time they moved caused his brother to begin to act out, which in turn shortened their stay, causing the cycle to shorten and repeat itself with the same problematic results. By the time his brother was 9 and he was 11, they had bounced around inside the system for almost 6 years. They had worn out their welcome in at least a dozen foster homes. The decision to separate them came with their next move. The boys were first taken to a group home. David was placed in a unit with 11 14 year old boys, while his brother was placed in a unit with 7-10 year old boys.

They were reunited briefly the day that his brother was assigned to a new family. The case worker told them that in light of the situation, it would be easier to place them separately, rather than together. He told them they could stay in touch with each other and that it would always be possible for each of them to know where the other one was. As they got older, they were promised they would be able to maintain their family connection with each other. David's brother cried and said he didn't want to get separated. David tried to reason with the social worker, but was told the decision had been made and was for the best. The boys hugged briefly as they said good-bye.

David was never placed in another foster home. It wasn't that the county agency didn't try. He seemed to have passed the expiration date. Over the next several years, he did manage to talk to Keith once or twice a year on the phone. Each time, however, his brother would be in a new home and his behavioral issues seemed to be worse. When David was 15, he asked to speak with his brother, but was told that he had run away from his last home and no one knew where he was. This was devastating for David. Until then, he had harbored a secret belief that his mother would come back and that the three of them would be reunited. Losing his brother was a heavy blow from which he never fully recovered.

There are many different approaches to foster care. In the county where David was institutionalized, he lacked for nothing physically. He had a warm bed and three meals a day. The facility basically functioned as a boarding school for children of various ages, although the older kids were the highest percentage of the residents. His days were a mostly dull routine of getting up, preparing for breakfast, being bussed to a local public school and back, supervised time doing homework, and an occasional recreation night or movie night. But generally, it was a boring routine. There was a little more free time on the weekends, but there was nowhere to go and nothing to do. Boredom reigned. Holidays were the worst time. The staff tried to decorate and make things a little less institutional, but in some ways it just made it worse.

The unit he was assigned to was made up of 12 boys. State law required that they be under constant adult supervision, but there were ways to evade the system. While fights were unusual in his group, there was a definite pecking order. The stronger ruled over the weaker. The older had seniority over the younger. If you were oldest, tallest, and strongest, you were the alpha. If you were the youngest, shortest, and weakest, you quickly learned your place as a follower. David was not the oldest or the tallest. He was a well-built kid for his size, but he wasn't the top of the heap physically. Even so, he garnered respect from the other boys for his intelligence and wit. If things got tense, he used his intelligence to bluff his way through a confrontation. The one time he was cornered and had to resort to defending himself, he took the initiative and surprised his taller aggressor. He gave better than he got, but ended up with a bloody nose. The other kid required stitches. There would have been payback, had it not been for the experience of the system in dealing with this sort of altercation. As a result, both boys were moved to new units. It did not hurt David's reputation that he had taken on a bigger kid and come out on top. That went a long way in protecting him from future fights, at least until some new kid felt he needed to prove something. In the meantime, David used his new found status to build a network of friends on lower rungs of the pecking order that kept him informed of who he needed to watch out for and when. His creation of a personal network of informants and allies was a skill he took with him into his later life.

As David moved through the system, he excelled naturally at his studies. Perhaps because his own personal history was so devoid of factual information, he loved history. All his earthly possessions were contained in a locker at the foot of his bed. He had no photos of his parents or of other family. He did have a couple of photos of he and his brother together. These were his most prized possessions, because they were all that he had that spoke of family and belonging. He had a couple of books, a baseball glove, some of his own baby teeth that he had saved. Once when the agency took the boys to watch a ball game, he had caught a fly ball. The ball and the ticket to the game were kept in a carefully sealed plastic bag. All in all, it wasn't much.

In addition to his love of history, he excelled in math. It was his ability in math that changed his destiny. He was pulled out one day from his normal class routine and walked to a room for special testing. He wondered if he had done something wrong or if there was something wrong with him, when in fact, this was the beginning of the path that would take him out of the system and open doors of opportunity that he could have never imagined.

The test he took that day was a national scholastic achievement test for kids that had tested well on the typical standardized tests that were administered on an annual basis throughout the state. His score had been flagged as being in the upper portion of the top quartile of all the kids in the school district that had taken the test. His score had been brought to the attention of the vice principal for instruction at the high school he attended by a phone call from a representative of the testing company. The vice principal had insisted that David be tested further as his score had exceeded all but one other test score in the entire state.

So as he walked into a classroom with several adults, he could not help being a little nervous. They told him that he had the opportunity to take another test, because he had done so well on the other standardized test. That did not really sound like an honor or privilege the way they described it and he initially deferred saying he would prefer not to take the test and to return to class with his classmates. If it were not for the intervention of his math teacher from the previous year, whom he knew and liked, he might not have taken the test. But this teacher saw in him a young confused kid with a screwed up background story not dissimilar to his own. He pulled David aside and told him how much it would mean to him if David would take the test. So David said, "Okay."

He spent the next 4 hours puzzling his way through math that he had never been exposed to in depth. Some of it made sense, but a lot of it was truly beyond him. But that is what a true test does. It presents a wide range of information, from simple to complex, to gauge the test taker's true knowledge. When David was finished, he apologized to his former math teacher as he left the room. He was pretty sure he had not lived up to his expectations. In fact, when the results came back, he had scored upper end of the top quartile for his age group and became someone the administration of his high school began to watch and guide very carefully. The system also reacted positively, providing additional resources for him to be able to attend special weekend tutoring sessions, take advanced classes at a local community college, even though he was still in high school.

By the time David graduated from high school, he had received acceptance letters from a number of prestigious universities. One of them came with the offer of a full scholarship, which made the decision regarding which one to accept very easy.

«»«»«»

Neil scrounged around on his desk and found the business card for Craig Stevens, the site superintendent for the construction company that he had promised he would send to Detective Andrews. He also found the e-mail address for Detective Andrews.

Neil had only briefly met Craig Stevens and didn't know anything about him, except he had been the site superintendent of David's project and was not on good terms with him.

In fact Craig Stevens had a temper with almost no fuse. He was a reasonably intelligent person, but he could be triggered into fits of fury over seemly insignificant, even trivial, issues. He had been a journeyman plumber for a couple of years and developed a reputation for not putting up with any crap and for getting things done. He found his home when he landed the position of site superintendent.

He started working construction right out of high school. He thought he would go to college, but some of his friends had gone to work after they graduated from high school and were making what seemed like good money to someone who had never had any. They made enough money to buy cars, burn on booze and cigarettes. He thought he would work a year and save enough to go back, but once he started working, saddled himself with a sizeable car payment and a hot girlfriend that liked it when he spent money taking her out, he never made it back.

He and his friends joked a lot about how much pipe they were laying. As a plumber's assistant, he laid a lot of pipe in every sense of the saying. The sub-contractor he worked for liked his aggressive self-confidence and his ability to motivate guys to get the job done. He didn't care that sometimes this was the result of Craig's hair-trigger temper, rather than positive reinforcement. So it did not take Craig long before he was more than just an apprentice. He became a journeyman plumber and eventually the foreman of a crew.

That was all great. He married his hot girlfriend, bought a house. Picked up another car payment and a couple of rug rats. He found himself driving to jobs all over the region from east of Sacramento, to down near San Jose, all the way up past Santa Rosa. He spent a lot of time in his truck early in the morning getting to job sites before the traffic slowed everything to a crawl. The money was significant, but so were his expenses. He had a number of really good years and then California went into an economic slump; the construction industry took a big dump, but his expenses stayed pretty much the same. The stress built up to a point that his temper flashed at his boss one day and he found himself without a job before he knew what hit him.

He lost the house and the cars. His wife was not far behind and she took the kids, but left most of the debt. He got another job, but it didn't pay as well. In the meantime, his ex-wife got an attorney and a child support judgement that made what little he did make disappear all too quickly. He knew something had to give, so he started looking higher up the food chain and managed to land a job with a general contractor as a site superintendent. He had the reputation of being a hammer and he knew what to do when he saw anything that looked remotely like a nail: he pounded it hard.

He got a new, younger, hotter girlfriend, and a newer, smaller house and he still drove all over northern California hammering every "nail" his employer put in front of him. So when his company needed a site superintendent to drive home a big new project for some rich guy named David Johnsson, they thought they had just the right tool in their bag to make it happen. It was a blunt force tool. A hammer meeting another hammer, both having been swung with their full force.

It did not take long for Craig and David to start butting heads. David initially liked Craig's aggressive nature. He liked it when he pushed hard for the outcomes that David wanted. But as things started to go a little sideways, he was not quite as happy when Craig started pushing back at David or he began insisting that the drawings were incomplete or that either David's meddling or other unforeseen conditions warranted the payment of change orders to his company.

Craig was a big guy and had learned at an early age how to use his size to intimidate others. Some might have called it bullying, but Craig was not self-aware enough to understand how his in-your-face bluster was a turn off to most people he met. He approached practically everything in life as a transactional, zero-sum negotiation. His imposing size was just another form of negotiating using "other means." His employers knew he operated at the level of a junk yard dog, but as long as he was their junk yard dog, they tolerated him.

David was used to getting his way no less frequently than Craig, but typically with much more finesse. His initial approach was smooth and only turned aggressive when the obstacle failed to remove itself at the desired speed. But David's aggression took the form of hired subordinates and legal action. He didn't like to get down into the fray and he avoided personal confrontations except as a last resort. He did not take kindly to Craig raising his voice to the man paying the bills and liked his "leaning in" during a heated argument and the associated physical bluster even less.

It seemed that both men lost no time beginning to see the other as the primary obstacle between them and success. The owner ultimately has most of the cards, because the owner ultimately has all the money. But that is not to say that a general contractor cannot exact a certain level of pain or extract an undue amount of money from an owner that wants to play hard ball. Once the ink on the contract is dry, both sides can retire to their respective corner to wait for the bell. In construction, the ringing of that bell is usually a weekly occurrence, but if you have an activist owner, it can be daily.

Craig started building his case for extras and delays and David started to doubt anything Craig said. As the chasm between them widened, the dollar amount of the breach of contract to which they each believed they were entitled grew larger. On a normal project, the architect tries to act as the referee. Sometimes that works and sometimes it doesn't. But on this project, there didn't seem to be a referee, so the slugfest continued until it devolved into a figurative bare knuckle brawl. They each bloodied the other. They each took a few rounds, and neither won by a knock out. It wasn't clear after it all fell apart who was going to win the decision when it wound up in court.

David thought Craig was a liar and a thief. Craig thought David was a blowhard who had money but not an ounce of reason.

It might actually have been interesting to have settled the dispute in a ring with some gloves. By the time everything came to a grinding halt, both men might have willingly climbed into such a ring. But instead, it turned into a cold war with hot rhetoric. Both sides were building their case. Both sides had been wounded. Both sides had drawn blood and had been bloodied. Both sides had lost money. Both sides were preparing to go to court.

«»«»«»

Neil drafted a short e-mail to Detective Andrews with Craig Stevens' contact information and then left for the day. Shelley had asked for a few days off and had left early. Judy had family visiting from out of state and had taken them to San Francisco. So there was no reason to stick around in the office.

«»«»«»

The next morning Neil arrived at the office about 9:00 a.m. As he parked his car and walked to the front door, nothing seemed amiss. However, as he inserted his key into the lock, the door opened slightly. That seemed odd, but not alarming. He pushed the door open wondering if he had forgotten to lock it. The house was always cool in the morning at this time of year, but never really cold enough to require turning on the furnace. Neil didn't usually have to do that until sometime in late November. But this morning he thought he might indulge in a morning fire to accompany his coffee and casual perusal of the day's news. Shelley's office also had a fireplace in it and had more space for storing firewood and the necessary fire tools, so he headed into her office to grab a couple of sticks of kindling and some matches.

Neil immediately sensed something wrong. Shelley was a neat freak and never, as long as he had known her, left her desk with anything out of place. She was sort of an organized-piles-person, so the top of her desk was always neatly arranged before she went home. This morning there were papers scattered about as if they had been rifled through. He immediately forgot about the fire and walked into his office and found an even bigger mess. His desk, which was never as clean as Shelley's, had nothing on it. All the paperwork that had been on it, was scattered around on the floor. The same was true of his drafting table. He quickly walked through the rest of the house and thought that it seemed as though someone had been through all the closets and storage cabinets. Nothing was trashed, but things just seemed a little out of place. All the jackets in the one closet where he kept a few old ones in the event that he needed to run out on short notice, had been pushed over to one side as if someone was looking for something.

Neil returned to his desk and dropped into his chair. Did this rise to a reportable event? Nothing seemed to have been vandalized or taken, not that there was really much to take. His not-so-new computers were still on the desks. None of his models or architectural books had been taken. His small computer server was still in its closet humming away.

After thinking about it, he decided to call the only person at the police department that he knew and tell him that he had been burgled.

“Andrews here,” the detective said.

“Good morning. This is Neil Thornton,” he said. “I was in your office yesterday.”

“I remember,” he said, laughing. “By the way, thanks for the e-mail with the contractor’s information. I got it yesterday and gave him a call. So what’s up? Did you think of something else you want to tell me?” he asked.

“No. Actually, this is a personal matter and you are the only person I know at the police department,” Neil said. “I think someone broke into my office last night.”

“Is it trashed or did they just take stuff?” he asked.

“Not really either,” Neil responded thoughtfully.

“Then what makes you think someone broke in?”

“Well, when I arrived this morning, my front door was ajar. I’m pretty sure I locked it yesterday when I left the office,” he said. “And stuff seems to have been moved around and paperwork that was on my desk is now on the floor.”

“But nothing is missing?” he repeated the question. “I don’t really do property crimes, but I’ll send an officer around so you can file an insurance report.”

While he was talking Neil scanned his office again and realized that in fact something was missing.

“Wait. There is something missing,” he said. “The roll of drawings for David Johnsson’s project is gone.”

There was a moment of silence on the other end of the line. “I’ll be right over,” the detective said, hanging up the phone.

«»«»«»

Detective Andrews did not walk. He drove. But he had an unmarked car, so at least there was that. Neil didn’t really want all the neighbors wondering why he had a police cruiser sitting in front of his office.

When the detective knocked on the door a few minutes later Neil ushered him into his office and gave him a brief tour, pointing out what he thought were the important indicators of grand larceny. The detective politely followed along, but

Neil got the impression he was not very impressed with his powers of observation. When they were done, they walked back to Neil's office and sat down. He had made coffee while he was waiting for the detective to arrive and they sat sipping their steaming mugs wondering why someone would bother to steal a roll of drawings.

"Why would someone do that?" the detective asked the question more to himself than to Neil.

Neil shook his head. He didn't know.

"Does the office have an alarm?" the detective asked.

Neil shook his head. "No."

"Hmm. So you have had both your car and your office broken into within a few days." Again he was talking out loud to himself more than Neil.

"The thing that connects the events is David Johnsson and his project. Someone takes your car registration, gets the address and hits your office. Wait," he said. "Do you live here? Was your car registered to this address?"

Neil shook his head again. "No."

"I think we had better take a trip to your house," he suggested.

"What? You're not suggesting someone has broken into my place, are you?" Neil asked.

He nodded. "I'm guessing they did it this morning. They might still be there right now. Do you have an alarm system at your house?" he asked.

Again, Neil shook his head. "No."

"You're making it easy for them," he said.

"For whom?" Neil asked.

"For whomever it is that wants to know what you know, or what you are doing, or what you have," was the detective's response.

"But that does not make any sense," Neil protested. "This guy calls me. I tour his partially built mansion. He gives me some drawings. I go back and see some more of his partially built mansion. Then I get broken into."

"When people commit crime, there is almost always a motive. Random crime is a very rare occurrence," Sean said. "To you or me it appears random at first.

But if you keep looking, keep asking questions, the puzzle pieces start to fit into place. The real trick is anticipating or even being able to establish correctly what information is hidden in plain sight between the puzzle pieces we have."

"So you think there was a crime?" Neil asked.

"You are sitting in the middle of a crime scene drinking coffee!" He laughed. "Yeah. There was a crime."

"I meant related to David Johnsson's disappearance."

"When you can't locate a high profile person, and their staff says they went backpacking on the Appalachian Trail – ALONE, something is definitely going on," he said.

Neil knew what he was referring to, it was the southern governor that was having an affair in South America and told his staff he was backpacking alone. It was a singularly dumb alibi.

"You ready?" he asked.

"I guess," Neil said.

They stood up and walked out the front door which Neil locked very carefully this time.

«‹›»«‹›»«‹›»

As they drove toward his place, Detective Andrews gave small talk a shot and asked how long Neil had been an architect.

"Too long," was his immediate reply.

"Do you have a lot of clients? Are you busy?" he asked.

"No. At the moment, things are slow. That is why I took David's thing. I didn't want to, but he was insistent and I did not have other work, so what the heck."

Detective Andrews nodded like he understood, but how could a public servant with job security and a biweekly direct deposit with a defined pension plan have any idea what income insecurity was like?

"But I did have a nibble yesterday," Neil said hopefully. "This guy from New York came to my office and asked about my winery design experience. He had spoken to a realtor that," as he spoke the words Neil stopped in mid-sentence. A puzzle piece that was there plain as day fell into place.

Detective Andrews looked at Neil with a puzzled look. "What?" he asked.

"Yesterday this guy from New York called the office about a possible winery commission. I was in your office at the time. Nobody ever calls about designing a winery or just walks into my office. It just doesn't happen. So when I got back to the office, I returned his call just as he was walking up to the office. It was all rather weird. He said he had spoken to a realtor who told him I was working with David Johnsson on his winery. He wanted to see drawings and asked if I had any from David's project." Neil paused, letting it all sink in before continuing.

"I told him I did have drawings, but that I could not show them to him without Mr. Johnsson's permission as I had signed a confidentiality agreement. The drawings were sitting right on my drafting table. He looked right at them."

"What was his name?"

"Karl Stroughmann," Neil said.

"Do you know where he is now?" he asked.

"He said he was returning to Long Island."

"Well, I bet you his name is not Karl Stroughmann and I'll bet you he is not in or from Long Island," the detective said.

«»«»«»

David majored in finance at college. He had landed at Harvard on a full scholarship and quickly made friends with young men from families with old money. He was ambitious, in the way that only an outsider can be ambitious, seeing what he did not have and wanting to rectify the situation. He established a tight knit group of friends and by the time he graduated four years later had managed to become engaged to one of the more sought-after young women in his class who, not surprisingly, was from an established east coast family.

In addition to his focus on finance and economics, David added a second major in antiquities. This was probably owing to his own lack of permanence. Everything in his life had been temporary and without a history. As a result, David developed a fascination with things that were old, and real, that had provenance, and just happened to be valuable. The value of old things was not the initial attraction. It was his own lack of provenance. Without even knowing it, he seemed to be seeking to find and secure a past. His first interest was in printed maps and letters; the older the better. His interest in art was a little slower in developing, but the collections and galleries that he visited looking for old manuscripts typically also had art pieces. The manuscripts had more meaning when there was an old master nearby that depicted the author or progenitor of the document in period plumage. Before long his interest in art was as strong or stronger than his interest in documents and books.

After he graduated, he headed to Wall Street. With a little help from his fiancée's father, he managed to land a spot in an investment firm making cold calls to prospective investors, trying to sell them on security instruments that were being underwritten by the firm. He did not love it at first, but he found that he could turn on his personality in a way that made him very convincing, selling questionable equities to people who may not have really wanted them. He had a small cubicle and was part of a sales team headed by an "old guy" of 34 who would gather the sales team in a conference room and raise hell about the weekly sales quota. He would single out the top and the bottom of the sales list. The top salesman of the week would get a good cigar and a small flask of gin. The bottom salesman would get a heap of flaming opprobrium dumped on his person and the empathy of anyone else on the sales force that had ever been there. Three consecutive weeks at the bottom and you were out. You would come back from the sales meeting to find someone else at your desk and a box with your stuff waiting for you.

His first week on the job he ranked near the bottom, but managed to escape the public shaming. He determined he would never be that guy. The next week he came in near the middle. The week after that he placed in the upper quartile. It took him three and a half months to make it to the top, and he relished every second of the limelight the week he arrived. After that, he routinely made the top five. Within a year he was at the top at least twice a month. His third year on the job he had a seven week run at the top. He became something of a sensation after that around the office. His bonus that year was stellar. About a month after his run ended, his boss, the old guy, suffered an aneurism and was not seen again in the office. Everyone knew the kind of stress he had been under and felt bad, but also knew he had made a lot of money, even if he never fully regained his ability to speak or walk without a limp.

David was called into the managing partner's office the next morning and asked to take over the sales team. He wanted to know the terms of the offer and was told that he would get a cut of each sale, along with the firm. The more the team sold the more he would make. Anything he sold himself, in addition to what his team sold, would earn a double commission. He was also told that his annual bonus would be based on the total performance of the team and that his predecessor, God bless him, had routinely pulled down seven-figure bonuses in addition to his mid six-figure salary and commissions.

David jumped on this opportunity with gusto. He increased the praise and rewards for the sales leaders and broadened the negative consequences and speed of removal for the laggards. The sales team doubled their performance the first year and tripled it their second year. They were on a pace to double again, but David did not remain at the firm to see it. He was lured away to the largest brokerage firm on the Street with an offer so sweet it almost intimidated him. But just almost. He set about making changes to the sales methodology and within a year had repeated his performance, earning one of the largest bonuses ever paid out on Wall Street to a non-equity employee. He bought his fiancée a nice diamond bracelet. The rest he invested.

As he made a name for himself on Wall Street, it wasn't all work. Life was hectic and followed the rhythm of the market. He married his fiancée and settled down. They bought an apartment in Manhattan and a place in the Hamptons. Whenever there was a market holiday, he took the time to get out of Manhattan. He had the money to fly to Tahiti or Bali for a weekend or to Europe for an art auction. His wife could fairly be said to have been the actual catalyst for his foray into becoming a collector. For their first anniversary she bought him a very small self-portrait sketch by Rembrandt. It sat proudly, if somewhat obscurely, on his dresser. He didn't care that it was small. That was not the point. The fact that it was a Rembrandt was what amazed him. He never tired of looking at it each morning as he put on his socks. He frequently picked it up and examined it closely, marveling at the individual careless strokes that belied the genius of the artist.

As the technology bubble of the 1990's expanded, his team rode the crest of the wave, consistently selling more equities than any other brokerage firm on the Street. As part of the machine that created the feeding frenzy driving the market to unsustainable highs, he sensed the party was getting close to an unpleasant end. Being on the inside, he knew the pressures driving the market and how that pressure plus the euphoria of a strong bull market caused investors to get caught up in what Alan Greenspan later described as irrational exuberance. Because of the destitution of his past, he tended to be conservative financially. He did have investment positions that were incredibly risky, but he also took positions that were very stable. As he felt the bubble's end approaching, and it was a feeling, he moved out of his riskier positions.

When the bubble burst, he was almost completely liquid and suffered very little from the massive drop in the NASDAQ and tech stocks in general. And because he was liquid, he was in a position to enter the market at a low point, snapping up bargains. Within several years, his patience was rewarded and he found himself to be financially set.

The impact of his upbringing could not be overstated. Owing to the extreme conditions he faced, he tended to have a somewhat cynical view of the world. After the market correction, he used some of his wealth to start a hedge fund with several colleagues. His experience selling equities came in handy as he reached out to investors and made the case for his fund's contrarian point of view. Within five years he had amassed a growing personal fortune that was only made larger when his hedging against credit default swaps and other derivatives proved prescient and made him his billions.

"Right angles don't attract me.
Nor straight, hard and inflexible lines created by man."

-- Oscar Niemeyer

Chapter Five

Sean pulled into the drive that ran up the hill to Neil's place. Neil hopped out to open the gate. Opening and closing a gate to your property is a lot easier when someone else is driving, especially when someone has cut the lock. When he climbed back into the sedan he held it up for Sean to see. "Looks like you were right," he said.

Neil had bought the land with the intent to build a house on it. The parcel was not suitable for growing grapes, so was in a price range that he could almost afford. He was still making payments, which given the variable nature of his cash flow, was always a challenge. Just like David Johnsson's parcel, his was located on the east side of the Silverado Trail. Just like his parcel, Neil's was on a hill, covered in pine and oak, it had a seasonal stream, and it had one spot where the local building department would permit the construction of a single family residence.

Neil had made his purchase offer contingent on his ability to get a building permit. The last thing he needed to do was purchase land that couldn't be built on. So after several months of working on the entitlements with the County planners and then the building department, he had the necessary entitlements for the sale to go through. That was about five years ago. Since then, he had been puttering around on his concept. Not having the money in the bank to actually finish a normally constructed building had limited his options. He either was going to have to wait until he had the money, or he was going to have to build it himself. At the rate his business was going it seemed that he might have to wait a long time, so he decided to look for a construction technique that he could handle with some occasional help and a design that would fit with the land.

Neil settled on a fringe construction technology that was just beginning to gain some acceptance, but really fit neatly into the northern California ethos. It was a simple technique but not used much. Known as hempcrete, it was basically a blown hemp fiber with a concrete slurry as a binder. He joked that if the thing ever burned he might be too high to bother getting out. But in fact, though hemp is a member of the Mary Jane family, you couldn't get high trying to smoke it. Hemp grows like a weed, because it is a weed. Nonetheless, it has a number of industrial uses, including rope and industrial fiber. The beauty of the material and technique, as far as Neil was concerned, was that it was affordable, sustainable, and something he could do himself without much experience or training. It didn't hurt that his use of the material to execute his concept was extremely forgiving and hid a multitude of sins.

The United States has always been blessed with abundant timber. California is no exception, so timber framed homes have been affordable and easily constructed from local materials using local labor. In the old days, architects did not have to include much in the way of detailing in their drawings. Their work was mostly conceptual: some floor plans, exterior elevations, a couple of sections, maybe several interior elevations and a site plan. But times have changed and it has gotten to the point where architects are almost showing every fastener on their drawings, making the process of creating architecture more cumbersome and less profitable. Part of what drove the change in the way drawings are prepared was the industrialization of the materials used to construct a building. And that, of course, was driven by economics and technology.

Plywood and gypsum board were not widely produced or used prior to World War II. Even after the war, you could still find examples of custom homes with dimensional lumber for flooring and shear elements and interior plaster. But the commercial builders that ramped up to build new single family homes in the suburbs for returning GI's quickly adopted standardized and industrial building components, making construction faster and less expensive. With the advances in materials technology came a reduction in the need for skilled craftsmen. In the days when the plans were more general, many of the building components were constructed on site by hand by groups of experienced tradesmen and craftsmen. When the materials changed, the designs changed, the building techniques changed, and the old craftsmen died out.

Most people are familiar at some level with what materials are used in building a house: concrete, of course, dimensional lumber, maybe a couple of timber beams, lots of wood studs, gypsum board or sheet rock as it is sometimes called, exterior plaster, perhaps some brick veneer, asphalt or concrete tiles. Then there are all the other components like wiring, piping, building systems like a furnace or central air, finishes like flooring and paint, and appliances. All of it mass produced, all of it available at your local big box builder's supply store. None of it very special or unique to the homeowner. And absolutely none of it lending itself to artistic expression.

Neil was not interested in going the typical route, even though the typical route does have definite economic and schedule advantages. No, he decided he wanted something more custom, more artistic. Something he could build, slowly, very slowly – and hopefully afford at the same time.

Sean and Neil bumped up the rutted road into the heart of the property, wondering what they were going to find. From the Silverado Trail, the road climbed about 150 feet in elevation through a series of twists and turns, hugging the terrain until coming to a clearing and a free standing carport. Neil had pulled a small trailer onto the property, which is where he actually lived while the house slowly took form. It was parked under the carport against the steep slope of the hill where a previous owner of the property had partially excavated the slope when clearing and leveling what was intended to be a building pad. This afforded the trailer some protection from direct sun, keeping it a little cooler in the summer, and keeping him dry from the drizzly and sometimes prolific rain events common during the winter months. He had also leased an old cargo container for storing his tools, equipment, and supplies. It was sitting adjacent to where the trailer sat, separated by ten feet or so. Neil kept a portable electrical generator inside which he used on an almost daily basis to power his trailer, his table saw, and other power equipment.

They got out of Sean's sedan and stood looking at Neil's folly forgetting for the moment why they had come. If he kept at it, one day it might be habitable. In the meantime, it was very sculptural. Neil had constructed an arched bridge across a deep ravine and had anchored a steel framework on the top. To that he had attached reinforcing steel bars and metal lath, blurring where the curved elements of the bridge ended and the massing of the house on top began. Neil had then sprayed the hemp slurry all over the steel skeleton, building up multiple layers that adhered to each other to create a thicker and thicker skin. Eventually, he had sprayed on several additional layers of titanium white cement plaster, bit by bit, troweling it smooth as he went. The massing of the combined piece was curved, sinuous, supple, and unearthly. There were no straight lines, which while creating the otherworldly look Neil wanted, made it more complicated to build. The hempcrete portion had been straight forward, it was the custom glazing that was currently killing him, both for time and expense.

As it stood now, it would keep someone dry in a light rain, but was not livable. It was essentially an open-air pavilion. He had not started much of the interior finish work, as he struggled to find the money to enclose the structure.

"Jeez . . . . ," was Sean's only response.

"It's for sale," Neil said with a laugh.

"Seriously?" was his response.

“No. Not really. It’s just taking so long and my budget is so blown that I would be better off selling it to someone that could afford to finish it in this lifetime,” he said.

“Well, it’s really cool. Can we walk out there?”

“Sure.”

«»«»«»

Neil had situated the house so that it bridged a ravine and the small seasonal creek at the bottom. And being focused on the natural lines of the terrain, the structure did not sit perpendicular to the ravine, but jumped it at an angle. The first and most expensive part of the process had been the construction of the bridge element. Neil had a number of materials to choose from, but given he was building in fire and earthquake country, he had opted not to design and construct a wooden truss structure, even though it would have been fitting to the site. Instead he decided to utilize a concrete arch which meant that he had to get some help engineering and then constructing this part of the structure.

Architects are their own worst clients. They keep changing their minds and they have expensive taste and no money. Parents should tell their kids, if they have any, that they should never, ever marry an architect.

Neil and Sean walked down an unfinished path dropping over the edge of the ravine to a point where the bridge element was anchored to a rocky outcropping on the bank. A slender element soared overhead, detaching from the main mass of the composition and disappeared into foliage above their heads somewhere along the top of the ravine. Below, another tendon flared out slightly and dropped to a lower point along the rock wall of the ravine. They walked into the flared end of what might have appeared to be something ripped from a larger organic element that had then settled in a fallen position across the ravine. The mass appeared to be settling slightly downward on the opposite side of the gully. Trees and shrubs grew up naturally, obscuring where the individual elements of the detached massing reached earth or rock and were anchored.

Shards of the “fallen” form opened and closed creating locations for future windows. Some of these would be buried within the mass, some would be butt-glazed flush with the outer edge of the skin. The main mass heaved up in the center, creating an opportunity for large expanses of glazing on either side of the shell and affording views looking both up and down the ravine.

They slipped through the overlapping tendons of the structure arriving at what would one day be the main entry, but now only a gaping asymmetrical hole.

They walked under the spine of the arching structure beneath a high ceiling space with arched openings on each side.

“This is crazy! I like it,” Sean said.

“Thanks.”

In studio Neil once had a professor that politely listened to his entire spiel about how he had come up with his design and what it was supposed to mean and how it was supposed to function. He had gotten ripped pretty royally by several other faculty members who had been invited to participate on the jury. They had found his drawings incomprehensible, the sections challenging, and the design too complicated. In addition to the drawings that admittedly were difficult to understand, Neil had built an amazing bass wood model on a mahogany base. He had not finished the base, partly because there was not enough time, and partly because if he had, the school would have kept the model. After the professor had listened to Neil’s presentation, he just said, “I don’t know about all that. I just like the way it looks.” He could not have paid Neil higher praise. Neil had long forgotten the rest of the comments, but not that one. He had finished the base the next semester in the midst of his other school work. The completed model was one of the projects on display in his office. Thus far, he had never had a client ask about it or seek to have Neil design something similar for them.

So if this emerging idea that would someday be a residence, hit Sean somewhere deep inside in a way that he could not express, Neil would take “it’s crazy” and “I like it.” Enough said.

Neil walked Sean through the rest of the unfinished spaces. Sean had a lot of questions about using something like hemp for construction. He said he had never heard of doing that and he clearly thought Neil might have flipped, but at the same time, he saw the sculptural advantages that it gave one determined architect with rebar and a rented plaster gun.

«»«»«»

They walked back up the dirt path to Neil’s trailer. The door had clearly been pried open. They had not noticed it, because as they drove up they were both fixated on Neil’s construction project and not the lowly trailer.

They walked cautiously up to the trailer and pulled the door open without touching it using the handle of a push broom that had been leaning against the trailer.

“Don’t touch anything,” Sean cautioned.

"I would guess you will only find my prints and maybe my assistant's," Neil said.

"Probably, but you never know," came his immediate and practiced response.

They peered through the door without going inside. Everything was dumped out on the floor.

"Fun," was all Neil could muster. There wasn't much in the trailer, except for the basic dishes, silverware, and food. Still, it would be a chore to clean up.

"I'll get my guys up here to photograph and dust everything. If we find anything, we'll let you know."

Neil just nodded. "I guess I'll be staying in town tonight."

They closed the door as best they could and propped a heavy timber that was laying nearby against it to keep it from opening. As they turned to leave, Neil noticed that the door to the cargo container was ajar.

He let out a long sigh. He could only imagine what that meant. While the mess in the trailer was annoying, if someone trashed his tools, or stole the more expensive ones, that would hurt.

"What's wrong?" Sean asked.

Neil gestured in the direction of the cargo container.

"I think someone may have broken into my storage container," he said. "It's where I keep my tools."

They walked the short distance to the door and Neil pried it open.

"Was it locked?" Sean asked.

"I thought so," Neil said feeling embarrassed. He picked up the lock from the ground in front of the unit. "But I guess not."

Sean didn't say anything, but the look on his face indicated his disbelief.

Neil was relieved to see that it looked like nothing had been taken. Things were scattered around a bit, but not as maliciously as in the trailer. Neil had lined the steel walls of the container with plywood. On one side he had installed steel shelving units that he had filled with all manner of construction related materials and supplies. There were power cords, and partially used rolls of flexible PVC piping. One section was devoted to fasteners. Another stored cans of paint, sealer, and the like. On the opposite wall he had built a series of brackets to hold straight lengths of pipe and lumber. He had also attached hooks on the walls where he hung shovels and rakes. Over all, it was fairly organized, if not entirely tidy.

With both of the doors swung wide open, a fair amount of daylight spilled into the container. But toward the back, shadows made it hard to see the condition of things.

"I'm going to crank up the generator," Neil said. "It's noisy, but it will give me a better idea if anything has been taken."

"Go ahead," Sean said.

Neil had mounted a long row of florescent shop lights on the ceiling from front to back. As soon as he had the generator humming away, he found a plug and the lights blinked on.

He surveyed the inside of the unit and walked slowly toward the back. His table saw was against the wall in its normal place. His power tools were in their cases on the shelf. He flipped the lid of his tool box. It looked like his hammers were all there. His hand tools appeared to all be there.

"Anything missing?" Sean asked.

"Doesn't look like it," Neil said. "As you can see, I have a lot of stuff in here, so it's hard to say for sure, but I don't see anything."

Sean held up a pick ax that had been leaning against the wall near where he stood.

"You put your initials on everything?" he asked. The ax had an "NT" carved deeply into the butt end of the handle.

"Yeah. Pretty much," Neil responded. "I volunteered with a non-profit that builds houses for a couple of years. I don't know that anyone would have intentionally stolen anything, but it just simplified the issue of knowing whose hammer you were heading home with or if you got your own hammer back at the end of the day."

"Makes sense," Sean said.

With nothing much else to do, Neil flipped the switch on the generator allowing loud silence to rush back to where they stood. They closed and locked the doors to the container. Neil checked the lock twice before getting back in Sean's car and heading back to town.

Both of them were silent for a while trying to put the pieces together in their own way. Neil finally broke the silence.

"This must have something to do with David and I think it has to do with the drawings he gave me for my report. Either there is something in the drawings that is an issue to someone or there is something in my report that they think I might have discovered that may mean something to them."

They were both silent again. "I didn't check my computers closely at the office. They didn't seem to have been touched, but I wasn't really thinking that my report might be of interest to whomever broke in. The fact that the roll of drawings was taken sort of sent me off in that direction."

"Do you have a laptop?" Sean asked.

"I do, but it is in my car. I don't really use it for business. Drafting and 3-D modeling require a big screen. That's more important than portability," Neil replied. "I do the bulk of my work on a desk-top computer."

"What are the possible angles with the drawings?" he asked.

"I don't know. They might show or quantify something related to his dispute with the contractor. But the contractor has their own sets so it wouldn't make sense that they would take them, unless there was something specifically on the set that David had added that they wanted. The original drawings are in France and could be easily reproduced or resent electronically, if they have been scanned – and I would bet they have been." Neil stopped to ponder why anyone would steal a set of prints.

"I would say maybe this Karl Stroughmann guy really did want to take a look at Johnsson's design and so he stole them, but there has been enough in the local papers and on line that he could get the basic gist without stealing the set. And even if that is not the case, why would he go to the next step and break in out here? That makes no sense, unless he was looking for something that David gave me. He only gave me the drawings and some keys."

They were arriving back in town, and Neil's office was only a few blocks from the station, so he told Sean he could just drop him there if that was where he was heading. It was, and so Sean parked in his assigned space and they said goodbye. Neil told him he would call him if anything seemed to fall into place.

Sean thanked Neil for the tour and complimented the design again. "Stay in touch. I think there are more pieces of the puzzle yet to be found," he said.

"Okay." And with that they parted.

Neil decided to grab a bite to eat rather than heading straight back to the office.

There really wasn't much in the way of food in the pantry and he didn't feel like trying to cook anything anyway. He had not really thought about his sleeping arrangements, but in the back of his mind he was resigned to sleeping on the sofa in his office. He would pop into a sporting goods store after dinner to buy a sleeping bag before settling in for the night.

«»«»«»

Sean returned to his office and was at his desk doing some paperwork when the phone rang. It was a detective working for the Napa County Sheriff's Department.

"Hank. How goes it?" Sean asked.

"It's going. How about you?"

"Same old same old," Sean replied. "What's up?"

"We got a call this morning from Julio Mendez over in Sonoma. You know him? He used to be on the Napa City force. He's a detective with Sonoma County."

"I might have met him once," Sean replied.

"He called to say they had a call about a burned out car off Long Branch Road. Know where that is? It's up toward Sugar Loaf off Spring Mountain Road."

Sean grunted.

"Not sure what kind of car it was. Never even seen one like this before. It was totally gutted. Not much left, but one of my guys thinks it might have been an old Ferrari."

Sean sat up abruptly.

"When was this?"

"When was what?" Hank asked.

"When was the call received?"

"He called me this morning, but they got the call yesterday. I think he said it was sometime in the mid-morning."

"Can you give me his number?" Sean asked.

"Sure." Hank rattled off a number and Sean scribbled it down quickly.

“Thanks. I’ll give him a call,” Sean said before hanging up.

Sean got up and was heading out of the station toward his police cruiser as he dialed the number.

“Detective Mendez.”

“Detective. This is Sean Andrews. I’m a detective with St. Helena PD. I just got off the phone with Hank Richards. He says you got a call about a burned-out car that might have been a Ferrari. I’m working a missing persons case for a ‘David Johnsson’. He owned a rare Ferrari. Looks like you might have found his car. I want to check it out and get copies of your notes and incident reports if you don’t mind.”

“Not a problem, detective,” Mendez said. “What works for you time wise?”

“I’m in the car now and could probably be there in 20 minutes or so,” Sean said.

“Sounds good. I don’t know what it is. We couldn’t find a VIN. There is not much to see ‘cause it burned pretty hot. Anyway, I’ll meet you there. You know where it is?”

“If it’s the car I’m looking for you won’t find a VIN. They didn’t start putting them in cars until 1981. The Ferrari I’m looking for was built in like 1964,” Sean paused. “I know the general area. I’ll see you in a few minutes.”

Sean drove from St. Helena up into mountains on the western side of Napa Valley. It took him a little less time than he had estimated. When he got there, what was left of a car was sitting off the road in a small clearing slightly below the level of the road that wound between tall pines and other low vegetation that screened the vineyards beyond. The clearing was surrounded by pine and fir trees and was not clearly visible from the road, unless you were looking. Sean might have missed it, except he was watching carefully as he drove up the hill.

A short gravel road from the paved roadway led down to the clearing. Sean pulled off the road and drove a short distance down toward the clearing before stopping.

The clearing was covered with low grasses that had somehow not managed to burn, probably owing to the recent rain. The grass under and around the vehicle went from burned to scorched. As Sean stood at the edge of the clearing wondering if there was any chance of disturbing possible evidence in the clearing, he heard the sound of Detective Mendez’s vehicle rolling to a stop behind his. He turned and waited for the detective to exit his vehicle and walk to where he stood.

Sean stuck out his hand. “Detective,” he said.

"Hey. You beat me," Detective Mendez said.

"I almost drove right past it."

"That would be easy to do," Mendez said.

"I think we've met in the past," Sean said. "But I don't remember when."

"You look familiar, too."

Sean turned toward the clearing.

"So what can you tell me?"

"We got a call from one of the property owners up on the hill yesterday morning. They had gone down to Napa on an errand and noticed the car on their way back home. They didn't stop, but just phoned it in. They told the dispatcher that it wasn't burning or even smoking when they saw it, so it must have burned out during the night."

"Who has been down here to check it out?" Sean asked.

"Just one of the deputies from my department and me."

The detective knew why Sean was asking.

"There isn't much to see, like I told you. The road is covered in loose gravel so there are no tire tracks. We walked the clearing looking for anything out of the ordinary, but didn't find anything. Finding footprints in grass is not likely. I took some photos of the car and the interior."

Sean nodded as he listened, his eyes scanning the clearing for anything that might offer the potential for gleaning any clues.

"Any evidence of human remains in the vehicle?" he asked.

"No. It's completely burned out. I doubt it burned hot enough to burn out a body, but it burned hot enough to burn out anything combustible. There were some golf clubs in the trunk. Nothing left of those but the shafts. Bag is gone, no shoes, gloves. Nothing."

Sean was still nodding.

"Come on. Let's go take a look and you can see for yourself," Detective Mendez said.

They walked toward the burned out car. Sean's eyes scanned the grass in front of them as they walked. He didn't notice anything beyond grass and weeds.

As they approached the remains of the Jag, Sean could see that Detective Mendez was right about the apparent heat of the fire. The exterior paint had burned off. The windows had all shattered out of their frames. The tires had burned down to the rims. Sean looked through one of the openings into the interior of the car. The paint on the dash and instruments were gone leaving just blackened residue on the metal supports. The seats were nothing but steel frames and springs.

Sean walked around the vehicle looking for footprints. There were several impressions in the soot on the dirt around the car, but it appeared they belonged to people who had been inspecting the vehicle rather than trying to get away from a crime scene. He poked around for a while and took several photographs. It was clear that if there was any evidence to be had it would be of the type that was scraped off and analyzed in a lab.

Sean stood up and turned to Detective Mendez. "You're right. Not much here."

"Yep. I'll send you copies of my notes and let you know if we find anything," Mendez said.

"If this is the car i'm looking for, it's what $35,000,000 looks like after it burns," Sean said.

"Wow," Mendez said with new appreciation for the charred remains. "What was it?"

"I think it was a very special Ferrari," Sean replied.

《》《》《》

Neil's favorite restaurant in the valley was a small place at one of the resorts along the Silverado Trail.

The resort itself was started as a health spa in the late-middle of the 19th century in the aftermath of the Gold Rush. Its location was dictated by the presence of hot springs on the property. The spring was located 50 yards or so up-slope from the bottom of the hill in an isolated ravine. The heated water from the spring trickled down the hill and commingled with the seasonal stream at the bottom of the ravine. An early hunter found the spring and named it after his horse, Bowler. Thus the name of the sanitarium that was started to exploit the spring was a foregone conclusion. Originally built to cater to the city folk of San Francisco, the Sanitarium at Bowler's Spring ultimately fell into bankruptcy and passed into new hands where it gained a new, if temporary, lease on life until the new investors suffered the same fate as the original business owners. Through a series of hopeful owners, while much about the resort changed, the name managed to survive.

So now an uninformed traveler could be forgiven for mistaking the name of Bowler's Resort and Spa for the lawn bowling that had been introduced at the resort sometime in the 1920's.

Neil and his late wife had visited the resort several times during their marriage. It was a favorite of hers. And while he had gotten beyond the obvious nostalgia for the resort, he found the familiar setting calming, like an old friend with whom you feel at home without feeling the need to say much. It didn't hurt that the restaurant was excellent and the bar was even better. He could not afford to visit very often, but every now and then it provided just the right respite.

He was enough of a regular that the staff remembered him and his preferred drink was usually placed at his table as he was seated. During the harvest or holiday weekends, Neil never bothered to visit the place, but on a weeknight in late October, he had no problem being seated without waiting.

The day's specials always made it hard to decide what to order. As he was in no particular hurry, Neil took his time re-reading the menu – as if he did not already know it well, and enjoyed a double martini. He finally decided to go with his usual and had just handed the menu back to the waiter when a small commotion at the hostess station caught his attention.

A slender, attractive woman was pitching a minor fit with the hostess. He could not hear the specifics of the conversation, but gathered she was not pleased about the service or not being seated. As Neil watched the drama that was beginning to unfold, a tall, muscular man with a healthy tan and short cropped hair joined her from the bar. He said something to her and they left the restaurant. Maybe it was the fault of his martini, but it did not immediately register in Neil's mind that the gentleman bore a striking resemblance to Karl Stroughmann. But he had only seen him from behind. When his waiter returned with his first course, he asked what the fuss had been about and the waiter said that the woman had said she had left her purse in the ladies' room, but that when she went back to retrieve it, the purse was gone.

Neil shrugged. That sort of thing was not unheard of.

"Do you have a security camera in the hallway?" he asked.

The waiter shook his head no.

"Well, that would have provided her with some clue. Why did she leave? Did Jake or Mike see anything?"

Jake was the manager of the restaurant. A super nice and a more laid back guy you could never hope to meet. Mike was the bartender.

“Carla offered to get Jake, but they decided to leave,” he said.

Carla was the hostess that night. She was a super-capable young lady working her way through a local college by working mid-week evenings at the restaurant.

“That’s weird,” Neil said. “Why would they just leave?”

The waiter just shook his head and turned to check in on another guest.

After dinner, Neil moved into the bar. October is football season and he thought he might pick up a game and enjoy another drink. As he entered the bar, Neil casually asked Mike what he had done with the lady’s purse. Mike just rolled his eyes.

“What, it wasn’t you?” Neil asked with a laugh.

“Not my color of nail polish,” he said.

Neil nodded.

“Seems kind of strange that she would claim her purse was stolen and then just walk out,” he quipped. “She was with a guy, did he say anything?” Neil asked.

The bartender was drying glasses and stopped for a moment. “She went to the restroom and came back. She got up and went back about five minutes later. After she came out she went straight to Carla and started to complain. Then the guy got up and went to talk to her and they left.”

“They left without paying?” Neil asked.

“They left without tipping,” he said. “The drinks were on her tab.”

Neil sipped his drink and thought about what the bartender said. Strange. It was then that it occurred to him that the guy looked like Karl Stroughmann.

“Probably none of my business, Mike,” he said, “but was the man’s name Karl by any chance? Karl Stroughmann?”

He shrugged. “No idea. Why?”

Neil had known Mike, as his resident dispenser of distilled spirits, for a couple of years. Neil didn’t drink a lot, but when he did, this was usually the place he imbibed.

Neil told him that he had been visited by a potential client that looked a lot like the guy that had left the bar earlier and that his name was Karl Stroughmann, and that subsequent to the visit his office had been burgled.

Mike thought about that for a moment and then leaned over the bar and lowered his voice. He did just what you would expect your bartender to do if you are a regular.

“I shouldn’t tell you this, so you didn’t hear it from me, okay?”

Neil nodded.

“I don’t know the guy’s name, but the woman’s name is Lydia,” he said.

Neil must have looked surprised.

“What?” he said. “Do you know her?”

He shook his head no and finished his drink.

«»«»«»

Outside, Neil fished for his cell phone and called Sean.

He answered on the second ring.

“Andrews here,” he said. He was on duty, even when he was off duty.

“Sean, it’s Neil Thornton.”

“Hey. What’s up?” His response was level and cool as if he didn’t really care.

“I’m at Bowler’s,” Neil said. “I think Lydia Mankovich was just here.”

“Probably,” he replied. “That’s where she is staying. She and David rented one of the bungalows. Why do you think it was her? I thought you had never met her.”

“I haven’t met her. Let’s just say I have been coming here a long time and I know most of the staff,” Neil said.

Sean grunted into the phone and Neil continued.

“She left with a guy that looked a lot like Karl Stroughmann,” Neil said.

“That’s interesting,” Sean said with a little more life. “How long ago was this?”

"Maybe an hour."

"Another interesting piece of the puzzle," Sean said

"Oh, one other thing," Neil said. "They were having drinks in the bar and she went to the ladies' room and left her purse there. When she realized it, she went back and found someone had taken it."

"Holy cow," Sean said. "We are having a regular crime wave."

«»«»«»

Two days later Neil was woken up when Judy got to the office. She tended to keep her own hours and came and went at hours that suited her needs.

"Oh, I'm sorry, Neil," she gasped. "I didn't know you were here. What's going on? Did you get kicked out again?!"

She laughed at her own joke, knowing he was not dating anyone and had no one to kick him out – of a trailer no less.

"Someone broke into my trailer, so I've been sleeping here," he said groggily.

"What?" Her surprise was genuine.

She had taken a few days off and did not know that the office had been burglarized as well. Neil didn't want to freak her out even more, so he didn't mention it.

"Yeah. I keep all the good stuff in the trailer," he dead panned. "What brings you in so early?"

"It's not that early. It's almost 8:00," she replied.

"I guess," he said.

"I remembered that I had some drawings in my car and that you might need them, so I wanted to drop them off. Today is the last day that my sister and her kids are here and they have never seen the redwoods, so we are getting an early start and are going to drive up to Ukiah."

"Wait. What?" he said. "What drawings?"

"Oh, the other day before I left the UPS guy came by. You and Shelley were both gone and I was pulling out of the driveway, so I had him just put them in my trunk. I've been driving them all over San Francisco," she said.

Neil sat up, rubbing his eyes.

"When was this?" he asked still not fully getting it.

"Last week," she said. "Are you dressed? I don't think I can lift them out of the trunk."

"Yeah, sure." He rolled out of the sleeping bag fully dressed in the previous day's clothes and slipped his feet into his shoes.

Once outside, he lifted the rolls out of her trunk one at a time as they were too heavy and bulky to lift out together. They were big sets of drawings and he saw immediately that they had come from David or his assistant. There was a smaller package that was probably the project specifications.

Neil took them inside and removed the packaging. The transmittal slip said they had been sent on the same day he had met David for his initial tour of his project. It wasn't clear who sent them, however, as the transmittal wasn't signed or initialed.

The drawings were packaged in heavy plastic shipping bags and had big, fat rubber bands on each end to keep the drawings rolled up. Neil removed them and laid out each of the sets on his drafting table. Volume 2 contained the construction drawings for the winery and surrounding site improvements. Volume 3 contained the construction drawings for the natatorium, the surrounding site improvements, and the fountain/grotto at the lower end of the cascading stairs/ fountain.

The third package contained the project specifications in book form.

Neil sat at his desk and wondered if he should bother completing his report for David. He had not been paid for more than his initial time. With two of the three volumes he could continue his review, but volume one was critical as the winery was apparently largely complete and the natatorium had not even gotten started.

He flipped through the drawings, but didn't bother with the specs. The natatorium volume was clean and basically a new set, but the winery set had been used by someone. It was dog-eared and several of the sheets had been torn and crudely taped together. It was dirty and had clearly been out in the field.

David had said he had been acting on his own behalf of late, but Neil had not asked him if this had always been the case. Additionally, Neil had not really pinned down at what point David had fired the architect, or who had been representing them during construction. Neil assumed that this set belonged to either someone from the architect's office, or someone else David had hired to represent him. He doubted that it had belonged to the general contractor, because they would have held on to their sets.

Neil spent most of that day looking through both of the volumes. Anytime an architect looks through another architect's drawings, he or she can't help but find things they admire and things that they feel should have been depicted or notated differently. Then, of course, there is the entire issue of the "design". The point of every set of drawings is to communicate the design intent to the general contractor. This can be done efficiently, and even elegantly, or it can be done in a wasteful, sloppy way. The volumes that David had sent him were both efficient and elegant. To some architects, there is artistry and an aesthetic even in the way the lines on the sheets communicate. This set had been prepared by a group of people that seemed to care deeply about how their drawings communicated the design intent.

The winery, in spite of the rusticated exterior, was laid out and fitted with the latest in wine processing equipment. The building was essentially a large rectangle in plan with large doors in the center of each long side. There were two smaller "wings" that extended off the main building and enclosed a "yard" on the south. The wings contained offices, toilets, and other ancillary spaces. The doors facing north, the direction of the lawn, were large and of solid oak. Tall windows were equally spaced on either side of the doors. On the opposite wall, there was an even larger roll-up door. A variety of crushing bins, pumps, and stainless steel tanks, occupied the perimeter of the room. The door to the tunnel was located on the west wall.

The plans showed the tunnel curving gently, terminating at the barrel room, the lowest level of the chateau. It appeared that the tunnel itself was wide enough to store barrels of wine on each side without restricting the width of the tunnel to less than what would be needed for a standard size truck.

There were things Neil might have done differently, but overall he thought it was a good set. David hadn't asked if it was a good set, however. He wanted to know if the contractor deserved to be paid what he was asking for based on a percentage of completion. The real driving motive behind Neil's review was professional curiosity, as well as a desire to understand the design intent so he could review the construction put in place to be able to estimate how complete it actually was.

By mid-afternoon, Neil's eyes were tired, his legs were stiff and his neck was sore. He called it quits and took a walk to clear his mind. The Valley had fogged in and a light rain had begun to fall.

The next morning, Shelley came bouncing into the office, and took a quick glance in Neil's direction before doing a double take.

"You look like crap," she said. "What happened?"

"I've slept here the last couple of nights," Neil replied.

"Why'd you do that?"

"My trailer is a crime scene," was his casual matter-of-fact reply.

"What?" she gasped.

"Yep, apparently someone thinks I have something of value. Not finding it here, they must have thought I took it there. So Sean wanted me to steer clear for a few days so his guys could dust it for prints. Only prints they are probably going to find are mine and maybe yours. Which leads me to the question of why you are breaking in when you already have the key?"

"I'm stalking you, man." She gave him the 'I'm watching you" hand sign.

He nodded.

"But who is Sean?" she asked.

"Detective Andrews. We're buds now," Neil said.

"Have I met him?" she asked. "Is he single?"

"I'll ask him for you," Neil said with a note of sarcasm.

"Why did you say 'they didn't find it here?' I'm not following what's going on," she said.

"Someone broke in here, too," he said.

"What!" She seemed shocked and even worried.

"You're going to love what they did to your office," he said.

She turned to look into her office as he continued.

"Someone seems to think this David Johnsson fellow gave me something of value. They broke in here and took the set of drawings he lent me and they also broke into my car and my trailer. The only other thing I have are the keys. They might have thought I left them in the trailer since they didn't find them here."

She looked very intently at Neil.

Just then, the phone range. Neil picked it up.

"Neil Thornton," he said into the receiver. "Hey Sean, good morning." Neil winked at Shelley, who gave him a look and walked away.

Sean wanted to know if there had been any other spotting of suspicious people after Neil had called him from Bowlers.

"Nope. Uneventful. Pretty boring," Neil replied. He asked if Sean had been able to talk to the staff at Bowler's about the missing purse. Sean said it was on his "to-do" list, but that he had not had a chance. He said that as far as he knew, no one had filed a police report, which he found rather curious.

"You would think that if someone stole your purse, you would call the police and file a report," Sean said.

"No one has ever stolen one of my purses, so I don't know," Neil replied, jokingly. "I guess that's right."

Sean laughed. "When it happens to you, be sure and give me a call, okay?" he said.

"You're the man," Neil said. "Did your guys find anything at my trailer?"

As Neil suspected, Sean told him they only found one set of prints. It was a no-brainer that they belonged to him, but agreed he would come down to the station to be fingerprinted.

Sean gave Neil permission to go back to his trailer any time.

"I think I need to go back to the chateau at least one more time," Neil said. "I never made it to the winery or the barrel room. "Wanna go with me?" Neil asked.

"Sure. What time?"

"What's good for you?" Neil asked.

"Anytime this afternoon would be fine," Sean said.

"How about I call you after lunch?"

"Okay."

Neil told Shelley that he needed to go down to the police station to get fingerprinted and that he was going to be going to David's winery later.

He returned to the set and flipped through the pages again, taking a closer look at the set itself rather than the information on the sheets.

As Neil flipped through the set, most of the sheets contained some mark-ups, indicating discussions or ideas about changes to the design that were being considered or made during construction. In a few places the plans had been marked on to indicate a change in design or perhaps a passing thought about how the movement of a wall or door might enhance the functioning of the winery. There were a few phone numbers, some idle doodles, and a coffee cup ring or two.

About half way through the architectural sheets, Neil noticed a neatly written set of digits on the back of one of the pages. It had not been scrawled randomly or in a haphazard fashion. It was written in the lower right hand corner of the sheet near the binding, in a clean, even hand.

"07 30 57 12 23 59"

Neil tore a small amount of the corner of the sheet off, folded it and placed it in his wallet. He guessed that it must be the combination to the winery's security system and might come in handy. It did not occur to him that he might be tampering with evidence.

"There is something about giving everything to your profession.
In Italian, an obsession is not necessarily negative."

-- Renzo Piano

Chapter Six

After being fingerprinted, Neil drove out to the chateau. However, this time he drove the long way around. There are no really direct ways to get from Napa Valley to points east. All the roads are narrow and twisting, having been built for the most part in the age of horse and carriage. But he wanted to see the estate from the east approach and to access the winery from the business end of things.

The drive was maybe forty minutes longer and took him over the hill and down into Pope Valley before climbing up the back side of Howell Mountain. He arrived at the east gate and found an unattended guard house and an imposing ornamental gate that was wide open. The gate was supported by two immense cut stone columns. Each column was topped with an elaborate, gilded ornamental iron sculpture of an eagle. Each side of the column had a similarly styled large, and elaborate light fixture mounted above the point where the adjoining stone wall terminated. Neil guessed that the light fixtures were antique and had been imported. Each one was at least four feet in height. A large bronze plaque indicated the street address. A highly ornamented metal arch spanned between the columns. Equally ornate gilded letters identified the winery as Chateau Mont Murat. He drove up a fully paved road, with beds of flowers and carefully manicured landscaping on both sides, up to the back side of the winery, and parked in a large flat service area to the south of the building. There were several trucks, but no sign of Sean's police sedan.

Neil got out and walked up to the wide-open side entrance of the winery building. Two fixed, massive rustic oak doors gave the impression of being functional, but were really just for affect. However, the large roll-up door Neil had seen on the plans was open allowing easy access to the interior of the building. The opening was large, capable of allowing large trucks to enter into the building. It had been a cool spring and that had pushed the harvest later than usual by a few weeks. All the grapes had been picked several weeks before, but the work was not yet finished for the season. Because this was the vineyard's first harvest, it had not been an overwhelming harvest. It was respectable for young vines, but was only a small fraction of what the vineyard would produce when it reached maturity.

Inside, several workers were engaged in cleaning the crushing floor. A large stainless steel vat used for crushing grapes to a pulpy liquid was draining pinkish colored water from an open valve onto the floor. A small pink river ran across the already wet floor to a drain in the center of the room.

"Monsieur. Please, you are not to be here."

Neil turned to see a man approaching him briskly, carrying a clipboard. He was dressed casually in jeans and a white shirt.

Neil smiled and extended his hand. "Good afternoon," he said. "I'm Neil Thornton. I'm Mr. Johnsson's new architect." He figured that if that was the way David introduced him, he might as well use it to his advantage.

"Oh, monsieur. My apologies. I did not know," he said.

"No it's okay. Not very many people know," Neil said. "Have you seen Mr. Johnsson?"

"No, monsieur. He has not come by in a week at least. I have been calling him and leaving messages on his phone. We are nearly through with the crushing and I need him urgently."

"Are you the manager of the winery?" Neil asked.

"Oui, monsieur. I am Philip Methier."

"Nice to meet you," he said. "So how was the harvest?"

Philip shrugged. "It is the first, so it is special even if it is not perfect. It will be a splendid winery one day, Monsieur Thornton."

"It looks like it is off to a good start and that you have the right facilities," Neil said.

"Oui. The best. Monsieur Johnsson did not spare any expense."

Just then they heard Sean's sedan roll into the yard. He parked next to Neil's old Bimmer and walked into the crushing room. He took a quick glance around the room as he walked in their direction.

"Sean, this is Philip Methier. He is the manager of the winery," Neil said. Sean and Philip shook hands.

"I'm detective Andrews." Sean introduced himself.

Philip seemed surprised.

"Escusez-moi? Detective? Is something wrong?" Philip looked at Sean and Neil with a worried expression.

"We are trying to find Mr. Johnsson," Sean said. "Have you seen him around here lately?"

Philip shook his head.

"I was telling Monsieur Thornton that I have been calling Monsieur Johnsson. I need to talk to him about the wine."

Sean was carrying a small tablet. He flipped it open. "Can I ask you a couple of questions?"

"Oui, naturally," Philip said. "Is Monsieur Johnsson all right?" he asked.

"That's what we are trying to find out," Sean replied.

Neil stepped away as Sean started asking Philip the basic questions about when he had seen David last. He walked around the edges of the open space in the center of the crushing room, inspecting each piece of equipment like he might have had some idea of what he was looking at. In fact, he did not, beyond the basics.

Eventually, Sean asked Philip if he would mind if they poked around and Philip of course said no. Neil walked back over and asked if Philip knew how to turn on the lights in the tunnel and the rest of the chateau, for that matter. Philip knew how to turn on the lights to the tunnel, but indicated that he did not know how to turn on any power to the chateau.

"Are you putting barrels into the barrel room?" Neil asked.

"Oui," he said.

"With no lights?"

Philip shrugged again. "The lift has lights. It is not a problem. We don't have that many barrels. Only less than 300," he said. "Next year, maybe we get 800 barrels. When the vines are mature, maybe we get 4,000. Come back then and we will be very busy." He didn't tell them that the only reason he had managed to get 300 barrels was because even though he had bought as many of the Valley's finest grapes as he could from one of the oldest vineyards, they would not sell him more than enough to fill about 250 barrels. In truth, he had only kept enough juice from the vines on David's property to bring the total to 300 barrels. The rest of the juice was not worth keeping and had been quietly discarded.

Sean and Neil walked over to the large doors at the mouth of the tunnel.

"Philip. You want to come with us?" Neil asked.

"No, Monsieur. But thank you," he said. "I have work to do."

There was a small man-door inset in one of the larger doors. Sean opened it and entered the tunnel. It was noticeably cooler in the tunnel. There was an interesting odor that was present in the crushing room, but more pronounced in the tunnel. It was both sweet and yet vaguely acidic and perhaps a little spoiled? They walked up the gently sloped and curving tunnel. It was wide enough for a truck. Both sides of the tunnel had been fitted with supports for storing barrels of wine stacked two high. They had been partially filled with the several hundred barrels of new wine that Philip had mentioned, taking up about two-thirds of the available space along the sides of the tunnel.

The tunnel was about 150 yards in length. When they reached the end, a dark looming void greeted them. They had both come prepared with flashlights and they turned them on and kept walking into the darkness of the barrel room.

Their flashlights only extended partway into the space. Intermediate columns could be seen receding into the distance. Empty barrels were stacked against walls and columns closest to the point where they had entered the room. Beyond that the room appeared to be mostly empty. It appeared that Philip had not produced enough wine to begin filling the cavernous hall and was tentatively using a small portion of the unfinished space to store barrels and other incidental materials and equipment. They walked the full length of the room following the shafts of light from their flashlights. The openings where elevators and stairs would descend from the floors above were open with pits below. Light from the top floors lit the upper part of the shafts, but quickly diminished before reaching the point where they stood.

"It looks pretty empty," Neil said turning in a full circle. His eyes followed the beam of light seeing nothing before or after the shaft of light momentarily illuminated the surface of a column or stack of barrels and then passed. There was a pallet with some neatly stacked cardboard boxes on it. Several large rolls of coiled 2 inch plastic food-grade pipe were stacked nearby. "Not sure there is anything here."

The room around them was basically empty. Neil pointed his light up onto the exposed concrete structure and slab of the floor overhead. There were electrical junction boxes embedded into the slab where future light fixtures would be installed. Bare wires protruded from the boxes and curled neatly into circles of wire, taped and ready for the next phase of the project. Stacked barrels were about the only non-construction related items in the room. They were stacked, waiting for a future harvest to be filled.

Neil walked from where they stood toward the west side of the barrel room. They had come from the south, so he had a rough idea of his directions. As he walked he aimlessly turned the beam of his flashlight from side to side. He passed another shaft and pit and kept walking west. He made it all the way to the west wall and found an opening to the immense barrel room that had been built below the parking structure above. It was so deep and wide that the beam of Neil's flashlight disappeared into the darkness.

He turned around pointing his light north and south along the wall and then continued back to where the beam of Sean's flashlight was moving through the barrel room. As Neil passed the elevator shaft and pit again, the beam of his flashlight fell partially down into the pit and illuminated part of the side of an oak barrel. That did not register as being strange for a moment, then he stopped and turned around and walked to the edge of the pit. It was full of oak barrels.

"Sean. Come here," he said.

Sean walked over to where Neil stood pointing his flashlight into the elevator pit and onto the oak barrels.

"This is not right," Neil said. "Seems like these barrels are expensive and probably not just tossed around or dumped into elevator pits accidentally."

The beams from both of their flashlights shown down on the barrels.

"Yeah. That's odd," Sean agreed.

Sean handed Neil his flashlight and leaned down to grab the end of one of the barrels. He couldn't get a good grip, so he moved, placing one foot down onto the fat curved side of one of the other barrels. It gave a little and shifted. Sean steadied himself, regaining his balance before he leaned over and secured a better hold on one of the barrels. He grunted as he lifted the empty barrel up onto the concrete floor slab.

Neil moved the beams of light to point onto the area where the barrel had been lying. A portion of the bottom of the pit was visible. It was dirty grey concrete with bits of construction litter scatted about and collected in the corner. A pant leg with a foot and shoe protruded from beneath the other barrels.

"Bingo," Sean said, without surprise or pleasure. "I think we found him."

"Oh, god," Neil said.

Sean's weight was distributed between one foot on the concrete slab and his other foot which was planted on a barrel that bore down on the body beneath. Sean stepped back onto the barrel room floor. He took out his smart phone and took a few photos with its camera. He then resumed removing the barrels one at a time.

David's body lay crumpled in the bottom of the elevator pit. He was on his back in an awkward position. His legs were twisted and he was lying completely on one arm while his other hand was partially hidden from view. A pair of bloody bolt cutters lay near the body. The broken remains of a hinged wooden case emerged from the shadows in a corner near David's head.

"Is it him?" Sean asked.

Neil nodded, but didn't speak. He turned his body away from the grisly sight and only looked down out of the corner of his eye. He had never seen a dead body and walked away visibly shaken by the gruesome sight and the shock of finding David dead. The body had been in the pit for perhaps a week or more and was showing definite signs of decomposition Blood had formed a pool under and around the body, but had dried into a dark, almost black, shape. As Neil stepped back away from the pit, the pit fell instantly into shadow and darkness.

"Neil. I need the light," Sean said in a matter of fact tone of voice.

"Sorry." Neil stepped back again toward the pit, but averted his eyes, looking instead ahead into the darkness.

"First time?" Sean asked.

"Yeah. Sorry. I wasn't really expecting it. I guess finding him this way caught me off guard."

"Don't apologize. Your reaction is completely normal. I'm sorry you had to see this," Sean said.

"So what do you do now?"

"I'll take a couple more photos and then I need to call the coroner and my office."

Sean began snapping photos from a variety of positions and angles. It did not take him long.

"So he probably fell from up there," Neil said, pointing his flashlight over his head into the darkness."

"Probably."

They walked back down the length of the tunnel in silence. Neil was thinking of his short acquaintance with David; the tragedy of a relatively early death, and all the things that David had hoped and planned for that were now completely irrelevant.

They walked out of the tunnel and into the crushing room. Sean told Neil that he would not be allowed back into the chateau until their investigation was complete. Neil understood. As a crime scene, the detective and his staff would be looking for clues throughout the building: footprints in the construction dust; a trail of blood; anything that might be another piece in the puzzle.

In the crushing room, they were greeted by Philip. Sean told him that they found David's body and that he and his men could not go beyond the crushing room and into the tunnel or into the chateau.

Philip was visibly shocked by the news. He and his crew had been brought from France by David to set up and operate his vineyard and winery. It was a long term project that would take years to complete and promised full employment for an indefinite period. The death of the owner and financier of the project posed obvious and immediate concerns for Philip and his staff.

Sean asked Neil to stay in the crushing room while he stepped outside to make several calls. He wanted Neil to keep an eye on the door to the tunnel.

He returned with a roll of yellow police tape. He taped it across the door to the tunnel from side to side so if the door was opened and the tape was moved, he would know someone had entered the tunnel. He also attached one end of a long piece of the tape to a vertical stainless steel pipe section and walked across the crushing room, tying off the other end on one of the crushing vats.

He said the coroner was on his way. While the St. Helena police department was small, it was not without resources. His call had summoned two associates who would marshal the necessary evidence kits, cameras, lights, and other tools that are a normal part of a homicide investigation.

Neil decided he did not need to be there for what lay ahead. He was not going to be of any use to Sean or his staff, and was more likely to be in the way. So he told Sean he would leave him to his work.

«»«»«»

When the coroner arrived, Sean returned with the staff to the barrel room to observe the removal of the body. He took more photos and retrieved and catalogued several bits of evidence, such as one of David's shoes that had come off his right foot either before or after the fall, and the broken wooden case. It had a lock that had been smashed. The interior of the case contained a semi-rigid foam liner that seemed to have been shaped to fit the contour of a specific object that was no longer in the case.

He took a number of photos of the bolt cutters before carefully picking them up. His gloved hands turned the handles as he positioned the tool to place it in a large clear plastic evidence bag. As he placed the tool head first into the bag and pushed it in, he noticed that the bolt cutters had initials carved into one of the handles. It was an "NT". He paused, a little surprised by the obvious implication. The tool had come from Neil Thornton's storage container. It was a new wrinkle. Either they were stolen from Neil or Neil was involved in David's murder. Sean doubted it, but sometimes the most obvious possibility pointed to the truth.

"In things to be seen at once, much variety makes confusion, another vice of beauty. In things that are not seen at once, and have no respect one to another, great variety is commendable, provided this variety transgress not the rules of optics and geometry."

-- Christopher Wren

Chapter Seven

Even before David had made his real money, he had become secure enough to use some of his excess capital to look for his brother. Not knowing what had become of him after they had lost touch had been constantly on his mind. His obsession with finding his brother was not all consuming, but it was something he was focused on resolving and he devoted significant resources to the effort.

The first step had been to hire a reputable private investigation firm to begin making inquiries. They had started with the County Child Protective Service records. There were the normal privacy issues to circumnavigate, but this proved to be only a minor obstacle for an experienced PI firm coupled with David's resources. He had been presented with a written report three months after he had retained the firm detailing all the families where his brother Keith had been placed, in addition to the official record of his descent into increasing significant juvenile criminal activity. The path went cold when Keith had been released at the age of 19, after serving a three year stint, from a juvenile correctional facility for assault and armed robbery. Because the weapon had not been loaded or discharged, coupled with the fact that he was a minor and it was his first truly serious arrest, he had not had to go into the adult prison population. Which was probably a good thing.

After his release, he seemed to disappear, probably as a result of living on the street in the shadows of society.

David was not content to leave the search there and agreed to continue the investigation. It was at this point that the progress became very slow with no real leads for several years. The break came when Keith was arrested and his case records were entered into the national criminal database system. A routine search the following month by the PI firm returned a hit and a call to David with the information.

It appeared that Keith had been arrested as part of a RICO sweep in Chicago and charged with being part of an auto theft ring. He was not carrying identification when he was arrested and this had complicated making bail as the system was inclined to hold him as a flight risk until it could sort out who he really was. This worked in David's favor, because had Keith made bail, he would have disappeared back into the shadows.

Within a day, David had dispatched a team of criminal defense attorneys to Chicago from New York. Everyone should be so lucky, in similar circumstances, to have a team of the finest criminal defense lawyers parachute into the legal system. Keith was summoned from his cell, having made bail, with some bewilderment. He was told that his representation was courtesy of his brother, which only heightened his surprise and apprehension. He was of course delighted to be rescued, but had not fallen so far that the source of his rescue came with a certain sense of embarrassment and shame. He had managed to survive on the fringes for a long time without getting caught. He had been careful, but mostly lucky. He had assumed numerous aliases and stolen identities that he had jettisoned after each phase of his criminal activity, managing to stay ahead of both local and federal law enforcement.

After his first juvenile incarceration, he had vowed he would not go there again. He made some friends while at the juvenile camp that he stayed in contact with after he was released. These contacts afforded a number of opportunities to be a part of one scam or heist or another. He stayed clear of any scheme that involved violent crime or weapons and typically chose to work alone, believing that his chances of eluding whomever might take exception to his activities were significantly better without the complications of trusting anyone. He survived mostly off the lucre from petty property crimes. Eventually, this led to larger schemes that brought enough money to survive for a while between heists. He managed to steal the identity of someone who was clean. He used it to get a job as a security system installer. This had the benefit of both teaching him how to disarm security systems, but also introduced him to a variety of properties of the affluent scattered around the suburbs of Chicago that contained significant items of value, like jewelry and art.

Keith's typical job was based on thoroughly casing a property where he had installed the security system. He kept the residence and property owners under surveillance until he could predict with certainty that they had gone on vacation. Sometimes this took up to a year. He then would visit the property, usually over a holiday weekend, and burgle it, removing just enough to make the score worth the effort but not appear to have been an inside job.

To cover his tracks, he would disarm the alarm, remove the items he wanted, trash enough of the house to make it look like a crime of opportunity, and then re-arm the alarm and leave. Sometime later, either the next evening or soon thereafter, he would return, break a window in a door, kick a door in, or in some other way create traces of a forced entry. He would then casually leave the area unseen.

The one time this strategy almost did not work, he hit a home whose owner had installed additional security in the form of cameras after his installation of the main security system. He had removed the items he wanted, including a small portrait that he sensed was valuable. When he returned to the house to trip the alarm, he realized that his previous visit had undoubtedly been captured on a multi-camera security recording system. He again disabled the alarm, searched the house until he located the recording server in a closet in the hallway between the kitchen and the garage. He could not spend the time to figure out how to erase the hard drive, nor could he be sure that the recording had not also been backed-up off site. Removing the server would have been an obvious clue as to the sophistication of the burglar, as would physically destroying it. So he assembled some flammable household solvents he found in the garage, being careful to avoid the cameras as much as possible in the event that his strategy for dealing with the problem did not work. He then doused the server, and the area around it, with an excessive amount of the solvent to ensure it would burn with enough intensity to destroy the hard drive. He did not, however, start the fire in the location of the server as that form of arson would have indicated that the crime was intent on covering someone's tracks. Instead, he started the fire in the garage. He regretted doing it, as the garage contained several high-value vehicles, including an original Shelby Cobra, but he was not going to get caught, burned out Cobra or not. He found a radiant heater in the garage and turned it on to high and left several rags on the floor close enough to ignite. The only other thing he needed to do was prop open the door from the garage to the house and move a five gallon plastic container of gasoline next to the rags. He then closed up the house, and re-armed the alarm. He waited to trip the alarm until after the rags and gasoline ignited. He then disappeared into the shadows. It was one of the few times he remained in the vicinity of one of his jobs after the hit. But he was concerned that the strategy might not work as planned, so he took the risk.

In fact, it worked flawlessly. By the time the fire department arrived, the house was fully engulfed in flames. The fire crew poured water onto the house, but did not try to enter it or to save it. It became an operation to ensure the flames did not spread to neighboring properties. The after incident report found the heater and the gasoline, which triggered an arson investigation and an insurance probe. The server was destroyed and no physical trace of the break-in was left.

The outcome of the job was troubling enough to Keith that he decided to lay low for a while, just in case. He moved his residence, changed his identity, and closed his only domestic bank account.

He did have a small, but growing account offshore, but as it only contained a number and no name or address, he felt fairly confident that it was not at risk. He also had a storage unit where he kept larger items and a safety deposit box for the cash, securities, jewelry, and other small, high-value items he stole. Mini storage places were not that rigorous when it came to asking for proof of identification. They just wanted their monthly fee. It was pretty easy to create a blind mailing address and then switch that to a post office box creating a second layer of separation. The names on both accounts were different and not his own. He had secured the safety deposit box with a false identity that he had only used once, and that was to set it up. If he was ever busted, he had prepaid both the mini-storage unit and the safety deposit box for a year in advance so that he would have time to arrange for continued payment while he was in the cooler.

As with most things, he was caught for something that was not expected. He always knew there was a risk of getting caught and had carefully planned his activities to reduce the odds of that and to contain the damage. He would never have imagined the stupidity of the thing that tripped him up. He was busted for trying to purchase a stolen car. When you are living under the radar, the things that can trip you up are things that cause you to provide information for a lease or mortgage or a credit card. Buying a car at a dealer requires a credit search and other complications that can be dealt with, but create complexities in maintaining a cover. So it was just simpler to pay with cash. But this also had obvious limitations. Buying a car was a hassle as it involved a registration, which requires a name and residence – even if you pay cash.

In the case of the bust, he had met a guy and was in the process of buying a car for cash not realizing that the seller was under surveillance for being part of an auto theft ring. Keith was careful to not carry identification with him when he did not need it. In the case of his arrest, this served him well, as his false ID would have immediately opened the door to other questions.

As it was, when asked for his identification, he answered truthfully that he did not have any. When asked where he lived, he said he was homeless. Disproving that is next to impossible. When asked his name, he also answered truthfully. His name came up clean as it had been years since his arrest as a juvenile. He was a blank slate. He was a real person, with no ID, but lots of cash. Clearly, something was going on, but it wasn't clear to the police what it was. He was not on their radar. The crew selling the cars was being rolled-up as part of an FBI investigation into a multi-state crime ring. He just happened to be a small fish that got caught up in the net. So it was not extremely difficult for a top flight defense attorney to pay his bail, file the appropriate not-guilty pleas, and move Keith into a nice hotel while the paperwork got sorted out. Since Keith had no prior arrests, the system was content to let him go with three-year's probation, in return for his testimony.

As soon as he cleared the system, David had Keith on a plane to New York where they were reunited over dinner at one of Manhattan's finer restaurants. He set Keith up in a nice hotel while they sorted out his long-term living arrangements. David eventually bought Keith a nice, but not opulent, mid-town apartment. He also provided Keith with a small bank account under his own name to pay for incidentals while he looked for work.

Ironically, Keith had been off the grid for so long, that he did not have a social security card or any of the normal forms of identification. Once he came into the daylight with no shortage of funds, it really was a simple task to establish his true identity and all the standard forms of identification, like a social security card, a driver's license, credit cards, and a passport.

Keith did have to return to Chicago briefly every six months to meet with his probation officer. After his three years of probation were completed, Keith was free and clear. In the meantime, he dispensed with most of the contents of his storage unit. He also emptied his safety deposit box. The precious stones from the individual pieces of jewelry were removed and sold. The remainder of the jewelry, the gold and silver, was destroyed. The cash was deposited in the Cayman Islands on a winter trip, leaving him clean and without a trail to connect him to his sordid past.

Keith and David spent a lot of time together catching up. David did not get into Keith's business and didn't really know much about how he had survived between his juvenile incarceration and when he had entered the system again. It was obvious to Keith that his older brother had done well for himself and had seemingly done it on the up and up. He had a lot of admiration for David and wanted to give him something to show his thanks for bailing him out and setting him up in a new life. Keith took notice of David's growing collection of art, old books, and manuscripts. While they came at their interest in these items from divergent points of view, Keith's own interest and knowledge of art was not entirely uninformed. His knowledge was more regional and focused on the interests of the owners of the homes he had robbed. Before he could sell a piece, he had to know what it is, who painted it, and what it was worth. He also had to know how to move it quietly and carefully, if he wanted to get top dollar. As a result, Keith had become self-educated in the value of art, mostly American masters and emerging artists of the mid-west.

Over dinner one evening, Keith presented David with a wrapped package containing the piece he had stolen from the house that had been destroyed in the arson fire. It was a small portrait painted by Edgar Payne. Payne was primarily a landscape painter, but he did paint several small portraits, including one of a friend's daughter Evelyn, when she was seven years of age. The piece is a sentimental impressionist painting, and as with most of Payne's other works, is notable for the way he captured the light surrounding the young girl as she sat on the floor playing with her dolls. It had remained with the girl's family until her death, when her children had sold it to settle the estate. They each wanted both the painting and the money it represented. Reluctantly, they had all agreed to sell the portrait. From there it had passed through several hands until it was purchased for the private collection of a wealthy commodity trader in Chicago. As far as the art community was concerned, it had been lost in the dreadful fire that destroyed a number of other notable pieces of art and several valuable automobiles.

David opened the package and was visibly pleased with the gift. He noted immediately Payne's distinctive signature.

"Keith, how can you afford this?" he said.

"Well. Let's just say it exceeds my means, by a wee bit."

"Yes, but where did you get it?" David persisted.

Keith shrugged. "You probably should put that someplace where you can enjoy it, but no one else will know you have it." Keith raised his eyebrows and nodded. David understood without anything else being said. He put it back in its wrapping and placed it discreetly beneath the table against the leg.

"Do you know who painted it?" David asked.

"Edgar Payne. It's probably worth a couple hundred." He didn't need to add "thousand."

"Well. Thank you." David leaned forward. "But don't get me anything else like that, okay?"

Keith nodded. "I don't have much as you know. But I wanted to thank you for everything. I've lived close to the edge for a long time. I might have even been over the edge in the view of some. You've made your money honestly. I totally respect that. The little I have, I've made by using my wits. Your recent help has put me on the straight and narrow, so to speak. So, I want to find something to do that is legit. I don't have much in the way of education, so I am probably going to have to find a non-traditional line of work."

"What do you want to do?" David asked.

"I don't know. Probably almost anything that does not include punching a clock."

"Are you interested in art or was this an aberration?" David motioned to the painting under the table.

"I know some about American art. I don't know much about European painters or most of the things you have collected," he said.

"I could use someone I trust to scout out pieces and close deals. I've had an agent helping me, but he recently passed away."

David paused, his sadness apparent by his expression.

"It's too bad. He was a great guy. And a friend."

David paused again, thinking about his friend.

"When the dealers know I am the buyer, I sense that the price goes up or stays up. We could work together if you are interested in that. The thing is Keith, you don't have to work if you don't want to. I have enough money for both of us."

Keith bowed his head to hide his emotion. He had been solo for so long, surviving by hustling, moving, hiding. To be able to come out into the light through the generosity of a long-lost brother was overwhelming.

He looked up. "Thanks. That would be great."

David smiled. He knew exactly what his brother was feeling and it pleased him to be able to offer the support.

"It will be fun," was David's only reply.

《》《》《》

Neil called Shelley and told her the news about David. He said he needed a drink and invited her to join him at Bowler's. Shelley and Neil had never crossed the line between employer and employee, not that they hadn't flirted a bit here and there. Neil wasn't so much asking her out now as much as he wanted someone to talk to as he unpacked what had happened to David Johnsson and tried to process what might be next.

He drove straight to Bowler's and settled in the bar near the bay window that looked out over the golf course. It was still early and the lounge wasn't full, so he had his choice of where to sit. He liked sitting by the bay window as it afforded lovely views of the valley, in addition to the lush green fairways of the golf course. He ordered a drink for himself and one for Shelley.

He had begun to think that she had forgotten when she breezed in looking a little more put together than usual. She never dressed up at work, so he was not accustomed to seeing her in a dress with high heels and make-up.

Neil stood as she came over and gave her a slight hug and a little peck on the cheek. "You look lovely," he said. "I didn't know this was a date or I would have tried to clean up a little."

"It's not a date, you dork, but it's not every day that I get to go out for drinks at Bowler's so why not? Besides, the last time you brought me here was on my first day at the office. I thought, wow, this is going to be a great place to work. The boss is taking me to a swanky bar on my first day. And then you have never taken me here again. So, I'm taking full advantage tonight, Neil. You are paying for lost time."

She saw that he had ordered her favorite drink and thanked him as she sat down.

"So. What can you tell me about what is going on?" she asked.

He had been focused on her new look and had not really heard the question.

"What?" he said.

"So. What can you tell me about what is going on?" she repeated herself.

"I haven't heard anything new. But Sean is pretty sure that the body was David," he said. "There was a pool of blood and his body was pretty messed up."

She grimaced, shaking her head as she nursed her drink.

"How do you think he died?" she asked.

"I think he fell down the shaft. If it had been an accident and he fell on his own, he wouldn't have been covered with barrels," Neil said. "So it seems clear someone killed him."

"Are you a suspect?" she asked innocently.

"I don't think so . . . ." The thought had not actually crossed his mind until she asked it. "Why would I be a suspect?'

"Because you were one of the last people to see him," she said. "I don't know. I'm just thinking out loud."

"I think Sean has more likely suspects," he said a bit defensively. "There is his girlfriend or that Karl Stroughmann guy. The real question is why did I see them together the other night here in the bar?"

Neil hadn't told her about that.

"What? You didn't mention that," she said in surprise.

"I'm sorry. A lot has been happening. I don't remember what I told you and what I didn't," he paused, a sly grin crossing his face. "Did I tell you how nice you look this evening?" He smiled self-consciously, knowing that his compliment was clearly, and baldly over the top.

"No. I didn't catch that," she said playing along. "What was that?"

"I think you look lovely tonight," he said.

"Thank you," she said, pausing briefly. "Why haven't you ever asked me out?" she asked.

"Because I shouldn't hit on someone who works for me," he posited.

"True," she agreed nodding her head. "But what if I hadn't been an employee?"

"No question. I would have hit on you," he replied.

"So if I quit, then you could, right?" she said laughing.

"That's not funny. You can't quit," he said seriously. "But maybe we could just go very slow," he offered.

"That's what we've been doing. And nothing has been happening. Any slower and we would be going backwards somehow. Look. Let me be clear. The lights are all green. But right now, let's go eat. I'm hungry."

«»«»«»

By the time Keith started working with David, he had already amassed a collection of several hundred pieces.

When David first started buying art, it was an occasional thing. He would typically hear about a scheduled auction that intrigued him from a friend and would just show up after dinner out. However, owing to the high value of some pieces, the sale commissions, and the potentially large sums of money exchanging hands, auction houses face significant risk if a transaction falls through. To avoid this, those interested in participating in a high-value auction are always required to pre-register, signing a sales agreement in advance that sets out the terms of any sale, the sales commission, and the hefty financial penalties that would result from failing to complete the transaction. Some auction houses require a deposit to be made before the auction against any sales made, others require a signed letter of credit from the buyer's financial institution attesting to the credit worthiness of the individual and a range of net worth. All auction houses require some form of partial payment at the time of the sale with the terms of completion for final payment spelled out in the agreement.

Filling out the paperwork on the evening of an auction is a tedious and time consuming process that ruins the spontaneity of the evening. So initially, if his attendance was not pre-planned, David did not register in advance. On several occasions this resulted in remorse when a piece came up that he would have liked to bid on, but was unable to owing to his non-participant status.

It didn't take long for David to realize that it was easier to establish a relationship in advance with several auction houses. This streamlined the process, but with it David's anonymity vanished. Now seen as a person of means and an occasional buyer, he received solicitations for future events through elaborate, glossy sales brochures mailed to him before the sale. Sometimes the sales material was printed as a limited edition book with the history and provenance of the piece documented through the reproduction of historical documents, interviews with historians, curators, preservationists, and the like. Sometimes there were high definition video presentations or even special websites to highlight a work or series of works.

Whether he bought anything himself, or not, it was always a fun evening out. As his attendance at various auction houses became noticed and associated with an understanding of his wealth and buying interests, he began to receive more focused and personal pre-sale marketing efforts. Sometimes he would be approached by a specific seller's agent or dealer and introduced to the piece or collection that was being offered. Quite often there would be the offer of a private inspection of the piece or pieces being offered, with the relevant experts and sales associates on hand to answer every question and cater to any need.

David hadn't amassed his growing fortune by being a gadabout. He worked hard and was extremely busy most of the time, putting in excessive hours. So becoming the object of interest of auction houses and art dealers, while interesting at first, quickly became a source of irritation. He simply did not have time to take all the calls and meetings offered, or to consider the merits of a piece or do the necessary research into the sometimes complicated provenance of the art that interested him.

He was at an auction with a date one evening for an estate that contained a work by William Hogarth that interested him. He didn't have any idea what the piece was worth. He just liked it. It was an interesting portrait of a common man painted with extreme humanity and candor. The man's face was lined from the toils of his life experiences, his clothes were ordinary and in need of mending, his hands were gnarled from the manual labor that had been his station, and yet the painter had captured him in a moment of happy contentment.

David had a self-imposed limit of several hundred thousand dollars when he didn't know much about a piece. In this case the bidding was opened at nearly two-hundred thousand, which gave him, and apparently others in the room, pause. When no one bid, the auctioneer reminded the audience of the quality of the piece before lowering his ask for the opening bid to one-hundred fifty thousand dollars. This prompted an auction card to be raised starting the auction, followed by several more cards and a slow increase in the bid price.

David weighed in at one-hundred eighty thousand dollars, but didn't feel he was on solid ground. He hesitantly participated in the bidding as it climbed over two-hundred thousand before reaching two-hundred fifty. He was aware that among the several bidders, there was an older gentleman on the opposite side of the room that was bidding consistently, but without any outward sign of emotion; almost as if bored.

David's mind was racing. The process of bidding was an intellectual and financial battle of wits. Was this a piece he had to have, he wondered. Was his excitement and competitive determination to win misplaced? He stayed with the bidding until it reached two hundred and eighty thousand. Then he capitulated and the older gentleman purchased the piece at two-hundred eighty-five thousand.

He sat staring at the gentleman as the painting was removed and the next piece was put in its place. The intent look on David's face could have easily been interpreted as a scowl. He was wondering if he had been had. He could have easily outbid anyone in the room. He was certain of it. So stepping back and letting someone else prevail was a choice. But was it the right choice, he wondered.

The older gentleman turned his head and caught David looking his way. He smiled politely and nodded in David's direction. But David didn't respond in kind. He was lost in his own thoughts.

After the auction was over and the crowd was filing out of the room, David and the older gentleman's paths crossed as they each approached the table at the back of the room where the sales paperwork and other details associated with the transactions were finalized.

David was considerably younger and taller than the stooped figure of the older gentleman who wore a rumpled suit. David motioned politely for him to go ahead. The man nodded and smiled.

"Thank you," he said, speaking to David. "You gave me a run for my money tonight," he said, referencing their having bid on the same piece.

"Yes I did. But I wasn't sure about the piece, so I let it go," David responded.

"I thank you for that," the man said. "I was near my limit. But I assure you it is an excellent piece and you would have done well to have taken it from me." The man was genuinely excited about his purchase.

"Really?" David said in surprise. In the financial world, he was not accustomed to talking to those with whom he competed. His transactions were largely anonymous.

"Oh yes," was the older man's reply. "A fine piece. Easily worth several times my bid. I thought you were from one of the museums. You seemed the most focused on the piece after me. And I was afraid you had deep pockets or the budget of a large museum behind you. So I was surprised that you let it go."

That made David curious.

"So how high would you have gone?" he asked.

"I had another thirty-thousand and then I would have had to call it quits," he said.

David could have kicked himself. Thirty-thousand. Damn it, he thought. But he just gave a thin smile in response.

"So what will you do with the painting?" David asked.

"Oh. This isn't for me," the old man said. "I am representing a client."

He turned and looked at David seemingly embarrassed by the admission.

"That makes it sound so transactional," he said. "And really it's not. I get a real kick out of doing this. I am an old retired professor that knows a thing or two about art and I have a couple of friends that trust me to come and bid for them. I don't have the money to buy pieces like this for myself, so this is fun."

"Really?" David said, his interest immediately piqued.

"Yes. That is how I know about this particular piece. You know, as they said before the auction, this work has been in a private collection since 1904. I was afraid it would be purchased by a museum. Once that happens, forget about it. You would never have a chance to get a hold of it again. And I am not against museums, or anything, mind you," he added. "But when something this special comes on the market I prefer to have a shot at it if I can."

They approached the table together.

“Do you take new clients?” David asked.

“I suppose I would,” the man replied. “I have a small circle of friends and my buying activities are mostly limited to that group. But, as the old saying goes, I guess you can never have too many friends.” He chuckled.

David asked if the man had a card, but he said he didn’t. David gave him one of his and expressed an interest in continuing their conversation in the near future. The man nodded and smiled and tucked the card in his vest pocket as the sales attendant asked him for his auction card. Since all of the necessary information was associated with the number on the card, there was no need to ask his name or seek any other form of identification.

Another sales attendant completed her transaction with another bidder and beckoned to David to move to her station at the table. As David moved to complete his own purchase of another piece, he said finally to the man.

“Please call me. I would definitely like to continue our conversation.”

“Perhaps I will at that,” the man said as he walked away. “Have a good evening.”

David would have preferred to rush after the man, but he needed to attend to his own purchase details. By the time he was finished and had collected his date’s coat from the coat check, the older gentleman was nowhere to be found.

Several weeks went by and David was too busy to give his brief conversation with the man much thought. His assistant, being an intelligent person, knew the interests of her boss and brought him the occasional piece of art news that made it into the papers. She had spotted an article about the sale of a work by William Hogarth. The article said that the academic art world was all abuzz over the recent re-discovery of the piece and the relatively modest price it had fetched at auction. She circled the article and left it with other documents requiring David’s attention in his in box.

When David arrived in the office the next morning he found the article. As he read it he realized how woefully ignorant he was about the art he was purchasing. He was just buying on hunches and probably overpaying for less than A-grade art or missing out to more informed buyers. He needed to find someone that really knew something about art, knew the pitfalls, and that was someone he could trust. The “old guy” he had met several weeks ago seemed to fit the bill perfectly.

David had his assistant call the auction house to see if she could discover the man’s identity. She hit a stone wall; the privacy of clients, etc. But she did get a name for someone interested in talking to David about a future sale. And as is often the case, when wealth returns a call, firewalls become less formidable and policies become less rigid. It took David a lunch, and a visit to a gallery presenting several pieces that the sales agent for the auction house was promoting, and would receive a commission on if David purchased one of them, but he got the name and contact information for Winston Tulles, PhD.

Doctor Tulles was surprised to be called on his private line at home. He was of an age that placed him in a shrinking portion of the population that insisted on having a land line. In fact, he had two lines. One line was reserved strictly for private business calls. He didn't give this number to just anyone. When David introduced himself, the man immediately remembered their brief conversation and agreed to meet with David.

They met at the Met the following week. As they walked through the galleries David was given a casual, but expansive lecture in art history. The old man was full of stories, insights, and knowledge about art that left David dazzled.

Dr. Winston Tulles was a retired art professor who had spent most of his career at Columbia. He had been active in the art world for over 50 years, travelling and lecturing extensively. His specialty was European masters between 1500-1700. He knew everything that David did not. In addition to possessing an encyclopedic knowledge about art, the man was humble and unpretentious. As they parted, David practically begged him to become his exclusive agent. The old man said he would give it some thought. He left David in suspense for about a month before finally agreeing, with two significant conditions.

"Anything," David said.

The man laughed.

"Son, you haven't heard them yet," the older man said not fully appreciating the flexibility that David's wealth gave him.

David had never been referred to as "son." It jolted him. Here was a man he was beginning to revere and he had unknowingly pierced deep into David's psyche with an offhand expression of an older man speaking to his junior.

"Okay," David said softly. "Try me."

"All right. First, I don't want to be paid," he said.

"What?" David said in astonishment.

"I want my commission to be in the form of art pieces you purchase, but that I keep," he said.

David thought for a moment.

"Okay. But then that could get kind of complicated later when you want to sell them."

"I won't sell them. A collector like me isn't in the game to make money," he said.

David understood that. His purchases were not about the money or the investment potential. Sure that was there. But each purchase was about possessing beauty and history. Two things that are elusive.

"It's really quite simple," Winston continued. "You'll reimburse all my purchase related expenses that I incur on your behalf. But for the commissions, we'll keep track of the value of the purchases I make for you. My commission will be five percent. But rather than exchanging cash, if I find something I want, you'll buy it, but it will be mine. We'll create an individual limited liability corporation to purchase and hold each piece of art. I'll hold the majority interest in each entity."

David sat back and thought for a moment, surprised that he had not thought of this strategy. But then, he had never needed something like this before. He planned to solely own everything he bought indefinitely.

Winston could see David running through the various issues before he spoke.

"So?" he asked.

There were a number of reasons, including tax avoidance, that made this an attractive approach. It came with a certain amount of ongoing paperwork, but it also made it quite easy to hide the identity of the real purchaser.

"In principle, I agree, But I will run it past both my attorney and accountants, just to be sure. What was the other thing?"

Winston gave David a knowing look. Even though he had only known him for a short time, he knew David was a true collector and very competitive as well.

"If I see something I want, you have to back off. I get first dibs. You can't bid against me."

"What if you can't afford it?" David asked with a laugh.

"In all probability, my budget will dictate what interests me. But if something comes up that is beyond my reach, we'll talk. It may be that I'll get possession of the piece until I go," he said, using a euphemism for his eventual death. "Then the piece would be yours."

'Seems fair," David said. He knew Winston's knowledge and taste precluded the possibility that he would be interested in anything less than stellar pieces.

"Let's do it," David said and they shook hands.

Over the next several years, David purchased a large number of pieces with Winston acting as his agent. Sometimes they would attend auctions together and sometimes not. But always, David would rely on Winston's knowledge to make the final decision about whether a piece was worth buying or not. And almost always, whether David accompanied the old professor or not, he let the man make the purchase. Sometimes, David would join the bidding briefly before dropping out. They never spoke or acknowledged one another at auctions. Occasionally, David would make a purchase, with the professor in the audience or in the wings on the phone guiding David toward the price they had agreed upon before the auction started.

Eventually, David began sending Winston to auctions in Europe with nothing more than a budget, and with the proviso that if he found something amazing that was more than the budget, Winston was authorized to make the purchase and David would find the money.

During this time, Winston found a number of special pieces that he deemed worthy and that David had to admit he would have liked himself. But by then Winston was his friend and David was happy to be a part of establishing his small, but outstanding collection. At the rate he was going, the balance in his commissions account was growing faster than his purchases. Winston was picky. He only bought the very best and he couldn't bring himself to overpay.

As a result Winston had purchased six paintings with David's help that had exceeded his self-imposed budget. David had readily agreed to assist in each purchase and subsequently became the part owner of each piece. David would have been proud to add each piece to his own collection, but he was also happy to help Winston.

Sadly, their relationship came to an untimely end. In one of the few times he spoke to Winston at an auction, he arrived to find him sitting in the audience, but uncharacteristically slumped over in his seat.

"Dr. Tulles, are you okay?" David had asked.

Winston had looked up and David had seen in his eyes a tiredness that replaced the usual twinkle that accompanied the excitement of entering the fray of an auction.

"Oh. Hello. I'm just extra tired today, I guess," he had said.

David knew that his friend was then in his early eighties.

“Do you want to skip this one?” David asked.

“Oh. no,” was the quick reply. “We’ve got to try to get the *de La Tour* in the first lot. I have been watching this piece for years. Did you know it was his last painting? He had been exiled from France the year before and this piece seems to capture his despair. We have to get it. See that gentleman over there?”

He gestured with his head to the other side of the room where a man sat alone reading the auction program. David nodded.

“He’s from the Getty. You know what that means.”

David nodded.

“We’ll just have to give him a run for his money,” David said, feeling the competitive juices beginning to flow.

Breaking tradition, he sat next to his friend. Together they outlasted the agent for the Getty. But nearly lost out to someone bidding over the phone. But after several tense moments, emerged victorious.

Winston beamed. He looked around the room with a self-satisfied aire. He loved the game.

He leaned over to David and whispered.

“I was talking to a friend. Don’t ask me who. I won’t tell you. But there is quiet talk about something truly special that may come to market in the next month or so.”

“What?’ David asked, his curiosity piqued.

“I can’t tell you yet. But it is important and big,” Winston said.

“You mean in size?” David asked trying to understand the riddle.

Winston gave him a look.

“No. I mean important. Maybe the most important piece to come on the market in several decades. And I want it.”

He paused looking tired and distant again.

“With all my heart and soul, I want this one,” he said, turning to look directly at David.

“Then you shall have it!” David said with a laugh.

Winston smiled thinly. David clearly did not understand the magnitude of the piece he was describing.

“I can’t afford it,” he said woefully. “I’m not sure even you can afford it.”

“What’s the balance on your commission account?” David asked.

“Thirty-seven,” Winston replied without emotion. It was counted in millions, of course.

“More than that?” David said with disbelief. “Jesus!”

“I’ll need Jesus, if I’m going to get it. But I think this might even be too expensive for him,” Winston said. “And we are not exactly on speaking terms these days.”

David laughed.

“Wow.” When are you going to tell me what it is?” he asked.

“My friend says that the decision to bring it to market is probably sometime in the next couple of weeks,” Winston replied.

“And you would blow your whole wad on this one piece?” David asked.

“Yes. And a chunk of money you may not even have - if you’ll let me.”

David was beginning to grasp how “big” this piece was.

“What’s your guess?” he asked.

“Maybe a couple hundred,” Winston said. “With a piece like this, the sky’s the limit. If you agree to chase this, you’ll probably never see anything bigger in your lifetime. This is a once in a generation opportunity.”

“I’m in,” David said with finality and conviction in his voice that caught Winston by surprise.

“David, you don’t even know what it is.”

“True. But I trust you. You don’t buy junk. If you say this is big. I believe you and I’m in. It’s simple.”

Winston bowed his head, smiled and let out a single laugh.

“Okay, my friend. Let’s see what we can do. I’ll call you when I can say more.”

«»«»«»

Over the next several years, the two brothers purchased a lot of art. Keith would do the behind-the-scenes work representing a silent buyer that was, of course, David.

David needed additional space to house all the pieces he was amassing. As the kernel of the idea to build a wine estate in the Napa Valley began to form, the art took on a different purpose. Instead of just being purchased for the sake of ownership and the impulse to collect, David came to understand that it would grace the walls of his chateau.

As the plans for the estate began to firm up, his marriage to his second wife started to fall apart. His first marriage had ended without children, a casualty to his endless hours at work and dedication to conquering Wall Street. He had been dirt poor when he had married his first wife. The concept of a prenuptial was beyond any reality he could imagine at the time, so when the marriage had ended, it resulted in a settlement that had taken a significant bite out of his growing wealth. He had recovered that and had made his real money after his first wife was long gone. When he met his second wife, however, he possessed not only significant wealth, but a raft of lawyers eager to help him protect it from any potential future divorce. So they had prepared for him a virtually bullet-proof prenuptial agreement that had been signed by his second wife without much joy. Prenuptial agreements are awkward things when juxtaposed against the love that is the presumed motivation for the planned marriage. David's agreement with his second wife was that she would receive a minimum of $10 million dollars in the event of a divorce and an additional $10 million for each year of the marriage. After a minimum of 20 years of marriage, and on the condition that the marriage did not end as a result of infidelity on her part, his wife would receive half the value of his estate, up to $500 million dollars, whichever was less, the Manhattan apartment -- but not the art -- and the weekend retreat in the Hamptons. At the time of his second marriage, his personal net worth was measured in billions, not millions. While this was a subject of much speculation in the press, he never acknowledged what he believed the true number to be. There was no point in that.

After eight years of marriage and no kids, David was ready to move on from wife number two. However, even after eight years of marriage, she was not. She had become accustomed to a standard of living that would not be supported by a mere $90 million.

While the details of the divorce were worked out, David had gotten busy on his next project, the Napa estate. He had hired a young, energetic assistant with a business degree from Wharton. She took care of many of his day-to-day details, without the need to see all of his holdings.

Lydia Mankovich, in addition to being smart, was attractive. She was able to keep up with David and was not offended by his brusque, and frequently tactless manner. She could give as good as she got. In short she was not intimidated by him or his wealth. She was, you could say, the flip side of the coin. She was his equal and he knew it. So it did not take long for them to end up in bed. It was not a torrid affair. It was a mutually self-gratifying physical and intellectual relationship. The employment was almost beside the point.

As the details of the estate took shape, Lydia took a room at Bowler's. What had started as a short stay eventually turned into a multi-year occupancy of one of the most sought after bungalows on the property. A private bungalow at Bowler's with daily maid service, room service, laundry service, and the restaurant and bar a short walk from the front door of the bungalow afforded all the conveniences and privacy of home with none of the upkeep.

She had managed the project's entitlement process with all the consultants. While David had become the focus of almost all the negativity and frustration for ramming the project through, in fairness, Lydia deserved a large amount of the credit. Where he possessed the vision and drive, with almost no tact, she managed to cajole or charm her way through the process with equal or greater success, and none of the animosity.

David was 58. Lydia was 39. She had been with him for seven years and had been his lover for six of those. She knew he was married. She knew he usually got what he wanted and that he wanted her. But in her case, she also knew she was getting what she wanted every bit as much as he was getting what he wanted through their affair. She also knew, because David was actually quite transparent once you got to know him, that his marriage was dead. It was dead before she arrived on the scene and she doubted her relationship with him had anything to do with his pending divorce. She had never asked him to get divorced. She had never even asked about his wife, for that matter. It just wasn't an issue.

For the last several months Lydia had been flying to Europe buying furniture for the chateau. She found the whole "chateau" thing a little amusing. She had been raised in an upper middle-income family. They weren't affluent by any measure, but she had never lacked for any of the basics. She had made it through school on scholarships and student loans. She had taken the job with David after her business school experience because she needed to retire her student loans and his job offer had come with a salary that promised to enable her do that in two years. After her first year on the job he had bonused her enough money to pay off the whole debt and stash some money in savings. After they started sleeping together, money was never discussed again. He just saw to it that a sizeable amount was deposited into her account each month, leaving her with no financial worries.

Now, as she was finding lovely old French antiques for the house, the task was more of a game than any sense that she might be furnishing a home where she might one day live. The challenge of furnishing nearly 100,000 square feet of "chateau" with period antiques and restorations was a fully engrossing endeavor. She had expended well over $18 million on the *piano nobile* and had secured only about 2/3 of what she needed. On the upper floor, the task was not quite as daunting as they had decided that only the master suite, the family day room, the private breakfast room, and two of the significant guest rooms would be furnished with period antiques. The balance of the rooms would be furnished with antiques of more recent vintage and commissioned reproductions. Still, she had managed to spend an additional $11 million and had to fly frequently to auctions and galleries in New York and Paris. She was now on a first name basis with all the buyers at all the major houses and was receiving preferential treatment, including private showings and advance notice of what was coming to market.

She had asked David repeatedly about the artwork for the chateau, as she was seeing a number of period pieces, including tapestries, that would have been appropriate purchases. But each time she raised the subject, he just said he had the art covered.

The other area of his life, besides his failed marriages, that she left alone was his relationship with his brother. She had never heard all of David's hard luck story, especially the parts about his mother or how he had been separated from her or his brother. She knew that he had grown up in an institutional setting, but that he had risen above the stigma and was a self-made man. She and Keith were essentially coworkers. Acquainted, but not really friends. Most of the time she spent with David was one-on-one. It seemed natural for two very busy people. The few times she had met Keith, had been on holiday weekends or to watch a Super Bowl game or the World Series.

Keith was always very quiet and seemed to be taking her measure. She was confident enough in her own abilities and her relationship with David, that she was not all that concerned about what Keith might think of her or her role in David's life. Their interactions were polite and even friendly, but not necessarily warm. Certainly not warm in the way that a sister-in-law or some other long-time family member would have been received. But it didn't matter.

As for David's project, she had only been on a tour of the construction site a few times: once when the site was being cleared and graded; once when the winery was about complete and the grapes were being planted; and once when the chateau's steel had been topped-out. She had never been on all the floors, and certainly not down into the bowels of the lower floors. But that is not to say she did not understand the project or the spaces that needed furniture. She had accompanied David on his trips to Paris as the chateau had been in design. She had sat in on all the design presentations and had seen and commented on all the design renderings, not that David had really listened. This project was his baby. He might ask what she thought, but whether he listened or incorporated anyone's input was unlikely.

When he began to express reservations about the architect's commitment to the project, she was too busy to be very concerned. She knew that whatever obstacle their performance or lack thereof presented, it would not be allowed to be a factor in the project's success. David would see to that. The same was true of the contractor. David had become quite concerned and very agitated by their inability to perform and had become increasingly perplexed by what he viewed as a calcification in their attitude. As his frustrations mounted, she began to hear about some fellow named "Craig" and what a complete asshole he was. A phone call from "Craig" would immediately send David into a fit of anger with shouting, threats of lawsuits, and very colorful profanity. David had finally had enough and had fired "Craig," only to discover that the contractor was not so easily dismissed. Where he had always been successful in dispensing of irritants, leaving his attorneys to exact the final revenge, here he found that his aggressive stance had been met with an unexpected belligerence and a form of retaliation he had not foreseen.

After firing the contractor and refusing to pay them, the contractor had the nerve to file a lien on his entire estate. After numerous phone calls to his attorneys he had begun the process of resolving the issue when he was unexpectedly called away by some urgent matter in New York. He had not returned for several weeks and then only for a short period before leaving for an extended absence. When he finally did return, several months later, he had set about finding a local architect to give him some idea of where things stood.

That was when Neil Thornton entered the picture.

«»«»«»

"A doctor can bury his mistakes, but an architect can only advise his clients to plant vines."

-- Frank Lloyd Wright

Chapter Eight

Sean's investigation of the chateau in the aftermath of the coroner's removal of David's body was taking longer than he had imagined. Not having power in the building made the process one of literally looking for clues in the dark. He had called the Napa County Sheriff for support as his office did not have the resources to illuminate such a large space. The sheriff had brought in a mobile generator and truck with lights and had driven right up the tunnel into the barrel room and flooded the space with so much light it was almost too much. But too much was better than none at all.

It seemed clear that David had fallen from an upper floor. Which floor wasn't immediately clear. The coroner's report would hopefully shed some light on that based on the damage to the body resulting from the fall. In a gruesome twist, the bolt cutters appeared to have been used to remove both of David's thumbs -- presumably after he had fallen, resulting in most of the bleeding. But even that was conjecture on Sean's part. Until they knew how the body had come to fall down the shaft and from which upper floor, they could not be sure that David had not been killed or rendered unconscious somewhere else in the chateau, his thumbs removed, and his body dumped down the shaft.

Sean and his small staff took lots of photos, they looked for footprints in the construction dust that covered the floor, and they began to carefully and methodically explore the upper floors, being mindful to limit their foot traffic to areas where they had determined that there were no footprints, or where they had already documented those that they could identify. The light situation continued to be a challenge. The presence of the generator truck helped. A long power cord had been plugged into the truck and extended up one of the shafts to the next sub-basement floor. Temporary lights had been strung and where the contractor had left a few lights in place, they were wired up to provide light. The largest problem with the truck being in the barrel room was that it did not take long before the fumes from the truck made the air in the space unbreathable. This was remedied by removing the truck and running the power cables from the exterior of the building and down through the shaft.

Sean was puzzled about David's missing thumbs until he discovered the security system guarding the roll-up door. They must have been removed in an attempt to defeat the security system. Without the thumbs, he was tempted to get a portable power saw from the County and cut through the door. But he decided there was no real hurry in breaching the door. Whatever lay behind it, if it was a factor in David's death, would be there when the time came and that information was needed.

Whoever committed the murder had not tried very hard to conceal the crime. Placing David's body under barrels, while bleeding heavily, was not exactly an effective form of concealment. It clearly had worked for a few days, but then as the basement was completely in the dark and there were few if any people in the building, the body could have just as likely laid on the concrete slab for that same amount of time without being seen. Sean had not jumped to any conclusions. It was also possible that David had fallen on his own and then his thumbs had been removed. The thumbs seemed to be key to understanding the sequence and whether the crime was murder or something else. The empty wooden case would suggest that he either had something in the case when he fell that had been subsequently removed, or perhaps it had been removed before he fell.

Neil called Sean early the next week to see how the investigation was going.

"Detective Andrews," Sean said with his usual efficiency as he answered his cell phone.

"Sean, it's Neil," he said. "Hey, I'm sorry for the interruption, but I was wondering if there is any way that I can be of assistance?"

Sean thought about it for a moment and said, "No. Although I am going to want to go over everything that has happened with you again to see if I missed anything."

"Is the coroner's report back?" Neil asked.

"No. I hope to get a preliminary this afternoon," he said in a weary voice. "Have you spoken to anyone about this?"

"Just my," Neil paused, "my assistant Shelley. We had drinks after we found him the other day. I needed to unwind with someone and sort of talked about it a little. Not that I know much, of course. I just have never discovered a body before."

Sean grunted into the phone. “Pretty normal. You were spared the really fun part, you know. But listen. Don’t tell anyone else what’s going on. Sometimes it’s useful to not have that information out there. I haven’t had a chance to inform David’s girlfriend, or others. I’ve asked Philip here at the winery and all his guys to keep the information to themselves for the time being as well. The last thing I need is the press up here camped out with news vans and that whole circus.”

“Of course. I hadn’t even thought about that. It would get crazy,” Neil replied. “Okay, well when you are ready to talk, give me a call.”

“I will,” he said. “Oh. One other thing,” he paused as if weigh what he was about to say.

“Yeah?” Neil asked.

“Since you are not presently a suspect I guess I can tell you.” He paused. “Someone cut off both of David’s thumbs.” Neil groaned and Sean paused again. “Sorry, that was pretty grisly.”

“No. I can deal with it. I suppose you have seen far worse. But it is a shock,” Neil said. Sean’s casual reference to Neil not ‘presently’ being a suspect did not go unnoticed and left Neil with an unsettled feeling.

Sean didn’t tell Neil about the bolt cutters. That information didn’t need to be volunteered without getting something in return.

“So look,” Sean said. “It seems clear that whatever is behind the security system is of interest to someone. Probably the same person that broke into your place looking for the drawings. They must have thought there was information in the drawings that would help them get through that door.”

It made sense. There was a fingerprint reader next to the key pad.

“But how would they know it was the thumb and not one of the other fingers?” Neil asked.

“I don’t know. That may be helpful, though in narrowing down the suspects. If we assume that the print reader needed a thumb and not a forefinger, then the person who cut them off must have been with him in the past when he opened it,” he said.

Neil thought about that for a moment. “Or else they just guessed, or they knew the specs for the reader or something else.” They were both silent for a moment.

“I suppose the thumbs are not just cut off, but haven’t been found,” Neil said.

"Correct," Sean said.

"Have you dusted the print reader?" Neil asked. "You know, I put my thumb on it the other day. That was dumb in retrospect, but it was just sort of automatic, like seeing a button and pushing it."

"We dusted it and it's not your print. Problem is, we don't have David's thumbprints to prove it's one of his. We do know it's not one of his other fingers. We got the prints from him for the other digits."

"Sheez. This was getting right down into the details," Neil thought. He guessed that Sean was probably going to tell him what was under David's fingernails next and what he had for lunch the day he died.

"So why haven't you informed his assistant?" Neil asked. "Seems like she had the knowledge and maybe a motive."

"That's one of the reasons I don't want you to talk to anyone. I want to see her reaction when she finds out."

"Maybe I should call her and ask her to walk the building with me so I can finish my report," Neil suggested.

Sean thought for a moment. "Let me think about that. I don't want to do anything that would mess up a case against whomever did this, and there would need to be an angle that includes me. You shouldn't be anywhere near the property or in the building now that it is a crime scene, unless I or one of my staff is with you."

"Trust me. That won't be a problem," Neil said. "What about this Karl Stroughmann guy? Anything on him?"

"Nothing."

Neil could tell something was up in the background of the call.

"Listen, I have to run. I'll be in touch." Sean ended the call.

«»«»«»

Neil was sitting in the office the next morning after talking to Sean. He was thinking about his dinner with Shelley and what might have been behind her question about why he had never asked her out. He would have liked to, but was sort of old fashioned and perhaps overly cautious since there were obvious employment issues. They had skirted the topic during dinner. They had driven to Bowler's separately and he had given her a little hug and peck on the cheek as they said good night and she got into her car.

Now as he waited for her to arrive at the office, he could not help but be a little nervous. Should he have brought flowers and left them on her desk?

"Yes! Damn it. I am an idiot. I should have done that," he thought. That would have been a nice gesture to reinforce his interest. She did say all the lights were green.

He could still make it down to a florist and get back to the office before she arrived, if he hurried. He would feel kind of dumb if he walked in and she was already there and he showed up with flowers, but he was going to feel dumb if she showed up and he tried to pretend nothing happened and it was just business as usual.

He grabbed his wallet and headed out the door, nearly plowing Judy down in the process.

"Whoa! Where are you heading off to in such a hurry?" Judy exclaimed.

"Morning. I forgot to run an errand, so now I have to 'run' my errand," he said over his shoulder as he dashed down the walkway.

Neil headed to the local florist and found it was closed. The local Safeway was open and usually had flowers so he dashed over there.

The nice thing about getting to the grocery store early in the morning is that for one, there are not many people in the store, and in addition, the store staff has spent the night getting everything restocked. He found a good selection of flowers and then faced a new dilemma.

"Should I get roses? Is it too soon for roses? Yellow roses would be lame. Isn't that a sign of friendship or something? But red roses are like dripping with romance. Is that the message? Daisies were out. All the other flowers were out," he thought. "What?" He had to decide. He knew he could not get her a potted plant. Even a potted orchid would be lame.

He hesitated for a few moments and bit the bullet selecting a nice dozen red roses. "Sheez. This feels like junior high," he thought. He was sweating slightly and felt a little weird.

He got in line, preoccupied with the roses in his hand and feeling a little flushed. He had not bought roses for anyone in years and felt extremely self-conscious, though undoubtedly no one was paying any attention.

It was not until he was right up at the cashier's station that he realized he was standing behind Lydia Mankovich. She had a few things in her basket and was placing them on the conveyor belt. It appeared to be mostly incidentals, some gum, some nail polish, some deodorant. Neil watched her intently not sure if he should try to start a conversation, when she turned to look at him. She smiled and said "excuse me" as she placed the basket on the floor in front of the belt.

Neil forgot all about the roses.

"Nice roses," she said. "I think someone is going to be happy to see you this morning."

"Oh," Neil said, at little embarrassed. "You think so? I feel sort of sheepish. You don't think that they are a little obvious?"

"I have found that most people are not 'obvious' enough most of the time," she said.

"You're probably right. I just haven't done this in a while and I am a little rusty," he said.

"Nonsense." She looked directly at him. "It's just like riding a bicycle." She smiled a sly little smile and Neil laughed.

"What makes you think *that* is what this is about?" he said.

"Trust me. It's what it's always about," she said.

The cashier had rung up her items and was waiting for her to pay. She inserted her payment card into the card reader and completed her transaction. She turned toward Neil and wished him luck.

He thanked her and slid his Safeway Bonus Points card through the reader while handing the cashier $20.

"Thank you Mr. Thornton. You just saved $1.23," the cashier cheerfully told him.

Lydia had not moved out of ear shot. She stopped and turned suddenly to face Neil with a surprised look on her face.

"Are you Neil Thornton?" she asked in surprise.

"I am," he said. "I don't believe we have met."

"No. No we haven't. But I know who you are," she said.

"I'm flattered! It's not every day that I am recognized here in town as a world class architect," he said dryly. "That *is* what you were thinking, right?" He laughed at his own joke.

"The reason that I know you, Mr. Thornton, is that I am David Johnsson's assistant. I was the one that sent you the drawings and specs."

"Oh," he said with feigned surprise. "It is nice to meet you. I am sorry, but I am not finished with my report," he said.

She nodded as if she knew this. "Can I buy you coffee?"

"I can do better," he said. "My office is right around the corner and I just brewed a fresh pot before running over here." He didn't tell her he was trying to get the flowers back to the office as quickly as possible.

"I know where your office is," she said. "I can give you a ride."

That made sense, so he said okay, not thinking to ask how she knew where his office was since they had never met.

As they walked to her car, she introduced herself as Lydia Mankovich. Neil continued to play dumb and said it was nice to meet her.

It took only a minute or so to drive the two blocks to Neil's office. He told her to park in the driveway and they walked to the front door. He had not managed to beat Shelley to the office and received a rather puzzled look as he walked into the office with a young, beautiful woman she had never seen before with a dozen red roses in his hand. This was not what Neil had in mind at all for the presentation of the flowers. He had hoped to have them on her desk in a vase when she arrived. That would have been more his style. So rather than make a big fuss, he simply handed the flowers to her and gave her a little peck on the cheek. "Good morning," he said, looking deeply into her eyes. She blushed and smiled and said good morning back.

Turning to Lydia he said, "This is Shelley." Nodding his head toward Lydia, he introduced her as "Lydia Mankovich."

"We just met at the store. She wanted to buy me coffee, but I am such a cheapskate, that I insisted we come to the office."

"I'll get the coffee and a vase," Shelley said and quickly disappeared down the hall toward the kitchen. "Oh, Shelley," Neil called after her. "Could you call Sean for me? He wanted to know when he could drop by this morning." Shelley, being very quick on the uptake, knew exactly what he was telling her.

Neil invited Lydia into his office and gestured for her to sit down.

She looked around the space in much the same way that Karl Stroughmann had. It gave him a distinctly odd feeling given that he had seen them together a few days before.

"So. What can I do for you?" Neil asked.

"Shelley is lovely," she whispered, looking toward the kitchen. He smiled and nodded in agreement, then turned to the business between them.

"As I mentioned earlier, I am not done with the report," he said. "But I have started," he added quickly.

"Good. What do you think so far?" she asked.

"I don't know how much experience you have with construction, so forgive me if this is all obvious. The thing about Mr. Johnsson's project is that it is very large and very complicated," Neil said.

"Tell me about it," she interjected with some exasperation. "I have spent the last six years helping David on this."

Neil nodded. "Well, estimating a level of completion for such a large project with so many different parts is difficult, especially if you don't have all the construction paperwork. David said he wanted me to give him some idea if the contractor was billing ahead, but without the schedule of values, change orders, and previous pay applications, I am kind of flying blind."

"I can get you all of that paperwork," she said.

"Okay. But it's going to cost more than I think David thought it would," he said. "Is that going to be all right?"

"It shouldn't be a problem. I have your contract on file and know that you signed a confidentiality agreement, so sharing more information under the terms of that agreement will be fine. When did David want you to complete the report?" she asked.

"He seemed like he was in a hurry, but I told him it would take a few weeks. It has been a few weeks and I am embarrassed to say I am not done, but I have not had all the information I need."

"David is always in a hurry," she said. "But I'll get you whatever additional paperwork you need," she reiterated. "Then how long do you estimate it will take to complete your report once you have the additional information?"

Neil was about to tread on shaky ground as far as Sean was concerned, because he assumed Sean did not want him to tell her anything.

"I am embarrassed to tell you that it may take longer than expected, because someone stole Volume I of the set," he said.

"What?" she exclaimed. She seemed to be genuinely surprised.

Neil nodded. "Someone broke in here and stole Volume I. It's very strange. Nothing else seems to have been taken."

Shelley popped in with the coffee.

"Thanks, Shelley," Neil said.

"Do you need anything else?" Shelley asked.

He looked to Lydia. She shook her head. "No, thank you. This is perfect."

Lydia took a sip of her coffee and thought about the missing drawings.

"What about the other volumes?" she asked. "Do you still have those?"

"Yes. They are right over there." He turned and pointed at his desk to the two thick sets of drawings rolled out and stacked on his drafting table.

"That seems extremely random," she said.

"Yeah. I've never had anyone steal drawings from me before."

Just then, there was a knock at the door. Shelley answered it and ushered Sean into the foyer.

"I'm here to see Neil," he said.

She knew why he had come, of course, having just spoken to Sean telling him who was in the office.

"Just a moment," she said. "He is with someone. I'll check to see if he can see you now."

This little theater was totally unnecessary as the foyer could be seen plainly from the living room. But Shelley walked gamely to the office and announced Sean's arrival and asked if Neil wanted to see him or ask him to wait.

Lydia had made the call to the police station to report David's disappearance. She had subsequently spoken to Sean on two other occasions and was briefly interviewed by him. So as she turned toward Sean her face expressed some surprise at seeing him in the office.

"Sean, come in," Neil said. He apologized to Lydia for the disruption. "This is Lydia Mankovich. We met this morning at the grocery store and we're having coffee. Would you like some?"

"Sure," he said.

The next several minutes were awkward. But Sean took the lead and broke the ice.

"Ms. Mankovich. Is there any new information about David?"

She looked down and shook her head.

"Have you told Mr. Thornton about David?" he asked.

Again she shook her head no.

Sean turned to Neil and said, "David has not been seen for about a week. Ms. Mankovich filed a missing persons report with my office."

"I'm sorry," Neil said. "I hope he is okay."

"Do you have any new information?" she asked Sean.

He ignored the question and sat down across from her.

"What do you know about the chateau?" he asked. "I assume you have been through it."

"I went through it a couple of times," she said. "I was there when we topped off the steel. Why?"

"There is a portion of one of the lower basement levels that does not appear to have a purpose," he said. "I was just wondering what that was for?"

"I don't know," she said. "It's a big house and there are a number of spaces in there that were what David wanted. Actually, it was all what David wanted. I sat in on the design meetings, but David drove the design. How does that factor into where David is?" she asked.

"It may not. It has a special alarm system on it and only one door in. Most of the house seems incomplete, but this area seems to be powered up and ready to go. But we don't know what it is for."

She looked at Neil.

"I toured the building with David and we didn't make it to that level. I went back later and have seen what Detective Andrews is talking about, but I don't know what it is either," he said. "It appears to be some sort of vault."

She pondered that for a moment leaning back in the sofa.

"I don't know what it is, but it might be a vault. I have spent a lot of time with David over the past seven years. It wasn't non-stop, but I think I know him pretty well. He is passionate about the project and while he has been open with me about practically everything related to the project, I do have a sense that he is planning a big surprise related to the completion and that he hasn't told me everything."

Sean and Neil exchanged a glance. Neil kept silent.

"If it is a vault, where would David have kept a key or security code?" Sean asked.

"I don't know. He had a key ring that he carried around with him, but I don't know if it contained a key for that. It did contain keys to the gate, though."

Neil walked to his desk and opened a drawer. He pulled out the keys that David had given him and tossed them to Sean. He caught them in the air.

"Have you had these the whole time?" he asked incredulously.

He nodded. "I told you I had them. How do you think I got back onto the project site?"

It was a detail, a piece of the puzzle, that had slipped Sean's attention. It didn't have significance until it did. Now seemed to be that moment.

He showed the ring and keys to Lydia. "These the keys?" he asked.

"I think so."

"Who else would know about the space?" Sean asked.

"Keith might," she offered.

"Who's Keith?" Sean asked.

"David's brother."

Neil looked at Sean, but he ignored Neil's glance.

"Can you describe what he looks like?"

"Of course. He's about 6'-3". Fairly trim. Tan. Short cropped hair."

"Younger or older?"

"Younger."

Sean looked at Neil. It sounded like his description of Karl Stroughmann.

"When was the last time you saw him?" Sean asked.

"A couple of days ago. Why? You don't think he has something to do with this, do you?"

Sean shrugged.

"You don't know Keith. He would die for his brother." She sounded like she had said all she was going to on this topic.

"I'm sorry to ask all these questions," Sean said, "but I am just trying to put some bits of information together."

She nodded and he continued.

"Did anything come out of the investigation into the theft of your purse?" he asked.

"No. The restaurant said they would report the incident to the police. I would think you would know more about that than I do."

It sounded like the interview was about over, as Lydia's tone had started to take on an adversarial edge.

"So does the name 'Karl Stroughmann' mean anything to you?"

"Never heard of him. Who is he?" she asked. Sean ignored the question.

"So the evening your purse was stolen, you left the restaurant with a gentleman. That was not Karl Stroughmann?" he asked.

"No. I don't know anyone named Karl Stroughmann," she said. "That was Keith, David's brother. We had agreed to meet for drinks before he left for a quick trip."

"Well. I've taken enough of your time. Neil, I am sorry for barging in and taking over your meeting."

Neil shrugged and held out his hands in a gesture of "it happens."

Sean thanked Lydia for her time and left.

Lydia looked at Neil and seemed upset.

"That was a lot of information for you to absorb," she said, believing that it was the first he was learning of the details relating to David's disappearance.

Neil nodded. "Yes. Again, I am sorry. Is it possible he just flew to New York or something and didn't tell anyone? He is probably fine."

Lydia shook her head. "I don't think so. We were on the phone constantly. If he had gone to New York or Paris, I would have known. He owned a private jet. I called them and asked when David had flown with them last. It was a flight from New York when he came out here last."

"Perhaps I should hold off on the completion of the report," Neil offered. "At least until things are sorted out."

"No," came her immediate and emphatic reply. "I don't know where David is, but I am certain that if he were here or could weigh in, he would insist that the project move ahead. You only met David the one time. He is a force of nature and he would not, WILL not, rest until this project is complete."

"Okay. Get me the paperwork we discussed and I'll keep going. I will send my invoices to you."

"Thank you," she said.

He walked Lydia to the door.

"If anything comes up about that space, I'll let you know," he said.

"I would appreciate that," she said.

«»«»«»

Neil closed the door and walked into Shelley's office. She had been leaning against the wall out of sight listening to every word and stepped into the doorway.

"Wow. That was weird," she said pausing. "Thanks for the flowers."

Neil suddenly got shy. "You're welcome."

"You're kind of old fashioned," she said.

"Sorry."

"No need to be sorry. It's kind of cute."

She leaned in and gave him a hug, lingering a little longer than one might have thought was necessary. "Hope that wasn't weird," she said with a smile.

"No. That wasn't weird," he said. But this could get distracting fast, he thought.

«»«»«»

Neil called Sean after Lydia left. He wasn't in the office and Neil left a brief message. Later that afternoon, Sean returned his call.

"So. Do you think this 'Keith' guy is the same person as Karl Stroughmann?" Neil asked.

"It seems likely. He matches your description, has been in the area and as David's brother, he had access to the house. He may have been the person that broke into your office and then your trailer, but I'm not sure he killed his brother. That piece makes no sense to me," he said.

"Why would he break into my office looking for drawings? His brother had the drawings and could get duplicate sets anytime from the architect, or off a disc – which he probably has somewhere. If there was something important about the drawings that his brother wasn't sharing with him, then that might explain the break-in, but it would also make him a suspect, right?"

Sean grunted. Neil took that as a yes.

"Maybe he didn't want Lydia to know he wanted the drawings," Sean guessed. "I'm trying to run down information on him now. Hopefully, I'll get something soon and we'll know who we are dealing with. A photo would be ideal so you can ID him," Sean said.

"So on a different subject, I found what looks like a combination on the winery set," Neil said.

"What?! Why didn't you tell me that?" he asked.

"I don't know" Neil paused. "It was a couple of days ago. I think it was before we found the body."

"Well that changes things," Sean said.

"How? You don't have a way to get past the print reader without David's thumbs," Neil said.

"The code and keys may work in lieu of the prints," he said.

"I didn't think of that. Probably couldn't hurt to try," Neil agreed. "So you want the numbers?" he asked.

"I'll come right over," he said, and hung up.

A few minutes later, Sean came back up the walk and knocked on the door. Neil greeted him and handed him the torn piece of paper from the drawings.

"Where did this come from?" he asked.

"The drawings," Neil said innocently.

"You tore this out of the drawings?" he said incredulously.

"Yeah. Why?"

"Neil, this is evidence. You shouldn't have done that," he said.

"But I didn't know it was evidence," he protested. "Really."

"Then why did you tear it off?" Sean asked.

"In case someone else broke in and stole these sets, too. It looked like it might be important, so I removed it from the set and put it in my wallet."

"Please show me where you found it," Sean said sternly.

Neil walked with Sean to his drafting table where the sets were still laid out. He explained how he had reviewed the sets after Judy told him they had been in her trunk. He showed Sean how the natatorium set had not been touched and was pristine, while the winery set looked like it had been used in the field during construction. He flipped through the sheets remarking on what he had noticed, both about the intentional marks on the set and the unintentional ones, like coffee rings. Neil then flipped to the sheet where the numbers had been written on the back of the sheet.

"So when I flipped to this sheet, I noticed that this page had the numbers written on the lower corner, here," he pointed.

Sean unfolded the torn piece of paper and fit it to the sheet. It was clearly the match.

"So without thinking much, I just tore it out and put it in my pocket," Neil said.

"So do architects do this sort of thing all the time?" he asked.

"What? Rip out parts of the set?" he asked.

"No write on the back of sheets."

"We draw and sketch on any blank surface we can find," Neil said. "We communicate through drawing. We think through drawing. It's what we do. So yeah. We draw on the back of sheets. But usually, it's a sketch and usually it's sort of messy. Neat hand writing like this? That is careful and intentional? That is something else. But I don't think an architect did this."

"Why not?" he asked.

"We don't have access to security codes and things like that during or after construction," he said. "If this is the code to that vault, assuming it is a vault, then this is either David's handwriting or it is the contractor's or someone that knew the code as the system was being installed. It is possible this was a temporary code that has been reprogrammed. It may not even be valid anymore," Neil said.

"Well, there is only one way to find out," Sean said, as he walked toward the door. "Is there anything else on the back of these sheets?"

"I didn't see anything," Neil said.

"Please check again. But don't tear anything out this time. I'll call you later," he said over his shoulder as he disappeared out the door.

«〈〉»«〈〉»«〈〉»

When Sean arrived at the chateau late that afternoon, he walked through the garage from one of the vehicle ramps. When you carry the full force of the law with you it must embolden you to go where others might hesitate to go or at least go in numbers. Perhaps Sean was too preoccupied with the code or had just not really thought about being in danger, but he strode into the garage with his flash light in his right hand and what he assumed was a code for the key pad in his left hand.

He headed straight for the print reader and was intently entering the code when he was struck from behind on the back of the neck. He was lucky that the blow did not break his neck or fracture the base of his skull, not that he would have been aware of it, as the impact rendered him immediately unconscious.

«〈〉»«〈〉»«〈〉»

Neil received a call the next day from one of Sean's colleagues who told him Sean had insisted that he be called. He informed Neil that Sean had been attacked at the chateau and was in the local hospital for observation. Neil asked if he could see Sean and was told he could see visitors. So Neil hopped in the car and headed to the St. Helena Hospital. It was a short drive up the Silverado Trail and then up Howell Mountain on Deer Park Road.

When Neil entered Sean's room, he did not look so bad. Sean was wearing a hospital gown and was under a light blanket, owing to the freezing temperatures inside hospitals. His head was lightly bandaged, but other than that, there was no other sign of any damage.

"So, what happened to you?" Neil asked.

Sean had a rather sheepish look on his face when he answered.

"I don't know, exactly. I was entering the code, and someone must have snuck up behind me and hit me with something. I guess they knocked me out. I don't know how long I was out, but when I came to, it was pitch black in the garage. My flashlight was gone. Luckily, whoever did this, didn't take my service revolver. They may not have known I am a cop," he said. "Taking my gun would have been a problem."

"So are you okay?" Neil asked.

"Yeah. The doc says I got clobbered pretty good. They took an x-ray in the ER and didn't see any real damage. I may need some physical therapy to work out the kinks, but basically, I'll live."

"That's good news," Neil said. "How long do you have to stay?"

"At least another night."

Neil nodded.

"They want to make sure there is no internal bleeding or clotting or something like that," he said.

"So do you need anything?" Neil asked. "Some real food, maybe?"

Sean smiled. "That would be great," he said. "How about a burger and some fries?"

"You got it." He turned to leave. "Oh. How about the code? Did it work?"

"I don't know. I got hit before I had finished entering it in. When I came to, it was dark. I hobbled out of there and back to my car in the dark. I've got some guys going up there to check it out," he said.

“So, ah, do you still have the code?” Neil asked.

He shook his head.

“That’s too bad. I’ll go get your burger. Everything on it?”

Sean nodded.

“We can talk some more later,” Neil said, and left.

«»«»«»

When Neil got back with the burger and fries from Gott’s Roadside, Sean was reading through a folder.

“Here you go,” he said. “A double cheese-burger with everything on it. If the head injury doesn’t kill you, between this and the fries, you may do yourself in,” he said cheerfully.

“You gonna be my mom, now?” Sean asked looking up.

“Nope. Eat whatever you want.”

“Thanks for getting this,” he said. He set the folder down. “I was just looking at what my guys found on Keith Johnsson. It’s pretty old. Looks like he was into some petty juvenile stuff and did some time in a juvie camp. Nothing after that until about 10 years ago.” He took a big bite of his burger. He held out his fries, but Neil shook his head.

“Is there a photo?” he asked.”

Sean nodded, but didn’t say anything until he had finished his bite.

“Yeah, but I don’t know if it will be useful. He was 17 or 18 when it was taken.” He thumbed through the file and held up a printout of a photo of a young man who glared at the camera.

“That look anything like your Karl Stroughmann?” he asked.

Neil looked at the image closely. “I don’t know. This is a young man and the man in my office was at least 20 or 30 years older.”

He nodded again as he continued to attack the burger.

“Not surprising,” he said finally.

“But you have prints on this guy, right?”

“Yeah, but so far most of the prints we have found have been yours,” he said giving Neil a look.

“I have an alibi,” Neil said.

“Not really you don’t,” he said. Neil’s reaction was what Sean had hoped for and he laughed. “I’m kidding,” he said.

“So what’s next?” Neil asked. He didn’t share Sean’s humor.

Sean shook his head as he thought about the question. “Keep an eye out for either of these guys, if they are two separate guys. Keep an eye on the vault, or whatever it is. Keep an eye on Lydia. Look for two missing thumbs.” He stuffed the last of the french-fries into his mouth. He did not really seem to be phased by any of this, including his injury.

“I’ll get out of here. Call me if I can do anything else. Really. Call me,” Neil said.

Sean nodded and Neil left.

«»«»«»

Neil’s cell phone rang. It was Shelley inviting him over for a real meal. How could he say no to that, not that he wanted to. He turned his car toward her place when the phone rang again. “Hey. Should I bring some wine?” Neil said.

“That would be nice,” Sean dead panned, “but I don’t think the doctor will let me have it. This is a teetotaling hospital. No booze and no cigarettes. Let’s just save it for another time,” he said.

“Sorry. I thought you were someone else,” Neil said a little embarrassed.

“I hope so. I don’t know you *that* well,” he said.

“So what’s up?” Neil asked, trying to change the subject.

“It looks like the code didn’t work. My guys just called. They said someone had beaten the crap out of the print reader and the key pad. Both had been broken off the wall and smashed pretty good. Looks like they were pissed off, so they hammered away at the roll-up door. It’s pretty banged up, but they didn’t get through it.”

“Hum,” Neil mused. “But they didn’t find the scrap of paper on the floor or anything like that?"

"Nope," Sean said.

"Have you reached out to the contractor? That might be worth a try," Neil offered.

"I did call the guy whose name you gave me to see if he had seen David around. He said he hadn't. He said that the last time that they spoke was when you were out there. I mentioned that you said it sounded like they were arguing. He acknowledged that was true, but said it was David who triggered the argument. He launched into a long tirade about David's meddling and failure to pay. He said all he wants is to get paid."

"I'm sure that much is true," Neil said. "Now that you have a specific focus in the building, his knowledge might be useful."

"Probably right," Sean responded. "I'll call him tomorrow. Go drink your wine." He hung up.

Neil stopped by the grocery store and picked up two bottles of wine. As you might expect, the wine selection at the Safeway in St. Helena is pretty good, if you are looking for a California wine.

When he got to Shelley's house, he could smell the aroma from her kitchen as he walked up to her front door. She let him in with a peck on the cheek and he handed her the wine. She seemed pleased that he had thought of it. "What did you bring?"

"I covered my bases with a Merlot and a Sauvignon Blanc," he said.

"Sounds good," she replied.

Neil told her the status of things over dinner. She was all ears, although she offered no better theory about who might be behind David's death than what was already obvious. They snuggled on her sofa and watched a movie. The thought of dragging himself back to his cramped trailer was not very appealing, so when she offered for him to stay over, he didn't need much coaxing.

«»«»«»

The next morning Sean received a call from Lydia. Keith had returned from New York and had paid a visit to the job site and was not happy to find the vault's security system vandalized. He said he would meet them the site at 11:00 a.m.

When he arrived, Keith did not look happy. Lydia was friendly, but business-like.

"Let's go inside," Sean said.

They walked down the ramp together. Keith carried a rather normal sized flashlight, while Sean had managed to come up with what looked like a portable search beacon.

Entering the darkened garage, they turned their lights on and paused momentarily to let their eyes adjust. As they continued deeper into the garage, none of them spoke. Keith pointed his light a little ahead and at their feet, making sure that they did not stumble over anything hidden in the dark. Sean, on the other hand, shined his light far ahead and from side to side. The beam of his light illuminated the far wall of the parking structure.

When they got close to the roll-up door, they could plainly see the damage from whoever had tried to pry it open.

"So, what is behind this door?" Sean asked.

Keith shined his light from side to side before answering, as if he wanted to make sure no one was there.

"My brother has been storing some artwork down here in anticipation of the completion of the house," he said.

"What's the hurry?" Sean asked. "Aren't there safer places to store art work than a construction site?"

"My brother is a collector. This space is going to ultimately house his collection, so whether now or later is not the point. Once it was ready and secure, there was no reason not to start using it."

"Did the contractor know about this?" Sean asked.

"Of course. They built it," Keith said

"But did they know David was starting to store stuff down here, even before they are finished?" Sean asked.

"That is an ongoing area of friction," he said. "They do not know what is inside, but they were not pleased that he insisted that this area be completed first or that it was being used now, given the state of the project."

"Who had access to the vault?" Sean continued. Keith looked at him like he had said something extremely stupid.

Lydia had remained silent, but did not seem surprised by these revelations.

"Only David can get in," Keith said.

Sean turned to Lydia. "So did you know about the art?" She shook her head.

"David is a collector. I have seen some of his collection. But he always said there was too much for his New York apartment and that a significant percentage was not really intended for display," she said. "My role has been to collect furniture and other furnishings for the house. I've been flying to New York and Europe on buying trips spending lots of David's money. But when I asked about artwork, because a house like this has to have significant art, he would just change the subject."

Keith smiled, but said nothing. He was probably sworn to secrecy.

"So how do we get in there?" Sean said, gesturing to the door.

"*You* don't. Besides, why do you need to? This is private property. You don't need to see in there without a warrant," Keith said.

If he was trying to get into a pissing contest with Sean he was heading in the right direction.

Sean looked at him and thought before he spoke.

"You are correct, of course. However, you can cooperate with me, or I will, as you suggest, get a warrant. I can have a warrant by this afternoon if I have to and I'll have an officer stationed here around the clock until I get inside. And if it isn't easy to get in, I'll call the contractor and have him cut or bore or grind his way in and then I'll have them send you the bill. And I will impound everything inside and keep it until my investigation is complete. It's your call."

"That won't be necessary," Lydia said, calmly bringing the temperature of the two men down a couple of degrees. "We will cooperate in any way we are asked." She looked at Keith, but he did not seem to share her good will, although it seemed apparent that he knew his confrontational approach was pointless.

"So how do we get in?" Sean repeated himself.

He looked directly at Keith. "I already told you. You don't. Not without David or getting a demolition crew out here."

Sean took a deep breath. "Then I guess I'll make some calls," he said.

Keith was annoyed. "What's the rush? There is no need to destroy the vault just to satisfy your curiosity," he said.

Sean had not informed them of having found David's body and would have preferred a more appropriate setting and perhaps thoughtful timing, but since the matter was being pushed he decided to delay the inevitable no longer.

"Let's walk outside," he said.

"If this is about David, tell us now!" Keith demanded.

Lydia had a concerned look on her face. She had not heard from David in weeks. It was not like him. She had, in fact, been more closely linked to David than anyone knew. While she did not show it, she was carrying his child. Even David had not known that.

"No," Sean insisted. "Let's go outside."

They walked in silence. Sean knew the moment had arrived to tell Keith and Lydia about David.

When they emerged, Sean directed them toward the cars. They stopped as they got close.

"There is no easy way to tell you this," Sean said. He was looking at Lydia. "As you know, I have been searching for David since you filed the missing person's report. We found David's car several days ago. It had been driven to a remote location and was burned."

Lydia gasped. "Was David in it?" she asked.

"No. There were no human remains in the car and it really hasn't yielded any useful information. But the bad news is that after that, we found David's body in the chateau in the barrel room. It appears he fell down one of the open shafts and died as a result of the fall."

Lydia gasped involuntarily. She quickly raised her hand to her face and her eyes welled up with tears. "Oh, David, David, David," she moaned. Keith put his arm around her. His face was ashen and pinched as the finality of Sean's words sunk in. David was his entire world. He was Keith's anchor in a new life to which he had not yet become accustomed.

"I'm sorry to have had to tell you this, and I am sorry for your loss," Sean said. "I was hoping to find a more opportune time, but the need to continue the investigation, and get inside the vault, will make more sense to you now that you know."

"Can I see him?" Lydia asked through soft sobs.

"I can make the arrangements," Sean said.

They stood there for what seemed like a long time. Keith looked around at the distant vineyard and the vines in their fall colors. The valley below was beautiful. The setting was peaceful and quiet, and David was not there to see it. The sky which had seemed so blue, now took on a grey hue as if rain might be coming. A cold wind ran up the slope catching them in their silent thoughts, flapping the netting on the construction fence and the torn waterproofing paper on the chateau.

At last Sean broke the silence.

"So you see, what has been a missing persons investigation is now much more serious. Someone seems intent on getting into the vault. It seems likely that David's death and the attempt to break into the vault are related."

"I'll make some calls. You are both welcome to be here when we cut through the door," Sean said.

"It's more complicated than that," Keith said.

Sean looked at Keith. "Why?"

"This is a very robust vault. The roll-up door is just the first deterrent. It is not really meant to keep anyone out for long. To get past it, you would need David and a security code. Inside the door, there is a sally port that is large enough for a truck and a second set of steel doors. They are very thick and are set into the reinforced concrete walls and floor system. You need a key and the security code for that, too. Then, once past those doors, you enter a series of lower security rooms for administering the collection. Inside this area, there is a large vault like you would find in a bank. It requires both David's finger print, a key, and a combination code."

Sean let the information sink in. He would need more than just a demolition team from the sound of it, unless David's thumb or thumbs could be located and the code which had been taken as a result of his own mugging could be found. Without those, the keys that David had given to Neil, and might or might not be the keys to the vault, would be of no use.

"Neither of you had access?" Sean asked incredulously. "Did David plan for something like this?"

Keith shook his head "no". "I helped design it. David wanted it secure, so I made sure it was."

"Neither of you have a back-up key or the code," Sean asked?

Again, Keith shook his head "no".

“What about the company that built and installed it?” Sean asked. “Would they be of any assistance?”

Keith shook his head. “No. The combination was set by David once the vault was installed. They told him how to do it and made sure he understood that if he forgot the combination, there would be no way in except doing what you suggest and getting a crew with the proper equipment. No vault can withstand a full assault like that for more than a few hours or maybe a couple of days.”

“Do you think he wrote the combination down somewhere?” Sean asked.

“I doubt it,” Keith replied. “David was pretty secretive about this.”

“Do you know which finger was needed for the scanner?” he asked apologetically.

“It was his left thumb,” Keith said.

Sean nodded, but said nothing.

Keith thought for a moment. “I suppose there is a way to transfer David’s thumb print to a media that the scanner could read,” he said. “But we would still need the key and the combination.”

Sean nodded. “That might be a possibility,” he said.

Lydia did not seem interested in the vault or what was inside. She had been standing nearly silent in her grief, except for the occasional sniffle, clutching at something attached to a small gold chain around her neck. Sean did not really want to tell her that someone had removed David’s thumbs, so he let it go.

“You’re sure the vault is impenetrable?” he asked one last time.

Keith nodded. “Unless they have a way to defeat each of the layers of security, it is,” he said, “or you bring out a crew with cutting torches and jack hammers. You will be able to get in that way, but it will take a while.”

Sean said he needed to go make some calls. He told them that they were not to return to the property without his approval as the whole place was a crime scene. He did not need to elaborate on that point. He offered to drive Lydia to the morgue, but she said Keith would take her and they would meet him there.

She had released the object she had been clutching. It was a small diamond encrusted pendant.

Sean offered his condolences and followed them in his car as they left.

«»«»«»

The next morning Sean called Neil.

"Well, the circus has begun," Sean said.

"I saw it on the internet this morning," Neil said.

"I had asked the coroner to hold off announcing David's death until I informed Lydia and Keith. I told them yesterday. Once they knew, there was no point in holding the information any longer. So the coroner's office put out a press release last night and my phone has not stopped ringing. There are news trucks parked in front of the station and more parked up on the hill. We've posted officers inside the gates to make sure they stay off the property. But there are drones flying around up there. I think we are going to file an enforcement request with the FAA to make sure that they are all registered."

"Sounds like you have had a busy morning," Neil said.

"Yeah," Sean answered sounding weary.

"Did Lydia notice that David's thumbs were missing?" Neil asked. It was sort of a tasteless question, but seemed relevant.

"No. The body was covered with a sheet. They only lowered it enough to see his face and shoulders."

"I don't think you are getting into that vault without digging into it," Neil said. It was an obvious point. "I wonder why it didn't work for whomever destroyed the scanner? Seems like it must have been the same person that killed David and cut off his thumbs. So if they took the code from you and had his thumbs, they should have been able to get in."

"No, because they didn't have the keys," he said. "I have the keys, but no code or thumbs," he said.

"I don't suppose that the interested party will have the time or resources to break into the vault with brute force," Neil offered.

"Not unless it was someone from the construction company," he said. "It would be too obvious. I think I owe the contractor another call."

"Let me know how it goes and if I can be of assistance," Neil said, although his offer had more to do with his own curiosity than with any delusions that he was helping Sean in the least.

«»«»«»

Later, as Neil sat in the office sipping his morning coffee, Shelley came breezing in.

“Hey there!” she said cheerfully. She gave her hair a quick tousle. She was wearing a favorite pair of old blue jeans and a fitted cotton blouse.

“Good morning,” he said looking up from his computer screen. “You’re late. I am going to have to write you up and put it in your file.”

She gave him a bratty look.

“What?” he said with mock innocence. “I read somewhere that is what a responsible employer is supposed to do,” he said.

He was sitting at his desk working on his computer. He was wearing a white button-down dress shirt and dark navy pants. He had no way of knowing that Shelley liked that particular combination.

She walked over pushing his rolling desk chair, with him in it, away from his desk. She sat on his lap, her legs straddling his. “I guess you’re going to have to write me up for this, too, then,” she said.

He put the coffee down and smiled. “I would, except I can’t seem to reach that pen over there. Would you mind getting it for me?” he asked.

As Shelley leaned over to reach the pen, the warm bosom beneath her freshly washed cotton blouse rubbed Neil’s face. She was wearing a small pearl on a silver chain around her neck. It dangled enticingly down into a chasm of youthful cleavage.

“I don’t think you are going to need it,” she said handing the pen to him before beginning to unbutton his shirt.

He tossed it back on the desk and neither of them spoke further. The office was silent for a long while except for the sound of papers rustling on his desk.

«»«»«»

"Architecture is not an inspirational business, it's a rational procedure to do sensible and hopefully beautiful things; that's all."

-- Harry Seidler

Chapter Nine

Special Agent Marcus Little was sitting at his desk reviewing his monthly expense account information preparing to send it downstairs to the accounting department. It was one of his least favorite things to be doing, but one of the many mundane activities that kept agencies of the Federal government, like the FBI for whom he worked, functioning.

It was a blustery, late-January morning. It was cold and clear with a brisk breeze. He knew this because he had walked from the subway station the last couple blocks to the FBI's New York office. His cubicle did not have a window or even a line of sight across the office to a window. So he didn't mind having a little outdoor time before being stuck indoors for most of the day.

When the phone rang he was both pleased and annoyed. He was pleased to have something to do other than review his expenses and receipts, but annoyed because it meant that he would not complete the task before the department staff meeting. It was Patti, the section administrative assistant.

"Someone is calling from Blackbridge about a painting," she said. Blackbridge was one of New York's oldest auction houses dealing in fine arts. There were other larger houses with higher profiles or with offices in major cities around the world, but none in New York were older.

"Okay. Send them through," he said.

The phone rang again and he tapped a button to accept the call.

"Agent Little," he said into the handset.

The voice on the other end of the call belonged to Jennifer Singh. She had a lovely English accent and informed Marcus that she was calling in regards to a painting that the house had received that they believed had been reported stolen about ten years previously. She asked if he would be able to drop by to see the painting?

He said he would and hung up the phone. He did not mind that he was going to "have" to miss the department staff meeting. He walked by Patti's workstation on his way to the elevator. He signed out and said he would not be back until sometime after lunch. Patti gave him a wry smile.

"I'm on to you, ya know," she said, taking the sign-in sheet from Marcus. She snapped her gum. "Yep. I know your type." She cocked her head and gave Marcus a knowing look.

Marcus chuckled. "I have no way of knowing when the public is going to need me to come to investigate a crime," he said. "Criminals don't wait until staff meetings are over, you know.'

"Uh huh. You keep talking," she said. "It won't do you no good. I got your number."

"So you want the grande or the venti, this time?" Marcus asked.

"You know what I like, sweetie. Just don't disappoint me. I can't take no more of that from men. Not even you."

"You drive a hard bargain, Patti," Marcus said. "But I just couldn't live with myself if I were to disappoint you. So don't you worry."

"You are one smart man, Agent Little," she said. "Now get on out of here and let me do my job!"

Marcus had been bringing Patti coffee and the occasional pastry since he had started working in the section. She was the glue that held it together and kept things humming smoothly. If Patti had your back, there were no surprises. If she didn't, you didn't see the bureaucratic truck that hit you until you were flat on your back with tire tracks across your chest. An occasional coffee was a small price to pay for that kind of cover.

Marcus took a cab from his office to the auction house which was located on Park Avenue. Ms. Singh requested that he enter the building from a side staff entrance, rather than the public entrance, to avoid any attention his visit might generate. Auction houses are notoriously sensitive about even the slightest hint of scandal, and this case had the all the markings of something full-blown about it.

Inside, he was met by Ms. Singh and introduced to the team that was responsible for evaluating and appraising the pieces of art that the auction house routinely sold. Typically, the firm assembled paintings and other works of art or furniture from a particular period or movement for a 'themed' auction as a way of attracting dealers and collectors. Curating an auction to maximize the sales value, from which both the seller and the auction house would benefit, took many months. In addition, the role and responsibility of the auction house was to authenticate and appraise each piece to be sold.

Marcus was ushered into a conference room and the painting followed soon thereafter. It was placed on an inclined shelf, meant to receive paintings of any size, that was bathed in bright, but appropriately filtered, light. They gazed upon the very sweet countenance of a seven-year-old girl painted by a gifted family friend.

His first question was how they had come to be in possession of the painting. He was told that it had been shipped to the auction house from San Francisco by a bonded courier and that all the paperwork had been in order.

Next he wanted to know how they knew it was stolen. Jennifer Singh told him they had access to a database of art objects, including paintings, whose information was maintained and provided as a courtesy by the insurance industry. As part of their normal vetting process, they checked the registry and thought it likely that this painting was one that was identified as having gone missing in a residential arson fire in Chicago about 10 years ago.

Marcus wanted to know if the painting had just shown up with no prior communication. Ms. Singh told him that a week or so prior to the receipt of the painting, an attorney for the seller had called her to make the necessary arrangements for the shipment and sale of the painting. She also told Marcus that the attorney informed her that he was representing a client that wished to remain anonymous.

"What was the attorney's name?" Marcus asked. He, of course, wanted to know the identity of the attorney as he or she would soon be paid a visit courtesy of the government of the United States.

"His name is Steven Jordan," she said.

"Is that normal? You get a lot of calls from attorneys for anonymous sellers?" he continued.

"I don't know that I would say it is normal," Jennifer replied. "But it's not unheard of. Wealthy collectors of art are typically eccentric in some way. Some are quite secretive. But that can take many odd ways of presenting itself."

"So you said you don't know who the seller is?" Marcus asked.

"Correct," she said.

"Then how do you know they are wealthy?" he asked.

"I don't," she replied. "But assuming they came by the painting legitimately, then they had sufficient wealth to purchase the piece. Compared to most people, that would make them wealthy."

Marcus just grunted, conceding the point as he scribbled notes.

"Do you know the attorney? Has he sent you paintings in the past?" Marcus asked.

"No. He has never sent us a painting in the past," she said.

Marcus had worked on a number of stolen property cases over the years, but this was the first one in which the stolen property had been offered up for a public sale by an anonymous person. It did not seem likely to him that the seller knew the painting was stolen. It wouldn't make sense to try to sell a highly recognizable painting at public auction that would be immediately identified as having been stolen. The person selling the painting probably had purchased the piece and was now trying to sell it.

When he asked who had been informed of the painting's recovery, he was pleased to be told that no one outside the auction house had been informed. When he pressed further about whether the attorney that had made the arrangements had been informed that the painting might have been stolen, Marcus was told that he had not yet been told what the auction house staff suspected.

Marcus asked that the secrecy surrounding the painting be maintained until further into the investigation. Ms. Singh readily agreed. If the attorney or anyone representing the seller approached anyone on the auction house staff about the painting, they were to be told that the painting was undergoing a rigorous process of authentication, but nothing more.

Marcus turned to the expert who had authenticated the painting. She was a middle-aged woman with bookish glasses.

"So you are certain this is in fact the missing Edgar Payne painting from the list?" he asked.

"As certain as we can be at this point," was her reply. "We would like to discuss the provenance of the painting with both the attorney representing the seller and the estate of the original owner, but we have not done that yet."

"Good. Let's keep it that way for a bit longer," he said.

The painting was rather small, measuring only about 10x12 inches. With the frame it may have been more like 16x18. Marcus was amazed that something this small could be worth so much.

"It's really worth half a million dollars? Are you sure?" he asked.

"At least that much," was the reply.

"Okay. I'll be in touch." He was given photo copies of all the correspondence, bills of lading, and other information that the auction house had on the painting. He took a quick photo with his phone before he left.

On the way back to the office he ordered a venti iced cappuccino with a shot of hazelnut. After returning to the office and making Patti's day, Marcus Little lobbied hard to lead the case. Even though he had seniority, he did not necessarily have the political skills to always get the cases he wanted. It took a week, but he was pleased to be assigned the case by his section's supervisor who was twenty years his junior, but had flown up the ladder owing to a couple of good suits and a degree from an outstanding law school. But Marcus wasn't really bitter. He didn't like agency politics. He just liked solving puzzles, crime puzzles to be specific.

«‹›»«‹›»«‹›»

Keith was not content to leave the investigation into David's death to the yahoos in a small-town police department. He knew from personal experience that they were not typically the sharpest bunch. He had, after all, managed to outwit them multiple times without much effort. He did some research and made a couple of calls. His last one was to the firm of Kurz-Wilder. There was more than one way to find David's murderer and he had money, David's money, to explore the areas in the shadows where law enforcement would not go and to use methods they could not. He would find David's killer and when he did, he was going to kill them himself, slowly, with his bare hands. He wrote a fairly sizable check and signed some paperwork to get things underway, and that was that. Now all he had to do was wait.

Keith was not very good at waiting.

«‹›»«‹›»«‹›»

As curious as Neil was about who might have killed David and what he had been storing in that vault, there really was nothing to do but wait for Sean to figure things out. His report for David, and now Lydia, was clearly on hold until case was resolved.

He spent the next several weeks working on his house. A local church called and asked for a proposal to assist them in refurbishing their fellowship hall and making ADA upgrades to their entire facility. Not sexy work, but he gladly took it.

November came and went.

The holidays were their typical blur.

It had started to rain, as it always does in January, almost nonstop. Neil decided he needed a fire with his morning coffee and had moved from his normal perch at his desk and was sitting next to a crackling fire, scanning the headlines on his tablet.

The Middle East was a mess, again. Fluctuating oil prices were causing concern on Wall Street. A large piece of one of the glaciers in Antarctica had calved and was causing scientists to be alarmed. The 49'ers were eliminated over the weekend from the playoffs by the Detroit Lions. Detroit? Really? There was an earthquake in Chile, and a rare frost in Mexico that was threatening the avocado crop. That would not be good, he thought.

He scanned back through the articles, reading a few and skipping a few. The piece on attorneys duking it out over a contested will caught his eye as he scrolled down and stopped for a look.

Neil had not thought about the late David Johnsson recently. He was thinking about how to get a wheelchair up onto the dais of the local Methodist church without having to put a large wheelchair lift in front of the entire church. As much of a problem as that might seem, it was nothing compared to what the Baptists were going to face when they decided to try to get a wheelchair into their baptistery.

He read the article.

> **New York** - *Attorneys in Manhattan are contesting the validity of a will signed by the late David Johnsson who was found dead from a tragic fall at the construction site of his Napa Valley mansion in early November. Georgia Johnsson, the billionaire's second wife, is contesting the will put forward by the estate of Mr. Johnsson that is reported to leave the bulk of his estate to his children and his immediate next of kin. Mr. Johnsson is survived by his younger brother Keith Johnsson.*
>
> *The attorneys for Mrs. Johnsson allege that the will produced by the estate was not properly executed and does not reflect the final wishes of Mr. Johnsson, who Mrs. Johnsson asserts promised her to be the sole beneficiary of his estate. Attorneys representing Mr. Johnsson's estate counter that the will was executed a year before Mr. Johnsson's death and is legally binding. They further point out that Mr. and Mrs. Johnsson*

were estranged at the time of his death and that Mr. Johnsson had filed signed divorce papers seeking a divorce from Mrs. Johnsson prior to the signing of the will.

While a spokesperson for Mrs. Johnsson has confirmed that the couple had been living separately, she contends that she was not aware of Mr. Johnsson's intent to file for a divorce or change his will. Attorneys for Mrs. Johnsson have not made public a copy of a previous will they contend will demonstrate that Mr. Johnsson intended to leave his estate to Mrs. Johnsson in the event of his untimely death.

Adding a further wrinkle to the case, Mr. Johnsson was not known to have fathered any children; however, Lydia Mankovich, Mr. Johnsson's assistant at the time of his death, asserts that she is carrying his child. Her attorneys have informed the press that Ms. Mankovich is due to deliver her child in June, and that she intends to file paternity documents with the court establishing her child as the primary heir to Mr. Johnsson's reputed fortune.

Police have not yet ruled out foul play in Mr. Johnsson's death, however no suspects have been identified and no arrests have been made. Reports from the Napa County coroner indicate that the cause of death was blunt force trauma to the head and neck, likely as the result of a fall. Mr. Johnsson's body was found in the as yet unfinished shell of his mansion outside St. Helena, California, a small community about 30 mile north of Napa.

Forbes Magazine listed Mr. Johnsson as one of the wealthiest men in America with an estimated net worth exceeding $10 billion.

Neil picked up the phone and dialed Sean. He had not spoken to Sean in months.

"Detective Andrews, here," Sean said as he picked up the phone.

"So how would a guy like me knock off a guy without getting caught by a guy like you?" Neil asked.

"Who is this?" Sean barked into the phone.

Realizing that Sean might not have a funny bone when it came to crime, Neil fessed up. "It's Neil Thornton," he said.

"That's not funny," he said.

"Sorry," he said. "I was just reading an article online about David Johnsson's disputed will," Neil said, entirely giving up on the humor. "Any leads on the investigation?" he asked hopefully.

"None. But I have cleared the last obstacle to enable me to open the vault," he said.

"What, you haven't gotten in there yet?" Neil exclaimed. "I thought you were just holding back on me."

"Nope. Nothing to report," he said. "It takes a while for all the paperwork to get cleared when there is not a direct link to a crime. Getting the warrant was more difficult than I thought. The whole probate and custody thing is a tangled web."

Sean was quiet for a moment.

"That's the thing that keeps this job interesting. It really is unpredictable." He paused and then went on. "So, as I said, I am close to getting ready to open the vault." He paused again. "I don't know if you have been keeping up with all the legal proceedings. Sounds like you haven't. But it has truly been a circus. After I filed for the warrant, an army of attorneys showed up. Apparently I started a big battle for the estate. Turns out David's second wife is protesting that the will is legit. And to make it more complicated, David had signed the final paperwork for the divorce with his attorneys, but his attorneys had taken their time informing his wife. Ex-wife, rather. So she disputed the legitimacy of the divorce papers, too. In the meantime, Lydia is claiming to be pregnant with David's child."

"That's what the article said."

"She is definitely pregnant with someone's kid and it would make sense that it was David's."

"So how are you getting to go ahead, if the estate isn't settled?" Neil asked.

"I convinced the judge, actually it was the district attorney, but anyway, we convinced the judge that waiting to open the vault was not relevant to who would inherit what was in it. And since we are in the midst of a homicide investigation, it might reveal clues relevant to the case."

"Oh," Neil said. "So it's not really Lydia or Keith that you are worried about. It's his ex-wife. She'll be there with her attorney's, huh?" he asked.

"She is invited, but I don't know if she will show," Sean said. "The judge has frozen everything until the paternity of Lydia's child is established. I guess if it is David's, then things roll one way. If it isn't, then things roll another way. In the meantime, I just want to solve this or close it cold or whatever. It is taking up all my time. They are supposed to get started around 9:00 a.m. on Tuesday. I doubt they will be through the steel doors that Keith described in less than an hour," he said.

“Am I invited?” Neil asked hopefully.

“No,” Sean said emphatically.

Neil tried to hide his disappointment, “Do they know you have the key?” Neil asked.

“No. Won’t do me any good either without the thumbs. I’ve given up on those. They are long gone, I fear.”

Sean was probably right.

«»«»«»

It was foggy the next Tuesday morning, which seemed to add to the suspense. The construction site was humming with activity. There must have been 50 cars and trucks gathered at the top of the hill. What had been a dirt lot late in the fall was now a muddy mess, made the worse for all the recent rain and the influx of vehicles. Sean arrived around 9:00 a.m. and stepped out of his car and down into the soft earth. He squashed his way to the entrance to the garage, looking for a path through the puddles and mud.

The entrance to the vehicle ramp to the underground garage had been cleared away. Several people were milling around the entrance and greeted him as he made his way down the ramp.

Sean did the best he could to stamp off the excess mud and dirt from his shoes and walked down the wet ramp into the garage. It was fully lit with temporary construction lights. A group of people were huddled around the entrance to the vault. The sound of their voices echoed through the empty parking structure. It wasn’t entirely empty, however. Sean had made sure there were at least a half dozen vans ready to move any evidence from the vault. They were lined up neatly against the wall nearest the vault’s entrance.

Sean walked up to the small crowd that waited in the garage near the vault. The roll-up door had not posed a real deterrent and that it had been breached easily. He could see the flashing light of the welders further up a tunnel as they slowly melted their way through the next door and its attachments.

The crowd was made up mostly of his fellow police officers and construction personnel hired by his department. There were several people that he did not recognize. He did not see Lydia there, however, Keith was standing near an outer edge, just as he was, with a slightly worried look on his face. Sean didn’t approach him immediately as there was little to say.

They all stood shifting their weight and casually looking around the garage, as if there were anything to see of interest inside such a utilitarian space. It was now approaching 11:00 a.m. and still there seemed to be no progress. The welding stopped for a period and then resumed, but no word had filtered back out to where they stood as to what was happening or to mark the progress of the demolition.

Several people started to leave, either bored to death or had other things to do more important than this. Sean was doing his best to be patient when Keith walked up behind him.

Sean turned toward Keith and said, "I thought they would have been through by now."

Keith smiled thinly. "I told you it would take some time."

"You did. But I still thought it would be faster," he said.

Keith nodded toward one of the men standing closest to the opening to the vestibule leading to the vault. "That's one of the attorneys for Georgia," he said in a low, almost hissing voice.

Sean just nodded in acknowledgement.

"Looks like she is not here," he said.

A few moments later there was a sort of squeaking sound followed by a very loud booming crash. Everyone was visibly startled.

One of the construction suits who had been standing nearby ran into the space asking in a loud shout if everyone was all right. Several shouts to the affirmative came back and the group pressed in a little closer to see what had happened. Sean pressed to the front of the group and asked everyone to stand back. No one really moved back, but no one pressed forward, either.

He came back momentarily and said that they would need to move some of the lighting into the vault before anyone could peer further inside. There was an audible sense of disappointment followed by an increase in the volume of the conversation and the group started to get excited about what was next.

The construction crew moved several portable lights through the opening in the garage wall and into the vault. The shape and contour of the interior of the vestibule became more distinct as the light dispelled the shadows.

Sean and several of his colleagues entered the next area of the vault and looked around. None of the assembled group could see what they were doing and it was beginning to feel a bit anti-climactic.

Keith wiped his brow with the back of his sleeve. He seemed even more nervous now.

They all stood there waiting for something. A few more people gave up and the group dwindled some more.

Sean was busy inside taking photos and determining if there was anything of importance inside. After a lengthy period he came back out and called for Keith. He then asked for the indulgence of those standing there and explained that he would need additional time in the space to ensure that there was nothing of importance to the criminal investigation before anyone else would be allowed inside. At that point, everyone but the attorney and a couple of the construction workers turned with a collective murmur and left.

The construction crews moved the portable lighting further into the next area of the vault. The harsh glare of the lights illuminated the rooms in bright white light that cast hard shadows against the distant walls and into the unfinished spaces. Sean and Keith walked past about two dozen large crates as they walked into the main room of the vault. Keith said these contained sculptural pieces. Keith followed Sean into the main room and stopped behind him as he took in the space. The outer edges of the room were lined with shallow rectangular crates leaning against the walls that were stacked five and six deep. The crates were of all sizes, but most were not more than about 9 or 10 inches in depth. There were hundreds and hundreds of crates.

Sean had expected the outer room to be empty and the collection to be inside the inner vault that Keith had described.

"If all the art is out here," he asked, "what is in the inner vault?"

Keith shrugged. "There is more than this. These are just the recent pieces David acquired for the estate. He also has an extensive collection in New York."

"Wow," was all Sean could muster. There must have been several hundred million dollars in art inside the room.

"David was a serious collector," Keith said. "These are mostly all pieces that I helped him acquire. He didn't like others to know that he was the person collecting the art, so he engaged various dealers to assist in the purchases so his identity would not be known. He was concerned that if the seller knew he was the buyer, they would increase the price."

"Still, what is in the vault?" Sean asked again.

"Probably some of his collection of rare books and manuscripts," Keith replied.

"Did he collect jewelry or precious metals?" Sean asked.

"Not unless it was of archeological significance. He did not care for contemporary pieces and he found diamonds to be of little interest. He always said carbon was too plentiful to bother collecting. I think there are some early Etruscan gold pieces and there are some artifacts recovered from sunken ships in the Mediterranean."

They walked around and looked in all the spaces. All of them were unfinished and all of them contained unopened crates.

"Did he have an insurance inventory?" Sean asked.

Keith nodded. "Lydia should have it somewhere or be able to get it from his files in New York. I'll call her."

While they were walking and talking, Keith was somewhat absentmindedly pulling the crates apart to inspect their labels. The crates were mostly stacked largest to smallest with the largest box leaning against the wall and the smallest being the outermost crate.

"Is there some order to the way they are stacked?" Sean asked.

"They seem to be arranged roughly by date, with the older pieces over there," Keith motioned over his shoulder, "and the more recent works heading over in that direction." He bent down to inspect a crate.

Sean looked at the crate nearest him. It was a painting by someone named Frans Hals and had a date on the front of 1664. He did not seem particularly interested in any of the art and began looking around the edges of the room. He spent several minutes in front of the vault door with his flashlight pointed carefully at the dial. He stepped away, making room for one of his staff with a fingerprint kit to begin dusting the dial and other surfaces on the face of the vault.

Keith had moved on to the far end of the room and was systematically pulling all the smaller crates apart, inspecting their labels.

"Are you looking for something in particular?" Sean asked.

"No," he lied. "It's been a while since I've seen some of these crates. I had forgotten there were so many."

Sean called him over to the vault door.

"I don't see any signs of forced entry or tampering. I don't think this room has been entered by anyone recently," he said.

Keith nodded. "I agree. If someone got in here, I don't think they took anything," he said. "The only way to be sure, though, is to inventory the collection."

"We are going to do that today as we move the pieces. I've got to let the lawyer for Mrs. Johnsson in," Sean said.

"Really?" Keith asked in exasperation.

"Yep. So is there anything else we need to see or discuss before I do that?" he asked.

"I guess not," Keith said. "I just want to make sure that nothing goes missing."

"I'm sure he wants the same thing, since his client is claiming a chunk of this," Sean said.

"A hundred percent is more than a chunk," Keith replied.

"True."

"Are you going to try to open the vault today?" Keith asked.

Sean looked back at the massive door to the vault. "It seems safe enough for the time being."

"I agree," he said.

"Keith, please get me a copy of the insurance inventory as quickly as you can. We'll cross-check that against what's here and see what might be in the vault. And I'll be in touch with the vault people to come out to see if there is a non-destructive way to get in to it."

With that he walked back out to the garage and spoke briefly with the attorney. The two of them returned momentarily with a couple of the remaining construction guys. There were a couple of low whistles and a crude, but respectful, exclamation of disbelief.

The attorney took a quick spin around the space with his camera phone recording the contents of the vault. He returned to where Sean was standing with Keith.

"I expect that all this evidence will be protected and that I will be furnished with a complete list of each item," he said.

Sean said that he would station two of his “best men” outside the door until the contents of the room could be catalogued and removed to a secure storage facility. The sarcasm was subtle and lost on Georgia Calhoun Johnsson’s attorney.

"Can't nothing make your life work if you ain't the architect."

-- Terry McMillan

Chapter Ten

The second Mrs. Johnsson was waiting in her hotel room at the St. Regis Hotel in San Francisco for a report from her attorney. She had spent a lovely morning in the hotel spa being pampered and refreshed from the stress she had been forced to endure all these months since David had died. She always found that a good massage by a strong, handsome young man was just what she needed, even if the young man in question was probably as gay as they come.

She had told the attorney to call the moment he was able to talk, but she thought he was ignoring her request and taking his time. She turned to her other attorney and asked him what could be keeping him from calling? He just shook his head with a worried expression and remained standing in the window where he had been looking out toward the cloud bank that was enveloping the city.

"I don't believe David signed those papers," she said for the thousandth time. "It was that woman!" She spat out the words. "And now she wants us all to believe that she is carrying David's 'love' child! What a crock of shit!"

Georgia Winthrop Calhoun was in high dudgeon. She had experienced a short and tumultuous marriage to David that for all intents and purposes had ended several years before the official separation. He had met her at a party after he and his first wife had divorced. He was in a vulnerable emotional state when they met, though he would never admit it. His excessive work-life imbalance had cost him his first marriage and he knew it. He had tried belatedly to put the pieces back together, but he had waited too long to make the effort and then she was gone and would have none of it. At the time, he still loved her and didn't really blame her for leaving. He walked into his relationship with Georgia with his eyes wide open, even though he was not fully cognizant of what he was truly getting himself into. Anyone around him could have warned him off, if he had asked or would have listened, but David was not one to seek much advice and accepted even less. When it came to relationships, he thought his barriers were a mile high.

So Georgia slipped into his life with little effort on his part. She saw the opening and exploited it fully. He saw the same opening, but from a different perspective and did the same, repeatedly. But he carried protection for this relationship in the form of his attorneys and their ability to craft a well-written prenuptial agreement. After things went south and they were formally separated, it had withstood a barrage of legal maneuvering to get it tossed out and had saved him several billion dollars. He said having it crafted was the best money he had ever, and he meant ever, spent.

Georgia was all laughs and giggles at first. She was the daughter of a prominent physician from Charleston. She had a flirtatious drawl and could use it along with some other rather prominently displayed Southern charms to get a man's full attention. She reeled David in like a play thing and believed she had him right where she wanted him. He of course thought the same thing and fancied himself quite the paramour. So they spent several months playing the game, flying to Europe, the far East, and South Pacific on excursions to five star resorts where the warm temperatures and secluded beaches made the physical intimacy all the more frequent and spontaneous.

David instructed the pilot of his plane to make a short stop in Las Vegas after one of their trips to Tahiti. Being a man of some social status in New York, David didn't want or need all the public speculation and titillation that a large formal wedding would generate. Georgia didn't mind the smaller faster version of the "I dos" so long as the result was a wedding license and a ring on her finger. David had not made much of the pre-nuptial agreement or its contents prior to landing in Las Vegas. He did have the presence of mind to have a copy of it with him in his briefcase along with several other consent forms that proved useful from time to time.

He had called ahead and reserved the penthouse suite at one of the newest casinos on the strip. They had made a brief stop at a Tiffany's in the casino mall before heading to the in-house Chapel of Love. As they stood at the counter signing the paperwork for the marriage license, she was gazing admiringly at the new, large, shiny diamond on her finger. He was fishing around in his briefcase for his passport and pulled another document out and placed it on the counter.

"I know we have not spent much time talking about the paperwork," he said, "but I need you to sign this."

"What is it, sweetie?" she asked.

"Something that my attorneys say that I have to have you sign."

"But what's it say?" she asked in her most innocent voice.

"It says that if this does not work for some reason, you will be well taken care of financially," he said.

"Oh, hun, we don't need this," she said and gave him a full body hug. She laid her head on his chest and said, "We don't need lawyers to define our love, do we?"

"No. But you need to sign it just the same." He said it kindly but firmly.

She looked up trying to gauge if there was any room for negotiation or bluff. "I don't know," she said. "My daddy said, 'Never sign a document you haven't read.'"

"Your father was right. If you would like to discuss this with him, you can. I'll have John fly you home this evening."

"Oh, but what about you, sweetie?"

David looked at her without saying anything further and she understood this was not negotiable. She could sign it and get screwed, but then she had already been letting that happen for several months. Or perhaps if she signed it she might find out it wasn't too terrible a deal. Or she could walk away and get nothing for her trouble, only to have to start the process of finding a wealthy man all over again. Or she could sign it and see if her attorneys could find ways to get around it; or maybe get it changed.

"I don't want anything to come between us, babe," she said. "Where's your big, thick pen?"

David laughed and handed her his pen. They both signed the agreement and the notary at the counter witnessed the document and stamped and signed it. They made it through the wedding mill in record time.

It had been fun briefly after that. They returned to New York, each having gotten what they wanted. It did not take him long to dread going back to his apartment. She found excuses to need to fly home to see her not-so-ailing mother. They both wasted no time connecting with the next, newer opportunity that soon presented itself to each of them. And she quietly began seeking legal counsel regarding the best way to get around the prenuptial agreement.

«»«»«»

When the phone rang, it was Georgia's attorney. The attorney that was waiting with her answered the phone and listened without speaking. He smiled and said, "That sounds good. No, stay there and stay close. If anything develops call me immediately. Good. Thanks."

He turned to Georgia. "Well, it looks like it's all there," he said.

“What did I tell you?” was her response “Oh, that is such a relief!”

Derek Storque was Georgia’s attorney. He walked over to where she sat and began rubbing her shoulders.

“You know that makes me crazy, when you do that,” she said.

“I know. I like it when you get crazy. Then let’s get some dinner.”

“You are so bad,” she said. “I’m not even divorced yet and my husband is dead!”

«»«»«»

As Sean and Keith left the garage, Keith walked a short distance behind. There was a rather awkward silence. There wasn’t a clear opening to any semblance of a normal conversation, so they both walked in silence.

As they exited the garage, Keith broke the silence.

“Detective. Have you found anything else about who might have killed my brother?”

Sean stopped and turned towards Keith, shaking his head.

“No, I am afraid not,” he said. “As you know we could find no signs of a struggle. A construction site is not exactly conducive to gathering fingerprints or other evidence, so there wasn’t much to collect. We did the best we could to try to determine where David had been in the days prior to our finding him and who he might have met with, but he seemed to have spent a lot of time alone.”

Keith was listening intently, nodding.

“Do you have any further ideas about what might have happened?” Sean asked.

“Not really. I don’t like his ex-wife. She’s always been a total bitch, but I don’t think she could have killed him. She might have paid someone to do it, but she would have been far away if she was involved.”

“Do you know her well?” Sean asked.

“Not really. Met her a couple of times when I was with David. It was always with a lot of drama and a big fight. I do know that she felt that David owed her more than she thought she was going to get as part of the divorce. She made no secret of that. She had hired attorneys to try to litigate the prenup, just as she is now contesting whether he signed the divorce papers and his will. She also seemed to have hired people to shadow David to try to catch him in some indiscretion."

"Really." Sean did not express surprise at this revelation.

"Yeah. David told me once that Georgia would get something like $10 million for every year of their marriage. There was some kind of formula. In the meantime, she basically had a blank checkbook. I don't know why it took him so long to sign the paperwork, because it was probably costing him a heck of a lot more not to sign it than if he had just gotten it over with."

They walked up toward where the cars were parked.

Sean hesitated for a moment.

"We've been through all this before, so I don't know that there is any point bringing it up again," he said. "But your background and time in the 'system' places you in a certain light."

Keith nodded. "Yeah. I already told you. David was my only family. He never stopped trying to find me and when he finally did, it changed my life."

"Did it?" Sean asked. "You had access and a motive. That keeps you on the list," he said.

Keith did not seem intimidated by the strong assertion that he might have killed his brother. He just shook his head.

"I didn't do it. I may have done some dumb stuff when I was young, but I didn't do this. I have been kicking myself that I didn't keep a closer eye on David. I should have protected him. A loaded guy like him was a mark for a lot of people. I talked to David about his security a couple of times, but he always brushed it off. Nothing had ever happened and he just assumed that nothing ever would." Keith paused. "I should have insisted and I should have hired some muscle."

Sean had been listening carefully. And though Keith may not have realized it, he had revealed a lot about himself.

"The most obvious scenario is that someone tried to get into the vault and killed him in the process, either before or after they tried to break in," Sean said. "Whether they knew what was in there is questionable. The list of people that knew about the vault seems to be very short. You, Lydia, the contractor, and the architect."

"So if you were going to steal from David, and I understand that you say you didn't -- so I am not accusing you, how would you have done it and for what? The money? Or what?" Sean asked.

Keith thought about it for a minute.

"Not the money. That would be too complicated, banks and the FBI and all that shit. But the art could be fenced," he said. "David had lots of valuable stuff. Most of it was locked away pretty tight, I made sure of that, but I think if I was going to try to score on David, I would have been looking for a way to snag a couple pieces of art. He had so much, he might not have missed it for a while."

"You helped David buy some of his art," Sean said.

"Yeah."

"So you know some people that buy pieces that have been stolen?" Sean asked.

Keith's eyes narrowed. "Maybe."

"Let's just say that after we do the inventory, and several pieces are missing. Then what?" Sean asked.

"If pieces are missing, it is not likely they will come up for sale anywhere," Keith said. "At least for a while. After that, they might be offered quietly to collectors who don't plan to show the work and don't care where it came from."

"So if some pieces are missing, how would we know? Are you the only one who had a clear idea of David's collection?"

"And Lydia," Keith said.

"So again. As far as you know, all David was moving into the vault was art, nothing else of value?"

"Correct."

"And you think that you and Lydia will be able to tell if anything is missing."

"Yeah. I doubt I saw everything, but I will certainly know what I helped him acquire. I also can get in touch with most of the dealers and galleries in New York where he made most of his purchases. But I won't know about any of the early stuff that he bought with Kelley. His first wife."

"All right. Get me the insurance list and we'll go from there," Sean said.

"And I can't help you with the dealer that died," Keith offered. "I have limitations when people are dead."

Sean didn't laugh. He gave Keith a hard stare before asking the obvious question.

"David had a dealer that died? When was this?" he asked.

"It was before my time. He was more of an agent, anyway."

"What does that mean?" Sean asked.

"He wasn't buying and selling pieces for David. Just buying and advising from what David told me. He was an old professor or something and he died of cancer."

"Oh. I thought maybe he was caught up in something related to David's death," Sean said.

"I doubt it. David was squeaky clean. By all accounts this professor guy was, too."

Keith got in his Mercedes-Benz and drove away.

In all the excitement, Sean had forgotten to try using the key on the steel doors. He looked at the keys in his hand rather sheepishly. He wanted to leave, but thought he had better try the keys while he was thinking about it.

«»«»«»

Sean walked back into the garage. The construction guys had cleared out and the only people left were with the local police and sheriff's office. Sean walked back through the taped off area and entered the corridor where the steel doors had been located and one was now laying on the floor in the middle of the tunnel. Once it had been welded off its hinges and had fallen, it was too heavy to move. They would eventually need heavy equipment to get it out of the way.

Sean fished the keys from his pocket and tried each one. The third key he tried slipped into the slot and turned effortlessly.

"Like butter!" Sean said under his breath.

Sean realized that they might not have found all of the locked doors that David used to lock away his prized possessions. It was possible David had a floor safe. He hadn't really been looking for that sort of thing when he walked through the building before. There was enough construction debris lying around that he could have easily missed something. Maybe he should go back inside and have another look, he thought. He sighed. He really did want to get back to the office. But there was no time like the present. So he walked back to his car and retrieved a flashlight.

He decided to start at the top and walk systematically through the entire building, room by room, floor by floor.

He climbed back up the partially completed stairs. The top floor was mostly dry, but near the edges it was wet. The concrete topping on the deck had not been poured dead level and small puddles of standing water were scattered about. By now it was early afternoon. Another front was moving in and even in the early afternoon, the winter sun could not dispel the gloom attending the dense cloud cover. It was not completely dark, but it seemed like deep twilight.

The stairs took him to the northeast corner of the top floor. He had been in the building several times, but didn't have the plan totally figured out. He decided to go from north to south and then to descend to the main floor. The entire west side of the top floor seemed to be bedrooms and guest suites. There was nothing to see in the area above the main salon, but he shined his light down into the deepening darkness.

As he poked around, Sean realized there seemed to be an endless number of places where someone like David could have installed hidden features like floor safes.

He pointed his flashlight between the metal studs and down through every opening in the deck he found. He kept nosing around, but began to doubt that he would find anything since he wasn't even sure what he was looking for.

The southeast corner of the floor was the master suite. It was huge. Even though none of the interior wall finishes had been installed, the rough metal framing provided a sense of the impressive dimensions of the layout.

He entered a vestibule to the master suite off the main corridor through an unfinished arch. The gaping hole of the shaft for a private elevator descended into blackness on one side. Beyond that, there was a private sitting room with a fireplace that had been roughed in. And adjacent to that was the bedroom itself. It must have been as large as Sean's apartment, he thought. Off the master bedroom was an expansive bath with a massive walk-in closet. A huge tub, carved from a single block of Carrera marble and bigger than your average spa pool, was already in place, along with a shower larger than Sean's office. He looked carefully throughout the master suite area. This seemed like the natural place to find a floor safe or some secondary vault; maybe even a secret stairway hidden in a wall cavity.

He found nothing, though he scoured every inch.

He walked back to the stairs by the family dining room and descended to the main floor and started his search of that floor in the same methodical fashion.

First the breakfast room, then the staging areas. He turned next to the ladies salon, powder room, and toilets. Nothing.

He walked back to the main dining room and into the main salon. Nothing. He peered into the dark shadows of the main stairway shafts, dodging puddles as he went. He found nothing in the main vestibule or stairs on the other side, or the billiards room, or whatever it was. Sean was sort of making up what he thought each room would be used for, or perhaps what he would have used each room for if he were the Lord of the Manor, or chateau, as the case might be. Nothing there. Nothing in the library. Nothing in the gentlemen's smoking room or the men's toilets.

It seemed like a bust and he began to sense that his initial impulse to conduct another "tour" was misplaced.

He trudged down the stairs yet again to the first sub-basement. He intended to start in the kitchen, but the depressed slab was full of water, yet again. So he did not go in. He walked through the entire floor and saw nothing. This left him with just the garage level, which contained the vault itself, and the barrel room level below that.

Sean was feeling a little despondent as he began to walk back from the south end of the floor toward the stairs. He tried to think back to when he had found the body. It had been dark then, too, and he wasn't sure he remembered.

"We came out of the tunnel and opened the doors to the space," he muttered to himself. The barrel room was divided with structural columns and bearing walls based on the layout of the floors above. "He was in a pit beneath one of the elevator shafts, so that would have put him under this area back here," he said to himself retracing his steps.

He walked back to the area where the private elevator descended to the floors below from the vestibule of the master suite. He directed his light down into the shaft. Sean did not really like the feeling of leaning over an open shaft, especially when it disappeared into darkness. He got down on his hands and knees and looked over the edge. He pointed the flashlight beam down into the pit two floors below. His light was not strong enough to see what was left over from both the time the body spent in the pit and the investigation of the disposition of the corpse.

He shined his light onto the barrel room floor around the shaft as far as he could before it was blocked out by the cut-out of the floor above. While doing this, Sean noticed that the shaft on the floor above the barrel room had not only been finished, it had been constructed out of poured-in-place concrete. That made sense as the shaft descended through the vault. He moved the beam of light around the edges of the shaft and realized there were only three sides.

Sean was no architect, but he understood that the shaft dropped right through the vault and it appeared that there was a stop for the private elevator.

Sean felt a rush of excitement. He pointed his light into the area that he thought might be an elevator landing, but he could not see much more than the concrete deck surface. He decided that the elevator must have been intended to open into a secure vestibule or perhaps into the vault itself. But that would not be very secure, so he discounted that possibility almost immediately.

He wondered how he could get down there. Then it occurred to him that David might have fallen down this shaft trying to get onto the landing.

Sean thought for a minute about making a call to get some support, but that would take time. He remembered seeing a cherry picker in the crushing room. If he could find a key, that would be faster, he thought. Either way, his excitement dispelled the doubt he had felt only minutes before. He felt sure he was onto something.

In the crushing room, he found the scissor lift he remembered. It was an all-electric unit and the key had been left in it, so getting it started was not difficult. Steering it with the little joy stick from six or eight feet off the floor took Sean a bit of getting used to. He steered the unit with one hand pointing his flashlight ahead. It took him a good twenty minutes or so to drive the lift up the inclined slope of the tunnel. When he finally made it into the barrel room it got easier to navigate. Once the lift was beside the shaft, Sean raised the basket up as high as it would go, which wasn't quite high enough. While the basket was close to the underside of the floor deck, the lift was positioned in a manner that was going to make getting out of the basket and onto the landing a bit of a contortionist's exercise.

Sean rolled the flashlight onto the floor overhead and then leaned backwards over the railing of the lift high above the pit. He eased onto the railing in a sitting position. From there he could almost see onto the landing, but not quite. He stood up slowly until he was standing on the lower crossbar of the basket reaching for a hold on the edge of the deck. Fortunately, there was an L-angle that had been welded to the edge of the deck to control the flow of concrete and to support the deck at the edge. It had just enough of a lip that Sean could get a little hold on it. He steadied himself and then hoisted up into a standing position on the top railing of the basket.

Sean gave a little grunt and hauled himself up over the edge and onto the landing. His flashlight had rolled away from the edge and was pointing into a corner at nothing in particular. The reflected light from its beam let him see that the landing was surrounded on three sides by poured-in-place concrete walls. The entire landing was perhaps eight feet wide and eight feet deep.

There was a steel door, with a scanner and a key pad. It looked like the security had been bypassed by cutting through the door.

"Damn it!" Sean thought.

He looked around the landing. There were several tanks of welding gas and the hose and other gear needed for an acetylene gas welder. The locking mechanism of the steel door had been cut out and the door left open. In addition to the tanks, there was a pair of gloves, a welding mask, and a starter.

Sean stood up, picked up his flashlight, and moved into the vault. It appeared to be empty and did not seem to have been completed. There were three rooms. The door from the landing was off the main space. Two additional rooms lay on the opposite side of the main vault door and looked as though they were intended to have yet another layer of security provided by a future security door that had not yet been installed.

He walked through the entire inner vault. It proved to be completely empty.

"Either they got everything, or there was nothing here," Sean said to himself.

He left the vault and moved the beam of his flashlight around the landing taking a closer look at the welding gear. He knelt down and shined the light directly on the valve mechanism on one of the tanks and then down the side. The light revealed the spot where Neil had carved his initials on the tank. Sean leaned down and took a look at the "NT" scratched into the steel tank.

"Oh, Neil," he said out loud. "Why didn't you tell me this gear was missing? This looks real bad, buddy. I may have to bust you yet."

Sean pointed his light to the opposite side of the landing between the wall and the door. There was a bloody rag and what looked like the tip of a finger, probably a thumb, poking out from beneath it. He knelt down and moved the rag using the end of his flashlight to uncover the thumb. There was only one thumb.

Sean stood for a moment and then reversed his contorted climb over the edge of the landing.

After lowering the lift back down to the floor, he decided there was no point returning the lift to the crushing room. He hiked back up the stairs to the garage level. Sean's team was still taking an inventory of all the art in the vault and loading it onto the vans. It looked like they would need more vans or have to make multiple trips. Someone had decided that the larger pieces could not be moved and were working on installing some temporary chain-link fencing. The pieces were so large, it was not likely that a casual thief would attempt to move them.

Sean called to one of his team. “Where’s Carlos?”

“Haven’t seen him,” came the reply.

“All right, thanks,” Sean replied. Carlos was his photographer. He walked out of the garage and pulled out his phone calling Carlos to come document what he had found. He had spent more time inside the building than he realized. It was dark as he waited for Carlos to arrive. He mulled over all the evidence, including what he had just found, and could not shake the thought that he was going to have to seriously consider Neil to be a suspect. It was not something he had seriously considered before, but all the evidence was pointing in Neil’s direction.

"Architecture is the reaching out for the truth."

-- Louis Kahn

Chapter Eleven

Marcus Little spent the next several weeks researching the works of Edgar Payne. He had flown to Chicago and discretely interviewed the widow of the collector from whom the painting had been stolen. She had a file of paperwork documenting her husband's purchase of the piece in 1986 and the insurance appraisal forms and receipts from the many years of having paid insurance premiums. The insurance had paid out on the claim, but the widow requested that if the painting was recovered, she would like to have it back as it held sentimental value. She said she would contact her attorney to see what would need to be done with respect to her insurance settlement for her loss. Marcus asked, and she agreed, to not discuss his visit or the possible recovery of the painting until his investigation was complete.

Being fully satisfied that the painting at Blackbridge was in fact the missing Payne, he set about discussing with Jennifer Singh how he might be able to discover the identity of the seller without showing his cards.

Jennifer thought it would not be remotely suspicious to ask for documentation of provenance on the assertion that the work was unknown and that the firm could not represent the seller and offer the piece for sale without further documentation.

Marcus agreed to have this communication sent to the attorney representing the seller to see what response was given.

The next morning, Ms. Singh e-mailed the attorney, a Mr. Steven Jordan, Esq., seeking the additional information. In the meantime, Marcus asked an old friend in the FBI's San Francisco office to see what he could find out about Steven Jordan.

«»«»«»

Steven Jordan was working on a divorce case for an orthopedic surgeon who had taken up with his physician's assistant in a less than subtle fashion. It had not taken his wife long to discover the infidelity and demand a divorce and a sizeable chunk of the doctor's accumulated wealth. The opposing attorney was a classmate from Berkeley and they were having an early breakfast at *Fitty & Smits*, a prominent San Francisco legal watering hole, to discuss the terms of the divorce settlement.

Being an attorney came with some perks if you had the right clientele and a lot of minutia if you did not. Steven had worked diligently after passing the bar exam to gain a position in one of the city's finest legal firms. After spending four years there watching and learning from the best, he launched out starting his own "firm" with several clients and a long list of wealthy potential clients that seemed to constantly need legal representation for one thing or another. It really wasn't a firm yet, but it would be one day. He just needed a few good clients with deep pockets in desperate need of good legal advice.

He made a practice of never checking his e-mail while having a meal with a client or colleague, but as soon as he had come to terms with the counsel for the doctor's wife, he checked his phone to see if he had any new messages.

He scrolled through the junk, deleting as he went, then opened the e-mail from Jennifer Singh at Blackbridge. She was asking for paperwork regarding the piece of art he had sent her. He would need to contact his client.

Steven opened an app on his phone that his client had instructed him to use. Other than the very first communication that had been via a Gmail account, all other communication had been via the app. He knew the app encrypted their communication, and that was fine. Client-attorney communications were privileged anyway, so encrypting their communications about the painting just added a level of confidentiality that he assumed any sophisticated client would expect, no demand, in this day and age.

He typed the message into the phone app:

> ----
>
> Good morning. I received an e-mail this morning from the auction house in New York seeking some additional paperwork to authenticate the piece. Apparently, it is an unknown work and they need more information about it before they can list it for sale.
>
> Let me know how you would like to proceed. Thanks.
>
> ----

«»«»«»

He hit send and walked the eight blocks back to his apartment. As he had just started his practice he had not yet built up a large enough client base to support an actual office. So he used an answering service, a mail drop at one of the most recognizable addresses in San Francisco, and e-mail. He had hired a local web designer to put together a very basic web page. It had already attracted one client out of the blue. He was encouraged that so far he had been managing to cover his monthly expenses and put a little extra away into savings.

The client that he had just sent the message to had reached out to him through his web site. They had exchanged one e-mail and then switched to the encryption app. He was intrigued at first, but the secrecy seemed routine in a short period of time and he had not given it another thought. They had exchanged the confidentiality agreement through the app and the contract for his services. He had provided an electronic routing number for his bank account and thus far, money had been wired into it like clockwork. It was all very slick and easy. Steven felt like he was on the bleeding edge of the legal services profession -- small, lean, and technologically savvy.

His new client had asked him to coordinate the shipment and sale of a piece of art in New York. They had wanted to remain anonymous and working through an attorney gave them the layer of confidentiality that they sought. He did not know anything about the client. It was unusual, but not unheard of. His client had indicated that they did not know which auction house to use and asked him to check into several. He did an internet search. Several large international auction houses popped up immediately, but he was drawn to a smaller, older house. Their website provided a list of their quarterly auctions. Their Spring Auction two years before had featured none other than six works by Thomas Payne. That seemed ideal and fromwhat he could gether from their website, they seemed to offer the more personalized approach that he wanted for this transaction as he didn't have any experience representing a client selling art.

It had been at least two months since he had sent the painting to New York. He did not know much about the art world, but it was interesting so far.

When he got inside his unit, he checked his e-mail again. Nothing new. He sat down at his computer to draft up the divorce settlement language agreed to over breakfast. He would earn enough from this client to pay his expenses for the next four months. With the work representing the owner of the artwork, he would probably clear enough to cover the whole year. All he needed was another client or two and we would be able to actually rent an office and start hiring some staff.

He had been working on the settlement language for about two hours when a pop-up message on his phone let him know that his client had responded:

Find out what they want.

“Fine. Whatever,” he thought. He drafted a quick e-mail to Ms. Singh:

----Original Message----
From: Steven Jordan
To: Jennifer Singh
Sent: 10:32 AM January 17
Subject: Additional Docs

Ms. Singh,

Good morning. Could you be a little more specific about the type of documentation you require? I am not sure what to ask for.

Thanks.

Steven

Jennifer Singh was on a conference call when Steven’s e-mail reply was received by her e-mail server, then she was off to a lunch with her assistant who was quitting to go back to grad school. She arrived back at the office a little before 3:00 p.m. and saw that Steven Jordan had replied. She picked up the phone and called Marcus Little.

“Go ahead and make something up,” he said. “You know the questions you normally would ask. Keep it straightforward.”

“Okay. Do you want to be blind copied?” she asked.

“Sure. But I have a different e-mail address for this type of investigation.” He didn’t tell her that the FBI was able to trace blind copies on e-mail and was not entirely sure that sophisticated criminal elements hadn’t figured out how to do the same thing, so the FBI used special ISP’s that would not link a message back to the FBI if the e-mail was compromised.

He gave her the e-mail address and they ended the call.

----Original Message----
From: Jennifer Singh
To: Steven Jordan
Sent: 3:11 PM January 17
Subject: RE: Additional Docs

Mr. Jordan,

After reviewing the painting with our curator, we have made discrete inquiries with several experts who specialize in the works of Edgar Payne. Your client's piece has generated an unusual degree of excitement as it is a previously unknown work.

As discussed, Edgar Payne is highly collectable in the current market and has generated a strong following and his work is experiencing a rapid increase in value. We believe that in order to maximize the value at auction of this piece, having more thorough documentation would be extremely helpful, as the market and discerning buyers reward thorough and complete provenance with higher valuations.

Our preliminary auction estimate with the present lack of documentation, and I need to stress this is very preliminary at this point, is that the painting is likely to attract favorable bids in the \$750k-\$1.0 million range. But this number could be increased significantly with the documentation of provenance that collectors and dealers favor.

The type of documentation that would be helpful would be a history of the piece while in the current owner's possession, any documentation about previous owners, any previous sales/auction values, appraisals, and the like.

Regards.

Jennifer

Steven received the e-mail a few moments after it was sent and immediately copied the text into the encryption app and sent it.

Steven had to wait several days for his client to respond. The encrypted message he received in reply indicated that the painting had been in the family for many years and had been purchased directly from the artist, passing from the parents to the current owners, who wished to sell the piece as part of the settlement of the estate between siblings. Jordan was instructed to indicate that the original sales paperwork had not been located, but that they were continuing to sift through their parent's belongings.

After digesting the instructions, Steven drafted a quick e-mail to Jennifer:

> **----Original Message----**
> From: Steven Jordan
> To: Jennifer Singh
> Sent: 4:17 PM January 21
> Subject: Additional Docs
>
> Ms. Singh,
>
> Apparently, the painting was purchased by the current owner's parents from Edgar Payne many years ago and has remained in the family ever since. They have looked for any sort of paperwork to document the sale, but since it happened so many years ago and their parents are now deceased, they have not been able to locate anything to substantiate the purchase. They are continuing to look and will send anything they find.
>
> Sorry.
>
> Steven
>
> ----

Jennifer forwarded the response to Marcus from her phone that same evening. He read it with little surprise. So the game was on. The cover story was patently false and the party attempting to sell the painting knew it, but didn't know anyone else would know it. The response was not bad as a cover story goes, but now the ball was in his court and he had to think of his next move.

If the painting was sold at auction, the seller would no doubt instruct the proceeds of the sale to be wired to some numbered account overseas where it would disappear into the murky sleaze of the international banking system. If the auction house acknowledged that the painting was stolen, the seller would probably just disappear. Marcus needed a strategy to bring the seller out into the light. A trip to New York would do it, but they were clearly too smart for that.

As a last resort, he could squeeze the mule, the attorney handling the sale, but that was risky if the seller had any additional layers obscuring their identity. He needed to get right to the seller straight away. He would have to give this some thought.

The next morning, he called Jennifer and asked her what she thought.

"Oh, it's a good story. It ties up all the loose ends in a tidy dead end, but the provenance of great pieces of art are rarely as simple as that," she said. "If we didn't have the details about the painting that we do, I might have believed it, or at least reserved judgment."

"Any ideas about flushing out the seller without spooking them?" he asked.

"Sometimes when there is one piece, there are more . . . ," she offered hopefully. Jennifer didn't care about this piece. She was fishing for something even better and was getting an inkling that there was more to the investigation than Marcus was telling her.

"Hadn't thought of that," Marcus said. "If they don't want to be known, though, why would they come out of the shadows for another piece? They'll just keep using this attorney as their front, and I don't want to spook him, either."

"I thought you Feds had all sorts of tricks up your sleeve?" Jennifer teased.

"We do. But getting a warrant to use them takes time."

"Why don't you just follow him?" she asked.

"That's one of those things that takes getting multiple approvals, but it might be just that simple. I'll get a tail in place and then you ask if he has more paintings. If he takes possession of another piece from the seller, either because he picks it up or they bring it to him, then we would have someone else to follow."

"Just tell me when you are ready," Jennifer said.

"Give me a couple of days. I'll call you back."

After hanging up the phone, Marcus filled out the paperwork to set up a tail and to "see" all the e-mail of one Steven Jordan of San Francisco. He also requested a temporary reassignment to the San Francisco office.

Marcus had spent his entire life on the east coast and had always wanted to visit San Francisco. He hoped that the case would afford him an opportunity to leave New York in January to fly to the warmer climes of California.

For her part, Jennifer gave Steven Jordan more thought than she had initially. "I wonder what he really knows?" she thought to herself.

Marcus' request took two weeks to get approved, not the few days he had asked of Jennifer. He called her when it came through and told her he was heading to San Francisco to lead the investigation from there. He told her he would need another week before he would be ready to have her ask for more pieces.

"Not to worry," she said. "This is your issue not mine. Take all the time you want. We'll be here."

"Have they contacted you?" he asked.

"No, but I would think they may be getting impatient. It's probably time."

"If they contact you let me know. It may be that we have to ask for the piece before I am ready," he replied.

Sure enough, two days later, Steven reached out for an update.

> **----Original Message----**
> From: Steven Jordan
> To: Jennifer Singh
> Sent: 9:23 AM February 10
> Subject: Sale Update
>
> Jennifer,
>
> I assume everything is proceeding nicely for the spring auction. If there is anything that is likely to interfere with the placement of the painting in the auction, please let me know immediately.
>
> Thanks.
>
> Steven
>
> ----

Jennifer decided to go ahead and broach the topic of additional pieces. She blind copied Marcus.

> **----Original Message----**
> From: Jennifer Singh
> To: Steven Jordan

Sent: 1:47 PM February 10
Subject: RE: Sale Update

Mr. Jordan,

We think that we will have enough similar pieces for the auction to garner the type of attention that we want for this piece. As I think I mentioned to you previously, we spend a great deal of time curating each auction to ensure that we attract collectors and dealers who specialize in particular artists, periods, and movements. Our spring catalogue will feature works from other relevant 20th Century American artists. We plan to include works by Georgia O'Keefe, Patrick Henry Bruce, Jackson Pollack, and others.

On a separate note, we are very appreciative of your business. We strive to maximize the value of our client's sales and the overall experience. I trust that we are exceeding your expectations as we move ahead and want to invite you to let me know if there is anything we can do to enhance your satisfaction with the services we are providing.

But beyond that, I would like to invite you to make Blackbridge your long-term partner in both buying and selling other pieces of art. We offer very attractive incentives for offering multiple pieces, either in the same sale or subsequent sales. The same incentives are available when you both buy and sell a piece at the same event.

So if your client is considering repositioning their collection or of making additional purchases please let me know. One of the other privileges that comes with a deeper relationship with Blackbridge is that we offer our most discerning clients special previews and advance notice of works being offered at future sales before this information is shared with the public.

If you would like to discuss the sale or purchase of additional items, please let me know.

Warmest Regards.

Jennifer Singh

"Blah, blah, blah," Steven thought as he hit the "enter" key on his phone, forwarding the message.

«»«»«»

Sean was sitting in his office when Lydia Mankovich called him.

"Where are you?" he asked.

"I flew back to New York a couple of months ago. I have been going through more of David's things, trying to resolve as many of the loose ends as I can. While doing that, I came across a list of art work in one of David's files. I honestly don't know if it represents everything in California or just some of his more recent purchases. Did you get the insurance list from Keith?" she asked.

"I did. And I assume that you received the list from our inventory," he said.

'Yes. I did not look at it closely. I have been so busy with other issues related to David's estate that it did not seem that relevant," she said

"That's fine," Sean said. "I compared the two lists and there were some significant differences. But there were also quite a few pieces on the list that were not in the vault."

"Oh, that's because they are here in New York," she said. "That is not surprising at all."

"So can I get a copy of the new list you found?" he asked. "It would also be helpful to have a list of everything in New York."

"I just scanned it and am about to send it to you via e-mail," she said. "I just wanted you to know it was coming. I'll get one of my assistants to indicate on the insurance list what is here in New York. I'm sure all of it was insured. Is there anything else new on your end?" she asked.

"Yes and no. We found an additional entrance to the inner vault. It had been compromised. There was nothing left in the vault, unfortunately. Although, we don't honestly know if there was anything in the inner vault to begin with," he said.

"You may find the list I am sending you to be of interest," she said. "It appears to provide a list of seven paintings in the inner vault and what was in the outer area."

"Really? Have you sent it yet?" Sean asked. His interest was piqued.

"I just hit send," she said.

It took a couple of moments, but an e-mail popped up on Sean's screen. It was from Lydia. Sean opened the file and the attachment. He scanned down the list, noticing the first eight or ten paintings:

. . . . – Bellini, Giovanni

1500 – Dürer, Albrecht

1503 – Dürer, Albrecht

1532 – Correggio, Antonio da

1535 – Salvoldo, Girolamo

1546 - Bronzino, Angnolo

1602 – Caravaggio, Michelangelo Merisi

1608 – Caravaggio, Michelangelo Merisi

1619 – Velázquez, Diego

1629 – Van Dyck, Anthony

1638 – Rubens, Peter Paul

1686 – Giordano, Luca

1688 – . . . .

The list went on for a number of pages. He wasn't an art person and the quality and expanse of the collection was largely lost on him. But he was impressed with the length of the list. There were several hundred paintings in all.

"Interesting," he said. "I'll compare this to the other lists and see what pops up. But if the seven paintings that the list indicates were in the inner vault were really in there, they are gone now," he said.

Lydia did not seem fazed or worried by the information. But why would she? There were hundreds of paintings in the outer vault, who knows how many more in New York, and an untold fortune in a variety of asset classes invested on various stock exchanges and several investment houses.

"Oh, one other thing," she said. "I had a call from one of the attorneys last week letting me know that David had created a number of LLC's to hold the ownership of some of the paintings.'

"You mean a limited liability corporation?" Sean interjected.

"Yes," Lydia continued. "She said so far they have found paperwork for 19 LLCs, but they are still looking. She sent me a list of paintings associated with the LLCs, but it's not clear why he did this. I did a quick check myself and most of the paintings on the LLC list are not on his other lists. However, it looks as though six of the paintings held by the LLCs were in the vault. So this is very confusing. Apparently there was a partner on the LLCs and the attorneys are going to try to find them and see if they can shed some light on this." She paused.

"Were there any other leads from the vault?" she asked.

"We found some things that might prove useful at some point," he said, but he wasn't specific. He thought there was no point telling her about David's thumb if he didn't have to. The information had been included in the autopsy, but she seemed not to know and he didn't want to be the bearer of that news. Her attorneys must have kept the details from her as they worked through the estate issues.

"All right, well I hope you catch them and lock them up for . . . ever," she said.

"That's my goal."

"Call me if you need anything else from me," she said.

"Will do," he said. "Please send me the list of New York paintings as soon as you can."

"Okay."

After he hung up, he set himself to understanding the three lists.

«»«»«»

Steven received the following encrypted message later the next morning:

> ---
>
> Tell art person in New York that there may be one additional piece. Ask what a sketch by Rembrandt is worth. Also, we require better terms.
>
> ---

"You have a Rembrandt?" Steven exclaimed to himself when he read the message. "Wow!" He quickly typed in a response without giving it much thought:

> ---

Why did you start with that other one? Rembrandt is going to get you the big bucks.

Perhaps. Remember stipulations and our agreement.

Got it covered.

Good. Keep it that way.

Steven couldn't help but be a little annoyed. "Who does this asshole think he is dealing with? Of course I'll keep everything confidential," he thought as he typed a new message to Jennifer Singh.

----Original Message----
From: Steven Jordan
To: Jennifer Singh
Sent: 2:47 PM February 14
Subject: RE: Sale Update

Jennifer,

My client has decided that they might be willing to part with one additional piece. However, this piece is likely to be even more eagerly received than the first. Your discretion is of the utmost importance.

All the same non-disclosure requirements will apply. I have attached another non-disclosure agreement for this piece. Please review as before, sign, and return.

Additionally, as this piece is of even greater public interest and will undoubtedly sell itself, my client insists that your fee be reduced by 50% of the customary commission.

Please let me know if you agree to these terms. If so, I will draft up the appropriate agreement.

Thanks.

Steven

—

Jennifer forwarded the e-mail to Marcus immediately as she dialed his cell phone. Her curiosity was piqued both personally and professionally. What could this new piece be? She could hardly wait to find out and was tempted to pick up the phone and call Steven. But knowing the FBI would be listening in kept that impulse in check. So she called Marcus instead.

The phone rang three times before Marcus answered.

"Jennifer. What's the good news?" he asked.

"Check your e-mail," she said.

"Sounds like they bit," he said.

"I think so. They are being even more cautious and greedy on this next one," she said.

"What is it?" he asked.

"He doesn't say."

Marcus opened her e-mail to him as they spoke.

"Okay. Sign the docs and let's see what it is. Maybe you should fly out here. Tell him you will be in San Francisco next week. I'll cover the flight and the room. Could you do that?"

"From the hints, it sounds like something interesting. I may not be able to sell it or make a commission on it, but that is not why I got into this business in the first place. Getting to see something special will make it worth it. I'll be there," she said.

She had a difficult time being patient, but she forced herself to wait until late the following day to respond.

----Original Message----
From: Jennifer Singh
To: Steven Jordan
Sent: 10:04 AM February 15
Subject: RE: Sale Update

Mr. Jordan,

I have signed and attached the new confidentiality agreement. I am not excited about the requested reduction of my commission, but will consider it. I would, however, like to inspect the piece being offered for sale before I agree to this condition. What is it?

I am planning to be in Los Angeles early next week and could catch a flight through San Francisco before I head back to New York. If this is agreeable, it will save you and your client the expense of sending and insuring the piece to New York for inspection. If I agree that the piece is as desirable as you suggest, and we can reach terms while I am in San Francisco, I am confident that the rest of the details can be subsequently hammered out to our mutual satisfaction.

Regards.

Jennifer Singh

—

Steven read the response. Jennifer Singh was no push-over. He would give her that much. But when she saw it was a Rembrandt, he was pretty certain she would agree immediately to cut her commission. He sent her this response:

----Original Message----
From: Steven Jordan
To: Jennifer Singh
Sent: 7:12 PM February 15

Subject: RE: Sale Update

Jennifer,

The piece is a small self-portrait sketch of Rembrandt. Will advise if seller prefers to preview the piece in San Francisco or send it to you in New York.

Any estimate of the value of a small piece from a well-known master?

Thanks.

Steven

——

Jennifer did not see the message that night. But in the morning as she was drinking her coffee, she glanced at her messages and nearly choked. A small sketch by Rembrandt. She forwarded the message to Marcus and blind copied him on her response.

----Original Message----
From: Jennifer Singh
To: Steven Jordan
Sent: 7:22 AM February 16
Subject: RE: Sale Update

Mr. Jordan,

You are right. An authenticated Rembrandt would sell itself. I would be happy to discuss my firm's commission and other sales expenses with you.

In the present market, a small Rembrandt, assuming it is in pristine condition, with full provenance, would probably start in the $4 million range and head north from there. There are a number of Rembrandt sketches in private collections, but if this is part of a series or the precursor to one of his great works it could fetch upwards of $7 million.

I look forward to the opportunity to preview this piece at your earliest convenience.

Regards.

Jennifer Singh

Steven didn't know what a small Rembrandt was worth, but he believed that Jennifer Singh did. He had asked for a small percentage of the sale of any and all pieces of art that he fronted and he quickly did the math. This arrangement was getting better and better.

He sent the message on to the seller.

«»«»«»

Marcus was beginning to like San Francisco. It was different than New York, but in some ways the same. The fog was trippy, but it beat the late winter blizzards in New York. He had settled into a temporary cubicle easily. They all seemed the same. Close your eyes, spin three times, and you wouldn't know which government office you were in when you looked around. He didn't know if there was an "official" U.S. Federal government beige color, or what. But it all looked the same to him.

He had gotten his team focused on Mr. Jordan and his daily routine. It was pretty routine, too. He had guys on Jordan's butt 24/7. So far nothing popped up of any interest. He had started reading Jordan's e-mail, too. That was just as bad. So far there had not been communication between Jordan and anyone trying to sell art. He had followed up his initial request to get into Jordan's e-mail with another request to broaden the dates of the search, going back a full year.

Reading through that had been a slog. The inanity of 90 percent of the e-mail was stunning. There were the e-mail messages that were work related. He had just quit his previous job. He had been planning his departure for several months before he informed his employer. That was probably the most interesting and telling part of the archive of e-mail messages. That and the messages with his now ex-girlfriend. They were pretty boring until he decided to breakup. Then things got more interesting. When would men learn, he thought to himself. It seemed pretty clear his girlfriend wanted a commitment and he wasn't ready to settle down. She seemed bummed enough that Marcus almost felt sorry for her. But just almost. At some point you have to move on. He had spent a lot of time reading lots of mundane e-mail. But he had to scan everything to make sure nothing slipped by.

Marcus slogged on through the e-mail for days. About nine months into the list however, he came across a single e-mail that caught his full attention.

----Original Message----
From: b47Xv22
To: Steven Jordan
Sent: 6:13 AM November 9
Subject: Inquiry

Mr. Jordan,

I am interested in retaining you for assistance with a confidential legal matter. If you are interested, please send me your phone number. Download the following app onto your mobile phone: "Conficomm". I will contact you via this app in two days. All future communication must be via this app.

I will make this worth your time. Details of our agreement and your compensation will be negotiated on the secure link.

—

Steven had waited about an hour to respond.

----Original Message----
From: Steven Jordan
To: b47Xv22
Sent: 7:22 AM November 9
Subject: RE: Inquiry

B47Xv22,

Thank you for your inquiry. My mobile phone number is 415.687. xxxx.

Sincerely.

Steven Jordan, Esq.

—

There was nothing after that. Marcus called one of the tech team guys in DC and gave him the Gmail address for b47Xv22.

"See what you can come up with and let me know. Start with today and go back two years at least," Marcus had instructed.

"Got it. I should have this back for you in like an hour."

"Great."

Marcus thought he had caught his first break.

An hour later his cell phone buzzed him. "Marcus Little," he said as he took the call. The tech was on the other end of the call.

"Got nothing for you, man," he said.

"Nothing? Really? Nothing at all?"

"Well, not entirely nothing. I got the two messages that you already have, one out and one back in, but that is it. The account was started about 10 minutes before the first message was sent and has not be used since the reply was received. What's more, whoever set it up was being careful. They set it up via a VPN, so there is no way to track their machine or the location where the set-up originated."

"Damn it! I thought we finally had something," Marcus said.

"Nope."

"All right. What's a VPN, by the way?" he asked.

"It stands for Virtual Private Network. It's a way to cover your tracks by routing through an internet service provider that does not keep track of who is using it," the tech explained. "They could be in Sweden or right next door and you wouldn't know it."

"Great. Looks like we are still two steps behind the bad guys," he said.

"Better luck next time."

"Thanks." Marcus ended the call with a sigh. This looked like it was going to take longer than he thought. He was dealing with a cool and savvy customer. "It would be all the sweeter to bust their ass," he thought to himself.

«»«»«»

Sean had started comparing the lists side by side. Lydia sent him the New York inventory about two days after they spoke on the phone. With it in hand he was able to determine that there were precisely eight paintings missing. They were the same paintings listed as having been in the inner-vault. Whatever else you might say about David, he seemed to be careful with his art. Interestingly, only one of the paintings in the inner-vault had been insured.

He called a contact at the FBI that he had known back in school. Sean had taken the local path, while his buddy had aspired to work for the Feds. The last he heard he had ended up at the FBI.

"Frank!" Sean hollered into the phone. "Put down the doughnut and step away from your desk!"

Frank laughed out loud. "*Fuck you,* Sean. It's you local guys that have a thing for doughnuts. I've got to pass an annual physical and doughnuts are not part of *THAT* regimen."

"How are you?" Sean asked.

"Good, man! Good. How are you? How come you haven't sent me any of that great California wine? I hear there is enough to share."

"Dude. There is more than you can imagine. We are practically drowning in it," Sean laughed. His old friend had not changed a bit.

"So what can I do you out of?" Frank asked.

"Hey. I'm working on a case with some missing artwork. I was wondering if you could point me in the right direction as to whom I should call inside the FBI on something like this," he said.

"Yeah, no problem, man. Let see . . . . That would be the High Value Division. That would be Eugene Greenburg. He's here in DC, but you could also call the guys in Frisco."

"That would work," Sean said.

"Okay. Then, hang on a second," he said as he searched through the FBI's on-line staff directory, "you want to call Timothy Phillips. He's the high value guy in San Francisco. Tell him I told you to call him. I met him a couple of years ago. He's a good guy."

"Thanks, Frank. Give me a call if you are ever out here," Marcus said.

"You do the same. You ever get out this way?"

"Not recently. All work and no play. You know how it is."

"Yeah, I do. But my wife would love to take a trip to the Napa Valley. Oh man. Did you know I got hitched?" Frank asked.

"No. But congratulations."

"Thanks. Got the kids, the dog, the whole thing. How about you?"

"I got the dog part," Sean replied.

"Hey. That may be the easiest part to deal with, man. Keep it simple."

"If you decide to take that trip, look me up," Sean said.

"I will."

"Thanks for the tip."

"Good to hear from you," Frank said.

"Yeah. Later." Sean hung up the phone. Life was too short.

«»«»«»

Sean called Timothy Phillips and explained what he was working on.

"Hmmm. That is interesting. You say there was an Edgar Payne on the list? I've got a guy out here from New York working on that case. His name is Marcus Little. Hang on, I'll transfer you over to his extension. He'll be interested in what you've got."

Sean waited to be connected. That seemed a little weird. The FBI was investigating a painting that no one knew was stolen?

Marcus answered the phone in his typical manner, "Marcus Little," he said.

"Agent Little. This is Sean Andrews. I'm a detective with the St. Helena Police Department. I am investigating a death and subsequent theft of some art work.

One of the pieces is an Edgar Payne. I just spoke to Agent Phillips and he said you are investigating the same painting."

Marcus was listening intently.

"I am investigating the theft and attempted sale of an Edgar Payne piece," Marcus said. "Not sure it's the same one, though. Where is St. Helena?" he asked.

"In the Napa Valley," Sean replied.

"Oh, okay. Sorry, I'm from the east coast and just getting acclimated."

"No problem," Sean replied.

"So you are chasing a missing Edgar Payne? It wouldn't happen to be a painting of a young girl, by any chance?" Marcus asked.

"I don't know. It's just a painting on a list," Sean replied. "It's one of eight that are missing. I suspect they may have all been stolen."

"Okay. Tell me more. It may be that our cases are connected."

"I'll give you the quick rundown," Sean said. "A couple of months ago we got a call about a missing person. Turns out it was a wealthy guy from New York. He was building a wine estate out here in the Napa Valley. His girlfriend reported him missing. We started our investigation and eventually discovered the body inside his partially completed estate. Turns out he was storing a bunch of paintings in an unfinished vault on the property. He was quite the collector. I have inventories of all the paintings he owned. It runs into the hundreds. Anyway, after we have inventoried the whole lot, it appears there are eight paintings missing. One of them is a Rembrandt. There is a Cézanne, a Vermeer, and, I'm not sure how to pronounce this one, a Vigée-LeBrun, a Rubens, and a Hals. Oh, and the Edgar Payne."

There was a low whistle on the other end of the phone. "That's quite a list," Marcus said. "But what is the eighth painting? Did you list eight? I tried to write them down as you were talking, but I think I missed one."

"We aren't sure yet what the eighth one is. We can infer that it was there, but we don't know what it was," Sean said.

"Okay. So there are eight and we have record for seven," Marcus summarized.

"Correct," Sean said. "I'm not an art expert, so they are mostly just names. I have heard of Rembrandt and Vermeer, but not the rest. Anyway, they seem to have been stolen sometime in the last several months. This is way outside my expertise and the resources of our department, so I need some help."

"You've come to the right place, even though our cases may not be the same," Marcus said. "I am looking into the theft of an Edgar Payne."

Marcus didn't mention the recent addition of the Rembrandt to the investigation.

"It's possible that our cases are related. It just came to the market a couple of months ago, so that fits nicely," he said.

"Who's the seller?" Sean asked.

"Don't know. They are using an intermediary and seem pretty adept at covering their tracks so far. Mind if I come up and pay you a visit?" Marcus asked.

"Be my guest. What works for you?"

"How about tomorrow?"

That'll work," Sean replied. "What time?"

"How's 10:00 or 10:30?" Marcus asked.

"Fine. My office is in the St. Helena municipal building. Just google it. If you have time, I'll take you by the vault."

"Sounds good. See you tomorrow," Marcus said as he hung up. Now, he thought, he had the break in the case that he needed.

«»«»«»

Late that afternoon, Steven received the following message:

> ---
>
> Green light on local preview. Get itinerary. Venue details to follow.
>
> ---

Steven read the message. "Excellent," he thought. "I'm going to get to see a Rembrandt up close."

> ---
>
> Got it.

He sent a message to Jennifer Singh.

----Original Message----
From: Steven Jordan
To: Jennifer Singh
Sent: 4:31 PM February 17
Subject: Itinerary

Jennifer,

Please send me your itinerary as soon as possible. Details on my end will follow.

Regards.

Steven

"Ha! They bit," she thought. She sent the message on to Marcus and decided not to respond until she heard back from him in case he had concerns or instructions. But she was pretty sure she knew whose art had been stolen. It had to be one of David Johnsson's pieces. She had not sold it to him, but after she learned that the piece was a Rembrandt, she went back and did some research. His wife had bought one at auction a number of years before. It was a well-documented sale. She knew he had been moving pieces to his new estate in California and suspected that she had sold him a couple of pieces through intermediaries. There was a high probability that these were from his estate. But only time would tell. Either way, it was not the piece she was interested in. There were other larger prizes to be had from David's collection.

«»«»«»

"Architecture is a service business. An architect is given a program, budget, place, and schedule. Sometimes the end product rises to art - or at least people call it that."

-- Frank Gehry

Chapter Twelve

Neil had finished his project for the Methodists and started another one for a local community college. It was good to have consistent work, even if it wasn't anything major. Every now and then he got a kitchen remodel or a family room addition. He really didn't like this sort of work as it was tedious, required a lot of hand holding with the client, and was low margin. Small jobs like kitchen and bath remodels took almost as much time at the building department as jobs many times larger. Not to mention that someone doing a $100,000 kitchen remodel thought that was a lot of money and thought his fee of $15,000 to $20,000 was outrageous. But Neil didn't get to keep a significant portion of the fee, depending on the complexity of the project. He might share some with a structural engineer. He might need to retain an electrical engineer if things got complicated. There were any number of consulting specialists ready to help him burn through his fee.

So in addition to his project at the community college, he had a small house addition. It wasn't enough work that he needed to hire anyone, but at least he would be able to pay Shelley and cover his mortgages.

As he got busy again, he forgot about David Johnsson and Detective Andrews.

«»«»«»

Sean met with Marcus the following day in his office. Marcus had never been to the Napa Valley, and while March is not its finest month, some of the locals thought that it was a nice time to visit the Valley. Most of the vineyards had mustard planted between the seemingly endless rows of vines. It was in full bloom making the valley a sea of bright yellow and green. Even on a day of drizzle and mist, the mustard blooms dispelled any hint of gloom.

Sean gave Marcus the full debrief starting from the beginning all the way through finding the inner vault compromised. Marcus took copious notes asking questions and grunting when he thought Sean had done some good detective work.

After they had spoken for about 90 minutes, Sean offered to take Marcus out to see the partially constructed chateau. On the drive out, Sean continued to fill in the blanks.

"So that's where we are now, and the reason I called Frank Mathews in D.C., do you know him? I went to school with him out here before he joined the Bureau about 5 years ago," Sean said.

Marcus shook his head indicating that he didn't know Frank Mathews and Sean continued. "Anyway, I called him because there appear to be eight paintings missing, as I mentioned on the phone."

Marcus broke in, "So how do you know this?"

"Because David Johnsson turned out to be a meticulous record keeper. I have four inventory lists of paintings that he owned. One is from his insurance company, the second is from our inventory of the outer vault -- those are the paintings we have in storage. Then another list that Lydia sent from New York last week . . . "

Marcus broke in again, "and Lydia is or was his girlfriend?"

"Right, and his assistant. She has been wrapping up some of the loose ends in New York and found the fourth list in one of his files. It is a spreadsheet that shows the name of the artist, the date it was painted, the name or subject of the painting, the date it was purchased, the amount he paid, who he bought it from, and where it was located. Actually, I forgot. There are two other lists she sent me last week. One is the list of everything he had in New York. The other list came from her attorneys and lists paintings he owned with a business partner."

Marcus absorbed the information, nodding and taking an occasional note or two.

"So I went through the lists and I can account for everything except eight paintings. And I think I know what all of them are except for the eighth painting. Of the eight, six were listed as being in the inner vault, but only the Rembrandt was insured. All the rest of the paintings on all the lists were insured," Sean said. "What do you make of that?"

"Hmm. That is a little odd I suppose," Marcus said letting all that information sink in. "But what about this eighth master. What do we know about it?" he asked.

"Nothing more than the date it was purchased and where," Sean said. "Several of the lists include a sales price so we have an idea of what each painting is worth. The eighth one was purchased by Johnsson for $310 million," Sean said. He had stopped being floored by the sums of money at David Johnsson's disposal early in the investigation, but this information stunned Marcus.

"What the hell?!" he exclaimed. "Are you serious? That puts it right up there on the list of the most expensive paintings ever sold. Was it a private sale?"

"Don't know. The lists don't include that information, but I would guess Lydia would know given the high value of the purchase, or she could figure it out with a few phone calls," Sean offered. "It was one of the paintings held by an LLC. So there were probably other partners, maybe a syndicate."

"All right. We'll dig into that later. Let me tell you what I know," Marcus offered.

"Okay," Sean said.

"The Edgar Payne I'm looking for was reported as having been destroyed about 10 years ago. It just disappeared from a collector's house that was probably torched to cover up the theft. Not a peep for 10 years. We were called by an auction house in New York about two months ago telling us that someone had brought it in through a third party to offer up at auction. They recognized it as having been stolen and called us. At this point the seller is anonymous. I am out here, trying to get the seller into the daylight so I can make an arrest."

"The timing seems to be right. Someone killed David Johnsson, broke into the vault and is trying to sell one of the paintings – assuming that there were, in fact, more than one in there," Sean summed up.

"There was more than one. It probably was all eight," Marcus ventured.

"How do you know?" Sean asked.

"Because they just agreed to sell a Rembrandt."

"Whoa," Sean seemed stunned. After so many months of glacial progress, the case seemed to have picked up startling speed.

"So what's the plan to get to the seller?" Sean asked.

"We're working on that. The seller seems pretty sophisticated. They have only communicated with their third party representative through encrypted messages on the internet. From what I can tell so far, the mule doesn't even know who he is dealing with. It's all at arm's length."

“And you don’t want to spook them,” Sean mused.

“Correct. But the seller has agreed to preview the Rembrandt for the auction house here in San Francisco next week. I’ve left out some details, but I am convinced that the seller knows the paintings are stolen. I didn’t think so initially, but we asked for provenance and got a tidy fabrication.”

“That would imply that the seller may have been in on the theft or the murder. . . ,” Sean said.

“. . . or both,” Marcus completed his sentence. “At the very least the seller knows that the paintings were stolen. They are also budget conscious, because they took the opportunity to save themselves a buck by having the painting previewed out here.”

Sean was silent for a few moments as they pulled up to the gate. He jumped out and unlocked it and swung it wide open. As they drove up the hill he could tell that Marcus was impressed.

“Quite the construction project,” Marcus offered.

“Just wait. You haven’t seen anything yet,” Sean said.

«»«»«»

Steven hadn’t communicated anything to the seller in several days. He wasn’t surprised to get the next message:

> ---
>
> What’s the plan?
>
> ---
>
> ---
>
> Just got the itinerary. She arrives Wednesday afternoon. Scheduled to stay through Friday if necessary. Booked into the Hyatt.
>
> ---
>
> ---
>
> Sit tight. Instructions to follow.
>
> ---

«»«»«»

Sean gave Marcus the tour of all the spots of interest to the investigation. It took about an hour. Marcus took a lot of photos and notes. When they emerged outside he checked his phone. Singh had updated him on the communication with Steven Jordan.

"Looks like we are going to meet with the mule next week. That should be interesting," he said.

"Any chance I could be there," Sean asked?

Marcus looked at him. "I don't think you can be seen anywhere near wherever the meeting occurs, but you might be able to be with me in our command center. We will have the representative of the auction house wired. Ideally, they would agree to meet in her room, so we could have it set up with hidden cameras. I doubt that is going to happen. My guess is they will say no to that offer and will probably set up a meeting venue, then change it at the last minute to try to ensure that no one has the time to wire it or follow or whatever. I have a plainclothes crew that will be wired and nearby, or as nearby as we can get at the time."

Sean understood and would do nothing to jeopardize the investigation.

"Get me a list of everyone you think might have known about this vault. What was the name of the guy that visited the architect? I'll run all their names when I get back to the office."

«»«»«»

Neil's birthday had passed for many years without much fuss. Shelley had decided that this must change and insisted on planning a surprise get-away. She would not divulge the details, and Neil played along. He kind of liked surprises, but he kind of didn't, too. But Shelley seemed excited about doing something special for him on his birthday, so how could he not play along? All he knew was that he was supposed to be able to go somewhere overnight.

This year, his birthday was on a Wednesday. He spent most of the week playfully trying to get clues out of her. Every attempt was met with a firm resolve to tell him nothing. Wednesday morning rolled around and Shelley told him it was time to get packed. They left mid-morning and it did not take long to guess they were heading to San Francisco. Heading out of the Napa Valley, there are really only a couple options, those that head south and west all basically take you to Highway 101, and that leads into the city across the Golden Gate Bridge.

As it turned out, Shelley had learned that there was a major retrospective on modern architecture being held at the de Young and had bought tickets with a reservation for dinner in the evening and a hotel for the night.

They parked near the museum and spent nearly the entire afternoon touring the exhibit. The museum had managed to piece together important original drawings and models from the Bauhaus down through Philip Johnsson. Neil's favorite architect from this period was Ludwig Mies van der Rohe. He particularly admired the simplicity and clarity of some of his designs. They seemed to embody the best ideals of modernism, yet still were aesthetically rich. To Neil, many of the practitioners of modernism had focused so completely on removing ornament from their designs that the resulting spaces seemed overly austere. He had always felt that Mies van der Rohe had managed to skirt the line between the impulse for modernity and a richness of materials.

Shelley to her credit tagged along and seemed interested in everything, or at least did an admirable job feigning interest. He caught her playing with her phone from time to time, but who didn't do that when they were bored?

After thoroughly reviewing the exhibit, and thoroughly exhausting themselves, they checked into the hotel and got ready for dinner.

«»«»«»

Steven had been waiting to receive the seller's instructions for the painting. He received them Wednesday evening.

> ---
>
> Meet Ms. Singh at her hotel Thursday morning at 9:30 a.m. Other instructions to follow.
>
> ---

Steven thought all the cloak and dagger stuff was a bit over the top. It was one thing to be anonymous, but this was sort of ridiculous. But he was being well paid. The payments were made on time with no fuss and if this sale went through, his fee would make the opening of his office a reality sooner than he could have ever imagined.

Jennifer naturally wondered what the arrangements were and knew that Marcus was waiting impatiently for her to feed him any and all news. As soon as she received Steven's e-mail, she forwarded it to Marcus.

Marcus got the ball rolling immediately. He had set up the surveillance team and it was on stand-by. Knowing the time and place of the meeting allowed the final arrangements to be put in place. He had given Jennifer a small device that would transmit her location to the surveillance team. He had also wired her purse so that he could hear the conversation. A miniaturized camera had been placed in the purse in a location that would not be detected and the battery and recording device had been placed under a false bottom that could not be detected without destroying the purse. Marcus felt he was ready, or as ready as he could be not knowing how things might unfold.

«»«»«»

The restaurant that Shelley had selected was great. She knew Neil liked Chinese and there were a number of excellent Chinese restaurants in Chinatown. The one she picked was one of his favorites. After dinner they took an Uber to Coit Tower and were treated to a romantic view of the city lights below. They walked back the mile and a half to their hotel for drinks. All in all it was an excellent day. To top it off, Shelley had made a reservation at one of the city's most exclusive hotels. She told Neil over dinner that she had a difficult time getting a reservation and that they were only staying there as the result of a late cancellation. And truthfully, she could afford no more than one night. But the night they spent was lovely and would be long remembered.

«»«»«»

At 9:30 a.m. Steven Jordan arrived at the Grand Hyatt San Francisco as instructed. He sent the seller a quick message.

At hotel.

Steven entered the lobby and waited only a few moments before spotting Jennifer. She was a tall elegant woman of Indian decent in her mid 30's. She was dressed to kill.

"Jennifer?" he asked, approaching her.

"Steven," she said. She shook his hand firmly. "Are we going to look at the piece here?"

"I'm not sure," he replied. "I am getting instructions as we go."

He glanced down at his phone. He had a new message.

Once you meet her, proceed to private car outside.

“I guess we are going for a ride,” Steven said after reading the message.

“Lead the way,” Jennifer said. “Do you know where we are going?”

“Nope.”

“Well this should be interesting,” she mused.

They got into the car.

“Can you tell us where we are going?” Jennifer asked the driver.

“No. But it shouldn’t take long,” the driver responded..

She turned and smiled at Steven. “I can’t tell you how much I look forward to seeing the Rembrandt,” she said.

“Yeah, me too,” he replied.

«»«»«»

Their departure from the hotel caused a slight stir, but they were not there to see it.

“Targets on the move!” someone on Marcus’ team squawked into their mic. This in turn caused a number of previously stationary guests in the hotel lobby to immediately leave their coffee or their morning paper and make a beeline for the main entrance of the hotel. Across the street, a van that had been parked in a loading zone left the curb in an attempt to follow the black town car that contained Steven and Jennifer. In the scramble that ensued, the agents on foot had no transportation and met in a slightly confused huddle at the porte cochere.

The black town car was followed by a second vehicle that had been summoned via Uber at about 8:30 that morning to accompany the town car and to ensure that if it appeared the town car was being followed, to slow to such a pace that the other vehicle would be in some way blocked.

The driver of the Uber vehicle was able to spot the van with little difficulty. As the town car made a rather unexpected left hand turn against traffic, the driver of the Uber simply slowed, blocked the intersection and waited for the light to turn.

The driver of the van, being impatient, leaned heavily on the horn, but to no avail. The light turned, pedestrians and the cross traffic entered the intersection, and the pursuit ended.

Steven and Jennifer were unaware of the drama in their wake and were busily discussing Edgar Payne and the art world.

After a short drive, they arrived at the St. Regis hotel and were greeted by a member of the hotel staff that seemed to have anticipated their arrival.

"Mr. Jordan, Ms. Singh. Please follow me," she said.

Steven looked at Jennifer and shrugged and motioned to her to go before him. They entered the hotel lobby and were shown to a small sitting room off the main lobby.

"Please wait here," the staff member said.

She stepped outside and a few moments later, another member of the staff entered the room with a small dark box. He set it on the table and said he would be back in 30 minutes to collect it. He then left them, closing the double doors to the room behind him.

«»«»«»

Shelley and Neil finished breakfast and began to gather their things in preparation for checking out.

«»«»«»

The box was custom made and had a thick black ribbon secured to the bottom of the box that extended up the sides. It was tied in a small bow on the top keeping the lid securely in place. Jennifer removed a pair of cotton gloves from her purse and positioned it rather nonchalantly to point one end directly at the box.

Steven watched but said nothing.

After putting on the gloves, Jennifer untied the ribbon, removed the lid of the box and smiled. There, nestled in a custom formed foam cutout, lay a small framed sketch of Rembrandt Harmenszoon van Rijn. The pencil strokes had a slightly rusty look on a faded white background. The sketch was of a mature Rembrandt with mustache and beard. A large hat sat upon his head, a ruffled cravat protruded from a high collared coat. It looked authentic. She gently lifted the piece from the box and turned it over. The back of the frame had been sealed. The front of the frame had a piece of laminated and tempered UV glass protecting the art work. Jennifer took a number of photographs of the frame, front, back, sides, nicks and dents. She documented it all. She took several photos of the sketch itself. She also took out a caliper measuring device and measured the frame in each of its dimensions. Placing it on the frame, she took another set of photos documenting its dimensions.

She pulled up a chair and sat down in front of the piece. She pulled a large magnifying glass from her purse and began to carefully examine the sketch. Steven had watched most of her inspection of the piece in silence. But at this point he had to ask, "So? What do you think?"

Jennifer looked up. "It appears to be genuine, however, I cannot be certain without removing it from the frame back and running a few tests. I can't do that here, obviously. So I'll need you to send it to me in New York for further study. We would also need to consult with a number of Rembrandt experts. Several of them are in Europe. One is in New York. That process could take several months. For something as special as this, however, the time and money spent is well worth it as the authentication will add tremendously to its value."

Steven nodded.

"What's next?" Jennifer asked.

"I don't know," he said. "Let me see if there are further instructions."

> ---
>
> Review complete. She is satisfied it is authentic. Further instructions?
>
> ---

Steven and Jennifer continued to chat somewhat awkwardly while waiting for the hotel staff to come retrieve the piece. Steven kept checking his phone to see if the seller had any further instructions.

In the meantime, Marcus and his team had regrouped and managed to identify the location of the transmitter in Jennifer's purse. Several rather sweaty FBI agents began to saunter into the lobby of the hotel while the van had taken up a new position in the service alley behind the hotel.

«»«»«»

Shelley and Neil finished getting their things packed away, left their room and headed down the elevator to check out. They walked to the front desk and Neil offered to take care of paying the tab, but Shelley insisted that this was her thing. So he left her to it and walked through the lobby, admiring the architecture. There is something about the grandeur of a fine hotel's lobby that he always enjoyed. As he walked through the space, Neil was impressed with both the attention to detail and the use of materials. Having walked to the far end of the lobby he turned to head back to the main desk and was surprised to see Karl Stroughmann sitting in one of the lounge chairs reading the morning paper.

"Mr. Stroughmann," Neil said in surprise. "Do you remember me? We met several months ago in my office. I'm Neil Thornton, the architect from St. Helena."

The man looked up in surprise. He said nothing and looked around the lobby.

Neil was thrown slightly by his lack of acknowledgment. "I'm sorry. You are Karl Stroughmann aren't you," he asked?

"Yes. I am. I'm sorry," he said. "You startled me. I am not recognized out here very often," he said.

"Have you decided to proceed with your winery?" Neil asked.

"I am getting closer," he said somewhat cautiously. "I have narrowed down the property search to several parcels. I have opened negotiations on the one I am most interested in and hope to close in the next six months or so."

"Have you hired an architect?" Neil asked hopefully.

"Not yet," he laughed, and looked around the room as if he were concerned who might be overhearing their conversation.

Neil turned around to see a hotel staff member emerge from a room with a small box. He turned back to Karl and he seemed a little self-conscious about Neil seeing what he was observing.

"You know where to find me," Neil offered. "If I may be of assistance, it would be my pleasure." Neil offered his hand and Karl Stroughmann took it. They shook hands and Neil walked away.

He walked back to the main registration desk as Shelley was finishing and they walked together out of the hotel, unaware of the drama swirling around them.

They were at the valet stand waiting for Neil's car to be delivered, when a young woman approached and asked them if they had a moment.

"A moment for what?" Neil asked.

"Sean Andrews would like to speak with you," she said.

"What? Sean's here?" Neil asked looking around.

"Please follow me," she said.

«»«»«»

They left their bags with the valet attendant and re-entered the hotel through a service entrance on the far end of the porte cochere.

She led them through a service corridor to the back of the hotel and out another door into a service alley.

There were a couple of delivery vans in the alley delivering food stuffs and other supplies to the hotel. The door to a small cargo van opened and Sean stepped out. Neil shook his head in disbelief.

"What are you doing here?" he asked in disbelief. He looked at Shelley, "Is this part of your surprise?" he asked. She shook her head emphatically.

Neil turned to Sean as he approached.

"The question is, 'What are you doing here'?" Sean said.

"What? We spent the night here and are just checking out."

"Your timing is a little suspect," he said. "You walked right into a major surveillance stakeout."

"Really? Wow. Sorry," Neil said. "I didn't know you investigated crimes all the way down here."

"I don't. I'm here with the FBI," he said.

"Oh . . . Must be something big," Neil said. "Listen. We were just leaving." Neil suddenly remembered bumping into Karl Stroughmann.

"Sean, you won't believe who I saw in the lobby. It was Karl Stroughmann."

Sean cocked his head. "What did you say? Karl Stroughmann was in the lobby?"

"Yeah. While Shelley was paying I walked through the lobby. When I turned around, he was sitting there with a paper. I said hello and asked if he had decided to build his winery. He looked a little startled. Anyway, he said he was closing in on a parcel to buy and hasn't hired an architect yet. But is that a weird coincidence or what?"

"Come here," Sean motioned for them to follow him to the van. He stuck his head inside and momentarily a man in a suit got out of the van.

"Neil, this is Special Agent Marcus Little. He is investigating the attempted sale of several pieces of art. We are here this morning trying to identify the seller. So far they have remained anonymous," he said.

He shook Agent Little's hand. "Good morning," Neil said.

"Marcus, this is the architect that David Johnsson hired and who was with me when I discovered David's body."

Marcus nodded in recognition. He gave Neil and Shelley a stern and not altogether friendly once-over. He was all business and wasn't in a particularly friendly or jocular mood.

"He says he just saw Karl Stroughmann in the lobby. That was the guy who visited Neil's office asking about finding an architect to design a winery, and what Neil knew about David's project and if he had a set of drawings for David's project. And then the next day, Neil's office was burgled and one of the volumes of drawings went missing," Sean said.

Marcus nodded again as if he knew the story.

"Why are you here, Mr. Thornton?" Marcus asked without emotion.

Neil looked at Sean and then back to Marcus. "This is my girlfriend, Shelley," he said introducing them to her. "Yesterday was my birthday. She surprised me with a night on the town and a stay here at the St. Regis."

"Nice to meet you," Marcus said to Shelley, in the same almost menacing tone.

Looking at Neil he said, "You know, you have knowledge about the plans for Mr. Johnsson's chateau, the vault, the code. You had the keys and the code in your possession after Mr. Johnsson went missing. I know Detective Andrews hasn't said you are a suspect, but it seems to me you stack up to be a prime suspect, and then you show up in the middle of a sting operation. I'm going to ask you to stay here until I sort this out. If you refuse, I'll arrest you. Agent Martinez," he motioned to the young woman who had led Neil and Shelley from the valet stand back to the alley.

She walked over to where they stood.

“Keep an eye on these two. If they try to leave, arrest them.” Marcus turned and got back in the van.

Neil looked at Shelley, she looked confused, a little afraid, but mostly pissed off. He gave her a little hug.

“Is there somewhere we could sit down while we wait, for whatever it is we are waiting for?” Neil asked.

Agent Martinez nodded, “This way,” she said. She led them to a government sedan parked nearby and let them sit in the backseat, closing the door after they got in.

She opened the door a crack and said, “Just stay here. Don’t try to leave, or as you heard Special Agent Little say, I’ll have to arrest you.”

She shut the door again and walked away.

Shelley pulled out her phone and started texting.

Neil found this behavior highly annoying. They were stuck in an FBI sedan, essentially under detention and Shelley is texting! “What are you doing?!” he exclaimed.

“Texting my mom telling her we might be getting busted. Someone needs to know where we are,” she said.

Neil calmed down a bit, but just a bit.

«»«»«»

Back in the lobby, Steven received a message from the seller telling him to ask Jennifer what the next steps would be. She had told him she would need the piece sent to New York for further authentication and that the seller should gather as much provenance as they had.

The painting had disappeared, presumably back into the hotel vault. Jennifer thanked Steven for having reached out to her for the opportunity to sell the pieces. He said it was his pleasure and asked if she had time for lunch.

“Unfortunately, I have to catch a plane. Perhaps we could do that the next time I am in town,” she said. “It was good to meet you, Steven. Take care of yourself,” she said.

“Thanks. You, too,” he said.

She would have liked to ask him a few questions about the painting, his client, and what other interesting pieces of art they might have and want to sell. However, knowing that the wire she carried was being monitored by the FBI kept her from being too personal in her interaction with Steven.

She hailed a cab, while Steven decided not to leave the hotel just yet and sat down to send an encrypted message to the seller.

> ---
>
> Jennifer Singh is gone. Says it looks like it's real. Wants to authenticate in New York with Rembrandt experts from Europe. Suggests you start to gather all provenance. Further instructions?
>
> ---

«»«»«»

> ---
>
> Done for today.
>
> ---

Back in the van, they watched as Jennifer and then Steven left the hotel. Constant visual reports from the undercover team were radioed to the van about the movement of people in the lobby. After several minutes, the surveillance operation was called as being complete. One by one, the undercover agents drifted away from the hotel.

Steven decided it was a nice day and he would walk back to his condo. He did not notice the two plain-clothes FBI agents shadowing him as he walked back through the city and disappeared into the lobby of his building.

«»«»«»

Marcus was visibly disappointed. He had consumed considerable resources on the surveillance operation, but had not achieved his mission. He would now have to write several lengthy reports and provide an accounting of the expenses. He did not look forward to any of these activities. "Okay, people, back to the office," he said.

He stepped out of the van with Sean.

"Let's talk to the architect," he said. They walked over to the sedan and motioned for Shelley and Neil to get out.

“Listen, I am sorry for this inconvenience,” he said. “I would like to talk to you further. We could go back to my office or find someplace nearby. Do you have a preference?”

“I don’t normally drink this early in the morning,” Neil said, “but under the circumstances, I think I might.”

“Okay, we’ll find a pub,” Marcus said.

“There’s a nice bar inside,” Shelley offered.

“That will do, I suppose.”

They went back inside, prepared for the inquisition.

«»«»«»

The décor of the main bar at the St. Regis was modern and sleek. Off to one side, there was a casual seating area, furnished in a luxurious, modern rendition of sophisticated comfort. They settled in and were momentarily visited by a waitress. Sean and Marcus Little declined, but as Shelley and Neil were not on duty, they each ordered something. Neil asked if Sean or Marcus might at least want coffee or water. Marcus agreed that water would be fine and Sean ordered a coffee.

While they waited for their drinks, Marcus got down to business.

“Tell me again why you are here,” he said.

Neil again looked at Shelley. She seemed to be content to let him do the talking as their skepticism seemed to be centered on him.

“Are you arresting us?” Neil asked first. It seemed like if that was what was next he should ask to speak with a lawyer. He knew nothing about being arrested, but knew enough to know that casual “interviews” with law enforcement could come back to bite you later if they did arrest you.

“Not necessarily. But if I did I think it would be just you at this point,” Marcus said. “So why are you here?”

“Yesterday was my birthday. Shelley and I have been dating for several months and this is the first of our birthdays that we have shared together,” Neil said as if reciting a well-known fact to a child or an imbecile.

“And if this is the kind of company you keep, it may be the last,” she said with a laugh. That lightened the mood a bit and Neil continued.

"So Shelley decided to surprise me with a day in the city and a night here in this great hotel. We spent yesterday at the de Young museum at a retrospective of the Modernist movement."

This bit of information was greeted with blank stares, either due to a lack of comprehension or acknowledgement of a statement of the obvious. He continued.

"We had dinner at a nice restaurant in Chinatown, and then came back here for the night. We had room service in our room this morning and were just checking out when your Agent Martinez asked us to come see you in the van. That's pretty much it."

Marcus looked at Sean and shrugged.

"I don't think these are your guys," Sean said. He looked at Neil. "Tell him again who you saw in the lobby."

"While Shelley was checking out . . . she wouldn't let me pay," Neil said looking at her. "I walked through the lobby and was surprised to see Karl Stroughmann. I don't know if Sean told you about him, but he came to my office the day before it was burgled looking for an architect to design a winery. He said he was from Long Island visiting the area and thinking of building his own winery. He claimed he had taken a tour of large parcels of land on the market and had met a couple of real estate agents, one of whom knew that I had been retained by David Johnsson to do some work on his emerging chateau. I was flattered at the time and didn't really give it much thought, but in retrospect, I don't think anyone but Shelley knew that I was working for David." Neil looked at her again. "Did you ever mention that to anyone?"

She shook her head. "No. I remember we were excited to get his call because we were slow, but it wasn't a large contract."

"So you saw this Stroughmann fellow this morning in the lobby," Marcus asked?

"Yes," Neil said.

"What was he doing?" he asked.

"He was reading the paper."

"Was he with anyone?" Marcus continued.

"I don't think so. He seemed surprised and maybe a little annoyed to see me."

"Why do you say that? Marcus asked,

"He didn't really focus on me. He kept looking around like he didn't want to be seen talking to me. I just took it that he wasn't pleased to be recognized or something," Neil said.

"What time was this," Sean asked.

Neil glanced at Shelley. "What time did we leave the room, like 9:45 or around then?" She nodded. "So it could have been like 9:50 or so."

Sean and Marcus looked at each other. Marcus pulled a phone from his pocket. He dialed a number and listened. "Could you join us, we are in the bar. . . . On the main level. Right." He ended the call and put the phone back in his pocket.

Agent Martinez appeared presently.

"Check with hotel security. I want to review their security recording for the main lobby this morning. I want to see all the camera angles from 9:15 to about 10:15. We may want the whole morning from as early as 6:00 a.m.," Marcus said. She nodded and disappeared.

Marcus addressed Shelley and Neil.

"We are in the middle of a very sensitive investigation. Your presence here is problematic to say the least. And personally I doubt it is coincidental. I am not at liberty to tell you exactly what we think is going on here this morning. At some point, if you are cleared, you may get to know."

Agent Martinez appeared again.

"Agent Martinez," Marcus said, "please read Mr. Thornton his Miranda rights. I am placing him under arrest."

Sean couldn't help himself. "Agent Little, I don't think this is your guy," he said.

"Fine. When we know that for sure, then he can go. But in the meantime, he is under arrest."

Agent Martinez approached Neil and asked him to stand. Shelley stood with him and gave him a hug. She whispered, "I'm sorry," into his ear.

"What should I do?" she asked.

"Get me a good lawyer. Know any?" he asked.

She shook her head.

“Sorry,” Agent Martinez said. “I’ve got to cuff you.”

“Seriously?” Sean said.

“It’s policy,” she replied. She pulled out a little card and read Neil his rights.

«»«»«»

Agent Martinez took Neil back to the sedan. Before Neil was placed in the backseat, Shelley asked what was going to happen and Miss Martinez briefly explained the booking and arraignment process. Shelley naturally wanted to know how long it would take and if she should come along.

“Up to you,” she said. “Sometimes it’s fast and sometimes it’s not. There is a possibility that he may have to stay overnight if he can’t be arraigned this afternoon.”

Shelley looked at Neil. “Why don’t you give me your car keys. I’ll get our stuff and hang out. When you know something, call me.”

Shelley looked at Agent Martinez. “Will he be able to call me?”

“Not until after he is arraigned,” she said. “Then he’ll either get his phone back or he’ll get one call.”

“Can I call you or someone at the FBI to keep up with what is going on?” Shelley asked.

“Sure. Here is my number,” she said handing Shelley a business card. “Call me in about two hours. I should know something by then,” she said.

«»«»«»

Sean and Marcus were shown into the on-site security office where the hotel’s security staff monitored the building’s entrances, public spaces, and hallways. A bank of monitors covered one wall. Two workstations faced the monitors while another two workstations faced the opposing wall.

The manager of the hotel introduced the two men to the security team on duty.

“Please show Agent Marcus the recording of the lobby from this morning,” he said.

Moments later, one of the screens changed to show a recorded video image of the lobby that had been recorded at 6:15 a.m.

The lobby was empty and remained empty for several minutes as the men watched.

"Okay," Agent Little said, clearly underwhelmed, "can we speed through this a little faster?"

"Sure," was the reply of the security staff operating the console.

The time and frame stamp sped up, but were the only indication of the passage of time, as the lobby was still desolate. At 7:17 a.m. someone scurried through the lobby.

"Want me to go back and slow it down?" the man asked.

"No. We'll probably watch it again later and have you do that. Right now we want to see what happens between about 9:15 and 9:45. When we get there, slow it down a bit," Marcus said.

The traffic in the lobby slowly picked up. Steven Jordan and Jennifer Singh scooted into view and disappeared into a conference room.

"Okay. Right here. Back it up a bit and slow it down to real time," he said.

The image stopped and reversed and then began again at normal speed. Steven and Jennifer walked through the lobby and were met by a staff member, then were escorted to an adjoining conference room.

Marcus noticed his agents hurriedly enter the lobby and take up various positions. A few moments later a staff member entered the view carrying a small object, and briefly disappeared into the conference room.

"Stop!" Marcus barked. "Who is that?" he asked pointing at the screen.

The image was in color and of reasonable clarity. The hotel security staff and even the manager leaned in to take a closer look.

"Don't know," came the first response. "Hard to say," came next. "Looks like it might be Julio Garcia, but he is on vacation."

The staff member in question was wearing a bellhop uniform complete with a little cap and visor. The visor provided just enough cover for the person's face that from the current camera angle, they couldn't be sure who it was.

Marcus had been so focused on the delivery of the package that he had not noticed someone sitting facing the camera with an open newspaper obscuring their face.

Sean leaned in and without saying anything, pointed at the person.

Marcus asked if they could rewind the recording to see when the person had come into the lobby.

“Oh, you would like to see Mr. Storque?” the security guy asked. “Hang on. I can do that. You could practically set your watch by this guy. He always comes in and reads the paper at about 9:20.”

He reversed the recording and sure enough, the man walked into the lobby at almost exactly 9:20 with a newspaper under his arm. He sat down and opened it.

“So you know this guy?” Marcus asked.

“A long term guest,” the manager offered with an almost reverent tone of voice.

“And what’s his name?” Marcus asked.

“Derek Storque,” was the manager’s response.

The security recording kept playing and before long, Neil Thorton came into view. He looked like a tourist gawking at the lobby. He didn’t see Derek Storque immediately, then as he turned he noticed Storque and approached him. The paper was lowered. The two men spoke. Storque looked around, just as Neil had said. They shook hands and Neil left the view of the camera. Momentarily, the unidentified staff member returned and disappeared again, briefly, into the conference room and then emerged with a small dark object, perhaps 10” or 12” square, and then disappeared from the screen. Nothing happened for several minutes, so Marcus asked that the recording be sped up a bit. After about thirty minutes of recorded time, which took only about six minutes to watch, Steven Jordan and Jennifer Singh emerged from the room and scurried, at the fast forward speed, toward the lobby entrance disappearing from view. Steven returned to the lobby a few seconds later, sat for a few more seconds, then scurried away.

Sean’s arms were folded. He felt justified in his initial instinct that Neil Thorton’s presence in the lobby was coincidental. But he didn’t say it. There is a pecking order in law enforcement. The FBI is at the very top, a detective from a small town is near the bottom and knew speaking his mind would not change the dynamic under the circumstances. So he bit his tongue.

“What can you tell me about this Storque guy?” Marcus wanted to know.

“He is our guest,” came the manager’s response. “Respecting our guests’ privacy is a hallmark of the outstanding service that we offer.”

“Seriously?” Marcus croaked out. “You’re going to give me that bullshit?”

The manager nodded.

“Okay. I can probably find out what I need to know without you,” Marcus said.

He pulled out his phone and hit a quick dial number. “Agent Branson. Marcus Little,” he said with annoyance dripping from his voice. “Get me whatever you can find on a Derek Storque. He’s staying at the St. Regis.” He paused to listen then turned to the manager. “How do you spell his last name?”

“It’s s-t-o-r-q-u-e,” the manager said.

“Did you get that?” Marcus asked into the phone. He paused to listen as Agent Branson spelled the name back. “Right, and it’s Derek with a ‘k’, right?” he asked looking at the manager again, who just nodded. “Start the paperwork for a warrant. The hotel isn’t playing nice.” He paused again to listen. “Correct. Call me or shoot me an e-mail as soon as you know something . . . . Thanks.”

Marcus turned to the clearly dismayed manager. “We can play this however you want,” Marcus said. “These recordings are evidence. Do not erase them or tamper with them in any way. I want copies made for all cameras for the last two weeks.”

The security guy looked at the hotel manager for guidance, but nodded his head in acknowledgement. The manager remained silent. He was going to have to notify his superiors for guidance. He didn’t like being stuck between the FBI and the hotel’s desire to accommodate a valuable client that had done nothing wrong as far as he knew.

«»«»«»

It took the hotel manager about ten minutes to get the green light from the upper echelon of the hotel’s management to cooperate with the FBI, interests of a very valuable guest not withstanding.

«»«»«»

The hotel manager really didn’t have that much to tell Marcus. He knew Derek Storque’s name. He knew that he was staying with Georgia Johnsson who was footing the bill. He knew they seemed to not have any budgetary limits, which was one of their most endearing qualities. He knew they availed themselves of many of the hotel’s outstanding amenities and services, but besides that and when they had come and how long they had stayed, he didn’t know much.

Marcus and his team got to work on unearthing information about Derek Storque and Georgia Calhoun Johnsson's stay at the St. Regis. They learned that the pair had been in residence for at least 6 months. They had one of the nicest suites in the hotel, but not the most palatial suite, either. They ate most of their meals in their room. They ventured down to one of the hotel's restaurants a couple of times a week. They frequently ate their evening meal somewhere outside the hotel. Georgia used the services of the hotel, like the masseuse, more than Derek. They sent their laundry out every morning. Derek frequented the bar and the hotel lobby on a daily basis. Georgia paid the bill.

When Marcus' team asked about the painting, they were met with blank stares. When asked whether either Derek Storque or Georgia Johnsson had placed any items in the hotel's safe, they were told that they had. Just that morning, in fact.

Marcus did not sugarcoat it. "What was it?" he asked the manager.

"I don't know, sir," he replied. "And it is against hotel policy to discuss the items left in its care by hotel guests with anyone other than the guest."

Marcus knew this of course, but it did not stop him from asking. So that's what he did. He asked questions and pushed to see what he could find out from whomever he thought had information he needed.

"I want to see it," he said.

"Sir. Have you discussed this matter with our guests?"

Marcus looked intently at the manager, his eyes drilling into the man in a way that caused him to shift uncomfortably. He doubted that this fellow was complicit in any crime and was just doing his job. But at the moment, he represented a road block to what was probably a critical piece of evidence.

"Mr. Ogilvie," the manager's name was prominently displayed on a brass badge on the lapel of his suit jacket, "we are in the middle of a very sensitive investigation involving the interstate transport of stolen property. Your guests are prominent suspects at this point, as would be anyone that chose to aide or abet them. This is a very confidential investigation at this point."

Marcus leaned forward toward the man and lowered his voice to a near whisper. "The FBI would welcome your assistance and that of this fine hotel in keeping this matter confidential."

He looked slowly around him, with a conspiratorial air before looking back at the manager. "And as you might imagine, your cooperation would be helpful in keeping this incident out of the media. I need to know what was placed in the safe. I can get a warrant and come back, but I would have to leave several agents behind to make sure that neither you nor your staff removed anything from the safe until the warrant was obtained. That would be an inconvenience to you and your staff and might draw unwanted attention."

The manager looked very serious and nodded intently to everything Marcus said.

"Actually," Marcus continued, "I don't need to see the object. I just need you or your staff to check to make sure it is secure and that your safe is appropriate for the object." Marcus raised his eyebrows and nodded.

The manager smiled and nodded his understanding of the request. "We pride ourselves in the high levels of service we provide to our clients. We, of course, will see to it that the contents of the package are carefully *looked* after," he said. "Please wait a moment."

The manager disappeared into the office area behind the reception counter. Tucked away down a hall and through a secure storage room, a large safe was embedded into a wall. The manager removed a key from his pocket and opened a small metal door next to the safe. Inside, there was a print scanner and a keypad. He placed his ring finger on the scanner and simultaneously typed in an eight digit code. Something beeped and he shut and re-locked the metal cabinet. He then turned the dial on the face of the safe door, entering in a simple four digit combination. The safe door swung open and Mr. Ogilvie reached into the safe and removed a small dark box. The box was sturdy and covered in the same material that the case for a stringed instrument would typically have been covered in. The manager had only seen the box briefly as it had been placed into the safe. It had a thick black ribbon secured to the bottom of the box that extended up the sides. It was tied in a small bow on the top keeping the lid securely in place. He untied the ribbon and removed the lid. Inside, he saw a small framed sketch. He was not an art enthusiast and it meant nothing to him. As such, it did not occur to him that this might be a nearly priceless piece of art and that he should not touch it without wearing gloves. He removed the painting and set it on a small table that was situated on one side of the open safe.

He took his phone from his pocket and took a photo of the sketch and then another of the inside of the box. He then quickly replaced everything as it had been, re-tied the ribbon and placed the box back in the safe. He shut the door to the safe, making sure it was secure and returned to the reception counter.

Marcus was still standing there idly fidgeting with his phone. He looked up to see Mr. Ogilvie returning. The manager's eyes quickly darted around the lobby as he approached Marcus. He smiled thinly and said "Mr. Little, I need to speak to you in my office. Would you mind joining me for a moment?" He continued looking around the lobby barely seeming to acknowledge Marcus, who was standing directly in front of him.

“Sure. I hope you found everything to be in order,” he said.

The hotel manager ignored the comment and motioned Marcus to join him at the far end of the counter where it ended and there was a space for the staff to enter and exit. Marcus walked to the end of the counter and followed the manager through a cased opening and into a short hallway. There were several offices along the hall. His office was at the end. The manager stepped aside, letting Marcus enter first. He then followed and shut the door behind them.

He motioned for Marcus to be seated as he unlocked his phone and searched for the photos he had just taken. He handed Marcus his phone without saying anything.

Marcus took the phone and glanced at the photo of the framed sketch sitting on the table. He looked up to see Mr. Ogilvie staring at him intently. “This was in the box?”

“What should we do?” the manager asked.

“Just sit tight for the time being. Are you the only person that can open the safe?”

The manager nodded.

“If someone comes asking for the box, have your staff stall for time. If you make yourself scarce, that will be a credible cover story.”

The manager furrowed his brow. “I have to be here,” he said. “I can’t just not be here,” he added with exasperation.

“I think you just got sick and probably need to take a few days off,” Marcus offered.

Mr. Ogilvie considered this for a moment. “I guess my staff could call me at home,” he said in defeat.

“Good.” Marcus stood and shook the hotel manager’s hand. “Thanks for your help. The FBI appreciates your cooperation. I’ll have one of my agents leave you with the information you will need to communicate with us. You can give them your contact info, too. I’ll need copies of the photos. One of my team will give you an address where you can e-mail them. In the meantime, I hope you feel better soon.” Marcus smiled.

The manager gave Marcus a thin, sarcastic smile and just shook his head. “I’m feeling lousy at the moment," he said. "No joke."

The next day, Marcus and his team were shown all the security footage again. No one at the hotel knew the identity of the hotel personnel that had greeted Steven Jordan and Jennifer Singh. The painting had been brought into the lobby and then retrieved by people wearing hotel uniforms, but they were not hotel staff.

One of Marcus' agents began to construct a time-line of events starting with the initiation of the operation. It all made sense until they got to the point where the package was deposited into the hotel safe. If Derek Storque or Georgia Calhoun were behind the "preview", wouldn't they want to have the painting in their possession? Why deposit it in the safe? Or why in the hotel safe, at any rate?

In order to determine that one of these two were behind the theft, he would need some physical evidence that tied them to the contents of the box. A finger print on the frame of the sketch would probably do it. But if they were being set up for some reason, then he doubted that he would find that.

Marcus called Sean Andrews.

"Detective Andrews."

"Detective. It's Marcus Little. We managed to confirm that one of the missing pieces of art is in the safe at the hotel."

Sean just grunted at the news. "So what do we know?" Sean asked.

Marcus rattled off the events of the morning from his time-line, "Neil Thornton bumped into the person he thought was Karl Stroughmann in the lobby. That person was in fact Derek Storque. Turns out he is David Johnsson's ex-wife's live-in boyfriend. He entered the lobby at 9:20 a.m. and ordered a coffee and the morning paper. He read the paper for about an hour before leaving and returning to his suite. Apparently, this is Mr. Storque's frequent morning ritual. He also had his phone out and was using it with some regularity to text or check messages. But everyone does that, so that is proof of nothing. But he was in the lobby during the time the painting was previewed. Either he was involved in some way or that is an amazing coincidence."

"I hate to say it, but the same is true for my architect friend," Sean said. "I have not really considered him a suspect, but his presence in the lobby pretty much falls into the same category."

"The thing about the architect is that he had the code, the keys, and the knowledge of the existence of the vault. The one thing he seemed to lack was the thumbs. As to a motive, millions of dollars in art is motive enough, I guess,"

Marcus said.

"You think he is trying to frame Derek Storque?" Sean asked.

"That is one possibility," Marcus replied. "But he didn't really seem to know who Derek Storque was and he told you about his encounter quite naively. If he was involved why tell you? We would have eventually figured out that the package had been deposited into the hotel safe under Storque's name. I looked at the security footage and I would say that the architect's account fits with the visual footage. He did seem to wander into the lobby and then seem surprised to see Storque sitting there. Storque for his part was not particularly friendly and did seem to be looking around while they were talking."

"But why be at that hotel?" Sean asked.

"I don't know. If anything else pops up, I'll let you know."

"Thanks," Sean said as he hung up the phone. The puzzle was getting more confusing with the additional pieces on the table, not less so, Sean thought.

Marcus filled out the paperwork to run a thorough check on Derek Storque and to get access to his phone and e-mail records. He might not be able to tell what he was doing exactly, but he might be able to tell when he had sent and received messages. He might also be able correlate this information with the information he was already receiving from Steven Jordan's phone and then be able to surmise if they had been communicating with each other.

«◊»«◊»«◊»

"Form follows profit is the aesthetic principle of our times."

-- Richard Rogers

Chapter Thirteen

It had been five months since David's death and Keith was nowhere nearer to finding the murderer and exacting his revenge than in the days and weeks since he had learned of David's death. Given the cold rage that consumed him, Keith could be considered to be fairly patient with the slow pace of Detective Andrew's investigation. But Keith had not been content to let the slow wheels of justice turn without taking the opportunity afforded him by David's resources to grease those wheels where he could.

Keith had spent the months since David's death puzzling through the details. He simultaneously felt guilt, anger, and remorse over the loss of his brother and a certain sense of helplessness. The official investigation into his brother's death had thus far not resulted in any satisfactory answers. Keith wanted to know who had killed his brother, and then he wanted to beat the crap out of them, or worse. But not knowing where to focus his anger, he had no outlet other than to channel it into his own suppositions and theories.

He cycled through the knowns and unknowns in his head. He couldn't stop thinking about it. He was consumed and determined to avenge the only family he knew. He would start with what he knew and work through the details until the strands of evidence began to fray into the endless possibilities.

The last time Keith had spoken to David, he had been in London looking at a Vermeer on David's behalf. It was a worthy piece, Keith had thought, but overpriced. He had tried to dissuade David from making the purchase, but David said it filled a hole in his collection and he told Keith to finalize the transaction. Keith was more interested in the price/value relationship. Whatever strategy David was employing regarding the entirety of the collection was lost on him.

"Okay. I'll sign the paperwork," he had told David.

"Good. I'll talk to Roger and have him wire the funds." Roger was David's personal banker.

Keith had spent another two days in London wrapping up the arrangements with the bonded courier, securing a secondary insurance rider from Lloyd's. He had planned to make a quick stop in Amsterdam before returning to New York, but he had received a worried call from Lydia asking if he had spoken to David, because he had not answered or returned her calls for several days. That was not like David, especially with Lydia. She had been in California with David and had sent some drawings for the chateau to an architect at his request before leaving for New York. But when she had not heard from him for several days, she called Keith. They had agreed that she should return to California and would call Keith if she had not heard from David or been able to locate him once she landed.

As soon as Keith ended the call with Lydia, he placed a call to David himself. David had not answered, so he left a message. Keith was used to waiting several days for David to return a call, so he was not immediately alarmed. However, when Lydia called later the next day and told him she had still not heard from him and that the staff at Bowler's had not seen him in several days, he became very alarmed. They agreed she should call the police and check with local hospitals. Neither action resulted in any news. It was at that point that Lydia filed the missing person's report and Keith quickly wrapped up his trip and purchased a ticket for a flight back to the U.S.

Keith had landed in New York and worked the problem from there for a week before he decided he needed to join Lydia in California, as that was where David had been when both he and Lydia had last spoken with him. Keith had reached out to the local police and had been questioned at length with little seeming to come from that. Keith typically would have stayed well clear of the police, but they seemed the logical place to start.

Over the next week he had interacted with a Detective Andrews several times, but had not learned anything. It was probably a week or so after that that he and Lydia had been informed that David had been found in the chateau. It was shocking news. He had not said much, but was furious; at himself, at David, at life, at whomever had done it.

As soon as the news of David's death broke and hit the papers, the media frenzy began and Keith's life of relative obscurity ended. He was immediately resolved to do something. Anything. So he had begun screening several private investigation firms, finally settling on Kurtz-Wilder.

It was a logical decision. They were located in San Francisco, they had resources, or so they claimed, in New York, and their founding partners were retired law enforcement with extensive contacts. Those connections and resources came with a high price, but Keith cared more about results than hanging onto David's money. He hired them without telling Lydia. She would probably have agreed, but there was no point in telling her.

It took almost no time for David's ex-wife, Georgia, to swoop in with attorneys and her 'fucking' boyfriend to try to get David's estate. He called the PI immediately after hearing that she had filed papers contesting David's will and upped the pressure for results. He offered them a reward on top of what he was already paying for information – along with a time limit.

Keith had seen right through her from the first time he had met her. There wasn't much he could do or say to David about his assessment of Georgia. David was married to her after all, and given the scant time they spent together, he suspected that David had a similar opinion about the hole he had dug for himself.

David had been too generous with her, Keith thought. Now she had the resources, plus the potential of billions more she stood to gain should she prevail, to retain a stable of high powered attorneys to do battle on her behalf and gum up the works in the meantime.

Her attorney's first move had been to file a petition with the court asserting her claim to all of David's assets and to block Keith and Lydia from continuing to act on David's behalf. This initial move had been partially successful in that she managed to win an injunction from the court restricting Lydia and Keith from disposing of any of David's assets. While many of David's business dealings could be handled by his estate's attorneys, this move did pose certain logistical problems for Lydia who had handled a fair portion of David's day-to-day affairs.

It had taken the attorney's for David's estate several months to successfully challenge key portions of Georgia's filing by establishing that David had written a new will and had, in fact, signed their divorce papers.

Keith had been left at the margins of the legal skirmishing with little to do but watch. He had to laugh when he learned the Lydia was pregnant with David's child and would have given almost anything to have been present when Georgia was told the news. He was fairly certain, and certainly correct, that the news had not been well received.

Because of the low esteem with which he viewed his ex-sister in-law, he was not averse to digging up some dirt on Georgia if he could find it. So he had added digging into Georgia's past and current doings to the PI's list of deliverables.

But now, some five months later, he was growing impatient. It was time for results.

Keith waited impatiently to be connected to Joshua. When he finally came on the line, Keith dispensed with the pleasantries.

"Why is this taking so long?" he demanded.

There was a brief pause on the line as Joshua Wilder considered his response.

"Good morning, Keith," he said.

"Seriously, why is this taking so long?" Keith said again. "It's been like five months. You have put quite a bit of my money down the shitter and I still don't know jack!"

Joshua Wilder had been in the private investigation business for long enough that Keith was not his first highly impatient and equally abrasive client. He might have been more blunt and acerbic than most, but it was not uncommon for clients to want immediate results.

"When you first visited my office, we discussed the difficulties in pursuing this type of case. I'm sure you haven't forgotten that."

Keith said nothing and Wilder continued.

"We have been methodically collecting, analyzing, and sharing with you the information that we have found," he said.

"You haven't found anything!" Keith shouted into the phone.

Wilder ignored the comment and the anger behind it and continued in a calm voice.

"Sometimes what we don't find is as useful as what we do find," he said.

"In the initial stages of an investigation we are looking for anything and everything that relates to the case. After we evaluate it, some of it is kept and some of it we can set aside. It is true that we have mostly been able to rule certain scenarios out, but we have also found a few things that we think are interesting."

Keith had seen the preliminary reports and had not been impressed. He knew that Wilder thought the architect was potentially involved. But he thought the factors pointing to Neil Thornton were weak. He knew that Wilder's people had spent time developing a relationship with Detective Andrews in an attempt to learn what he knew that had not yet been disclosed. But all the background work was slow and not getting to a conclusion fast enough for Keith. While he was impatient, he also knew he really didn't have many other options. So he waited.

"Keith. I know this is hard for you. Every investigation I have ever done for the family of a murder victim has been hard. But there are no short cuts. It just takes time. So go do something. Take a trip or whatever you can to get your mind off the case. We'll keep plugging away and when we find something, we'll call you."

Keith knew he was right, but that didn't keep him from letting his anger get the best of him.

"I expect results," Keith spat into the phone before abruptly hanging up.

«»«»«»

Neil returned home after his arrest in a foul mood. Posting bail about bankrupted him. Paying for a decent defense attorney was going to finish him financially. His architectural practice was only barely treading water. He had managed for some time to shuffle things around without really getting ahead. His arrest promised to cause a financial hemorrhage from which he might never recover. In addition, as a licensed professional being arrested, for anything, was something that the licensing board would look at every two years when he renewed his license. He knew he would be trying to explain his innocence for the rest of his life. And all because he agreed to assist a rich dead guy determine the completeness of his pet project for a few measly dollars. "Damn it!" he thought. He meant it in all the ways it could be interpreted.

He tried to go about his business as usual, staying focused on his own problems rather than those of the investigation. His project at the community college turned out to be a royal cluster. It was always the little unassuming projects that turned out to be problematic. After he had signed the contract, it was all downhill from there. He had set up a meeting with the program manager that was running the project for the college to discuss unforeseen scope, but had been met with a disdain that bordered on open hostility. It didn't make sense. He pulled out his contract and read it again carefully. It was rather vague on provisions for how to handle the issue at hand. He also reread his own proposal to see if he had excluded the type of scope creep he was facing. He sort of had, but as he had not known it was going to be an issue he had not addressed the specifics. How could he have excluded it? He didn't know it was going to be a problem.

The project involved renovating the lobby of the administration building. There were several obvious issues that needed to be rectified, in addition to upgrades to finishes that the college wanted, in order to accommodate the public and to be in compliance with the Americans with Disabilities Act. One was the reception counter which could not accommodate a person in a wheelchair. Another issue was a non-compliant drinking fountain that posed a hazard to people with impaired vision. The front door was not compliant, but could be mitigated with an automated door opening mechanism. And then there was a short flight of stairs that required a lift.

He had set about to start the design process and had met with college personnel several times only to discover as he dug into the original drawings for the building, that the lobby had been "de-rated" as a result of a previous project. The lobby, which functioned as part of the building's egress system, had its plaster ceiling removed. Apparently, the architect for that project had thought that the lobby would be more interesting without its low plaster ceiling. Unfortunately, the ceiling was part of a fire rated assembly and with its removal, the lobby could no longer function as part of the emergency egress system. So the college would have to reinstall the ceiling or install fire sprinklers. And this would have to be accomplished under a new version of the building code rather than the one under which the building had been constructed many years before and other "code-related issues" would probably be found and altogether it was going to be an expensive fix.

While none of this was Neil's fault, he could not get his project approved through the State Architect's office if he did not have the proper paperwork showing that the previous project had been constructed per the approved drawings and the building code in effect at the time. The issues associated with the removal of the ceiling had been discovered at the time the ceiling was removed but had not been resolved. This put the project it was a part of into a bureaucratic limbo from which it had not emerged.

None of this had been disclosed to Neil and it should have been pretty obvious that the issue was the college's and not his. But the program manager seemed determined to make it his problem and had threatened to withhold payment on his outstanding invoices if he didn't buckle under and fix the problem as part of his project at no additional cost. So it was looking like a fight lay ahead. A design fix could not be generated without additional consultants and his fee was already too tight. He had been selected because he had proposed the lowest fee. So he had no additional money in his fee for more consultants. He could hire the consultants and lose money or he could stop the project and get his attorney involved and lose money that way. Either way, it was not pretty.

While Neil was fighting fires on multiple project fronts, Shelley dropped a bombshell in his lap by announcing that she was quitting. Beyond being indispensable around the office, she had become an important part of his mental well-being. The single last bright spot. A source of comfort and solace.

After his release from jail, she had been the one to pick him up. She arranged for his attorney, and had managed to find a good one, he thought. She had been a patient, understanding friend and lover through this most recent mess.

"How could she go?" he thought. He needed her desperately.

"So there is nothing I can do or say to change your mind?" he asked.

She shook her head. "I need to get my career back on track," she said. "You've been great and I have enjoyed working here, but it's time."

"Shelley, I really need you. I need you to stay." He paused. "Is this about us?" he asked.

He thought maybe this was a way to breakup without having to actually say so.

"No, Neil. You have been great. I mean, it may sort of be about you. Working here has helped me understand what I want. I could stay here. It's comfortable. You're fun to work with. It's pretty uncomplicated and until recently, there has been no stress. But there is nowhere to go with this job. I'm not an architect. After working here, even if that had ever been an option, and we both know it's not, I would not want to do what you do and put up with what you have to put up with for the kind of money you make. As I have watched what you face here in the Valley trying to build a business I just realized that I want to accomplish some things on my own terms and I don't think I can do it here."

"Here, as in 'with me,' or here as in 'the valley'?" he asked.

"Both."

He nodded, thinking about what her leaving would mean for him in terms of his practice, his legal hassles, and for him in terms of their relationship. He wasn't ready to get super serious as in getting remarried. He had thought they were on the same page about that, but maybe that was it. But then, Shelley was open enough about things that if she had wanted to get hitched and start a family he knew that she would have pretty much put that out there front and center.

"So this is not about us?" he asked again.

"No," she said.

"Is it about the arrest?" he asked.

"Of course not. I know you didn't do it," she paused. "It's about me. I need to move on. Not away from you, but I know you can't leave what you have here. It may not be everything you had hoped for, but starting over somewhere else is not really in the cards, right?"

Neil nodded and shrugged.

"The timing sucks." he said. "Having you go at all sucks. I don't want you to go. Everything seems to suck right now and losing you is . . . ." He didn't finish the sentence.

"And I can't support you. Either here or wherever I land, so that won't work either," she said.

"Yeah. I need a rich wife or mistress to support my architectural 'habit'. A patron," he said. She didn't laugh at his attempt at humor.

"So what are you going to do?" he asked trying to cover his emotions.

"I think I will go to New York. When I went to college, I thought I would get a job working on Wall Street or for a Fortune 500 company or something. I just think I need to get back to it before that door is closed. This is just too comfortable. You are just too comfortable. I could stay here. We could settle down and have kids. But that would be it. No career. All that education, just to be an architect's book keeper."

"Ouch. You make it sound so limiting. I guess I didn't realize that this was such a downer."

"Neil, it's not like that. And that's not what I said," she said in a scolding tone of voice.

"I don't know exactly what to say. I don't want you to go, but that is just my selfishness talking. I need you here at the office. I have enjoyed our relationship. I need our relationship. I am better at everything with you around. You have filled a part of my life that was empty for a long time. But I also want you to be happy." He paused for several moments before continuing. "If this what you need to do, then it's what you should do. But it sucks for me."

She leaned in and gave him a hug. "I'm sorry Neil. I need to try this. I need to take a risk with my own career. How will I know if I don't try?"

"You're right," he said in a wounded voice.

Neil wasn't convinced by her logic. They had fallen together and now it looked like they were going to fall apart.

"You can come visit me in New York and I can come back once in a while," she said.

"Right," he said without conviction. "It won't be the same. But I'll most likely be here slogging away or I'll be in jail."

They embraced for a long while.

"So when are you pulling the plug?" he asked.

"I know I should give you a couple of weeks, but I thought I would start packing up my office tomorrow. "

"What! Tomorrow?!" This caught him by surprise. "Can you stay until the end of the week at least? It's going to take me a couple of days to get caught up on the billing and stuff. Actually, I need you to stay through next month's billing. Or why don't we just say you'll stay until the end of the fiscal year. That's only a couple of more months."

"Nice try," she said.

"Isn't there anything else I can do to convince you?" he asked.

"You can try. There is that one thing you do that might work," she said with a laugh.

She packed her stuff with her usual efficiency and he had to start answering his own phone.

«»«»«»

Jennifer Singh had not heard from Marcus Little for several weeks. She was not sure what was happening or what she was supposed to do. She had not heard from Steve Jordan either. She was just sitting down to draft an e-mail to Marcus when an e-mail popped up from Steven.

> **----Original Message----**
> From: Steven Jordan
> To: Jennifer Singh
> Sent: 1:59 PM May 8
> Subject: Auction
>
> Jennifer,
>
> Is everything still on track?
>
> Thanks.
>
> Steven
>
> ----

She sent the message to Marcus asking if he had further instructions. Her auction was scheduled for late May and she needed to print the catalogue and announce it. If the Edgar Payne was to be included she needed to know soon.

Marcus didn't bother to reply by e-mail. He picked up his phone and called her.

"Jennifer, it's Marcus Little," he said.

"Hi. I thought you had forgotten me," she said.

"Not even," he said. "It's been busy out here. What's the drop dead date for including the piece in the auction?" he asked.

"If you are going to do it, I need to know by the end of the week," she replied.

"The thing is, that piece was in the press 10 years ago as being stolen. Someone is going to remember it and make a fuss about it being stolen. How do we deal with that?" he asked.

"I don't think we can," she said. "If we list it and that comes out, we'll have to pull it. I would prefer not to have to do that as it makes us look like we don't know what we are doing. It wouldn't be good for our reputation."

"So what are our options?" he asked.

"I could tell them that we discovered it was stolen. I could say that we determined it was a forgery. I could say we have shown it to a reclusive private collector and that they had made an offer and would the seller consider it," she said.

"Okay. Let's consider each approach. If we say it's stolen, the seller is just going to disappear. Right? They won't ask for it back. I think given all the secrecy, they know it is stolen, either by them or by someone else or both. Right?"

Jennifer indicated she thought that was correct.

"If we tell them that it is a fake, we could send it back and try to track it. That has an upside," Marcus said. If we tell them that someone wants to buy it, they might jump at that. But I would need to figure out how to transfer the money in a way we could track it. That might be a trick. I think I like the forgery scenario better. What do you think?"

"I can create the letters from 'experts' indicating that they think it is fake," she said. "I would have to send it wherever they asked. What if they want it sent overseas?" she asked.

"There is a law against that," he said. "I'll look into that. There has to be a law that restricts the transport of . . . whatever we call it."

"If it wasn't for the fact that you wanted to use the painting as bait, you could just refuse to return it. You could claim it was stolen or something else."

"That's interesting. Just refuse to return it and let them sue you and see if you could coax out the identity in court. I like it, but I don't think it would work. What it would do, though, is make the attorney some money, assuming that the seller has money. I might be able to track the payments." Marcus was thinking out loud and talking himself into returning the painting as a fake. That seemed like it would offer the highest probability for finding the seller.

"I think we tell the attorney it is fake and ask for instruction on where to send it," he said.

Jennifer didn't really care. She would have loved to have sold it, but knew that could never happen to a piece that was known to have been stolen. "Okay. I'll do it and let you know what happens. So whatever happened to the Rembrandt?" she asked casually.

"We're still watching it," he said. "We know where it is, but no one has claimed it yet. Sort of a chess game with multiple pieces on the board."

"Listen, I want to sell that one if that is ever a possibility," she said. "I have dibs!"

"I bet you would," Marcus laughed. "I would like to win the lottery, too, as long as we are throwing our pipe dreams out there."

"I'm just going on the record."

"Noted," he said. "Let me know what happens."

"Of course," she said. "We'll talk soon."

«»«»«»

----Original Message----
From: Jennifer Singh
To: Steven Jordan
Sent: 6:04 PM May 12
Subject: Auction

Mr. Jordan,

I have some bad news. As you know we have been working to authenticate the painting. We have shown the piece to a number of experts. As I shared with you previously, it generated considerable initial excitement, but as the investigation has continued, it has also begun to generate some controversy. I did not share the concerns with you previously, as it was only a single expert and the process was not complete. However, at this point, I fear our experts have reached a consensus that the painting is a forgery.

The factors that have led each of them to arrive at their respective finding(s) are technical, but I am happy to share them with you separately. If you or the seller would like to come to New York, we could arrange for our experts to review their findings with you in person.

Or if you prefer, I will simply return the painting to you to an address of your choosing.

I am personally very sorry to have to share this news with you as I was very excited and hopeful, as was everyone at Blackbridge, about the prospects for such a promising piece of art at auction.

Furthermore, I would like to add that even though the piece is not an original by Edgar Payne, it is still a lovely work of art and could be proudly displayed for what it is. I think there must be an interesting story behind the work and the accomplished painter that painted such a convincing and compelling portrait.

If you would like to discuss this further please call me.

On another topic, I am very interested in continuing to explore how we may be of assistance to you and your client regarding the sale of the Rembrandt. We need to have the work authenticated as well and suggest that you send it to our preservation/restoration unit in New York to start that process at your earliest convenience. I know that the disappointment of our findings about the first painting may diminish your client's desire to pursue the sale of another piece, but the chances that a second painting would fail the authentication process seem extremely remote.

Please tell me how you would like to proceed.

Regards.

Jennifer Singh

Steven Jordan read the e-mail with considerable alarm. "Great," he thought sarcastically. If the painting was a fake, there would be no commission for him. He couldn't imagine anything good coming out of this new wrinkle. He sent the message on to the seller and waited.

It took a week before he received a reply.

Have Ms. Singh send the painting back to us. Address to follow.

"Okay. Whatever you say," Steven muttered to himself as he drafted the e-mail to Jennifer.

----Original Message----
From: Steven Jordan
To: Jennifer Singh
Sent: 11:26 AM May 18
Subject: Painting

Jennifer,

Instructions for return of painting to follow.

Thanks.

Steven

«»«»«»

Derek and Georgia decided that they needed a change of scenery. They had been in San Francisco for most of the winter and as it was warming up in New York, they thought it would be nice to get back to civilization. Georgia was putting the last of her things in her luggage when Derek returned from the lobby. He handed Georgia a note that had been left at the reception desk addressed to her.

She read it and asked if this was some kind of joke?

Derek had sat down and was watching Georgia intently.

“No, I don’t think so,” he said.

“Well, why not? Let’s do it. They belong to me anyway, don’t they?”

The note had offered to send Georgia five paintings from David’s collection in return for $1 million in bitcoin. After that, if Georgia was interested, there were two additional paintings she could have for $1 million each - again in bitcoin.

“Someone got into the vault,” Derek said. “And they got whatever was in there. I don’t know. There may have been more than seven paintings. A million is a lot of money for something you have never seen. They could be worthless.”

“David didn’t collect paintings that were worthless. He spent a considerable amount of money on artwork while I was with him. I went to several auctions with him. I thought they were boring at the time. The most fun was the first time when he let me bid for him. We bought an old painting for $6 million.”

“What was it,” Derek asked?

“I don’t remember. It was an old painting of a king or something.” She looked at Derek.

“What? Why are you looking at me like that? It was just a painting, hun. He had lots of old paintings,” she said. “Besides, if they were junk, why would he have kept them in the vault? No I think they must have been special.”

“Maybe. Still a million is a million,” Derek said.

“I’ve got a million. You like to tell me about investing. This is a kind of investment. I bet $1 million gets us $10 or $20 million in art. Once it’s ours, we can sell it.”

Derek had not known how they were going to liquidate anything they had managed to take from David. That was a problem for another day. The real gold mine would have come if the estate had been decided in Georgia’s favor. Without that, the paintings represented a second way, but nowhere near as lucrative as getting all or even a piece of David’s estate.

“Derek, honey. Just take care of this for me, okay?” she said in her best pouty-voice.

He nodded and thought about all the ways this could go wrong. He had not told Georgia about what had happened in the chateau.

Derek got up and pulled her laptop from a case. He opened it and began typing on the keyboard.

"What are you doing?" Georgia asked.

"Setting up an account to move some of your money around. Before we do this deal, I want some proof. But I'll get it set up first."

The note had said that if they agreed they should send their cell phone number to an e-mail account and download an encryption app. Derek did both. He e-mailed the seller Georgia's cell phone number and then downloaded the app onto Georgia's phone. While he waited, he opened an electronic wallet account on a bitcoin trading site. He then wrote down what he wanted Georgia to say and then called Georgia's personal account executive at her bank in New York.

Her personal banker was an earnest young man. He was not going to be excited about Georgia transferring three million dollars into bitcoin. There was nothing illegal about it but the transaction would be reported to the Treasury Department and the IRS, just as it would be if Georgia opened a brokerage account with an investment broker. Moving money tripped certain reporting requirements. But once the money had been transferred into bitcoins, it would become almost transparent.

It was before noon on the West coast so the bank was still open in New York, but they did not have much time. Derek called down to the front desk and told them they had a change of plans and would be staying at least a few more days. The hotel clerk graciously accepted the news and asked if they needed anything sent to their room. Derek told her that they were fine for the moment, but they would need housekeeping to come by later to freshen things up.

As the banker's phone rang, Derek handed the notes to Georgia. She had a direct line to her banker. He placed Georgia's phone on the coffee table between them with the speaker phone turned on.

"Hi this is Gordon," the voice on the other end said.

"Gordon, honey, this is Georgia Johnsson. How are you sweetie?"

"Mrs. Johnsson. I'm fine. Thank you for asking. How are you and more importantly, what can I do for you today?" Gordon, though young, had mastered his role quickly and had the patter down to an art form.

"Gordie, I want to move some money into a new account," Georgia said.

"Okay, Mrs. Johnsson. Do you have the routing number?"

"I sure do sweetie," she replied. "Are you ready?"

"I am. Fire away," he said.

Georgia read off a long list of digits that Derek had written down for her. When she was finished Gordon read them back to make sure he had written them down correctly. He then asked for the name of the bank and a contact person and phone number.

When she told him it was a bitcoin exchange he did not seem concerned. When she told him how much she wanted to transfer, he hesitated.

"Mrs. Johnsson. That is a lot of money. As your personal banker, I feel I need to ask you if you have considered the risks of transferring this much money into a bitcoin account. Bitcoin has been fluctuating quite dramatically over the last year and you could potentially lose a significant percentage of your money."

"Oh yes, Gordie. I knew you would be concerned, but I have thought this through very carefully and everything is going to be fine."

"Mrs. Johnsson. I have a number of clients that are moving funds into bitcoin accounts. Some are doing this because they like the convenience and simplicity of doing business in bitcoin, but there are others that are moving money into bitcoin as a speculative hedge. I don't know how closely you have been monitoring the secondary market for bitcoins, but it has been very volatile lately. If you are making this transaction for the purposes of investing, I would like to recommend that you discuss this decision with one of our financial advisors. They would be happy to answer any questions you may have about bitcoin investing."

Derek shook his head "no".

"Gee, Gordon. That is what I love about you. You are always watching out for me. But I am not really interested in this money being used for investing. Well, maybe some of it, but I just think it would be easier sometimes to make purchases in bitcoins."

She had no idea what she was talking about, but it seemed to placate Gordon so he said he would go ahead and make the transfer.

"Oh thank you, Gordie," she said.

Derek was scribbling a note which she read. "Oh. Do you think the transfer will go through today?" she asked. "Today or first thing in the morning?" she repeated. "Okay. Great. Thank you, Gordie. How is your mother?" She always asked about his mother, for some reason. "Oh good, good," she said. "Thank you. Good bye."

Derek hit the end call button on her phone.

"All right. We'll be in business soon," he said.

They sat in the room watching Georgia's phone for an e-mail or other message on the new encryption app he had downloaded. Nothing came through. They decided to have lunch, and since the room had not been cleaned, they called housekeeping and informed them that they would be stepping out.

They called down to the bell captain and had him order up a private car. He called back in a few minutes and they went downstairs.

They had been seated at Georgia's favorite restaurant for less than five minutes when they received a message.

Are you ready?

Almost. Want visual proof. Will transfer funds as each painting is received. $200k each.

They waited several minutes before they received a reply. They did not know if this was because the person on the other end was considering their terms or if they had not been able to respond, or if that is just how long it took the encryption software to do its thing.

Will send photos. $200k each for each of first three. $400k for number four. Number five sent when funds clear. Will discuss final two after that.

Okay.

«»«»«»

Jennifer Singh called Marcus.

"So our buddy Steven responded that the seller wants us to ship the painting back and to wait for instructions."

"That's it?" he asked.

"Yep," she said.

"I will send someone over with the crate I want you to use. We want to hide a tracking device in one of the wooden planks," he said.

"Better get it going. I could receive the address at any time."

"I'm on it."

«»«»«»

First thing the next morning, Georgia received an e-mail confirmation that her transfer had taken place. At around 10:30 a.m. they received five photo attachments to an encrypted message.

Derek opened each attachment. The message also contained a brief description of each painting, the artist, and the year painted. Derek then googled each artist and each painting. None of the paintings showed up specifically in a google search, but there was considerable information about each artist.

Paul Cézanne was a post-impressionist painter who rose to prominence in the late 19th century. There were ample visual examples of his work online and details of several pieces sold at auction that confirmed the worth of an authentic piece. The image he received of the painting being offered was of a nude woman reclining on a settee.

Derek recognized the painting by Jan Vermeer. He had not spent a lot of time looking at art, but somehow the Vermeer stood out as something he recognized. Perhaps it was the perfection of the painter in capturing light and reflections on objects. The image included in the group was of an interior still life table setting.

The painting by Viǵee-LeBrun was a portrait of a young woman. It appeared to be very old. While he could not find the same image, the one he was sent seemed to be very similar to the paintings online. Viǵee-LeBrun painted in the late 18th and early 19th century and was quite accomplished, although she did not receive as much recognition as her male contemporaries. According to what he could find online, her work was gaining in popularity for its long overlooked excellence.

He had no problem finding information about Peter Paul Rubens. Clearly any work by him was both highly collectable and valuable. The same was true for the Frans Hals, a Dutch master that painted in the early to middle part of the 17th century.

He wondered who they were dealing with. David's brother? Someone from one of the contractor's crews? He didn't know who they were, but they had beaten him to the punch on getting inside the vault.

Derek transferred $200 thousand from Georgia's bitcoin account into the electronic wallet of the seller. It took a few moments for the transaction to be authenticated. Derek wondered if they had just been scammed. There was only one way to find out, and the upside seemed to be worth the risk. The first painting being offered was the Cézanne. Derek had checked and other works by Cézanne had sold at auction for upwards of $6 million. So it seemed like $200 thousand would be a reasonable investment, if the painting was delivered as promised. If it was a scam, it was only a $200 thousand scam and Georgia could afford that.

The next morning, they received a call from the hotel concierge. He said that a package had been delivered for Mrs. Johnsson care of the hotel. He wanted to know if Mrs. Johnsson had any instructions?

"Bring it up, Harold," Derek said. "I think Mrs. Johnsson would prefer to have it up here for the time being."

"My pleasure, Mr. Storque."

It took about ten minutes for the staff to bring the package up. Derek tipped the bellhop after he brought the box into the suite. It was a wooden shipping case that measured about 40 inches, by 30 inches, and was about 10 inches thick. The box was fastened with four metal straps, two in each direction. There was a clear plastic sleeve taped to the box. There was a transmittal inside that indicated that the package was to be delivered to Mrs. Georgia Johnsson at the St. Regis Hotel. The sender was not identified.

He asked the bellhop to bring him a pair of wire cutters and a pair of pliers. That took another ten minutes and resulted in another tip.

After the bellhop left their suite, Derek began the process of cutting the metal straps. Georgia sat nearby watching the process. When the last strap had been cut, Derek removed a number of screws and then the top of the crate. The painting was encased in a foam surround that protected it on all sides.

Derek removed the foam cover, then the painting. He held it up for Georgia to see.

"It's an old painting," she said, "of an ugly naked woman!"

"What did you expect?" Derek said with a laugh. "Of course it's an old painting. This was painted about a hundred and thirty or forty years ago, at least."

"Do you think it's worth what we paid?" Georgia asked.

"I think it is worth 30 times what you paid," he said.

"Really?" Georgia squealed. "That's wonderful! How many more are there?"

"At least four more," Derek said. "You want me to send the money for the rest?"

"If it's the only way to get what David owes me, you bet I do," she said. "He owes me a lot more than this."

"All right. I'll send the next $200."

Derek retrieved her phone and sent a message with the encryption app.

First one arrived. Ready for second transfer.

It took a few minutes, but he received a reply faster than he thought he would.

Good. New information for next transfer to follow.

It took another five minutes before he received information for a new bitcoin transfer account. In the parlance of the bitcoin world, this was referred to as an electronic wallet. There were a number of clearing houses for bitcoin transfers. It appeared that the seller intended to create a new electronic wallet for each transfer. This would make it much more difficult, if not impossible, to trace the transactions. Derek wasn't fully up to speed on bitcoins, but recognized that they probably represented the future.

He transferred the next $200 thousand as before into the new wallet. He had read enough about bitcoin to know there was a public registry of all bitcoin transactions called the block chain. After the second transfer, he did some research on bitcoins and bitcoin transfers. He figured he might find bitcoin useful for a transaction or two of his own one day.

Just as with the first transfer, a delivery was made the next day. Harold, the concierge, called to inform Mrs. Johnsson that a crate had been delivered and was directed to send it up.

And as before, Derek cut the metal straps, removed a number of screws, and opened the wooden case to reveal an old painting. As before, Georgia was not impressed until Derek told her how much he thought it might be worth. She gave her blessing and the process repeated itself two more times. The last transaction was a double payment, $400 thousand. The next day two crates arrived at the hotel for Mrs. Johnsson.

《》《》《》

A message came later that morning.

> ---
>
> Assume all is satisfactory. Price for last two is $1 million each. If interested, reply. Instructions will follow.
>
> ---

Derek was inclined to send the funds, Georgia was not so sure.

"How do we know we won't get taken on the last two?" she asked. "A million each is a lot."

"You don't. But look at it this way, you have shelled out $1 million so far and are now sitting on paintings worth at least 15 or 20 times that much, or more. If you roll the dice again, you may increase your tally to 30 or maybe 50 times."

"I want to see what they are," she said. "I want to know."

"I'll ask," Derek said. "It can't hurt."

He sent the request and they waited. It took two days to get a reply and during that time they were nervous. They quarreled a bit with Georgia forgetting it was she that had insisted that they be shown images for both paintings. Derek didn't hesitate to remind her that it was her money and that he was only following her wishes. She had asked for proof and that was what they were waiting for.

"What if they don't come back?" she fretted.

"Then they don't come back. You still did pretty good."

It was late evening when Georgia's phone chirped that she had a message. It contained no message, but two image attachments. One image was of a young girl, the other was a crude drawing of a man in an old-fashioned costume wearing an outlandish hat. Or that is how Georgia would have described them.

"See! I told you we should ask for images! Who would want either of these?" she squawked.

Derek was a little more educated about art than Georgia and possessed a slightly calmer demeanor. So he said nothing and turned to the internet to see if he could figure out who the artists were. He did not know who Edgar Payne was and was unable to think of any search terms that narrowed the search. With all the famous and would-be famous painters in the world, it was difficult, without some training or experience, to identify a painter just by the style of the work. The paintings did not have any visible marks indicating who the artist might be. And even so, the images were not of a sufficiently high resolution to have made reading a signature or a mark a simple task.

The sketch of the gentleman in the ruffled shirt, with a high collared coat, a broad rimmed hat, and a rather rakish mustache and goatee, was a little easier to deduce. It did not take Derek more than about 15 minutes to determine that the sketch was, in fact, a self portrait of none other than Rembrandt himself. He sat back in his chair and thought about the piece. This one was worth many millions by itself.

"Georgia," he called.

She had been in the bathroom getting ready for bed. She came to the door of the suite that separated the bedroom from the living room.

"What is it, hun?" she asked.

"Come look at this." He had the laptop on the small breakfast table in the living room. He was wearing reading glasses, sitting in the dark peering at the screen. She walked over and looked over his shoulder.

"But that is an actual painting," she said. "Ours is a sketch."

"The image we were sent is of a sketch by the artist before he painted the final work. This is an image of the painting when it was finished."

"Still just looks like an old painting to me," she said.

"That old painting might be worth forty or fifty million," he said.

She gave the image another look.

"I like it. I like it a lot," she said changing her tune. "But the sketch is probably not worth very much."

"Here. Look at this."

Derek clicked on an open tab and the screen blinked to a different page. It was of an auction house in New York that had sold a similar sketch, several years previously. It showed the auction price of a sketch by an old master as having sold for $12 million.

"Oh. Well that's not too bad," she said. "So this could be worth that."

"Or more. No guarantees, of course."

"Okay. I get it. Tell him we want it."

Send instructions.

Fifteen minutes later, the transfer details for a new electronic wallet appeared in a new encrypted message. Derek's research had informed him that there was a way to monitor bitcoin transactions, as this was one of the security features of the virtual currency. The authentication of the bitcoins being transferred actually added unique code to each bitcoin making it more secure as the result of the transaction. Derek opened a website for following the transfers in real time as they were made.

He opened a second window and began the transfer of the final two million dollars. He then clicked to switch sites and watched as a stream of data scrolled across his screen. He had quickly jotted down his confirmation number and a long stream of digits. Looking at the torrent of numbers cascading across his screen it was impossible for him to recognize the transaction as it was coded and authenticated. It would have taken a much more sophisticated computer geek than he was to have noticed the numbers slipping by, or to have known how to capture and record the stream.

If someone had been watching and comprehending in real time what was happening, they would have seen the transfer of the bitcoin, the exact number determined by the value at the time the transaction was made, move from one electronic wallet to another. Then they would have seen that number of bitcoin split into 13 separate transfers heading into 169 successor accounts. It would have been impossible for the average person to follow more than one of the transfers after the initial split. Only a large, sophisticated company or a fully-funded watchdog agency of a nation state would have the resources to vacuum up all the data and the analysts to reconstruct the transaction, months or weeks later, as it split into successively more and more opaque routing.

Unbeknownst to Derek, there were multiple government agencies and several private companies recording every digit that was sent and received. But there was no real time intelligence to be able to parse the data stream and to know who was doing what and from where and with whom.

Eventually the bitcoin was converted into US dollars and deposited into a numbered account in the Cayman Islands. That is where the visible data stream ended. The funds, however, would continue their journey through the international finance system bouncing through two numbered bank accounts in Switzerland. The funds would be loaned to an offshore subsidiary of a bank in New York for 13 minutes, before going back to a third Swiss bank, and then end up in a numbered account in the Virgin Islands. Eventually, the money would be removed in several significant chunks of cash and physically redeposited in 7 different banks with lax banking oversight in the Caribbean.

But Derek and Georgia were ignorant of where her money went. They were busy planning how to move the paintings they had already received and thinking about the ways of converting them to cash.

«»«»«»

The next day came and went and the normal call from the concierge did not occur. Georgia was starting to worry. She pestered Derek all the next day until he relented and sent a message to the seller.

> ---
>
> What gives? Nothing has arrived.
>
> ---

Thirteen minutes later they got a response, but not the one they wanted.

> ---
>
> Patience.
>
> ---

«»«»«»

"Architecture is the learned game, correct and magnificent, of forms assembled in the light."

-- Le Corbusier

Chapter Fourteen

Jennifer Singh had grown up in London, raised by a single mother who struggled to make a living as an art dealer in one of the most expensive cities in the world.

She never knew her father and didn't know much about him other than fragmentary information gleaned from her mother over the years. Her mother had been raised in a moderately affluent family in Britain. Both of her parents were of Indian descent who had emigrated to Great Britain as newlyweds after World War II. They had arrived in England with some means and had worked hard to make a way for their children, but the entrenched social structure and the color of their skin proved to be significant obstacles to a complete integration into British society.

Determined to create a better life for their children, they sent Jennifer's mother to the United States where she studied art in New York at Columbia University and met a dashing and highly acclaimed professor. As is too frequently the case, the two developed a fondness for each other that blossomed into a romance, in spite of the young professor's existing marriage. That romance resulted in an unplanned pregnancy that abruptly ended Jennifer's mother's education. She returned to London to have and raise her daughter, never remarrying. She rarely mentioned Jennifer's distant, estranged father.

Sadly, while Jennifer completed her 6th Form, her mother succumbed to cancer. Jennifer was close to her mother and devastated by her death. Both of her grandparents had passed away years before, thus leaving Jennifer without any living relatives in Great Britain. This fact was undoubtedly an influential factor in Jennifer's decision to go to the United States for university. Unbeknownst to Jennifer, her parents had communicated shortly before her mother's death. In her father's defense, he had never been informed of the real reason Jennifer's mother had ended the affair and returned to London. It was only through the belated communication with Jennifer's mother in the late stages of her illness that he was informed that he had a daughter.

Subsequently, he had tried to reach out to Jennifer in New York, but she was not interested in developing a relationship with a long-absent father for whom she harboured many resentments.

She had attended the University of Pennsylvania and earned both a bachelors degree and a Master of Fine Arts in Art History. She landed a job at Blackbridge right out of grad school and moved smoothly up the ladder. She loved her job and loved the firm.

Now she was waiting for instructions regarding the return of the Edgar Payne painting. She was starting to wonder if the seller had bolted. After getting a good look at a Rembrandt the seller had not followed through in sending it to New York for authentication. Coupled with the recent instructions for the return of the Edgar Payne it seemed to her that the seller might be getting nervous.

She had received a visit from some geeky FBI agents who brought a new crate for the painting. She was told it contained a location transmitter hidden inside. She fretted that if it was discovered, it would be assumed she had placed it in the container and that there might be unwanted and unpleasant ramifications. The FBI agents told her not to worry as the device was a micro device nearly too small to see and integrated into the construction of the case in a way that made it difficult to find and impossible to trace. She was on the verge of calling Marcus for new instructions, but didn't need to as Steven Jordan finally responded with an address.

When she read it, she couldn't believe it. It was simply the St. Regis Hotel in San Francisco. No name and no address. That seemed pretty bizarre. Who would send a high value painting to a hotel not addressed to anyone?

After she read the message, she called Marcus.

"You won't believe where they want to send the painting," she said.

"The Louvre," he dead panned.

"Not quite. The St. Regis Hotel."

"What?"

"And, get this, addressed to no one."

Marcus was silent for a moment. "Okay. I think we are ready on our end. I understand our guys came by and gave you the new case."

"Correct."

"Then go ahead and send it," he said. "We'll be tracking it with or with out a listed recipient."

Jennifer Singh shipped a lot of art work around the country. Her team had specialized capabilities and personal relationships with the carriers that specialized in the transport of high value objects, like paintings. She called in an assistant and gave the go-ahead to start the process. "Be sure to send copies of the billing and insurance expenses to Marcus. And be sure we mark it up. We are assisting in this investigation, but we are not doing it for free," she said.

The painting started its journey west. It left Blackbridge's highly secure shipping department via a bonded courier. From there, it went to JFK where it was placed on a direct flight to SFO via a major package shipping company. In San Francisco, it was removed from the plane and taken to a secure holding section within the cargo facility. The next morning, another bonded courier with an FBI agent riding along for good measure, picked up the painting and delivered it to the St. Regis Hotel by 10:00 a.m.

«»«»«»

Keith handed the keys to his Mercedes-Benz SLS AMG GT to the valet attendant and walked to the elevator. The private investigation firm's office was on the 19th floor of a tower on Market Street. When he left the elevator lobby he was greeted by a member of Kurtz-Wilder's staff and shown to a smallish conference room. He declined the offers of water or coffee and stood absorbing the view for a few moments until Joshua Wilder gently closed the door behind him.

"Mr. Johnsson," he said as a greeting.

Keith turned. "Morning," he said in a tone of voice devoid of emotion. "What have you got?"

Joshua Wilder motioned for Keith to be seated. He took a seat himself and slid a bound leather portfolio across the conference table toward Keith. Wilder was a founding partner of the firm. He was in his late 60's, but would have passed for a man 15 years younger.

"We have found a few things of interest," he said. "It's all in the report."

Keith was thumbing through the portfolio looking for a summary or something to justify the hefty fees he was paying these guys.

"Okay, let's hear it," Keith said.

"As you know," Wilder began, "you requested, in addition to the broader investigation into your brother's death, that we look into your brother's wife and companion."

Keith momentarily paused his page flipping and gave Wilder a look of annoyance. The mere reference to Georgia was immediately annoying to Keith. Coupled with a mention of her 'companion,' and his annoyance bordered on anger.

Wilder continued.

"We placed a tail on her immediately. We also took a room in the hotel where she and Mr. Storque are staying and have been monitoring their movements. Through various means that are better not discussed, we have also been intercepting some of their electronic communications," he said.

Keith put the portfolio down. Mr. Wilder had gained his full attention.

"I won't go into all the details, as much of what we have observed is entirely mundane. Every detail, however, has been provided in the report before you," he said gesturing at the now closed portfolio in front of Keith.

"The most interesting thing we have learned is that she has moved several million dollars into a bitcoin account."

"What?!" Keith exclaimed.

"There is more. Apparently, she has been using these funds to buy several works of art."

Keith felt as though a bolt of electricity had struck him in the back of his head. "I'll kill her!" he said involuntarily.

"Calm down," Joshua Wilder advised in an even voice. "You have only heard the first part of it. She seems to be under surveillance by the FBI. They are actively watching the hotel."

"How do you know this?" Keith demanded.

"You are paying me to know this. Look," he said pausing, "we have eyes and ears in the hotel and we have used your funds judiciously," he said.

"How?" Keith wanted to know.

"You know better than to ask that question," came the reply.

"You're right," Keith sighed. "I don't need to know."

"There is more. The FBI has been watching a painting being held in the hotel safe. It's a small one."

"Probably the Rembrandt," Keith muttered.

"What? Do you know the piece?" Wilder asked.

Keith nodded. "If these are David's, the one in the safe is a Rembrandt. It was one of his favorites. Probably the first piece in his collection. Georgia banished it when she learned his first wife had given it to him," he said. "So what else?"

"The paintings she has been purchasing have been delivered by a bonded courier service. We have traced it back to a company in Richmond."

"Where's that?" Keith had never heard of it and had not spent much time in California beyond going from the airport to the Napa Valley.

"It's across the bay."

"So tell me you know who has the paintings and who is selling them to her," Keith demanded.

"Not exactly. We are on it, though. I have a couple of people looking into that now, but so far, we are not seeing anything unusual coming into the warehouse. Additionally, we are not able to track every delivery coming and everything going out. We are able to see that what shows up at the hotel has come from their warehouse," he said.

"How is the security at the warehouse?" Keith asked.

"It's solid. Besides, there are easier, less messy ways to find out what is going on in there than that."

"Then do it," Keith said. "I'll pay your expenses."

"I thought you might feel that way. We have already started putting out the feelers."

"How long do you think it will take?" Keith's impatience had not diminished with time.

"It's anybody's guess," Wilder replied. "But we will watch closely." He changed the subject. "I need you to tell me about the paintings. How many are there? What are they? It will help us understand the likely sequence."

"Okay," Keith said. "David bought a lot of paintings. Mostly before we reconnected. He had extensive lists and everything is accounted for except eight paintings. I gave him one of those and I'd kind of like it back."

"What is it?" Wilder asked.

"Doesn't really matter does it? It's a painting. I'm a sentimental guy."

Wilder shrugged and Keith continued.

"David told me once that he had an old guy, an art dealer, helping him decide what to buy. I guess he helped David buy a lot of the pieces. David paid him for his help by helping this guy buy pieces of art he wanted, but couldn't afford otherwise. I think he said the deal was that if the old guy wanted a piece, David would back off. If the guy didn't have enough credit from previous commissions, David would help out and the guy would keep the art until he died or something and then David would get it."

"Did you tell the police this information," Wilder asked.

"Nah," Keith said.

"Why not?" Wilder wanted to know.

"Screw the police and the FBI. They can do their own job," Keith said with obvious contempt.

"So what else? Wilder asked.

"David also told me there was this one really big piece that the guy wanted," Keith said.

"And?" Wilder asked.

"And David helped him buy it," Keith replied.

"So what was it? How are we going know if it is one of these pieces?" Wilder asked. "And does it make a difference, either way?"

Keith shrugged.

"If these people got it, I doubt they will sell it to Georgia," he said.

"Why's that?" Wilder asked.

"Because she doesn't have the cash for it, even at a deep discount, unless she gets David's money, and so far that ain't happening."

"So what's it worth?" Wilder asked, not really caring.

"Something like $300," Keith said without a trace of emotion.

"Three-hundred thousand?" Wilder asked in disbelief. He knew from what Keith had told him that Georgia had that kind of money.

"Hell no," Keith said almost angrily. "$300,000,000!"

"Oh," Wilder said in a matter-of-fact tone, as if the information had been plainly in front of him. "That is big."

They were both silent for a moment.

"You know, people get murdered for a lot less than that. Who else knew he had it?" Wilder asked.

"I don't know," Keith said shaking his head. "That's the problem. I don't even know *if* he had it. It doesn't appear on any of the insurance lists. David had a separate spreadsheet, but I'm not even sure Lydia knows about it."

"What was it?" Wilder asked finally.

"A work by Michelangelo di Lodovico Buonarroti Simoni," Keith said by rote.

"You surprise me," Wilder said.

"Why? Because I know the name of one of the most famous painters to have ever lived?" Keith asked.

"I guess. Yeah. Most people don't know his full name. I mean I didn't. I mean I don't. I assume that's right," Wilder said trying to cover for revealing that he had underestimated Keith's knowledge.

Keith grunted.

"I didn't know it. But I learn fast when a painting is worth that kind of money. It's a study he did before finishing the statue of David."

It was Wilder's turn to grunt. Keith continued.

"So these rich dudes in Florence had bought a huge chunk of marble and paid to have it hauled from Carrara. They wanted a statue of David because he was an underdog that kicked ass. They were in some sort of political struggle with the Medicis or something and were trying to send them a message. Anyway, shit happened and it was left partly complete for like 35 years or so until they selected Michelangelo to finish it. The painting that my brother bought with his professor friend is of a young teenage boy in the same pose as the statue. I guess you could say it is more of a sketch, because it is not finished."

Wilder had been listening intently but had taken no notes. He didn't need to as every moment of their time together was being recorded by a very discrete and virtually undetectable audio/visual recording system. It was illegal, but then some of the other things he did for his clients happened in a grey area, so who were they to complain – if they ever did find out.

"Aren't you going to write any of this down?" Keith asked.

"It's better if I don't."

Keith nodded.

"Okay. So Mrs. Johnsson," Wilder began, causing Keith to grimace, "has received five paintings, so you think they are from David and that there may be as many as three more to go?" he asked.

Keith nodded. "Assuming they are David's".

"We don't know what paintings she has received. But there may be two more, plus the Rembrandt in the hotel safe," Wilder summarized.

Keith nodded.

"We will keep watching. We will tail the truck and see if we can get close to the driver. We'll also see what we can do about hacking into their . . . ," Wilder's voice trailed off. "We will see what we can do to monitor their internal phone and data systems," he said.

"I don't care what you do or how you do it. Just find out who is selling her the paintings," Keith said. "I'll cover everything."

"That's what I like to hear," Wilder said. "If you'll excuse me, I need to get back to some other issues. But rest assured we are covering all the bases. Oh," he said as he left the room, "please leave the report on the table when you are through looking at it. It wouldn't do either of us any good if it ended up in the wrong hands."

«»«»«»

When the painting from New York arrived, the concierge asked whom the crate was for. He was told that it was for one of the hotel's guests. It did not take much imagination on his part to realize that he only had one guest who received crates such as this. He called Mrs. Johnsson's room and was greeted by Derek Storque.

"Ah, Mr. Storque. Are you and Mrs. Johnsson expecting another crate this morning?" he asked.

"Actually, we are expecting two of them. Is there only one?" he asked.

Yes sir. Just one."

"Well, send it up.

"Yes sir. It will be up shortly."

Derek waited impatiently for the bellhop to bring the crate up. It took no more than a few minutes before there was a knock on the door to their suite.

When he answered the door, he was slightly surprised to see two other men with the usual bellhop. They apologized, but said that they were required to get a signature in order to leave the case. Derek didn't think twice and signed the paperwork. He then showed the bellhop where to put the crate. He tipped the bellhop as he left, shutting the door behind all three men.

He then called to Georgia to see if she wanted to watch him open the crate. While he was finding the wire cutters and screwdriver, he heard Georgia's phone chirp with a new message. He located the phone on one of the coffee tables and checked to see who had called him. It was another encrypted message.

"They better not being trying anything funny," he thought to himself.

Final painting at hotel. Hotel staff expecting your call.

He picked up the handset in the room and called down to the front desk. He asked for the manager.

When the hotel manager answered the phone, Derek Storque got right to the point.

"Mr. Ogilvie. This is Derek Storque. I believe you have something of mine."

"Good morning, Mr. Storque. To what would you be referring, specifically?"

"A painting. You have a painting that belongs to me." He caught himself. "Rather, to Mrs. Johnsson."

"Ah, yes. Mr. Storque. What would you like me to do with it?"

"Send it up, please."

"Very good, sir." Mr. Ogilvie ended the call and then called Marcus Little directly.

"Marcus Little."

"Mr. Little. Good morning. Your package has been claimed."

"I'm not surprised. Let me guess. Georgia Johnsson or Derek Storque."

"Correct."

"I have a team on-site. I'll be there myself in 10 minutes. Please hold on until I get there. Do you have some sort of form you can ask them to sign?"

"We do."

"Please use it. It's important in this case."

"I'll get it ready," Mr. Ogilvie said.

Derek cut off the metal straps and opened the crate. He and Georgia were inspecting the painting of a young girl, when there was a knock on the door. Derek strode to the door and opened it to find the bellhop with a small package. He reached for the package, but was handed a clipboard with a claim slip instead. He quickly signed his name and was given the package. He handed the young bellhop yet another tip.

"Thank you, sir," he said and disappeared down the hall.

He passed at least six men waiting near the elevator. He had no idea who they were, but they had a vaguely official look to them and he didn't pause to find out. Had he turned to look again, he would have seen large yellow letters "FBI" emblazoned on the back of their black coats.

The agents walked briskly toward the door to the Bay View Suite.

Derek and Georgia were examining the Rembrandt with barely concealed excitement. The sketch looked authentic and Georgia, in particular, was exultant.

"I remember this one!" she said on seeing it up close. "David had this on his dresser when we first got together. He said his first wife gave it to him and it had special sentimental meaning. I told him to get rid of it and it disappeared. This was one of his favorites!"

They were both startled when there was a loud knock on the door. Derek assumed the bellhop had forgotten something and walked to the door with a slight degree of irritation. He was not prepared to be confronted with a badge and six large men bursting into the room.

"FBI!" Marcus Little announced.

Georgia gasped and looked more than just surprised.

Someone read them their rights and both were very quickly handcuffed and seated in separate rooms, Georgia in the living room and Derek in the bedroom.

The agents quickly and methodically began their work. One of the agents had a camera and began taking numerous photos. Another sat down and began questioning Georgia, while a third agent began to question Derek. Two other agents donned gloves and began looking through the suite. Two of the paintings were wrapped in hotel bath towels and placed behind their clothing in the closet. Three others were similarly wrapped in towels and placed under the bed. The most recent arrivals were still sitting near their opened crates in the living room of the suite.

Marcus put on a pair of latex gloves and looked at each painting closely. It turned out that his transmitter was an unnecessary precaution. He picked up the Rembrandt and looked at it and decided it would be safer in its custom case. It was a deep case, deeper than it needed to be really. It did have foam in it, but it seemed like there was excess depth. He asked one of the agents if they had a flashlight and pointed the light down into the box. There was a small indentation on one side of the bottom for removing a layer of foam. He placed his finger into the slot and lifted out the bottom. He looked in again with the light pointing down into the box. There, in a custom, made-to-fit slot lay a dehydrated thumb with traces of dried blood coating the torn flesh. He called the photographer over who began taking close-up photos of the box. Marcus walked over to each of the other agents and whispered what he had found. They all exchanged glances, but no one said anything to Derek or Georgia.

«»«»«»

Derek Storque sat seething in a holding cell in the U.S. Marshal's office located inside the Federal Courthouse in downtown San Francisco. He was waiting to appear before the U.S. Magistrate, however, because the initial processing had taken so long, it was beginning to look like he was going to have to spend the night in this or some other god-awful cell. He was also waiting impatiently for the arrival of his attorney, who unfortunately had to fly out from New York. He had never been arrested before and subjected to the indignities that are routinely meted out to those deemed worthy of such treatment. It had been a long day.

First there was the arrest at the hotel which seemed to take much longer than necessary. Then there was the perp walk to a waiting FBI vehicle and a ride through traffic to the local FBI office where he was fingerprinted, photographed, and read his rights, again. He had insisted that he was not answering any questions without his counsel being present. He was then moved to the U.S. Marshal's office where he was waiting for his initial appearance before the court.

Naturally, because of the time difference between the east and west coasts, his call to his attorney was made after office hours in New York and he was reduced to explaining the particulars of his situation to an answering service. Now, it was god-knows-what-time and he was lying on a cot in a cell that was perhaps the most uncomfortable thing he had ever laid on. The food the U.S. Marshal offered him was pathetic. The whole experience was a living nightmare.

He had no idea where they had taken Georgia. She might be in a cell elsewhere in the same building for all he knew, or out for a lovely meal and drinks drowning out and forgetting the day's unsavory events.

When the FBI burst in on them, he and Georgia had been immediately separated in their suite in the hotel so he had not been able to tell Georgia to keep her mouth shut. He was worried she would start blabbing and try to pin everything on him. He had been careful to make sure that she had personally been the one to pull the trigger on anything that came close to crossing the line of legality. But he had been by her side and had been complicit in her attempt to get her hands on any and all of David's estate. At least he had a good personal lawyer and was developing a short memory.

The FBI had tried to question him at the hotel, but they didn't know who they were dealing with. They read him his rights and he remained silent except to insist on contacting his attorney. Georgia on the other hand had been wide-eyed with fear. She had remained quiet while casting furtive glances in his direction, but they had not been able to speak. He hoped she would keep it together, but feared she would not. He focused his thoughts, as the lawyer he was, on the case against him, the case against Georgia, the case against them both, the case against him if she implicated him, the case against her if he did the same. None of the possible outcomes were good, but some were worse than others. His days as an attorney would be over if convicted. He had some money put away, but an aggressive defense would put a significant dent in that. Had he been able to get more money out of Georgia he would have been better off, but he had managed to siphon what he did without her knowledge or leaving a trace. He turned all the scenarios over and over in his mind until he was eventually rescued temporarily by sleep.

For their part, Marcus and his team of agents had photographed the hotel suite and collected evidence that would establish that a certain Georgia Johnsson Calhoun and her associate Derek Altus Storque had been in residence at the hotel for some time and were present when the FBI had raided the suite. His agents took photos of the paintings and dusted them for prints. They collected all of Georgia and Derek's personal effects, cataloguing everything. The laptop and cell phones were placed in separate evidence pouches for further examination at the crime lab. Eventually, all the necessary procedures were completed and the suspects were removed from the premises by separate teams of agents. Everything was packed up and moved to FBI vehicles for a short trip across town to the FBI's San Francisco office. Eventually, everything taken from the suite would be re-catalogued, photographed and either sent to the FBI's crime lab in Virginia for further forensic examination, or simply held in a crime evidence locker pending handing the material over to the Assistant US Attorney for trial.

It had been a hectic day for all involved and while the U.S. Marshal's office had tried to get Derek and Georgia before one of the U.S. Magistrates, it didn't happen. Derek was awakened by one of the U.S. Marshal guards and instructed to stand near the edge of the cell with his back facing the guard and his hands behind his back. He groggily did as he was asked and was soon rewarded with the cold pinch of a set of handcuffs. The door to his cell buzzed and then opened. The guard and a companion entered the cell and soon he was also sporting a set of leg irons. You would have thought he had committed some heinous crime and was some sort of violent felon. Momentarily he found himself waddling down the corridor that ran between cells. After a seeming eternity, he was brought to an elevator and then out into a secure sally port to a waiting van. He had managed to learn that he was being taken to the San Francisco County Men's Correctional Facility for the night – or whatever was left of it. Because San Francisco is both a city and a county, his accommodations for the night would be courtesy of the County of San Francisco. If he thought the U.S. Marshal's holding cells were awful, his next stop was, he thought, a descent to hell itself. He was glad he had managed to get a bit of sleep before landing in the County facility. He was certain he would not sleep the rest of the night.

The next morning the process was reversed. He was summoned fairly early, although he had no idea what time it was until he was out of the holding cell. He was directed to a shower facility where he was given the opportunity to take a short shower in what was the dirtiest shower he had ever seen. He did not take off the standard issue flip flops for fear of what he would catch by stepping on the wet floor. However, it woke him up and washed away some of the exhaustion that marked his countenance. He had been given a small plastic bag with a little speck of soap, a safety razor and a bit of squeezable gel for shaving, and a disposable comb. He was instructed that each of the items in the bag had to be returned to the bag when he was done. And sure enough the guard checked the bag to ensure that all the contents were back in it before he was allowed to leave the small shower cubicle. His attire for the day looked to be a festive, but clean, orange jumpsuit.

After a quick breakfast in a large prison cafeteria of more pathetic food and something dark and watery that they assured him was coffee, he was reintroduced to his handcuffs and manacles. After waiting again for what seemed like forever, he was escorted back to a bus and taken to the U.S. Marshal's office. While he had no idea of the time, his morning activities had brought him back the federal courthouse in time to be ushered into a court room for a 9:00 a.m. appearance before the magistrate.

As he hobbled into the courtroom, he could see that Georgia had arrived before him and appeared not to have managed to find representation before the hearing. Derek scanned the room and was relieved beyond words to see his attorney sitting at the defendant's table reviewing the paperwork containing the charges.

Georgia looked over her shoulder as he shuffled in. From the look on her face, the lack of makeup, and the uncharacteristically disheveled appearance of her hair, he could see that she had endured her own level of hell leaving her marked beyond the mere physical toll of a night without much sleep.

The judge entered and they all rose to their feet.

«»«»«»

Neil sat at his desk staring at his computer screen. It showed his account balances, or rather what was left of them. Unopened bills sat in a haphazard stack to one side of the keyboard. Invoices from his consulting engineers, bills from utilities, the mortgage for his office, the mortgage for his land, an invoice for his architectural license fee, a quarterly life insurance payment, . . . he didn't need to open them to know he was screwed. The newest addition to the stack was an invoice from his defense attorney.

He was on thin ice financially. After his arrest, his expenses skyrocketed while his cash flow had fallen off a cliff. He had found it difficult, with Shelley's departure, to keep track of his accounting and get the work done on his projects. He was lucky to have projects, but the lag between getting them and collecting for the work he did created an inevitable period where there was little money coming in. To make matters worse, his focus on the work and inattention to sending out invoices just made the problem worse.

He sat back in his chair and scratched the stubble on his unshaven chin. He had not left the office in a week and had taken to sleeping on the sofa. He had been wearing the same faded pair of jeans and a rumpled shirt for the past three days, at least. Or was it four days? He couldn't remember.

He only had to clean up and get presentable on days when he had a meeting on-site with a client. In between, he didn't bother to shower or dress up.

He was momentarily startled by movement and the crossing of a shadow across his front porch and then the abrupt, although polite, knock on the front door.

He got up and walked to the door, opening it to find Lydia Mankovich staring at him in surprise. The look of surprise quickly faded as he smiled and welcomed her into the office.

"Good morning," he said in embarrassment, knowing he looked the wreck. "Come in. Come in."

Lydia stepped through the doorway peaking into the darkened interior. "Have I come at a bad time?" she asked.

"No. Of course not. Come in," he said yet again.

Lydia looked around the office taking it all in. It was quite a different scene from her last visit. In polite terms it would have been described as reflecting the creative energy of its occupant. Papers were strewn about, articles of clothing were hanging over furniture. A vacuum, which did not seem to have been used, sat in the middle of the room.

In less polite terms, it would fairly have been described as an unholy mess. A man-cave. A disaster.

Lydia's quick survey had not missed the fact that Shelley's office sat dark and empty.

"Where is your assistant?" she asked.

Neil had followed her gaze and knew what she must be thinking as he understood the reality of the cluttered scene through her eyes.

He motioned for her to follow him and cleared a spot for her to sit down in his office. He tossed a jacket and a pillow aside and made a seat for himself before speaking.

"Yeah. She quit," he said looking around. 'Kind of obvious, huh?"

"Well, to be honest, your office seems a little less organized than the last time I was here," she said. "Is everything all right?"

Neil looked at her not quite sure if he should laugh or cry - but certain he wasn't going to tell her how bad things really were.

“I have been so busy that I have not taken the time to tidy up. Clearly, I’ll have to do that,” he said. “It will be tough to replace her, though. She was great.”

“So what happened? Where did she go?” Lydia asked with seeming genuine interest.

“Not sure exactly. She said New York, but she hasn’t called, so I am not really sure,” he replied.

“New York?” Lydia said in surprise. “Tell her to call me. I could use a good assistant. You know, I am splitting my time between here and there. David’s affairs were so complicated. I had no idea. So I have been spending about two weeks each month there.”

Neil just nodded and gave a polite smile. He loses his bookkeeper, office manager, receptionist and lover and all Lydia can think about is giving her a job, he thought. That’s nice.

“Looks like you need to replace her,” Lydia offered.

“I do. And I will. It just takes time,” he said awkwardly, aware of the defensiveness in his voice.

They sat for a moment without speaking.

“So the reason I dropped by,” she said, “is to see if you would be willing to assist me in completing the chateau.”

Neil was stunned. “Of course. I’d love to. That would be great,” he said in rapid succession. He realized immediately that he sounded desperate.

“There are some things we would need to discuss first, of course,” he said in an attempt to recover from his embarrassment.

Lydia just smiled. “If you are too busy, I’ll understand,” she said, knowing from the look of things it could not be true.

“No, no. I like to finish whatever I start. I feel like I owe it to David to see this through,” he said.

“Good.” She reached into her purse and pulled four thumb drives, looking at them carefully.

“This one contains Volume 1 of the drawings,” she said handing him the drive.

"This one contains Volume II." She handed it to him next. "And this one contains Volume III. And this one," she said, holding it up, "contains the project specifications and all the construction related paperwork that I could find."

"So what about the contractor and the dispute about the level of completion?" Neil asked.

"I would like you to be a part of that negotiation once you have had a chance to review all the files. If we can't reach an agreement with them, I assume you can assist me in finding another contractor willing to complete the project." She looked at him earnestly. "This is what David would have wanted. I will not feel like I can rest until we have finished it."

She looked down to hide her emotions.

"I'll get started right away," Neil said. "Too bad Shelley is not here to help me," he thought.

«»«»«»

Keith read the new report from Kurtz-Wilder carefully several times. It seemed improbable, but he had to admit there was a certain convergence of data points that lent credence to its conclusions. He was sitting in the bar at Bowler's having a drink. It was just after noon, not too early he thought to settle into a nice chair with a beer, in the late spring sunlight. He had received the report via an overnight courier service earlier in the morning. He had scanned it quickly and was left with a latent sense of skepticism about parts of it. He had met with Lydia later to go over some details relating to David's estate, then decided to have some lunch. He had walked to the restaurant with the report tucked under his arm after Lydia declined to join him. As a new mom, and a single one at that, she had her hands full with caring for her new daughter, finalizing details related to David's estate, and making preparations to restart the construction on the chateau.

She had told him of her decision to hire Neil Thornton, the architect David had retained, to assist her in completing the project. Keith didn't care much one way or the other who she hired for the task – as long as it got done and was finished in a manner consistent with David's original vision.

But now as he sat sipping his beer, he wasn't sure what to think. Wilder's report suggested that a young woman fitting the description of Neil's assistant might have been a key player in sale of the art to Georgia.

Keith turned the beer glass on the table absentmindedly as he mulled over the implication of the findings contained in the report. Light scattering over the table from the cut glass went unnoticed as his mind revisited each detail and each possibility.

Wilder had apparently used his money to good effect. He knew that Wilder had learned that the FBI had been watching two of the paintings from David's vault that had been offered in New York for sale. Reading further that one of the paintings was none other than the Edgar Payne he had given to David caused Keith to break into a slight sweat as he digested the report. "The FBI is tracking the Edgar Payne. Shit," he thought. He was relieved to find out that it had been sent back to the original owner after Georgia and Derek's arrest. It looked like the FBI was not that interested in learning how a dead man had acquired a stolen painting.

The report outlined, via some facts and some conjecture, what had happened to the paintings in a reverse chronology starting with their recovery at the hotel with the arrest, working backwards through an auction house in New York. Then the trail went cold.

Where the FBI had focused on the obvious and arrested the architect, Wilder's team had turned their attention to his assistant. What they found was largely circumstantial, but it was interesting:

- Shelley Marston was 28 years old.
- Caucasian, 5'-8" in height, approximately 120 pounds, auburn hair, green eyes, wore contacts.
- She graduated magna cum laude from the University of Pennsylvania 6 years ago with a degree in finance.
- She moved to the west coast with a boyfriend starting law school at Berkeley. They dated for a couple of years while he was in school.
- After they broke up she moved from San Francisco to the Napa Valley.
- She landed a part-time job working for Neil Thornton, AIA, where she worked for 20 months. She became romantically involved with Thornton during her period of employment.
- She also worked part-time as a wine sales associate for a local winery.
- She was an avid cyclist.
- She had no prior arrests and no outstanding warrants.
- She had a clean credit history.
- She did not have a California driver's license.

Probably the most interesting part of the whole circumstantial connection linking her to David's art was that the attorney, Steven Jordan, who was the mule between the seller and the art house, was her ex-boyfriend.

Wilder had found little else to connect her other than this, but it seemed fairly likely that this was an important connection, rather than a mere coincidence.

But if this Shelley person was involved, did that mean that the architect knew more than he was saying? He had been one of the last people to see David. He had been to the chateau a couple of times before David's body had been found. His bolt cutters were found with David's body. His welding gear had been found at the location where the vault had been breached. He was at the hotel with his assistant, supposedly for his birthday, when the FBI watched the Rembrandt sketch show up. While the FBI had initially arrested him, no charges had been filed and they seemed to think he was not involved after all.

That was all a bit too coincidental for Keith. Could the architect be that brazen? Or was he that stupid? Was he just being used by his assistant or whomever she worked for? There were many possibilities to consider and somewhere within them all was a thread that connected one singular set of details into a neat, if obfuscated, narrative that would exactly match what had happened to David and how his art had been lifted. He just needed to let it all sink in, and maybe sleep on it. It was a puzzle and he was determined to figure it out.

«»«»«»

The next day, Keith knocked on the door to the house where Neil Thornton had his practice. It had not been difficult to find. He had driven past it several times during his many visits to the valley, but had never paid any attention to the sign in the middle of the lawn identifying it as an architectural practice.

Neil answered the door and seemed a little surprised to see Keith standing at his doorstep. He invited him into the office.

Keith stood in Neil's office and surveyed the space in a manner that seemed vaguely familiar to Neil and brought back a sense of something not entirely pleasant. He had tidied the place up a bit after his last visitor, but it still was not as organized as he would have liked.

"Sit down, sit down," Neil said, gesturing for Keith to get comfortable. "Can I get you anything? Some water or coffee?"

"No, I'm good," Keith said.

"So, what can I do for you?" Neil asked.

"I wanted to discuss Lydia's intention to hire you to assist her in completing David's project," Keith said. It was a plausible lie.

"Okay, but wouldn't it better to discuss it with Lydia?" Neil asked.

"No. I'm fine with you helping her get it done. I just want it done the way David planned it," Keith said.

Neil seemed relieved. "You and Lydia are on the same page on that. I told David the first time we met that I admired his vision and commitment to getting it right." Neil paused, "He seemed to be a stickler for details."

"He was," Keith said. "A real control freak." Keith looked around the office. "I'm going to bring in a security consultant from New York to advise Lydia on rebuilding the vault. She may not think it is necessary, but I want to make sure that whatever weaknesses were present in the previous design are resolved before we move ahead on that part of the construction."

Neil nodded. "Seems reasonable, but I've got to tell you I can only have one client. I know David was your brother, but the fastest way for me to get sideways with both of you is to get between you on this. So if you don't mind, I am going to have to run everything you request past Lydia. Or even better, once you guys are on the same page, just have her give me the direction. That would be the simplest thing."

"Oh, of course," Keith said. "That makes total sense. But there is one other thing I wanted to ask you. "

Neil waited.

"So you were arrested by the FBI. Have you been cleared?" Keith asked.

Neil thought he now understood the real reason for the visit. He shook his head.

"I am told by my lawyer that it is unlikely that the FBI will clear me while the investigation is going on. It's a major hassle," Neil said, realizing he sounded like he was whining. "Look. That sounded rather pathetic. Compared to your loss, my issues are nothing. But the answer to your question is 'no'."

Keith looked at him for a moment. "So what can you tell me about the day they arrested you?"

"I don't know. What do you want to know? I was at the hotel with my girlfriend for my birthday. We had gone to an architectural exhibit the day before and then spent the night. As we were checking out I noticed a man I knew as Karl Stroughman in the lobby. It turns out it was some guy named Derek Storque."

Keith nodded.

"You know him?" Neil asked in surprise.

Keith ignored the question. "How do you know him?" he asked.

"He visited my office claiming he wanted to build a winery. Said he was from the east coast."

Keith let out a low curse, "Son-of-a-bitch. What else did he say?"

"He wanted to know if I had any winery experience. We talked for a while and he said he wanted to buy land and do something similar to what your brother was doing. He asked if I had any drawings of wineries, like your brother's, that he could look at. I told him I could not let him do that without my client's approv-al."

Neil paused. "So who is he?"

"He is David's ex-wife's current boyfriend," Keith said. "I know her well enough. But I have never met him. I didn't know she had shacked up with a new guy after my brother. I was just glad David had moved on. I didn't like her much."

Neil continued his tale of being arrested.

"Anyway, I guess we were in the wrong place at the wrong time. And because I was one of the last people to have seen your brother alive, it was too much of a coincidence for the FBI."

"Did they arrest your girlfriend, too," Keith asked?

"Shelley? No. They let her go, but she was pissed."

Neil noticed the surprise on Keith's face. "What?" he asked.

"Oh, I just thought I had heard they arrested two people, so I assumed it was her, but wasn't sure," he said.

Neil seemed satisfied with Keith's lie. "No they arrested just me. It was a real pain. Have you ever been arrested?" he asked.

"No," Keith lied again. "But I imagine it would not be a fun experience."

"Exactly. And it is expensive. Innocent or not, it costs money to navigate through the process." Neil shook his head again in disbelief of what he had been through.

"So what's her take on all this?"

"It wasn't helpful to our relationship. She dumped me about a month ago and moved to New York," Neil said.

"Ouch," Keith said. "So much for loyalty."

"I'm probably putting too strong a spin on it. She said she needed to move on and get back to her own career aspirations. But her reasons didn't really add up. You know how it is when a woman wants to end it. There really isn't a good explanation. And even if there is they won't tell you anyway."

Keith nodded.

"So we split up. But it is probably just as well." Neil didn't elaborate and Keith didn't ask. In truth, Keith didn't care. His mind was jumping ahead to the possibility of tracking Shelley down in New York.

"Listen," Keith said. "Getting back to the chateau. I'll talk to Lydia and make sure she is cool with me bringing in the security guys I want."

Keith stood up and extended his hand to Neil who also stood.

"Let's make David proud," Keith said.

"Naturally," Neil said, somewhat embarrassed to have ended up their conversation on such a personal note.

"I'll be in touch," Keith said as he left Neil's office.

«»«»«»

"You know what really burns my ass? A flame about this high.... Actually, your design would look better if you turned it upside down and added a tower."

-- Roy Bennington

Chapter Fifteen

Derek and Georgia were arraigned and released on separate bail the day following their arrest. They had both endured their own separate hell after being arrested. Besides being trundled through an abrasive system of detention and conditions that were beyond abhorrent to both of them, they each faced a long night of uncertainty and mental anguish. Georgia was certain she was going to be sexually abused in some violent manner, while Derek was certain he was being compromised legally by his dim-witted co-defendant. He was not entirely sure which fate was worse, although he was prepared to defend himself against either.

The next day, after their initial appearance was complete and arrangements for their bail had been satisfied, they finally were allowed to leave. Georgia's attorney arrived late, but had managed to make housing arrangements for them. The wheels of justice being what they are, they naturally were released separately.

Once outside of the courtroom, they were whisked away in separate private cars by their attorneys. Derek's first question to his attorney was whether he had been able to find out what Georgia might, or might not, have told the FBI.

Instead of answering, his attorney held up his hand, gesturing for silence and instead asked an innocuous question about Derek's treatment. Derek understood the gesture - that their conversation might not be secure, and began a long, and authentic rant on the travails of spending the night in a holding cell in a county jail.

Georgia, for her part, sat silently, almost weeping during her ride. She didn't ask where she was being taken and didn't really care. It was all just too horrible.

Because the Saint Regis declined to extend their stay further, they were driven to a tall residential tower, with a furnished condominium that Georgia's attorney had quickly leased for a month. The terms of their bail required that neither of them leave the city on the threat of being re-incarcerated. Both had suffered enough during their short encounter with the penal system, that neither was remotely tempted to violate the conditions imposed by the court.

Georgia had arrived first and was sitting in a stupor staring into a corner. When Derek entered the condo, she didn't react immediately. She had a drink in her hand that was nearly empty. Her clothes were a rumpled mess. Derek had never seen her hair and makeup in such a sad state of neglect. She almost could have been mistaken for someone who might have been living on the street, he thought. Her attorney had been moving her things into one of the bedrooms and retuned to find Derek staring sternly at Georgia.

"You found it," he said in a statement of the obvious. He had shared the information about the arrangements for the condo with Derek's attorney as they had both waited for the process to grind to its conclusion.

Derek's attorney followed him into the unit.

"I'll have someone bring up your things later," he said.

"I could use a drink," Derek said. "What is Georgia drinking?"

"Scotch," her attorney said, gesturing toward a bar on the opposite wall.

Derek walked to the bar and poured himself a half glass and downed it straight. He found an ice bucket and poured himself another glass.

He turned back towards the attorneys.

"I have just spent the night in hell. I truly hope you have some good news," he said.

The attorneys looked at each other, each willing the other to speak, but neither one making the effort.

"Nothing?" Derek asked. "You have nothing?"

"Right now, we need to focus on the positive," one of them finally said.

"And what would that be, exactly?" Derek asked taking a long slow sip of Scotch.

"Well. You are out on bail. That's a good start," the other attorney said.

"I have no intention of doing time," Derek said. "So I suggest you both get to work immediately devising a strategy for refuting the charges. This was unlawful entrapment. We were lured into this, weren't we Georgia?"

She didn't respond.

"Georgia. Tell them. You were lured by the FBI into this whole mess."

She roused herself slightly. "What?"

Derek knew Georgia well enough to know she had access to a variety of sleeping aids and prescription pain killers. She seemed unusually groggy, he thought. Perhaps she had self-medicated using what she had available before he had arrived. An understandable, if unwise action. "Georgia. Are you all right, my dear," he said without a trace of tenderness.

"What, hun?" she replied.

"Are you all right? Do you need another drink?" he asked.

"That would be nice," she said, lifting her glass in an unstable motion.

He walked to her and retrieved her glass, handing her his.

"It looks like Georgia could use some rest," Derek announced. "Why don't you come back in the morning and we can discuss our next steps then."

The attorneys agreed and left them alone. Derek walked out to the balcony of the condominium and stared out toward the bay. It was a beautiful day. From the upper floor of the tower where their rented unit was located, Derek could see the Bay Bridge heading to the east toward Treasure Island and Oakland beyond. It was early afternoon and the sun bathed everything in his view in a warm golden light. The distant hills were still green. The bay sparkled. A few early sails dotted the water. Yet he saw none of it. His thoughts were focused on the mess he found himself in and the multiple emerging possibilities that presented diverging avenues of escape.

He knew he could not entertain any of them without knowing what Georgia might have said to the FBI. If she was silent, he had options for how he characterized his involvement, what he knew, and how much he could blame on Georgia.

On the other hand, if she had said too much or had blamed him for everything, he would have to decide how to deflect her accusations and paint her as the guilty one.

He dialed his attorney's cell phone and waited for him to take the call.

"So what do you know?" Derek asked. "Did she talk?"

He grunted. "Are you certain?" There was a pause as he listened. "Good. You had better be right. I'll call you later. She is pretty drunk at the moment and will probably go to bed early this evening. I can step out after that."

«»«»«»

Derek had met Georgia while she was still married to David. He didn't know who David Johnsson was. He didn't care. She had caught his eye over dinner one evening at his club. He was not aware that she was a member, and indeed she was not. She was simply adept at utilizing all the perks and benefits that came with being married to a wealthy man. David was the member and anything she spent went on his tab. It was a very convenient arrangement, she thought.

Because she was alone, Derek felt free to send a drink to her table. She had accepted the gesture and then invited him to join her. They had flirted shamelessly and she made no pretense of hiding that she was married, but didn't feel particularly limited by that reality. He had suggested she accompany him to his room and was surprised at how readily she had accepted. The rest was fairly automatic. She needed him and was content to have him lavish attention on her as he discreetly probed her for ways he might profit from their acquaintance besides the enjoyment he derived from routinely bedding her.

Derek quickly came to realize that David's estate dwarfed any previous machinations he might have been devising for swindling Georgia. He became even more attentive to Georgia's every need and inserted himself into every conversation and decision she made regarding David's estate.

Georgia didn't really know a lot of the specifics about David's wealth. But like anyone with time and access to the internet, Derek was able to learn a lot about David from the volumes of articles on the internet. He had learned that David was a significant collector of art. That soon became a focus of his interest. Small, high value objects that are easy to hide, move and sell had a certain attraction, compared to other forms of wealth that were harder to acquire.

He eventually read about David's construction project and decided to pay a visit before it was too far along. He told Georgia he had some business to attend to, and disappeared for a couple of weeks. He surveilled the property and when he was satisfied that he would not be discovered, he quietly toured the construction site. It wasn't a difficult thing to do, as the project had been stopped.

It was on his initial visit that he had encountered someone in the garage. He did not know who it was that was poking around. He had been in the chateau for at least an hour when he became aware that he was not alone. He had been in the underground garage looking at a curious security system when he heard footsteps. He had found a particularly dark corner in which to hide and waited, motionless, for the unknown person to leave, when instead they practically walked right into him. So he had bolted.

Not knowing if he had been identified, and seeing a lone car parked near a construction fence, he had the presence of mind to rifle through it, taking the registration. Interestingly, the car belonged to a local architect. As a precaution, he decided to pay the architect a visit, which yielded a set of drawings for the chateau that only heightened his interest in what lay behind the security system.

He returned to the chateau several times over the next week and was in the house watching from the shadows as David put paintings in the vault on several occasions. He was trying to figure out the required sequence of entry. He knew that there was a print scanner and a key and code. He hadn't worked out how he was going to get all the parts. But he felt he was very close to all the pieces he needed.

He was in the chateau on the main floor late one afternoon, when heard someone climbing the construction stairs. It was a new person. In the still silence of the cavernous space, each person brought with them a unique presence. This was not the architect, nor was it David. He listened as whoever it was stealthily climbed the stairs and quietly disappeared on one of the upper levels. While he couldn't see who it was, he had the distinct impression that it was a woman.

He froze with indecision. Should he follow? Was there something he had missed on one of the upper floors?

He had just left his hiding place and started up the stairs, when he sensed that another person was climbing the stairs below him. He froze again, trapped on the landing between floors. His body was flooded with adrenaline as he prepared for the expected fight. The sound of the foot fall was different, probably a man, and he was breathing heavily. He pressed himself hard against the shaft wall as if in the near total darkness it would make him less visible than he was.

He was relieved when the person disappeared without making a sound onto the floor he had just left. But now he was trapped with someone he couldn't see both above and below the landing.

He inched his way up the stairs, feeling his way as he moved as quietly as he could toward the landing on the next floor. He was moving slowly up the service stairs on the north side of the building and emerged onto the residential level between the private dining room and the sitting room. But not knowing where the first person had gone, he had to be careful. He stayed close to the edge of the shaft and listened, barely breathing, for several minutes.

Momentarily, he heard someone speak softly. It sounded like, "Unit two in position."

He could feel his heart rate elevate as his sense of danger grew, fearful that he might give his presence away through some inadvertent noise. He knew that the other person's hearing would eventually acclimate to the silence and his position would be betrayed by little more than the sound of his own breathing.

He could not tell where voice had come from or if they had moved. Being uncertain of their position, he dared not move.

If the people he encountered were in radio contact, it seemed highly probable that they were part of a surveillance team. Derek kicked himself for not being armed. He had not thought it necessary. He had significant martial arts training, and was confident in his abilities against an average opponent. But someone with a handgun, was well above average if they knew how to use it and did not hesitate. But at the moment he had the darkness and the element of surprise and he did not intend to surrender either advantage unnecessarily.

Time seemed to crawl very slowly. He thought perhaps an hour, maybe two, had passed. It seemed endless. He wanted to sit down, but dared not. Just as he thought that he could take scarcely more, he heard the person nearest him speak again in a pressured voice.

"I heard that, but does he have it?"

He couldn't tell if it was a man or woman. Whoever it was, they were in the private family sitting room.

"But where is he heading?" the voice paused. "All right. I'm moving."

The next sound he heard came from below him. It was the sound of heavy, rapid footsteps ascending the stairs. His position was about to be compromised. He had to move. He ducked into the pre-function alcove near the open elevator shaft between the dining room and the family sitting room, hoping that his movement would not be noticed as the surveillance team monitored the person racing up the stairs.

He assumed it was David.

Derek could not see the other person, but was fairly certain they were mirroring David's pace as his exertion from climbing the stair took its toll.

David seemed unaware that there was anyone on the floor, and when he reached the landing, he briefly turned on a flashlight to orient himself.

Derek could see in the reflected light that David was carrying a case.

As David moved his flashlight in a quick, jerky arc, the beam of his flashlight briefly illuminated the silhouette of someone hiding between the metal studs. David froze and turned his flashlight off. However, the sudden burst of light caused the black shape to reflexively step back, bumping something in the darkness that emitted a loud metallic thud.

David's momentary indecision vanished and he sprung into action.

What happened next was chaotic. From his position, Derek did not fully comprehend what occurred. But he knew David crashed through an opening in the studs and into the main corridor. His sudden motion was anything but silent as his body and the case impacted with the metal studs. His progress was momentarily slowed and then he disappeared further into the darkness.

An angry voice called after him.

"You know why I'm here, David!" it screamed.

He didn't respond and Derek thought he could hear the sound of David's running footsteps fading somewhere down the corridor.

"You can't get away!" the voice screamed.

Still there was no response.

Derek sensed David was being followed, however, he could not see or hear when the person left their position.

Derek didn't move as he quickly recalculated his options. Following was not possible without considerable risk. He assumed that there were other members of the team and that they were likely to be converging on David's position. That would mean he would confront them on their way up the stairs if he tried to escape immediately. But he did not want to be found in a vulnerable position as they mopped up their operation.

Derek's mind was racing.

His thoughts about his own escape were interrupted with distant shouting. Then the sound of running in his direction. He crouched, coiled and ready to strike, but only saw a dark shadow disappear down the stairs.

Several long moments passed as Derek strained to hear anything that might pose a threat. Then he heard a shout from below and a few seconds later he was aware of the sound of yet another person running toward his position and again he braced himself. But instead he heard shouting into the radio as someone passed him.

"Don't let him escape!" a voice screamed.

He sensed movement past his position, but it was nothing more than a dark blur.

"I don't know! But he must have the painting!"

Then the sound of a vehicle's engine revving.

Derek did not move for perhaps another five minutes. He listened carefully, but heard nothing else.

Finally, he decided he had to risk making his own escape.

He made his way slowly down one flight of stairs and eased out between the studs on the east side of the building, disappearing over the ridge into the fog.

«»«»«»

Two days later, Derek slipped back into the chateau before dawn. He used the cover of darkness and the lingering fog to his advantage. He was dressed entirely in black. He carried a small flashlight and a newly acquired 9 mm handgun. He suspected that there had been some foul play and that David might have been its victim, but he wasn't sure. He poked around on the upper levels of the chateau and was surprised to find a small stash of tools on the upper floor hidden in a wall cavity. He didn't bother to take any of them, but noted there was a sledge hammer and pair of bolt cutters, among other tools.

Derek eventually made his way through the chateau and down to the barrel room where he discovered David's body. He lay crumpled in the bottom of the elevator pit. He was laying face down as if he had done a belly flop into an empty pool. Derek stood for a moment taking in the scene. He had seen dead bodies before, a couple being the result of his own efforts. He had never met David and was unmoved by his death or the manner in which it had occurred. His primary interest was in discovering the means necessary to gain entry to the vault. He realized that David's thumbprints were never going to be more readily accessible.

He formulated a plan as he hiked back up to the cache of tools to retrieve the bolt cutters. He harvested the digits, turning over the body to search in David's pockets for his keys. As he did, he contorted David's rigid corpse, leaving his legs twisted and his torso lying completely on one arm. As he climbed from the pit, he decided to roll several barrels into the pit to conceal the body.

«»«»«»

Keith dropped by Wilder's office a few days latter to receive the next update about his investigation. He hoped there would be something new to break the investigation wide open. Thus far, it seemed to be moving very slowly.

"So what can you tell me?" Keith asked as he settled into a chair in Wilder's now familiar conference room.

"She didn't have a car registered in her name in California," Wilder said for starters, "We are checking with all the other states, but that is going to take a while. We have also been checking to see if we can determine if she flew out of either the San Francisco or Oakland airport. But that is a bit more complicated than it used to be. Since 9/11 it is difficult to get that sort information. We can still usually get it, but it takes more time and more discretion as there are multiple agencies scrutinizing who is accessing the data. But we'll get it."

Keith nodded. "What about credit cards?" He figured Wilder could get that information.

"Same issues. Nothing so far, but we'll get it. It is a bit tricky if you don't want to raise any red flags or leave a trail. I'm not going to tell you how we do it though. So don't ask," he said.

"I don't care. I've told you before. I don't care how you do it. Just get me the results."

Wilder nodded. "If she was involved, I doubt she is in New York. She wouldn't be that stupid to tell him where she was really going."

"Probably right. So where would she be?" Keith asked more to himself that Wilder.

"If you stole several high value paintings and managed to sell them, where would you be?" Wilder asked.

"Close to my money," Keith said.

"Yeah. And . . . ?"

Keith shook his head.

"You did read the report?" Wilder asked.

"Of course," Keith bristled. He resented being patronized.

"Sorry. I thought you might enjoy connecting the dots," Wilder said.

"Just tell me," Keith said.

"Bitcoins. The FBI has indicated that Georgia purchased the paintings with Bitcoins at the insistence of the seller."

Keith rubbed his face. "So it's untraceable."

"Basically. But think about it. If you scored several million dollars in Bitcoins through a transaction that was, if not untraceable, at least problematic for anyone to trace, how would you get the Bitcoins back into dollars?"

"That assumes that I would want to. You can pay for a lot of crap with Bitcoins," Keith said.

"True. But leaving that much in Bitcoins takes a true believer. The value of Bitcoins is not that stable and a collapse is possible. So if it were me, I would want to transfer a big chunk of it, or maybe all of it, back into dollars. And I would want to do that in a place that would not ask too many questions or file too many reports with the US government."

Keith was listening intently. 'So you think it's off shore. You're probably right."

"So if you wanted to disappear with your money or reconnect with it once it was wired somewhere where would you go?"

"Russia, Cypress, or the Cayman Islands or someplace down there," Keith said. "I could probably get to the Caribbean without a passport."

Now Wilder was nodding. "It's the logical place to start looking, which means it's improbable. On the other hand, if you are young and don't have the social connections that would include an attorney that you trust, or are willing to split the money with, and who is willing to go down there on vacation to take care of some business for you, discretely, then you have to go down there yourself."

"Man. That could be a wild goose chase. That might be what happened, but if she takes her time getting down there, your investigation might be six months too early and miss her."

"Or several months too late," Wilder interjected. "But from what we have been able to learn about her, she does not have the luxury of being patient. If she did this, she is going to live off the proceeds. And she may try to move the last painting, assuming she has it. My source at the FBI says they did not recover it. So if she makes a mistake, one of those things is going to potentially make it possible to find her. But I agree. If she parks the money and does not touch it, and sits on the painting, you may never find her. And if you do, you will not be able to determine she was involved," Wilder said.

"I could beat it out of her," Keith said, his anger exploding.

Wilder was quiet for a long moment before continuing. “I hope you are not going to do anything dumb in the future. I understand that you are still grieving. But think carefully about what you just said. You don’t need the money. I don’t need to be involved with a case that ends unpleasantly. If you cannot assure me that you will let the authorities handle this if we figure out who did what, then I am going to walk away today and you can keep your money.”

Keith slouched down in his chair like a scolded child. He had not had a father and was not accustomed to being spoken to by someone who sounded like a father. His history of relationships with authority figures was not positive.

He didn’t say anything. But just sat there and stared at the tabletop.

“Do we understand each other?” Wilder asked.

“Yeah,” Keith offered without conviction.

“Good. So what are you willing to pay for next? I suggest sending someone down there to ask around.”

“Fine. You go,” Keith said in an aggravated tone of voice.

Wilder considered the suggestion. He was busy running an active investigation firm and didn’t need the distraction. He had staff who could go on an extended trip, make the enquiries and get back efficiently – leaving him to manage his business. On the other hand, he hadn’t taken a vacation in a while and it might be a nice diversion.

“I don’t have the time. But I could send someone or you could go yourself,” he said.

“Why would I do that?” Keith asked.

“I think you could use a vacation,” Wilder said. “But you have to promise me you won’t do anything rash if you find her.”

“We’ll see,” was all Keith could offer.

«»«»«»

When the news of David’s death hit the papers, Georgia rushed to California to insert herself into the chaos as his wife. California being a community property state, she hoped to assert her position as the rightful heir to his estate. She had attorneys in New York contesting David’s will and the divorce papers while she played the part of the heartbroken widow. It was all so tragic.

Derek never told Georgia what had transpired at the chateau. The less she knew the better.

The days after Georgia and Derek were released from their brief incarceration, were not happy ones. Derek was fixated on planning his defense and naturally suspicious about what Georgia and her attorney might be up to. Georgia, on the other hand, set about drowning her anxiety in booze. She had sent out for a delivery service to bring her a variety of hard liquor and had amassed quite a collection in just several days time. If she had been willing to share, she could have opened a well-stocked bar.

The further she slipped into an alcohol induced haze, the more perplexed and suspicious Derek became. He knew that in addition to her supply of booze, Georgia also maintained a respectable supply of both over-the-counter and prescription pain killers. It was a lethal combination, the possibilities of which he could not ignore.

He set about his plan to simplify his legal defense by expressing his concerns about Georgia's heavy drinking to both of their attorneys on several occasions. Then several days later he arranged to meet his attorney for a late dinner to review his legal strategy. As the early evening wore on, he very helpfully kept Georgia's glass full, helping her edge closer to a state of full drunkenness. By 8:30, as he helped her transition to bed, she was pretty well gone. He had prepared a cocktail for her of a lethal dose of her prescription pain killers mixed with a half a glass of the finest whiskey on hand. He was careful not to touch the glass or the medication bottles with his bare fingers.

He sat down next to Georgia and roused her.

"Georgia, darling," he said. "I made you a night cap."

"Oh, sweetie," she said in a slow and heavily slurred voice, "that was sweet of you. You have always been so good to me."

"Here," he said carefully handing the glass to her without touching it directly. He steadied her hand as she took it and held it to her mouth. "Take a big sip, it's your favorite whiskey."

She took a long draw on the glass. "One more," he said urging her on.

She finished most of the glass and he helped her set it on the night stand. She closed her eyes and turned her head into the pillow.

"Good night my dear," he said, kissing her on her forehead. "Sweet dreams."

Derek stood and went to the kitchen where he had prepared the cocktail. He carefully removed the caps from mostly empty bottles and returned to the bedroom, he set a few on the nightstand and tossed the rest on the floor. A few pills spilled out on the nightstand and onto the floor.

After reassuring himself that he had not touched anything and that the condominium was ready for the onslaught of visitors that would be summoned later in the evening, he checked to make sure he had his phone and that Georgia's was on her night stand. He then left to join his attorney for dinner. There was no turningback now. Plan B was in full swing.

«»«»«»

The sun was setting on another perfect day in the Caribbean. The sky near the horizon was a bright yellow, but faded to a deep gold, then multiple shades of darkening blue. Large puffy clouds of grey and white stood out from the evening sky with brightly illuminated edges of brilliant white and gold. A soft, warm trade wind rustled in the brush while warm turquoise waves lapped up on clean white sand. In the distance, Shelley could hear the soft melodic rhythm of a steel drum band at Drake's floating down the beach in her direction.

She closed her laptop, shutting down her computer. She had gotten into an almost obsessive habit of checking her account balances several times a day, just to make sure nothing was amiss. So far, everything seemed normal. Her account balances at all seven banks were in line with her expectations. She had about US $400,000 in each one.

She threw her water bottle and the laptop into her bag, along with the paperback she had been reading. The nightlife was better further up the beach, but she had opted to stay in a less expensive and less touristed hotel. It was showing its age and seemed to attract the budget conscious traveler, but she didn't mind.

She had been in Saint George for about a month. Prior to that she had hopped around from island to island, never staying in one place more than a few nights. She always stayed in hotels that were off the beaten path and she always paid in cash. She had picked up a deep tan that matched her recently darkened hair color. To anyone casually observing her, she look like any other day tripper off one of the large cruise ships.

For the first several weeks she had been constantly worried that she might be followed or that when she checked her bank accounts, the money would be gone. But slowly, over several months, she began to relax and settle into her new life of financial security. She knew that her $2,977,416 would not last forever, but if she was careful it could last for a very long time. And she knew that number only because she checked it four times a day.

When she left California, she had made the rather unorthodox decision to take public transportation as far away from San Francisco as it would take her. So she had taken BART to Concord. From there she picked up a low-cost commuter bus to Sacramento. From there she had taken a hotel commuter van to the airport, where she picked up a casino shuttle that took her to a casino in Reno. She was never asked for ID or to pay using a credit card for any leg of her trip. In fact, most of her trips were free, courtesy of a hotel or casino.

When she got to Reno, she boarded a bus to Salt Lake City. From there she picked up an Amtrak train to Chicago. Someone had told her that if you got on a train without a ticket you could buy one on the train. If you only intended to go one stop, the conductor would accept cash and not ask to see identification. This proved to be true, however, it took her a good week to make it from Salt Lake City to Chicago, a trip that normally would have only taken 36 hours or so if she had gone straight through.

From Chicago, Shelley took a bus to St. Louis where she answered an advertisement looking for a cook on a barge heading to New Orleans. From there she had found her way onto a sailboat being delivered to the US Virgin Islands.

The whole trip had taken a month, but she had managed to find her way to the banks storing her newly, if illicitly, acquired wealth, without leaving a trace.

She had decided that since her money seemed to be secure it was time to head back to the States. This would require one last unorthodox mode of transportation if she was to evade US Customs and Border Protection personnel on her way back into the US. She had a plan, but needed to find the ride. So she headed back to her hotel to get cleaned up and ready for a night out.

One of the benefits of staying in one location for several days was that she had a chance to meet the locals in their favorite watering holes. It was not surprising that she had met a number of young enterprising men whose eye she had caught who also happened to own charter fishing boats. After a few drinks, which they, of course, were happy to pay for, she had come to learn all about the local waters, the best fishing spots, the length of time to travel between various ports of entry and the ins and outs of evading the US Coast Guard and even the Department of Homeland Security, when that was necessary. Although all the men said they had never needed to do that.

One of the men seemed less than convincing in his denials that he had ever personally "run" anything or anyone to shore. This was the man she would be looking for tonight, and it didn't hurt that he was also the best looking, in a rugged sort of way, of the whole lot.

Shelley showered and put on a flowered print dress and some sandals, hopping on a rented bike for a short ride to Drake's. The sultry evening air of the Caribbean perfectly matched her mood.

She peddled along enjoying the sights and smells of the evening. The ride to Drake's would only take a few minutes. Shelley's phone emitted a single, low, beep. She was startled by the unexpected sound. She had not received a call for some time. In fact, it was a pre-paid phone with fairly limited functionality. She had purchased this particular unit after arriving on Grand Cayman, using a name and address for someone on one of the islands that she had selected at random from a local phone book. She had not put any personal information on the phone, so it was "clean" with respect to anything that could be traced to her. However, she had downloaded the encryption software on the phone and had signed in once.

She coasted to a stop and reached into her bag fumbling to find the phone. When her fingers felt the familiar shape, she pulled it out and glanced at the screen. She had received an encrypted message.

> ---
>
> Clever girl.
>
> ---

Shelley froze. She had used the app to communicate with a number of people in setting up the sale and shipment of David Johnsson's art. Who could this be? It was from a number she did not recognize.

She ran through the list. Steven, Georgia, the bonded courier, various drivers, a temp agency? Who could this be? It was obviously a fishing expedition seeing if she would bite. But that screamed danger.

《》《》《》

When Derek returned from dinner, about midnight, he checked in on Georgia and found that she was not breathing. He called 911 to report that he needed the assistance of paramedics immediately. When asked what the problem was he reported that his girlfriend was not breathing. He was nervous as he made the call and had little difficulty feigning genuine anxiety over the situation. He was a grown man and obviously would not cry or get hysterical, but he did manage to convey deep concern and near panic.

"Hurry!" he demanded as he finally hung up the phone.

Next he called his attorney and bid him to come immediately and to call Georgia's attorney on his way.

It took only a matter of minutes for the paramedics to arrive. They tried valiantly to resuscitate Georgia, but it was to no avail. They took note of the medications on her nightstand and the nearly empty bottle of whiskey. They knew what they were dealing with and the slim odds that she could be revived.

The police arrived shortly thereafter and then the two attorneys, just in time to see the paramedics taking Georgia from the unit. Derek was sitting by himself with his head in his hands. He was tired. It had been a long and emotionally draining day. As he addressed the police officer that needed to ask a few questions, he said he blamed himself.

He knew that Georgia had been drinking heavily and he knew that she had always had painkillers to help her sleep. But never before had she ever mixed alcohol with the medication. In retrospect it was clear that their recent arrest had taken a devastating toll on her psyche. He told the officer that he regretted not being more attentive to her needs.

It's always easier to tell a lie when it's the truth.

«»«»«»

Marcus Little stepped out of the cab and into a wall of humidity. It was a warm evening in the Big Apple and he had been away for long enough that he had not expected to be surprised by stepping from a frigid cab into the damp evening air of mid-summer, mid-town Manhattan.

He tipped the cabby and lugged his carry-on suitcase onto the curb and toward the entrance of his building. It was late and his usual door man had relinquished his post to someone Marcus did not recognize. He had left San Francisco on a mid-afternoon flight, but between the long flight, crossing multiple time zones, and the cab ride from La Guardia, his arrival home might have been better described as being early, rather than late. But late more aptly fit the fatigue he felt as he exited the elevator and fumbled for his keys.

His apartment had a warm stale smell as he walked in. He flipped on a few lights and surveyed the main living space in his small flat. It was both familiar and foreign to him as he looked around the room. He had been living in San Francisco for the past several months and had been in a slight rush when he left, so he had not taken a lot of time to straighten up the place before he left. He had managed to empty both the trash and the refrigerator, but that was about it. A jacket he had needed in the late winter was hung over the back of a bar stool. A couple of old magazines sat on the counter. A few rinsed, but unwashed dishes sat on the drainboard. He was too tired to worry about any of it. He headed to his bedroom. He brushed his teeth and laid down on his bed fully dressed. He was tired and thought he would lay there for just a few minutes before shutting off the lights and making a proper effort to climb into bed.

The next thing he knew, his phone was buzzing and full daylight was pouring in from windows that normally would not be admitting direct daylight until sometime after noon. He rolled over searching for the source of the buzzing. His phone had fallen to the floor beside his bed and was just out of reach. By the time he sat up, it had become silent and he decided that if it was important, the caller would leave a message. He laid back down and rubbed the stubble on his chin and decided he was hungry.

It took him some time to slowly rouse himself. He looked at the clock on his nightstand and was surprised to see that it was 1:37 p.m. He kicked off his shoes and walked to his bathroom to start his typical morning ritual. The reality of being back home was a rather sudden transition that left him slightly nostalgic for the slower pace of San Francisco. But as he looked in the mirror and contemplated his jet lagged countenance, he knew it was time to get back into the swing of things. He turned on the shower and began to erase the stubble.

When he was dressed, he decided he needed coffee before tackling any of the tasks associated with "digging out" after his extended absence. He headed downstairs and was pleased by the friendly and surprised reaction from his usual doorman, who was back at his post.

"If it ain't Mr. Little in the flesh!" Eddie croaked as only someone from Brooklyn could do. "I thought you might be dead and gone!"

"You thought wrong, Eddie," was Marcus' quick reply. "But at least you was thinkin'!"

"Good to have you back, sir."

"Good to be back," Marcus replied.

He crossed the street in the middle of the block, dodging traffic expertly, arriving at the Starbucks closest to his apartment. Directly across the street was as close as the corporate real estate experts were able to get it. They had tried, he was sure, to get a lease inside his building lobby, but the local neighborhood council had thought that any more than three Starbucks on the same block was pushing the limits.

He ordered his usual, which was somewhat unusual for Starbucks, as he seemed to be a member of a small minority of their vast customer base that didn't really like the taste of their coffee. He ordered Eddie an iced latte. It was sort of a ritual that Eddie seemed to appreciate and somehow seemed a little less awkward than the occasional tip.

While he waited for his order to come up he checked his phone. He found the voice mail from the missed call. It was from his office. He had hoped to have been able to spend at least a day getting back into the swing of things, but it looked like that was not going to happen.

"Marcus, this is Dave Hughes in Cyber. I got your name from Tim Phillips in San Francisco. He said you were chasing a bitcoin scam. We posted a recent hit on the events log. He noticed it and gave me your name."

"Cyber" was the inter-department FBI slang for the cyber crime division. They were tasked with monitoring and chasing down an exponentially expanding universe of online crime. The "events log" was a daily posting of tips and leads created after 9/11 and published on a secure internal server for the purpose of breaking down the silos between the various internal departments. Occasionally it helped connect the dots, but usually, most people within the FBI were simply too busy to read it.

"So I don't know if you knew this, but we have been collecting and recording all the bitcoin transactions for about the last 6 years. Mostly it's a waste, but every now and then we manage to correlate something our algorithms notice on the data stream with something in the real world. Listen. I'm sorry this is a long message. Call me back or I'll try you tomorrow. Thanks."

Marcus did not pretend to understand any of the cyber lingo, but the word 'hit' would cause any old FBI agent to perk up with or without caffeine in his system.

He picked up his coffee and headed back to his apartment. Eddie's grin at receiving his favorite iced coffee and Marcus' nod and slight smile communicated more than words. Anyone living in New York knows that being 'in' with your building's door man or woman has a non-monetary value that is not to be underestimated.

Marcus had not bothered to dress up for his jaunt to the Starbucks as he thought he would be heading out to run errands, restock his fridge, and generally ease back into his old routine. With the call from Dave Hughes, he wondered if it was worth putting on a suit and tie and heading into the office for the last hour of the day. He decided it wasn't, but returned Dave's call to see what was up.

Dave did not pick up his phone, so Marcus left a message and headed back out with a cloth grocery bag to pick up a quart of milk and a six pack of beer. There were other food stuffs he needed, of course, but those were the essentials.

He was at the checkout in the middle of paying when his phone rang. He assumed it was Hughes and as he was slightly preoccupied, did not bother to check the caller ID to be sure.

"Dave, it's Marcus. What do you know?'

"Well for starters, I'm pretty sure my name is not Dave." It was Jennifer Singh. She sounded amused.

"Ah, Miss Singh. Sorry. I was expecting a call from someone in my office. To what do I owe this pleasure?" he said.

"I tried to call you in San Francisco, but they said you had flown home yesterday. I thought maybe we could grab a drink and you could bring me up to speed on everything," she said.

"Did you know I am standing in line at the grocery store buying beer or are you just a good guesser," he laughed.

"I did not know and actually had something other than a six pack in mind," she said.

"Okay. Like what?' he asked. "A pint?"

"Where are you?" she asked.

"At a small market on 83rd street. Where are you?"

I'm in midtown. Do you know where Phillipe's is? It's a nice wine bar near Bryant Park," she said.

"I'll find it," Marcus said. "What time?"

"An hour?" she asked.

"Sure. See you in a bit."

Marcus had only met Jennifer Singh once, but he had not forgotten that he thought she was stunningly attractive. Here he was in his grungy, Sunday morning's best being invited to drinks. He had not bothered to iron his shirt before heading out for coffee and had just thrown it on, pulling on his favorite pair of faded jeans and a comfortable pair of loafers. At least he had showered and shaved.

He walked out of the store and hailed a cab. He passed a homeless guy digging through a trash bin on the curb. "Hey, buddy. Here's a two-fer." He handed the surprised man his shopping bag with the beer and milk. Not exactly a balanced meal, but perhaps something that would fill a need.

He got into the cab as the man opened the bag. Marcus heard him call out after him as he shut the door. “Whoa. Thanks man.”

“Where to?” the cabbie asked.

“You know where Phillipe’s is? It’s a wine bar near . . .”

“Bryant Park.” The cabbie finished his sentence. “Of course. I know this place.”

The cabbie pulled into traffic while sizing up Marcus in the rearview mirror.

“You go there before?” he asked.

“No,” Marcus replied, attaching no particular significance to the question. He didn’t notice the cabbie nod at his answer or his occasional glance back at Marcus as he headed uptown.

The cabbie broke the silence after several minutes.

“Phillipe’s is nice place,” he said looking in his mirror back at Marcus.

“Good,” Marcus replied, still not grasping that the cabbie was trying to communicate something to him.

“Is fancy.”

“Great.” He still didn’t get it. “Have you been there?” he asked.

The cabbie laughed. “Oh no. I think too fancy for me.”

Marcus nodded, but said nothing. It was about 5:45 p.m. and the streets and sidewalks were jammed with people and cars. As it was late spring, the sun would not set for another two hours or so, but was below the skyline. This time of afternoon was Marcus’ favorite time of day in the City, no matter what the season. The streets were in dark shadow, but shafts of golden sunlight burst into every intersection, creating dazzling reflections off the store windows. All the colors of the city streets seemed to be intensified as if the day was making one last vibrant stand against the inevitable deepening of the coming evening’s shadows. He was enjoying the ride and not really thinking about what the cabbie had said.

It took about 45 minutes to make the 30 or so block trip. He paid the cabbie who left him with a seemingly indifferent wave. He stood for a moment before a large, elegant building, then approached the doorman and indicated he was looking for “Phillipe’s.” The doorman gave him a not-too-subtle once-over. And indicated that it was inside.

Marcus entered a spotless, elliptical lobby decorated in classic streamline Moderne. The walls were clad in a light mahogany terminating at a high ceiling in a layered scalloped coving. Several large, white marble columns with inverted flutes punctuated the space. They terminated at the white plaster ceiling with the same layered scalloped coving as the walls, except here they were executed in polished black marble. A huge modernist pendant chandelier was suspended in the center of the space over an elliptical ebony table with shiny brass feet. Situated in the middle of the inlaid table top, a huge floral display dominated the room. On one side, the wall was taken up by a large, streamlined fireplace surround. Above it a huge mirror was hung expanding the sense of the room's volume. On the other side of the room, a simple elegant reception desk beckoned to those not belonging in such a refined environment. Behind the desk, an impeccably dressed young woman looked up and gave Marcus the same scrutiny as the doorman. He immediately comprehended, with a sickening sense of inadequacy, the meaning of the cabbie's remark. "Fancy."

"May I be of some assistance, sir?" the young woman asked.

"Yes. I am looking for Phillipe's," Marcus said with a flushing embarrassment.

"Certainly, sir. Did you have an appointment?"

"No. I am meeting someone whom I believe made the arrangements," he said feebly.

She pressed a button beneath the edge of the desk and momentarily an equally impeccably dressed young man appeared.

"Armando, this gentlemen is meeting a friend at Phillipe's. Please show him the way. I'll let George know you are coming."

They seemed to exchange a knowing glance and Marcus could swear he was once again given the treatment. He knew he was underdressed, but this was getting ridiculous.

"Please," Armando gestured to Marcus to accompany him toward a bank of elevators. They stepped into an elevator cab as elegant and spotless as the rest of the lobby. Armando swiped his ID badge across a security device beneath a key pad and entered a code, then pressed a few other buttons. This was like no other elevator Marcus had ever been in. The elevator moved so smoothly that Marcus could barely discern that they were, in fact, moving. It took them about a minute to complete their ride.

When the doors opened. They were greeted by a tall young woman holding a black jacket with a deep burgundy tie. The young woman handed them to Marcus, while George, it had to be George, Marcus thought, welcomed him.

"Good afternoon, and welcome. Would you be Mr. Little?" he asked.

"Yes," was all Marcus could find to say.

"I believe you will find the jacket to be your size. You may try it on in the gentlemen's lounge," he said gesturing to Marcus' left. "You may leave it and the tie with the attendant before you depart. When you are ready, I will show you to your table. Ms. Singh is already here."

Wow. Marcus didn't know if he should be impressed or creeped out. His immediate reaction tended towards being creeped out. He headed to the "gentlemen's lounge" and put on the jacket. It fit him perfectly. He put on the tie and tried to straighten his hair. After a couple of swipes with his fingers, he gave up and headed back through the elevator lobby to the maître d'hotel. George beckoned him to follow and Marcus immediately realized that he was in for a treat. As they walked through the restaurant, he was greeted by floor to ceiling windows looking out over New York from what must have been the 70th floor of the building.

"Excuse me, but what floor are we on?" Marcus asked.

"This is the 83rd floor, sir." George did not stop walking or slow down. "Ms. Singh requested a table on our garden terrace."

He opened the door for Marcus and ushered him out onto a terrace with about a dozen tables. There were a number of boxed planters with small trees just beginning to bud out. Blooming flowers surrounded the base of each tree. Each table had a small bouquet of fresh flowers and a lit candle in a cut crystal votive. Jennifer was seated near the parapet sipping a glass of wine. She looked up as they approached.

"Marcus. So you found it," she said.

"Yes. I don't know how I could not have known about a place like this. What a view," he said looking past her to Maine, or was that Canada?

"Please. Sit down. I want to hear everything. But let's get you something to drink. What would you like?" she asked.

"Honestly?" he asked. She gave him an uncertain glance. "Yes?"

"You said this is a wine place, but I am more of a beer guy, honestly," he said.

"Then beer it is," she said motioning for the waiter. "I think honesty is an important trait in a man. Especially in your line of work." She laughed as the waiter approached.

"What may I get for you?" he asked.

"Beer. Lots of beer," she said.

«»«»«»

Maarten Visser packed all his clothing and personal effects into two suitcases. He placed his old phone, driver's license, credit cards and, passport in a small satchel apart from his other belongings.

He was not scheduled to appear in court for another week, so the plan he was about to set in motion would find him many miles away before his failure to appear was noticed.

He left the condominium he had been staying in with Georgia since their arrest and her unfortunate death and walked several blocks to a retail store that specialized in shipping and post boxes. He used a credit card in the name of Derek Storque to pay for standard shipping and sent the two suitcases to another similar store in Chicago. He wondered how long they would be there before someone realized no one was going to pick them up.

He hoped it would be at least several weeks.

After leaving the store, he used his new phone to summon an Uber that took him to Walnut Creek where several days earlier Maarten Visser had purchased a new car that was ready to be picked up.

He had solved one problem with Georgia's passing. Now he intended to settle the score with whomever it was that had turned the tables on his carefully laid plans. He carried a Saint Kits and Nevis passport and planned to pursue the leads he had from the safety of a tropical island nation, far from the US court system, where he just happened to have all the correct paperwork to prove he was a citizen and access to a sizable bank account.

«»«»«»

By the time Shelley got to Drake's the night had overtaken the tropical sunset and it was pitch black. She parked her bike and stowed her helmet and head lamp before entering the bar.

The atmosphere inside managed to replicate the nightly party vibe as though it had not ended the night before at closing. To the occasional tourist it seemed like a rollicking good time, but to the regulars, it seemed like a slow Tuesday night.

Shelley scanned the bar and was disappointed that Rick wasn't there. Rick was the captain and owner of a 42-foot Pursuit S 408. It was a fairly new boat with a top cruising speed of 47 knots and a range at speed of 350 nautical miles. At a more leisurely pace its range approached 700 nautical miles. Rick had added two additional 100 gallon fuel tanks as insurance when he ordered the boat. The additional fuel significantly expanded the boat's range to southern Florida, without refueling. And it was fast – if it needed to be.

She settled into the bar and ordered a beer. She could not shake the nagging worry that she felt after receiving the cryptic message. She hadn't felt nerves or fear since having arrived in the Caribbean. Things had seemed to fall in place and with money squared away, she had felt secure in her new life.

The bartender was friendly as usual. She was an American, one of the few Shelley had met, owing to the complicated residency and work-permit requirements that had been put in place to keep the island from being overrun by foreigners.

Shelley thought the bartender might know if Rick was likely to come in. Bartenders know who their regulars are, as their tips depend on it.

"Think Rick will be in tonight?" Shelley asked innocently.

The bartender was wiping down the bar.

"Hard to say. It kind of depends if he had a charter today. If he did, he probably won't be in as there are a bunch of things he's gotta do after getting back." She glanced up at Shelley who was studying her beer as if there were some deep wisdom hidden in its shallow depths. Shelley just nodded.

Trina had worked in the Islands in a variety of establishments. She had been at Drake's for longer than most. It seemed to have a longer season and more steady tips. She had seen just about all the different types of people you could imagine drift through the bar and was usually pretty good at sizing someone up. A young single woman at a bar alone asking for a hunky guy wasn't too hard to figure out.

"So you've been in before a couple times. You here for the whole season?" Trina asked.

"No, I'm on vacation. It'll come to an end eventually."

"Yeah. That's the problem with vacations. Where are you from?'

Shelley looked up and momentarily pondered if she should go there.

“Phoenix,” Shelley offered smoothly. Her tan certainly could have been acquired locally or in Phoenix.

“Cool. Never been there. What’s it like?”

“Not as nice as this. It’s a desert. If you like warm winters, it’s a nice place to be. But the summers are all about coping with the heat. So you have warm winters here, right? And it never gets too hot, so I’d say this beats Phoenix.”

“I was born in Michigan,” Trina offered. “I went to college and got a degree and teaching certificate thinking I would be an elementary school teacher. But I came down here on a cruise over spring break with a girlfriend and was hooked. I went back, finished out the year and turned in my resignation. The fact that I married this hot guy who lived down here probably had something to do with it,” Trina said with a smile.

“What happened?” Shelly asked.

“He turned out to be a jerk.”

Both women laughed.

‘Sounds familiar,” Shelley said. “Tell me about Rick.”

“Well, he hit on me pretty hard when I first started. I try not to hookup with customers, but I will make an exception from time to time,” she said.

“And . . . ?” Shelley asked.

“He turned out to be a jerk.”

Both women laughed again.

“Okay. Fair warning given,” Shelley said.

“He’s smooth, so watch yourself,” Trina offered as she moved down the counter to refill another patron’s drink.

Shelley’s phone emitted a single, low, beep. She felt a pang of fear as she fished the phone out her bag.

> ---
>
> Think you’re safe? I know where you are.
>
> ---

Shelley stared at the screen, her mind racing. Who could this be? She decided not to respond. If this was a head game, she was not going to play. She tried to ignore the message and ordered another beer. But she could not stop thinking about it.

She finally gave up as the evening grew late. If this "Rick" fellow was coming, he would have probably shown up by now. She put some money on the bar and headed outside. She put on her helmet and started to peddle away, when she realized that she had a flat tire. 'Oh great," she muttered to herself. She got off her bike to inspect the tire and quickly realized the tire wasn't just flat. It had been slashed.

She felt a jolt of adrenalin shoot up her spine and into her neck. The skin on her neck tingled. She looked quickly around her, beyond the pools of light into the deep shadows. She couldn't see anything. A car approached and she quickly turned with the bike and ran pushing it into the bar.

"Hey. What's wrong?" Trina asked.

"Oh. Just a flat," Shelley said breathlessly.

Her almost frantic glances around the seating area of the bar did not go unnoticed by the bartender.

"You sure you're okay?" she asked again.

"Yeah. I'm fine. You don't happen to have a tire repair kit handy?" she asked.

Trina looked at Shelley as if she had asked a stupid question.

"No," she said finally, after giving Shelley a long hard look. "You're going to need a taxi tonight, I'm afraid.'

Before Shelley could respond, she added, "And you can leave the bike here tonight and get it fixed tomorrow."

Shelley seemed relieved.

"That would be great," she replied.

"You need me to call a taxi? Trina asked,

"No I can do it," Shelley replied.

It only took a few minutes for the taxi to arrive. As Shelley climbed in, she gave the driver the name of a hotel a few blocks from where she was really staying. She didn't know if she was being watched as the threatening messages had claimed, but she wasn't going to risk finding out. As she walked back to her hotel after being let out of the taxi, she dodged the pools of light along the way. At one point she found a deep shadow in the recess of a shuttered store and pressed herself into a corner and held her breath. She waited and watched to see if anyone or anything stirred or seemed to follow. The night was quiet. A car approached from the opposite direction and didn't slow as it passed.

After several minutes her heart rate returned to normal and she realized she was breathing again. Even though she was pretty sure there was no one behind her, she still stayed in the shadows as she approached her hotel.

She slipped into her room seemingly unnoticed. She could not shake the feeling that something worse than bad was brewing. And while it focused her thinking on the need to escape the island, it also left her feeling unsettled and with a pervading sense of danger.

She did not sleep well that night.

«‹›»«‹›»«‹›»

Jennifer Singh wanted to know how the investigation was going. She had read in the paper about the arrest of Derrek Storque and Georgia Calhoun Johnsson and the recovery of multiple paintings. Because of her involvement, she knew about the Edgar Payne and the Rembrandt, but learning that there were other paintings recovered made her curious. She had checked. Georgia Calhoun Johnsson was David Johnnson's ex-wife. So it seemed likely that the other paintings had to be from David Johnnson's collection.

"So I guess that's it," Jennifer said. "You got the two paintings back and arrested some bad guys. It was a weird and sort of exciting experience for me. But I was really hoping to get to sell one of those paintings."

"There were more than two," Marcus offered, "and it looked like you might have gotten to sell one of them for a while," Marcus said.

"There were more than two?" Jennifer asked. "What were they?"

"You know, you're going to laugh. But they were just names on a list to me," he said.

"Oh come," she exclaimed. "You can't remember any of them?"

He shook his head.

"Sorry."

"You are talking to an art person, right. I am very curious," she said.

He apologized again.

"Sorry. I owe you one, though. We could not have pulled it off without you and your firm's cooperation."

"It's what we do. Once we decided the Payne piece had been stolen, we had no choice but to call you. But if you want to owe me, I'll let you. For starters you could get me the list of those other paintings and tell me where they went and if they might be for sale," she said hopefully.

Marcus just smiled. He knew that it was unlikely that he would be in a position to pay off the debt with an opportunity for him to push a high profile painting her way.

"I can get you the list, and I'll keep my eyes open for another painting for you to sell, but don't hold your breath," he said. "Actually, there is one more painting that is unaccounted for, but if we ever find it – it will go back into David's collection – assuming it's not stolen."

"Really?" Jennifer asked. "What is it?"

"Mr. Johnsson kept pretty accurate records. There is one painting on one of his lists that does not appear to have been in either part of his vault and it was not one of the paintings we recovered. So we don't know where it is. He never reported it as missing," Marcus said. "All we have is a purchase date and an amount. It must be something incredible given the price he paid."

"But what is it?" Jennifer asked impatiently leaning forward in her chair.

"So it's this canvas with a bunch of colored paint on it," Marcus said

Jennifer leaned back in her chair giving Marcus a look of exasperation she had perfected as a teenager. She wasn't going to play this game with Marcus.

"We don't know what it is. But we know he paid $310 million for it."

She stared at him intently before speaking.

"I think I know what it is," she said. "There was a rumor a couple of years ago about a study sketch by Michelangelo that changed hands in a private sale. The rumored sale price was in the range of between $200 to $300 million."

Marcus looked at her carefully. She could see he was evaluating what she told him and probably the source as well.

"You are not the only one with sources," she said slyly.

He still looked surprised as he processed the information and wondered what else she might know.

"Okay. I might have been in on the sale of that one." she said.

"Really?" Marcus seemed relieved.

"Yeah. It was about six years ago. It was through an intermediary after a pre-auction preview. It's not uncommon for a buyer to retain an agent to represent them at an auction. It was probably his brother. We showed him the painting. He had someone on the phone as he looked at it. He must have been Skyping with David while he listened to my staff present the piece and its extensive provenance. He said the buyer was interested and would be in touch. The next day we received a call from an attorney with terms of a pre-auction purchase offer significantly higher than our internal auction estimate."

"So he bought it before it went to auction?" Marcus asked.

"Correct. And as part of the sale, there were very specific limitations on all the parties with respect to confidentiality. So the painting came to market from a private collection and then disappeared back into another private collection," she said.

"Was that disappointing?" Marcus asked. "Maybe you could have done better if it had gone to auction."

"Maybe," she said thoughtfully. "But we did fine. And essentially we did what we do best. Our involvement resulted in two satisfied clients. One or both of whom will undoubtedly bring us return business. Our firm is not the oldest in New York by accident."

"Did you meet the agent" he asked.

"No. I was on vacation at the time," she said. "So I only know this from what my staff has told me. But it was a big deal, to say the least."

"After you sold it, where did you ship it?" Marcus asked.

"I'd have to check. I really don't remember," she said, fudging a bit. She had checked. In her line of work she definitely wanted to know who had that kind of money. It had been shipped to a warehouse and then moved. All she had found out at the time is that it had been sold to an LLC.

"Well, it's more information than I had a few minutes ago. I guess that means I can pick up the tab."

"Don't be silly," Jennifer responded. "This was my idea."

"Yeah, but since you have provided a new lead, this is not a date anymore and I can turn this in and expense it," he said. He didn't know how she would take that not so subtle attempt to frame the meeting as something personal. Nor did he tell her that it was unlikely that the accounting department in the FBI's New York Bureau would accept a $300 tab for wine and beer. Maybe the Director could get away with that, but not the likes of lowly Special Agent Marcus Little.

"Nice try, Agent Little," she said with a smile. "I will be picking up the tab. And don't forget to send me the list. Or maybe we could do this again when you have it," she suggested.

"You are relentless," he said.

"It's how I make a living."

«»«»«»

"Architects of grandeur are often the master builders of disillusionment."

-- Bryant H. McGill

Chapter Sixteen

Keith's plane landed at Lynden Pindling International Airport, Nassau, The Bahamas. En route he had opened a map app on his phone and had been dismayed to realize that what had seemed like a fairly simple exercise in the comfort of Wilder's conference room, looked rather more daunting on an actual map.

He had never been to the Caribbean before and assumed it was a couple of islands off Florida. Looking at the map, he realized it was actually hundreds of islands stretching from the east of Florida all the way down to South America. Wilder had made it sound like he could walk into a few banks and bars, flash a photo, ask if anyone had seen his "sister" and get meaningful information in maybe a week or two. When Keith asked Wilder where he should start, he had suggested Nassau as it had a thriving banking sector, was close to Florida, and was heavily visited by tourists. All things that might be attractive to someone on the run like Shelley.

In the taxi on the way to his hotel, the work ahead of him seemed distasteful. Finding his brother's killer was not a game. This was not a holiday and schlepping around a bunch of hot muggy islands wasn't his idea of fun. The scenery whizzed by as his taxi driver tried to make small talk. He had been lost in his own thoughts and had largely ignored the prattling banter of the driver.

"You come to the islands alone?" the driver asked.

"What?" Keith asked having barely registered that he was being addressed.

"You come to the islands alone," the driver said. This time a statement based on observation.

"Yes," Keith replied.

"No missus. No lady friend?" he asked.

"No. I am traveling light," he said.

Keith could see the driver sizing him up in the rearview mirror.

"You a businessman." the driver said.

"Right," Keith said. "I'm here on business."

"You need a guide?"

Keith saw where the interrogation was going. This was about extending the driver's fare.

"Actually, yes," Keith said. "I do. I assume you know the island well."

"Naturally. I can show you everything."

Keith looked out the window. "I'm looking for my sister," he said pausing. "She came down here on a cruise last month and we have not heard from her. It's not like her. I'm worried. So I thought I would come down and see if I could find her."

Keith saw that the driver had been watching him as he spoke, shifting his gaze quickly back and forth between the road and the rear view mirror.

"That sounds worrisome," the driver said. "I take you to police station, first," he said.

Keith hadn't expected that to be offered.

"No," he said slowly. "I would prefer to start elsewhere," he said. "At least at first."

They both remained silent for a few moments before Keith added, "This is kind of personal. But my sister is an alcoholic. She is probably in a bar somewhere drinking her inheritance."

The cabbie was nodding. "Okay," he said. "I know all the drinking places."

Keith was surprised how easily the lie was falling into place. He could almost believe it himself.

"She has been taking money out of her bank account and then probably hitting the bars. So I need to visit banks and bars."

"I take you to both. It is my pleasure," the cabbie said.

Keith unlocked his phone and googled the number of bars in Nassau. According to Trip Advisor it was 51.

Wilder had given Keith a photo of Shelley from her college yearbook. It was several years out of date, but it was the only thing they could find. She did not have any of the typical social media accounts so had not left any easy way of finding a photo.

“Do you know a place to make copies of a photograph?” Keith asked.

“Of course,” the cabbie said.

“Great. Take me there first. By the way, what’s your name?” Keith asked.

“Charles,” the cabbie said.

“Keith,” he said.

“A pleasure to meet you and to be of service,” Charles said.

«»«»«»

Architecture has been described as lurching unpredictably between feast or famine. This certainly was an apt description for the dramatic change in the prospects of Neil Thorton’s practice. He had been on life support, unsure of how he would be able to pay his bills. With one new client he was back in the clover. Lydia Mankovich was not just any new client, however. She was perhaps the dream client. She had a large, complicated project that needed to be completed. Her resources were seemingly endless. And the drawings had been signed by someone else.

Neil met with Lydia to sign the contract at Bowlers. She had brought a document prepared by her attorney that was nearly a half-inch thick even though it had been printed double-sided. He looked at it, but didn’t open it.

“Is something wrong?” Lydia asked.

Neil hesitated for a moment before answering. “Well,” he said sliding the contract slightly away from him, “I am afraid to open it. I’m sure your attorney believes he has provided you with a great service, but he has probably over-complicated things a bit.”

“What makes you think it was a man?” She asked.

“Good point,” he said. “But either way, it’s over the top.”

Lydia gave Neil a long contemplative look. “This is a complicated project, Neil. So what would you suggest?”

“I think we could write something on the back of this napkin that would work just as well," he said.

"Really," she said.

"Yeah."

She pushed her cocktail napkin toward him. "Show me," she said.

He wrote a few sentences and signed the napkin. Lydia read it and said, "Okay. We can start with this."

She took his pen and signed the napkin and laughed. "Now get to work."

They talked for a couple hours about the project, David's passion for excellence, the quality and authenticity that both David and now Lydia would insist upon for every aspect of the project. They made a plan, talked about next steps and then parted ways.

The next morning, Neil enjoyed his morning coffee while he read the news on his phone. He then called the contractor to start discussions for the project restart. It was the last quiet moment he would enjoy for the next two years.

«»«»«»

The bartender knew that Rick Collins always started off his evening with a beer. He had barely sat down as she slid a tall glass of icy cold beer in his direction.

"Thanks," he said.

He made an honest and even comfortable living on his boat running a charter service. But it hadn't been easy at the start.

Like some of the locals he was a transplant. He came to the islands while working a boat for a wealthy client and quickly realized he liked the climate and the lifestyle. When the owner, whom he liked, sold the boat to another wealthy, but less likeable person, he quit rather than staying on. He assumed he could quickly find another job, but that proved to be impossible.

Not being from the island, he hadn't counted on the work rules that kept the island from being overrun by people from all corners of the globe that came to Grand Cayman on vacation and then decided they wanted stay. It turned out to be almost impossible to get a job without a work permit and a work permit required at least eight years of residency before being issued. So the only people who could gain residency were wealthy retirees or others with sufficient wealth to start a business or remain idle.

But Rick had an advantage that most other boat hands didn't have. He had some money.

He had managed to save most of his salary while working on the yacht. So he used his savings to buy a small fishing boat and set out to offer charters. Things were going great until he ran into the next barrier. He had placed an advertisement in the local paper offering his boat for charter which was spotted and carefully read by someone from the Caymanian Status and Permanent Residency Board who informed him that he was not authorized to provide charter services because he was not a resident. The official brought with him members of the local constabulary who then proceeded to impound his boat.

He had no choice but to find and retain a local barrister who helpfully revealed the intricacies of the immigration law. There was a loophole, albeit a unhappy one, that would allow Rick to get his boat back and to resume preparations for guiding others to catching fish. As his options were explained to him, he wondered if he could get his money back from the seller of the boat - as the only means for starting a charter business seemed to be in finding a local business partner who would be entitled to retaining 60 percent of any and all profits for basically nothing. This wasn't an attractive option to Rick.

The next day he returned to the docks and managed to locate the previous owner of the boat who seemed to have anticipated Rick's return. He listened patiently as Rick asked if he would consider buying back the boat. Much to Rick's surprise, he agreed immediately. The relief Rick felt was short-lived as the man then offered Rick a small fraction of the previous sale price to repurchase the boat.

It didn't take Rick long to realize he was caught in a government-endorsed hustle that his ignorance had allowed him to walk into unwittingly. Rick declined and took out yet another add in the local paper offering his boat for sale. He ran the add for three weeks and received exactly zero interest as he quickly burned through the balance of his savings on housing costs.

He returned to the owner of the boat and asked if instead of repurchasing the boat the man would instead be his local business partner. The man agreed and so began eight years of financial servitude to a worthless leach.

But Rick was not a quitter. He had been through worse. The weather was good. The fishing was good. The tourist babes were good, and plentiful, as plentiful as the fish. It was simply that he had not been rewarded for the full value of his efforts that sucked. Rick kept good books and knew the full measure of the sweat equity that he was investing in his business as well as every Cayman dollar that he paid for his ultimate freedom.

Rick had listened carefully to the barrister he hired to walk him through the residency regulations. It had not escaped his attention that there was a Residency Commission charged with formulating and enforcing the Island's residency requirements. Membership on the commission was a matter public record and as the island was small, it did not take long for him to become friendly with a couple of the commission's members at the Yacht Club. He offered to take them out whenever they wanted and made sure his coolers were always full of plenty of booze.

To save money, he slept on the boat. He rarely ate out, eating what he caught instead. It was during this time he became a local at Drake's. And it was at Drake's that he plotted his revenge. As he approached the end of his eighth year of servitude, he took out as large a loan as he could secure using the business and boat as collateral. The proceeds of the loan were ostensibly frittered away on women and booze. It was a plausible cover as he had a reputation for both. In truth, the money went into several numbered bank accounts that the Cayman Islands are so famous for.

He also stopped spending any money on routine maintenance letting the boat fall into hideous disrepair. He also failed to make his last two insurance payments. Such was the state of things when a hurricane struck the island sinking the boat after it inexplicably slipped its moorings. It was a tragedy. The boat was lost. The insurance refused to compensate the owners, either of them, for the loss. The bank that gave him the loan seized the business's bank account which had slightly more than the exact amount he owed them.

Sometimes bad things happen.

After he lost his boat, he spent more time at the Yacht Club. He found that his friends on the commission were very sympathetic as he related his story of woe. They felt so bad for him that he was able to get his permanent immigration papers several months later, way earlier than was usual. To celebrate, he rewarded himself with a brand new boat. He called her the *Cayman "At Last"*. And life was indeed good.

He was on his second beer when Shelley arrived.

She sat a bit down the bar from him and waited for an opening, preferring that he start the conversation, but he seemed content to nurse his beer. Eventually he looked around and noticed her. He slid over to a seat next to hers, letting his beer glide down the bar.

"Drinking alone tonight?" he asked.

"Not any more," she said with a laugh.

He smiled. “I haven’t seen you in here in a couple of weeks,” he said.

“You haven’t been looking,” she said. “I was here last night. Where were you?”

“I was prepping my boat for a charter,” he said bit defensively. “And when I have a charter I go to bed early. So no Drake’s for me.”

“Too bad. I was here,” she said.

“Just my luck.”

“So did you catch anything today?” she asked.

“I didn’t personally catch anything. I don’t fish during a charter. I’m too busy. But my clients caught plenty,” he said. “If they are staying in a hotel, they usually don’t want what they catch, so I always have plenty of fresh fish. More than I can eat, actually.”

“What do you do with the rest of it?” Shelley asked.

“I sell it. It goes to the local fish market,” he replied, taking a long sip of his beer.

“So what’s the farthest you have ever gone out?” Shelley asked with all the innocence she could muster.

“I try to keep it to about 50 miles,” he replied.

“Do you ever go to the other islands?” she asked.

He shook his head as he took another long swig of his beer.

“How about the States? Ever go that far?” she asked.

“Oh, hell no,” he said. “No time for that.”

“So it’s not that you can’t, it’s just that no one has ever paid you to do it?”

“Pretty much,” he said.

They both fell silent for a few moments.

“So, just out of curiosity, what would it cost?

Rick cocked his head and gave her a long, careful look. Up until that moment, she had appeared in his bubble of reality as a possible target for consensual sex. She was young, attractive, and apparently alone. Those were all things he considered prerequisites for some uncomplicated sex. But if she was interested in hiring him for a charter, that was business. And he did not mess around when it came to business.

"I doubt you could afford it," he said without meaning it as an insult. "It would be cheaper to fly."

"If I wanted to fly," she said with a laugh. "I think it would be much more fun to take a cruise. Here we are surrounded by some of the most beautiful scenery in the world, and everyone is in such a rush to get here and then in such a rush to leave."

"You have a point," he said. He looked at his beer for a moment or two. "I could probably squeeze in a run later this week, but I have a charter scheduled for Saturday and Sunday, so I would need to time it to be back in time to prep my boat for that."

"Seriously? You'll do it?" Shelley asked in fake surprise. "I don't have a set schedule, so whatever would work for you would be fine," she said casually.

"Well, as long as you have the cash and want to spend it," his voice trailed off as he contemplated the journey.

"So seriously. How much would it cost?" she asked.

"I'd say it's about 600 nautical miles to Key West. So double that. My fuel costs will be about five grand, plus it will take a full day of sailing to get there and another to get back. I typically charge $2,500 per day for the boat, but that includes a fuel charge. But that is a lot of time on my engines."

He thought for a moment before giving her his final price.

"I'll tell you what. I'll make you a screaming deal. I'll do it for an even ten grand," he said.

"Ten thousand for a once-in-a-lifetime experience or $500 for a commercial flight," Shelley mused aloud.

It was a Sunday evening.

"So we could leave by Wednesday?" she asked.

"I would prefer to leave Tuesday morning. Very early and by that I mean before first light. It'll be a full day of cruising. Then I'll need some time to clear US customs and refuel and provision the boat to return. Ideally, I would be back here by Thursday night so I would have the time on Friday to get ready for my Saturday charter."

Shelley needed to avoid customs, and had thought that this mode of transport might make that possible. She didn't want to ask if avoiding customs was possible for fear he would back out or double his price.

They both sat at the bar nursing their drinks. He wondered if he had asked for enough, she wondered if he could be trusted with skirting the law and be, in essence, untrustworthy.

"I need cash up front," he said finally. "By Tuesday morning at the latest."

"Of course," she said breezily. She decided she would need at least twenty-five thousand in cash. She was travelling with about ten thousand. So she would need to withdraw some more.

On her way back to her hotel, her phone buzzed with another threatening message.

"Who is this?" she typed into her phone. It took several minutes to receive a response, but her phone buzzed again.

> ---
>
> "So. You have finally decided to play. Who do you think?
>
> ---

"I don't know," she replied. "How did you get this number?"

It took several minutes between each message and a response.

> ---
>
> "Of course you don't. You don't know how deep you are in over your head. I have resources you can't even imagine. Finding an amateur like you was easy. Have you spoken to your old boyfriend lately? Hope nothing else bad happens to him. "
>
> ---

Shelley was stunned. Who could this be and how did they know about Neil?

> ---
>
> What did you do to Neil?
>
> ---
>
> ---
>
> Ah yes. Neil. I wasn't referring to *that* old boyfriend. I'm referring to Steven. But your concern about Neil's longevity might be useful, too.
>
> ---

Shelley powered off her phone. She felt ill. If something had happened to Steven Jordan on her account she would feel terrible. He had dumped her and been fairly mean about it. But she used him to connect with the auction house in New York because he was a known intermediary, not because she was trying to hurt him. She knew how ambitious he was and how he would react to the possibility of getting a lucrative client. He was so arrogant, and yet still green, that he wouldn't ask a bunch of pesky questions. And in fact he hadn't.

"Great." She realized she had offered up Neil too. But if they knew about Steven, they probably had also already known about Neil. She was really scared for the first time and resolved to ignore future messages.

«»«»«»

Charles had proved to be very helpful. He knew Nassau like the back of his hand and had contacts that Keith had been able to exploit. They had been able to circulate the photo of Keith's "sister" very efficiently and within two days had come to a fairly certain dead-end. Far from being dispirited by this outcome, Keith seemed energized. It was a process of elimination. And he had stumbled on a strategy of moving ahead that he thought he could replicate on other islands.

"Charles. You ever travelled to the other islands down here?" Keith asked.

"I got no money for that, sir," he replied.

"You have been very helpful. If you're interested, I could use your help. I intend to keep looking for my sister on every single island until I find her," Keith said.

“Mr. Johnsson,” Charles said, “there are over 700 hundred islands down here. You going to go to all of them?” he asked incredulously.

“No. Just the ones with banks and bars. How many do you think that is?” Keith asked.

“I don’t know. Maybe 50,” Charles replied.

“Then if you are willing, I’ll pay you to help me cover as many as we can until we find her.” Keith paused. “How about it?”

Charles was silent. “How much money?” he asked. “I got a wife and kids. If I leave this job I don’t know how I would be able to pay my bills.”

“How much money do you make each year?” Keith asked.

“Last year I made about twenty thousand US,” he said lying. It was closer to eleven thousand and it had been his best year ever.

“I’ll tell you what,” Keith said. “I’ll pay you twenty thousand now and twenty thousand if we find her. And,” Keith paused, “I’ll pay all the expenses.”

Charles didn’t speak. He wasn’t sure if this Keith Johnsson was telling the truth. But twenty thousand US dollars up front for something that didn’t appear to be illegal seemed too good to pass up.

“What do you say?” Keith asked.

“I need to talk to my wife,” he said. “And I don’t have a passport.”

“I’ll pay for your passport, too,” Keith said.

“That is not the part that I am worried about,” Charles said.

Keith laughed. He understood. “Would it help your lovely wife if she were able to count the money first?”

“Most definitely,” Charles said grinning.

“Then take me to the nearest bank.”

While waiting for Charles to count the money with his wife, Keith spent some time considering his next move. He looked at the map again.

While it was true that there were over 700 islands in the Caribbean, they were not all likely to be places that Shelley might have landed. Half were uninhabited or certainly did not have banks and bars. She wouldn’t have gone to Cuba, or Haiti, or the Dominican Republic. Jamaica seemed unlikely. He doubted Puerto Rico was on the list. She might have been able to get there without raising suspicion, but their banking laws must mirror those in the United States, he thought.

He decided his next move would be either to the British Virgin Islands or the Cayman Islands. He pondered each, but had no real basis for a decision.

Charles emerged from his house smiling.

"I take it she said yes," Keith said.

Charles nodded.

"I think the next island is either the Virgin Islands of the Cayman Islands," Keith said. "What do you think?"

"I say you go to one and I go to the other," Charles said.

"Now you are talking," Keith said. "You go to the Cayman Islands and I'll go to the Virgin Islands. You'll need a cell phone and a passport," Keith said.

"I got a cell phone," Charles said reaching into his pocket.

«»«»«»

It took Neil about a month to get everything squared away. He called the general contractor and along with Lydia's attorney set up a meeting to hash through the outstanding issues. The contractor was initially skeptical, but eventually came around when they realized Neil's only agenda was to find a way forward. He told them that he would not be the one to settle their previous dispute with David. That seemed to make them nervous, but he said he would endorse a settlement, if he thought it was fair. And that fair meant that they could expect to be paid for the work in place, their de-mobilization and re-mobilization, and an adjustment to their contract to reflect a change in market conditions while the project sat idle. But that they would have to set aside all their claims for damages. He also told them they had a week to decide and get their paperwork in order. If they chose to litigate, and here he turned to the attorney, they would be dealing with David's, and now Lydia's team of attorneys. If they chose to move ahead, he would get them paid within a month and work would start immediately after that. It was their choice.

They all shook hands and seemed like they were leaning toward staying with the project. And in fact they did. Neil had to challenge them on some of their pricing, but as it was water under the bridge and they were nursing a grudge, he convinced Lydia that they should let bygones be bygones and press ahead, a couple of million dollars not withstanding.

Once the contractor re-engaged, the project site began to hum again. Neil insisted that the contractor bring a large construction trailer to the site. How they had managed to get as far as they had without one was surprising. He also tied their new contract to specific milestones with both incentives for timely completion and liquidated damages for missing the schedule.

Weekly on-site meetings, access to engineers from San Francisco, an on-site team of architects (which Neil had needed to hire to support the effort), and deep pockets to smooth out all the problems - and it was no surprise that things started to hum along.

Lydia had access to an amazing group of artisans and had no reticence to fly them in for consultations or to engage them in providing custom pieces of work.

Neil was so busy he had to hire several new people as he soon realized he would be unable handle it alone. He hired a new receptionist. With some effort he convinced Judy to help him with his books. She resisted claiming she was too busy and could not take him on as a client. But he persisted and eventually she agreed. Finding an architect with extensive construction phase experience willing to move to the valley would seem like an easy sell. And it was until the interviewee checked the cost of housing. It took a while to find the right person and ironically, when he did, it was an acquaintance he knew from his local AIA Chapter whose wife was a local physician. He had stopped working to design their home (and hobby winery). That project had wound down and he was bored. Neil happened to bump into him at the grocery store and when he explained his predicament was surprised by the almost immediate offer to help. He found a construction administrative assistant through Judy whose neighbor had a friend at church that was working at UC Davis in their facilities department but was tired of the drive.

Neil didn't really have time to think about whether serendipity was an appropriate hiring strategy. He had too much to do.

«»«»«»

So where is the eighth master? It better be safe or you won't be for long. It would be better for you to hand it over quietly.

«»«»«»

Keith took a short flight to St. Thomas, Virgin Islands. He connected with another driver and started making the rounds. St. Thomas seemed to be more spread out than Nassau and it didn't take long for him to wish that he could stay and have a drink in the places he was visiting rather than moving from place to place. Most of the bartenders seemed suspicious. The bankers were downright hostile. He stopped visiting bank branches after the second visit when he thought his questions were attracting unwanted attention. Eventually he got his patter down and usually ended the pitch by making a contribution to the tip jar. Wherever he went, he left a photo of Shelley with a cell phone number on the back.

Charles didn't have the advantage of claiming Shelley was his long lost sister as the pretext for his inquiry. His dark complexion made that ruse seem unlikely. Instead he simply asked if anyone had seen Shelley. If asked, he said he had been retained by Shelley's parents to look for her. If things got weird he just beat a hasty retreat and moved on.

He had been busy all day long when he finally made it to Drake's. He was tired and needed something to eat and ordered the catch of the day and a cold local beer.

As a cabbie, he did not get the chance very often to frequent places like Drakes. He was either sitting in a taxi stand waiting for a fare, or driving. When he did get off, he went home where his wife and son waited. His wife would not have endorsed him stopping for a drink on the way home. Money was tight and paying tourist prices for alcohol was not in their budget.

So sitting in a bar, away from Nassau, drinking beer and a restaurant meal would have been exciting, if he were not so tired. His weariness wasn't just physical, it was emotional. He was tired and sat in a stupor eating his shell fish combo. He didn't much care for the chips and was about to say something when a young woman breezed in and sat down at the bar. She was tan and wore a flowered print dress. She struck up a conversation with the bartender and ordered a beer. She didn't look around and only occasionally fidgeted with her phone.

It took Charles a few minutes to realize this could be the woman he had been searching for all day long. Eventually he got up and went to the men's room to give him a chance to see the woman's face. He didn't get a clear view, but decided it was her.

He returned to his table and pulled the phone from his pocket and sent Keith a quick text.

Keith was sitting in the bar at the Four Seasons enjoying a martini when his phone buzzed. He turned the phone over and stared in disbelief.

“I think I found her. Should I introduce myself?”

Keith tapped a quick reply, “No. Where are you?”

“A bar named Drakes.”

“How does she look? Is she okay?”

“She looks fine.”

“Good. I’ve been so worried,” Keith lied.

“I can just go say hello and tell her you are coming”

“No. Stay with her as long as you can, but don’t approach her or follow too closely.”

“That makes no sense, she’s your sister.”

“I don’t want her to run. She may not be happy to see me. Is she with anyone?”

“Alone.”

“Keep me posted.”

“Okay.”

«»«»«»

"An important work of architecture will create polemics."

-- Richard Meier

Chapter Seventeen

Progress on the chateau was moving rapidly. A small village of trailers had been brought on site and arranged on the top of the parking structure. A significant number supported the general contractor and the major sub-contractors. They would eventually have to be moved before the *Avant-Cour* could be constructed. Several dozen trailers had also been placed on the south side of the chateau, where one of the formal gardens would be eventually located, to house the team of skilled crafts people that Lydia had brought from France to support the detailing of the interiors. There were metal workers, carpenters, plasterers, furniture makers, interior designers, seamstresses, and painters - all experts in the creation and/or restoration of the Baroque arts. Together they did not nearly resemble the innumerable artisans assembled by Fouquet, but Lydia's team had modern tools and other resources their ancient forebears did not.

No detail of the chateau had been ignored. Everything was being custom fabricated either on site or by crafts people in workshops all over the world. Doorknobs, light fixtures, light switches, cover plates, call buttons, everything was being made by hand, specifically to order, of the highest quality materials available.

Neil walked through the chateau with Lydia and a team of interior designers and four or five of the crafts people that were relevant to the day's walk. One of Lydia's assistants carried a large tablet device with a photo of every painting, piece of furniture, sculpture, tapestry, and rug keyed to the location on each floor plan of the building where the piece would eventually be placed.

Another assistant carried a laptop prepared to capture whatever thoughts or direction that Lydia might make. Another assistant carried a digital camera documenting everything.

The whole scene was over the top, as far as Neil was concerned, but the gathering of so many resources did need additional layers of management to be effective, and Lydia was a marvel of effectiveness.

Inside the chateau, the infrastructure supporting building systems had been installed allowing work on interior wall and ceiling finishes to begin. At the time that the original Vaux le Vicompte was constructed, masonry was the most commonly used construction material. As a result both interior and exterior walls were load bearing and sized, based on the intuition of the master architect, to take the structural dead load of the floor or floors above. As high carbon steel had not yet been discovered, the means of spanning openings was limited to either masonry arches, or perhaps cut stone. But as masonry was more economical for a variety of reasons, stone lintels were used sparingly if at all.

In the case of David's chateau, steel was doing all the real structural work. In some locations it was paired with concrete in the form of columns. Arched openings and indeed most of the columns were necessary only stylistically, rather than structurally. The thickness of the walls, which were hollow or concealed mechanical ducts, plumbing, or other infrastructure, were for effect rather than necessity. The interior steel studs that Neil had seen on his first visit had been completed and were being covered with cementious board. Wall cavities were filled with insulation to deaden sound. And while the insulation would help, it could never replicate the sound-stopping qualities of a thick masonry wall. But the entire wall assembly when complete, would be sufficient.

Ornate interior plasterwork or wood paneling or a combination of both would eventually cover every wall and ceiling surface. These materials would then be covered with paint, textile, or gold leaf.

As Lydia's entourage worked its way through the chateau, they dodged construction workers, ladders, scaffolding, materials, power cords, temporary cutting and fabrication stations. While Neil was present and available for consultation on a moment's notice, his attention was focused on the progress of the construction, rather than concerns related to interior finishes and furniture. He largely delegated the task of coordinating with Lydia to his assistant.

There was still so much to do, yet it was all coming together. The finishes in the salon were beginning to take form. The ornamental plasterwork below the spring line of the dome was complete and had been painted. Carpenters and stone masons dodged each other as they jockeyed to complete the wall paneling and marble door and windows surrounds. Scaffolding filled almost the entire room, leaving a four or five foot open space around the perimeter of the room, while providing the platform for the painters working on the fresco on the underside of the dome.

Every floor of the building was a beehive of activity. Neil and his recently hired staff could barely keep up. Each day started early with an all-team meeting in the largest trailer, where the GC and representatives from each sub-contractor would gather and review the day's scheduled construction activity. Issues related to the previous day's work that required corrective action were discussed. Coordination between the trades was reviewed to ensure that each sub could do its work without impacting other subs that needed access to a given area of the building. It was a fast-paced, high-pressure meeting where progress was tracked, problems were solved, solutions were found, and gallons of coffee and several dozen donuts were consumed daily.

The construction trailer was predominantly male, with all the odors, foul language, and off-color humor one might expect. The women in the meetings, and there were a few, were treated like one of the guys and had learned long ago to give as good as they got and to not be offended by the not infrequent sexist joke or metaphor.

Neil typically arrived at the meeting shortly before it began, having just completed an early-morning walkthrough of the entire chateau. The rest of his staff were already there, typically huddled in a corner with one of the subs pouring over the drawings or other paperwork trying to resolve some recently discovered construction issue.

Neil could not remember having so much fun. Ever.

«»«»«»

Shelley met Rick the next evening at Drake's and finalized the details for her charter and then downed the last of their beers. Rick was tempted to ask her what her sleeping arrangements were for the night, but as she was about to be a paying customer, thought better of that and simply bid her a good night.

Charles who had been trying to observe them nonchalantly, was caught off guard by their sudden departure and was not able to get to the door casually in time to see how or where they departed the premises.

He had been texting Keith occasionally throughout the evening, with a particular flurry of texts being sent and received when Rick arrived and he and Shelley began their conversation. He wasn't close enough to hear what they said, but he sensed that the conversation was more business than pleasure. This suspicion, he thought, was confirmed when they said good night.

Keith monitored the texts as he frantically gathered his bags and checked out of the hotel. He hailed a cab and went straight to the airport only to discover that there were no late evening flights from St. Thomas to the Cayman Islands. It seemed there really was such a thing as "island time" and it included inter-island transportation.

He sheepishly returned to the hotel and checked back in to the room where he had been staying. He couldn't get to sleep as he was too wound up. So he called

Wilder and told him the news.

"What do you know? Wilder said. "That hunch paid off." He paused. "Now listen, Keith. Don't do anything dumb. You are in a foreign country. You need to play this real cool. When you get there tomorrow and you find her, you have to keep your temper under control." He paused again. "Can you do that?"

Keith was quiet. He wasn't sure what he would do. He knew he might not be able to keep his temper in check.

"I'll try," he said.

"That's not good enough, Keith. You have to do more than just try. You want to spend the rest of your life rotting in prison? Your brother would not want that. You don't want that."

"I said I would try," Keith hissed into the phone.

"Keith, if you can't convince me that you can control your anger before we end this call, I will call the police and the FBI and have them arrest her before you can even get to the airport."

Keith was silent.

"What do you say? You gonna control yourself?" Wilder asked.

Keith let out a long sigh. Wilder was right. She wasn't worth it. He would see her behind bars and make sure she stayed there a long, long time.

"All right, dad," he said sarcastically. "I'll behave."

"You had better and you had better keep me posted or my next call will be to inform the police or the FBI of your whereabouts. Do we understand each other?"

"Josh. I understand," Keith said. "She isn't worth it. I'll only talk to her. Besides she probably doesn't even know who I am. So I'll have the upper hand."

«»«»«»

As Shelley rode her bike back to her hotel through the darkness, she could not help but feel she was being followed. The messages she had received starting the previous night and continuing through the day had spooked her. And although she had managed to hold it together while at Drake's, now that she was alone, riding through the darkened streets on the way back to her hotel, she could not relax.

"What had the messages said? 'Clever girl.' and 'We know where you are.'"

"Did they? Who were they?" They seemed to know about the stashed painting and assumed she had it. They knew about Steven and Neil. It seemed like someone had put most of the pieces together. "Shit." She was scared like she had not been scared before.

«»«»«»

Shelley managed to get some sleep, but it wasn't deep, relaxed sleep. It was anguished sleep. She awoke feeling tired. Daylight flooded the room. She walked to the French doors that opened onto a small balcony. She had made sure they were securely locked the night before, but she threw them open walking into the breezy sunshine of an absolutely beautiful sub-tropical Caribbean morning. Kids were already playing in the pool. The chaise lounges were nearly all spoken for. The cabanas were full. The towel boys were busy attending to the needs of the hotel guests and as far as she could tell, the equilibrium in the universe was undisturbed.

She relaxed and decided to order room service. This was her last day on Grand Cayman and she decided she deserved to be pampered a bit for having arranged transportation off the island.

"Maybe I'll have a massage, too. What the heck?" she thought. "Then I'll take care of packing for the trip."

She checked her phone.

> ---
>
> I know you are reading these messages. You don't have much time. If I have to get ugly with you I will. I also know you were there when David died. So let's keep it simple. Give me the painting and I may go easy on you.
>
> ---

Shelley froze in fear. Who is this person and how do they know she was in the chateau when David died?

«»«»«»

Keith was about as impatient as he had ever been his whole life as he waited to board the 11:20 a.m. flight from St. Thomas to George Town on Grand Cayman. He had about lost it when he realized there were no direct flights and that he was going to have to stop in Kingston, Jamaica. It was going to take five and a half hours to get there. He could imagine all sorts of scenarios that resulted in his missing the opportunity to find Shelley.

He texted Charles again.

"Anything?"

"No."

«»«»«»

Shelley gathered her things in preparation for her trip the next morning. Rick said to meet him at his boat at 4:30 a.m.

She was looking forward to leaving in the dark and watching the sun come up over the eastern Caribbean. The recent threatening messages induced a nearly primal instinct to get away as quickly and invisibly as possible. It couldn't happen soon enough.

She had not accumulated much as she hopped from island to island. Now she decided she was going to ditch everything, but one shoulder bag and it would only contain the barest of essentials. She had committed the information she needed to access her numbered accounts to memory so she needed nothing physical related to her nest egg on her trip. But there were a few things she decided she had to have - like cash and a phone.

She had been planning for this trip for weeks and had visited a fabric store and purchased two yards of black, nylon cloth from which she had sewn a dress. She had carefully sewn pockets with Velcro flaps on the inside of the dress that were sized to match the items she intended to keep. All that was left to do was to pack those items into small, flat packets that would not add unnecessary bulges to the dress when she put it on.

She decided to wear a dark blue one piece swim suit beneath the dress she had made. She had been wearing a wide-brim, straw hat all over the island and a sensible pair of flip flops. Both seemed ideal for the trip.

She carefully wrapped a new pre-paid phone, her contingency cash, passport, and a Pennsylvania driver's license into individual zip-lock bags. She laid out everything on the hotel bed before placing them into the pockets in the dress. She then tried everything on, smoothing out the dress in front of the full length mirror in her room. As an afterthought, she tied a floral wrap around her waist as added insurance to hide any bulges from the contents of her interior pockets. If everything went to plan, she would not need the dress for long and would be able to discard it upon reaching Florida. Satisfied, she removed the dress and hung it up in preparation for the next morning's trip. She then placed her sunglasses, and a second, new, unused pre-paid phone, sunscreen, a wallet with a little cash, some lip gloss, a woman's fashion magazine, a paperback novel, and a bottle of water in her shoulder bag.

The rest of her clothes she neatly packed into a small carry-on size rolling suitcase. Everything else, including her existing phone, phone charger and all other unnecessary items, she put in a plastic bag. She then made a final trip around George Town on her bike depositing the bag's contents in several dozen separate trash receptacles.

«»«»«»

Charles was waiting for Keith when his flight finally arrived, an hour and a half late, at the Owen Roberts International Airport.

Keith was in a fine state of agitated exhaustion. He had not wanted to arrive in the early evening. The day had been wasted in travel. He had considered chartering a plane, but found that it was not easy to do on short notice. Thus he had been relegated to flying on a small inter-island service which boasted all of 5 twin turbo-prop Bombardiers.

"Any new information?" Keith asked immediately.

"None," Charles replied.

He had been in nearly constant communication with Keith all day and there was nothing about his day that Keith did not already know. He had started canvassing the area in the morning and found plenty of people who had seen Keith's sister. But none of them seemed to know her name or where she was staying or how she filled her days. Strangely, he thought, none of them described her as an alcoholic or a pathetic lush. Charles assumed there would be plenty of information about her imbibing.

Charles had rented a car and he and Keith headed directly to the heavily touristed part of town. They spent the entire evening driving to and then walking through various beach-front bars, a night market or two and several hotel lobbies. Charles had spent the day doing much the same thing, but there was no point in trying to dissuade Keith from giving it a go. It was Keith's sister after all.

Finally Keith had had enough and decided to call it a night. Charles had found affordable accommodations at a small hotel. He drove Keith by it, but he turned up his nose so they headed back to one of the fancier places on Seven Mile Beach. Keith, for all his other shortcomings, at least had the presence of mind, or decency, to offer to buy Charles dinner. Not having the chance to eat at such a pricey restaurant except on the rarest of occasions, Charles accepted and ordered a steak, as he could have excellent seafood anytime.

«»«»«»

Shelley woke early and showered before 4:00 a.m. She had purchased a box of energy bars that was probably going to be her sustenance for the trip. She ate one as she cleared out of her room, giving it the once over before she let the door close and latch behind her.

She slipped quietly down the fire stairs and out the side entrance of the hotel to her bike. She secured her suitcase to the bike rack and peddled silently through the deserted streets, weaving her way toward the marina, avoiding the pools of light created by the occasional street light.

She found a bike rack and parked her bike, leaving it unlocked for whomever would finally take it.

Rick had given her instructions about how to find his boat. They were fairly basic. The public marina was adjacent to the Yacht Club, across the street actually. There were four docks. His boat was at the end of the longest one, which was the first one she would come to, or the most westerly.

He had not added that his boat was also one of the newest and most well kept. Had she been able to see this in the dark it would have been reassuring given the long trip that she was about to take across open ocean.

As she walked down the dock, she could see his boat even before she got close. Rick had powered up the twin diesel motors and turned on all the bridge lights, illuminating the deck. He was busy scurrying around the deck preparing his baby for the trip. Everything else on the dock, and in fact out into the surrounding darkness, was silent and still. There was a warm, gentle trade wind blowing from the west. Lights from houses surrounding the marina defined the distant edges of the early morning.

As she walked up to his berth she stopped and waited until he came aft before bidding him good morning and asking cheerfully for permission to come aboard.

“Hey, you found it,” he said.

“Couldn’t miss it,” she said from the dock. “You have this thing lit up like a Christmas tree. I think I spotted it from my hotel.”

“I doubt it,” he said with uncertainty looking beyond her toward George Town as if what she said might actually be possible.

"Are you ready?" she asked.

"Almost. I have to do one or two more things. Why don't you hand me your things and come aboard."

She handed her suitcase over to him and stepped over the gunwale. He took her things and headed below. "I'll give you the quick tour," he said.

"The head is in there," he said gesturing toward a closed door. "If you are hungry or thirsty, this is the galley. Feel free to help yourself to anything."

She followed along peeking into the nooks and crannies of the boat as they moved toward one of the forward compartments.

"If you get tired or seasick and want to lie down, you can rest in here," he said as he placed her small suitcase on a bed.

"This is great," she said.

"I'm going topside to finish up. If you could come up in a couple of minutes you can help me cast off the lines."

"Sounds like fun. I'll be right up," she paused. "Oh, before I forget. Here is your money," she said.

"Thank you," he replied taking an envelope containing a thick stack of cash she offered him. "I wasn't expecting cash."

"Is that okay? I just assumed you would want cash," she said.

"No. It's fine. Cash is good," he said as he turned and disappeared back up onto the deck.

«»«»«»

Keith met Charles for breakfast on the veranda of his 4 star hotel to chart the day's activities. They decided to continue to work the island separately. Charles would continue to troll the bar scene while Keith would see if he could make any headway with the local banks.

By noon it was clear to Keith the banks weren't going to talk. He tried his missing sister routine at the first bank and was met with polite, but complete non-cooperation. He had entered the bank and asked to speak with someone about his missing sister who might have opened an account. He was asked to return later to speak with the bank's vice president who had not yet arrived. They thought he might arrive in about 30 minutes so he waited. Ninety minutes later he was still waiting and losing patience when he was shown into an office that had been occupied the entire time he was there. Then when he made his pitch, the banker just politely declined to discuss any matters related to any of the bank's clients.

Being something of a scammer himself, Keith knew it wasn't going to be an easy sell. It was a numbers game. Get through enough "nos" to eventually find a helpful "yes." What he didn't have time for was 90 minutes at each bank. Nor would he have been happy to know that immediately after his visit, a phone call would be made to the intelligence service of the local police (it's a small island nation, after all), along with the electronic transmission of a photo of him sitting in the waiting area.

At the second bank, he could not gain access at all. The lobby was accessed via a locked door. A video phone sat on a nearby hallway table. He picked it up and requested admittance. After being questioned about his reason for wishing to enter, his request was declined.

At the third bank, he decided to change tactics and asked how he might open an account. This line of inquiry resulted in his being graciously and immediately invited to enter the premises. However, after the initial round of questions and answers about logistics and desired services were dispensed with, he hit the same stone wall. When he tried to gingerly ask how he might find a sister who was missing and may have opened an account, he basically got the response from the first bank and was summarily shown to the door.

And so went his day.

Charles, however, had a lovely day. He visited several really nice bars. He enjoyed lunch in one with perhaps the best crab cakes he had ever eaten and an incredible view, besides. By 4:00 p.m. he had tasted all the islands best rums, distributed all of his photos of Keith's sister to bar tenders in a dozen bars and made unsolicited tips of between $20 and $50 to each. All in all, he felt completely self-satisfied. He could get used to this kind of work.

«»«»«»

By that same afternoon, Shelley and Rick had made reasonable progress. The sunrise had been under-whelming. But by mid-morning the sea and sky were beautiful as Rick guided the boat to the northwest and into the Gulf of Mexico. The sea started out relatively calm. By midday they had hit some swells, but the sky was sunny with big puffy clouds.

The trip from Grand Cayman to southern Florida was about 600 nautical miles. The length of the trip was dependant on which port they headed toward. Key West would be the shortest, but posed certain logistical issues for Shelley as there was only one way to get from there to the mainland and she could be easy apprehended. Naples was farther but not ideal either, she thought. Miami seemed to offer the most potential for disappearing, but is was also the farthest. She rightly assumed that their boat would be greeted by an official representing US Customs and Border Protection. Her worst fear was that they would be intercepted and boarded by the US Coast Guard and asked to produce identification. She had managed to slip into the Caribbean on a boat and was hoping to be able to reverse the process. She had no way of knowing if she was on an FBI watch list, but didn't want to risk it. Moving undetected was her goal. Hopping a ride with Rick was the entire plan so far. She guessed she would have to improvise when the time came. But she was good at that and tried not to dwell on all the unknowable risks.

Rick had agreed to take her to Key West. If they made good time, the trip would take about 16 hours, meaning they should arrive between 8:00 p.m. and 9:00 p.m. At least it would be dark. Beyond that she didn't have a plan.

Throughout the day Rick had let her steer the boat. There wasn't anything to hit, so there wasn't any real risk. Her first opportunity came when Rick shouted to her asking if she had ever steered a boat before and if not would she like to give it a try. They were cruising at full speed. The throbbing of the powerful twin diesel engines drowned out all other sound. There were three foot swells coming out of the Gulf, but because the wind was only a few knots, they were separated by 50 yards or so. At the speed they were travelling, this introduced only the slightest rocking motion to the boat. So she found it easy to handle.

Rick shouted explanations of what all the instruments were for and how to read them. She found it all very interesting and asked lots of questions.

"Try to keep her heading here on the compass," he shouted pointing to the dial. "Want a beer or water?" he asked as he headed below.

"I'm good," she yelled back over the sound of the engines and the wind.

He soon returned and stood over her shoulder for 30 minutes or so until he offered to resume his normal position at the helm. She had made lunch for them both and took a short nap.

The afternoon wore on as they rounded the tip of Cuba and changed their course to a northeasterly heading. The sunset was glorious. The sky turned from a deep blue through shades of aquamarine, to chartreuse, to brilliant gold that eventually faded to black. The clouds were lined with golden edges and the surface of the sea sparkled like scattered diamonds. She was sorry to see the day disappear until the stars emerged and in the utter darkness of a night at sea they presented their own dazzling display.

«»«»«»

As it got darker, Rick began to be much more alert. During the daylight hours a collision at sea was possible, but not as likely. From the bridge of his boat he could scan the sea ahead and have time to make a course correction. In the dark, while the odds were still low, there would be no warning unless he kept a close eye on his radar screen. Since he was trying to make good time, the weather was clear, and the sea was relatively calm, they had been cruising at or near the boat's rated speed. In the dark, that speed could be a killer.

"Technically, I should slow down," Rick yelled to Shelley over the roar of the engines. "But as a practical matter, since we are in international waters, there is no one to enforce it. When we get closer to Key West, we'll have to slow down. But for now I am going to keep pushing it."

The night air was warm as they motored on into the deepening night. To the east beyond the horizon, they could see the faint glow from the lights of cities along the northwest coast of Cuba. Ahead of them they could see the brighter glow of Key West. Eventually they left international waters and entered the twelve mile limit of US territorial waters surrounding Key West. Rick throttled back the diesels and they slowed to 20 knots. It would take them another half hour at least.

"We're getting close," Rick said. "Should be pulling in by 9:00. We made decent time."

"This beats a plane ride, for sure," Shelley replied.

During the heat of the afternoon she had taken off the wrap she had brought along as she sat in the sun. She retrieved it from below along with her flip flops. She threaded the wrap through one of the flip flops so it wouldn't blow away and set them together near where she was sitting on the bridge.

Shelley became more and more nervous as they could begin to see the coastal lights of Key West ahead. Her instinct to flee became almost unbearable.

"So where are we heading?" she asked as innocently as she could.

"I haven't been here in a while, and never at night," Rick said. "Everything looks different than I remember. But I looked at a map before we left and I think I am going to head to the marina east of the airport."

"So is there a specific place that we are supposed to go, since we are coming from another country?" she asked.

"Yeah. I have to radio in to the Coast Guard and then get instructions about which dock to tie up at so that Customs can be there."

"How long do you think that will take?" she asked.

"We are still about a mile out, but I should call in now," Rick said. "Could you take the helm?" he asked as he throttled back the diesels yet again. "I need to get the instructions and a better map. Just keep us pointed at that red light. That's the control tower for the airport. Just head toward that. I'll be right back."

He disappeared below deck and Shelley realized this was the moment of opportunity she had been waiting for. She grabbed her flip flop with the wrap threaded through and immediately tossed it overboard into the dark sea. Rick had given her the obligatory safety tour of the boat while they were underway, including the location of life preservers and fire extinguishers. She left the bridge, grabbed a life preserver, and hopped overboard into the sea.

She surfaced, bobbing in the water, to see the boat moving away in the direction that Rick had pointed to. Holding the ring in front of her she began kicking toward the shore as hard as she could. Being a biker, she had strong legs that she hoped would last until she hit the shore. She also knew she needed to get as much distance between her and Rick's boat as she could before he returned topside and found her missing.

She was a good swimmer and probably would not have needed the assistance of the ring, but having the ring gave her the ability to channel all her energy into kicking. If Rick pulled about and trained his flood lights on her, however, he would be more likely to spot the ring. Same thing if he put in a distress call and a Coast Guard chopper managed to spot her. She could worry about all the possible ways her move might back fire or she could just press on. Her legs began to burn, but she kept kicking.

She had been in the water for about five minutes when she sensed that Rick must have discovered that she was missing. She could barely hear the sound of his engines over the sound of the wind, but she thought she heard the engines get cut, then about a minute later, she thought she heard them throttle to full power.

She kicked harder. She had to get away.

She had managed to get about 300 yards from the point where she had left the boat. However, in the time before Rick stopped and turned around, the boat had continued on perhaps another half a mile.

Charter fishing boats frequently have large flood lights mounted above the bridge. Rick had turned the flood lights on as he slowly retraced what he thought was the course the boat had taken while he was below deck.

As she kicked through the swells she could look over her shoulder and see that he was going to miss her. She kicked harder, just to be sure. Her legs hurt and she feared they would cramp up and that she would have to stop. She slowed a bit, but didn't stop.

Back on board the *Caymen "At Last"*, Rick radioed in a distress call. This was answered by the US Coast Guard Key West Sector. A rescue helicopter was airborne in three minutes. It was hovering over Rick in four and a half minutes and began a search pattern ahead of his course. Several minutes later, the pilot spotted Shelley's wrap floating on the waves and a more intensive search of that area of the coastal waters commenced.

Rick didn't arrive in that area for a few more minutes and then throttled back to almost a full stop. He had never lost anyone on his charters and was baffled how it could all go so wrong.

In the meantime, Shelley kept swimming, making straight for the shore. She had been in the water about 15 minutes and could begin to hear the pounding of the surf. A new fear arose within her. What if there was no safe place to land? She tried to see ahead, but the salt water stung her eyes and she could not see anything in the dark. She kept swimming, hoping that she would find a safe spot.

She slowed and rolled over on her back. She could see the Coast Guard helicopter slowly moving over the water, using its search light to illuminate the surface of the sea. Soon she saw the light of several other rescue vessels moving toward the area.

She resumed swimming, slowly drawing up to the shore. It was not until the last several minutes that she realized she would land on a sandy beach.

When she had made it through the surf and to shallow water, she tried to stand and walk, but her legs were like jelly and she collapsed and was knocked over by a wave and momentarily pushed under. She clutched the ring and crawled to shore, dropping onto the sand at the high water mark.

She knew she could not stay on the beach for long, but didn't immediately have the strength to move. She laid there for a minute or two and then managed to pull herself up and walk with as much speed as she could muster to the edge of the beach.

The spot where she made land fall was along a section of beach south of the airport and along Highway A1A. She had studied a map of Key West before the trip and had a rough idea of where she was. It was about 9:15 p.m. She was soaking wet and had nothing on her feet. Being barefoot and wet in a place like Key West was not that unusual. Being barefoot and wet while walking along a highway leading from the airport at that time of night was unusual and likely to draw attention to herself.

She could see what looked like a resort across the highway and decided to try to make her way there, hoping to perhaps be able to duck into a ladies room to straighten up. She stashed the life preserver behind some bushes and headed for the highway.

As she walked toward the highway, she encountered a rather pathetic lawn and realized that she was walking through a coastal park and that there were public toilets nearby. She ducked into one of them and did the best she could with her hair. She checked the contents of her inner pockets and was relieved to find that everything was still in its proper place. She removed several hundred dollars and left the rest room.

As luck would have it, the resort was a Sheraton complete with a taxi stand. She entered the lobby hoping to find a hotel gift store, but it had already closed. So she returned to the concierge desk and asked the staff member on duty to summon a cab. She felt extremely conspicuous, but no one took note. She had the look and demeanor of just another ordinary tourist on holiday.

The cabbie asked where she wanted to go and in turn she asked what might be open at this time of night. He said the K-Mart was still open, he thought, so she asked to be taken there.

It was open and she asked the cabbie to wait while she made straight for the women's clothing section where she put together an outfit, shoes, grabbed some essentials, like make-up and something for her hair. Within ten minutes she was out of the store and back in the cab. She noticed that there was a car rental place on their way to the store, but it had looked closed.

Back in the cab, she asked how much it would cost to go all the way to Miami? The cabbie turned in surprise. "That's a long way, lady," he said. "Are you sure?"

"If it gets me away from the jerk that I came down here with, yes I'm sure," she said.

"It's gonna cost you like $400 bucks. You sure? That's a lot of money. You could fly tomorrow morning for less than that."

"Yeah, maybe," she said with disdain in her voice. "But then I would have to go back to the hotel and I don't want to do that."

He looked at her through his rear view mirror. "You wanna get out of here? I'll get you out of here," he said. "But I got to stop for gas first."

«»«»«»

Rick and a Coast Guard vessel stayed in the area where Rick thought Shelley had disappeared for several hours. The Coast Guard helicopter had to return to its base after about 45 minutes. Eventually, the search was called off and Rick was instructed to proceed to port to file the necessary reports. He felt terrible. He was tired. And he dreaded the several hours of questioning that he knew lay ahead of him. For all the authorities knew, he had made the whole thing up. Or maybe they would think he killed her or something sinister.

The search and rescue effort made the local eleven o'clock news. There was no photo of the missing person, but Shelley was described as a woman in her thirties who seemed to have fallen overboard. The Coast Guard had sent several rescue teams to the area where the woman was reported missing. An unsuccessful search of the sea had been conducted where the woman was believed to have fallen into the ocean. The search had been called-off for the night, but would resume in the morning. Local authorities were questioning the boat's captain who was from Grand Cayman. More news would follow as details became available.

In the morning, the Coast Guard, who has jurisdiction over investigations of people missing at sea, placed a call to authorities on Grand Cayman to check into Rick's story and background. He had turned over Shelley's things to the Coast Guard. She had left her purse, which contained a wallet with several hundred dollars in it, a cell phone, and some cosmetics. Her suitcase contained ladies clothing and undergarments. All the things one might have with them if they were travelling. It was odd, however, that neither the purse nor the wallet contained any form of identification.

At any rate, Rick checked out, so they told him he was free to go. This came as a huge relief. He had managed to get a few hours sleep on his boat after he had answered every question at least twice and filled out a whole bunch of forms. With nothing else to keep him there, he refueled his tanks and headed home. He had another 15 hours to think about how his client could have fallen overboard. He finally decided some things are unknowable. Sometimes shit just happens.

«»«»«»

Keith and Charles spent another fruitless day searching for Shelley. It had sort of been fun at first. The thrill of the hunt. Getting close, certain that he was going to find her. He had been planning for that eventuality in his head for months. Part of him wanted to beat the crap out of her and part of him just wanted to know what exactly happened to David. Then he would beat the crap out of her.

Two days later, Keith was reading the paper when he came across a story about a woman who had been lost at sea off the coast of Florida on her way to Key West from the Cayman Islands. She had chartered the trip on a local fishing charter boat and had vanished.

Keith read the piece several times.

It had to be her. It had to be. Shit! He couldn't believe it. He had to find the captain of the boat. The article said the boat was named the *Caymen "At Last"*.

He didn't bother to call Charles. If she was dead, the search was over and Charles could go back to Nassau.

Keith asked the concierge where he could find a fishing charter. Keith said he wanted a taxi to take him there and within a few minutes he was on his way to the marina.

When he got to the marina, there was no sign of the *Caymen "At Last"*. Keith went across the street to the yacht club and asked around. He was told that the boat was likely to be out all day, but was given Rick's phone number so that he could arrange a charter on another day.

He went back to his hotel and impatiently waited for evening to come. He spent several hours online scouring Key West news papers, but most were weeklies and only one even mentioned the incident. It provided no additional information.

Frustrated, he called Wilder and sent him a photo of the article he had taken with his phone while they talked.

"Let me see what I can find out," he told Keith. "I have some contacts in Florida. Sit tight."

"Stupid comment," Keith thought. "What else could he do?"

By mid-day he had decided to pay Charles what he owed him and to send him back to Nassau. Charles wasn't ready to give up looking, but realized Keith was done. So he thanked him, took the money, and flew home.

By late in the afternoon, Keith decided he might as well wait at the Yacht Club as at his hotel. Waiting was waiting wherever you had to do it. So he settled into a corner of the bar where he could watch the boat traffic heading into the marina and ordered a drink. Then he ordered dinner. And then another drink.

Rick didn't return from his charter until after dark. Keith didn't even need to ask if it was the right one. He walked down the dock passing the tired and sunburned party that had rented the boat. They were loaded down hauling their gear. They drug their catch in coolers with wheels, although it might have been unused beer.

Rick was busy stowing gear and cleaning the boat when Keith approached. So busy, in fact, that he didn't notice him standing on the dock watching him for several moments.

"Can I help you?" he asked Keith.

Keith hadn't decided exactly what story he was going to tell Rick. The one about his sister or perhaps a new one. Instead he just went with the truth.

"I'm looking for someone. I think you might have taken her to Key West the other day. I heard she is missing, so I wanted to know if we could chat?" Keith said.

"You a cop?" Rick asked.

"No."

Rick had stopped what he was doing and considered the stranger on the dock asking questions about his recent and most troubling experience with a paying client. He hadn't done anything wrong, but maybe she had and he didn't need any part of it.

"So what's it to you?" Rick asked. He wanted to know a bit more before he volunteered anything.

"She stole something from me and I have been trying to locate her for several months. I heard she was down here and I was hoping to have a chance to talk to her. So this is bad news, I'm afraid."

"You can say that again," Rick said. "Nothing about my involvement with her is positive."

"Had you known her long?" Keith asked.

"No. Bumped into her a couple of times in a bar. Thought maybe I'd hit on her. You know she was kinda hot. Then she asks me to take her to Florida and offers me good money, so I thought, why not?"

Keith pulled out the blown up print of the black and white year book photo he had been passing around and held it out to Rick. "This her?" he asked.

Rick stepped to the edge of the boat and took it. He looked at it closely.

“Yeah. I’d say that was her,” he said handing the photo back

“What happened?” Keith asked.

“I don’t know, exactly. But it appears she ended up in the water and hasn’t been found. We, and by that I mean it wasn’t just me looking - it was the Coast Guard, too. We looked for several hours. Didn’t find anything but a flip flop and a wrap she was wearing.”

“So you didn’t see her fall overboard?”

“No. I asked if she could take the helm for a minute. We had been taking turns all day. She seemed to enjoy it and since she was paying the freight, so to speak, I was fine with it,” Rick paused. “So I thought she could handle it. I needed to go below to find a map of the harbor at Key West. When I came back topside, she was gone.”

“Who else was on the boat?” Keith asked.

“Just the two of us,”

“What time did this happen?

“About 8:30 or 9:00. It was dark.” Rick looked around his boat. It had a different feel to it now. The bright possibilities and strength he felt before, seemed diminished. “Anyway. It’s terrible.”

“Did she say why she was down here or where she intended to go?” Keith asked.

“We mostly engaged in small talk before the trip. During the trip it was mostly explaining the boat and logistics. She might have said she was on vacation or something to that effect. I didn’t really ask what her business was.”

Keith nodded. He wrote his name and phone number on the back of the photo. He handed it to Rick.

“If you hear from her or what happened to her or if she is in a hospital, whatever, I would appreciate it if you would call me at this number.”

Rick just looked at him blankly.

“You want me to call you when they find her body?” he asked.

“Yes. Or anything else.”

"Okay," Rick said shaking his head. "If I get a chance, I will."

With nothing else to do, Keith booked a flight to Miami and then to New York. There was no point in sitting around in the Caribbean. Shelley, if she had survived her fall into the ocean, wasn't there. If she had not survived, he would eventually hear about it, but Wilder could keep tabs on that.

Keith's short period of purposeful life was at an end. Or that was the way it felt to him. After David bailed him out, he set Keith up in New York. But that wasn't really home. The hunt for David's killer was about the only reason he had to spend time in Napa Valley, even though his only known relative, his brother's infant child, was there. But Keith hadn't put down roots there. Truthfully, he hadn't put down roots anywhere. He didn't have a home and knew he needed to find one somewhere.

"What people want, above all, is order."

-- Stephen Gardiner

Chapter Eighteen

Progress on the chateau was coming along. The exterior stone cladding was on track and about 80 percent complete. The roof was nearing 100 percent completion. The glazing was nearing 100 percent completion, with a few challenges on windows with irregular shapes. On the interior, all the building systems had been installed. All interior wall and ceiling finishes had received cementitious panels and interior plaster. Final wall finishes were being prepared. In some cases this included elaborate carved wood panels and molding. Elsewhere, primarily on ceiling surfaces, equally elaborate decorative plaster elements were being applied, or were awaiting the application of hand painting or gold leaf. As rooms neared completion, flooring was being laid and then covered for protection until the rest of the painting and final moulding was completed.

Neil walked through the chateau several times a day. He was pleased with the progress. He was also pleased that Lydia enthusiastically embraced the work. There was still much to do, particularly on the exterior where the final construction of roadways and the auto court and gardens and water features had not even begun.

On one of his early morning walks, he passed an area on the main floor in the central corridor where one of the subcontractors had left a mess. There were chunks of plaster scattered on the floor. The baseboard had been removed, torn off was a more correct description. And nothing had been cleaned up. There was a gaping hole in the wall through both the plaster and the cementitious board. This was both highly unusual and upsetting. He took out his camera and snapped a few photos. Outrageous. He was going to be sure someone heard about this at the morning meeting or sooner.

He completed his walk and headed to the trailer. The project was going well enough that the atmosphere in the trailer was relaxed and even jovial. Money was flowing. Everyone was getting paid. Things were going well. There was a box of fresh donuts on the large folding table in the middle of the room. The smell of freshly brewed coffee filled the trailer.

The contractor and several subs were standing around in twos and threes joshing about professional sports, trucks, and fishing. Neil's assistants were both there. A city building inspector was there. No one was in any hurry to start the meeting, even though there was a lot to do. The project was progressing so well that the meeting was a formality.

As they all settled in and meeting minutes were distributed, Neil asked who had been working on the main floor the previous day. The GC looked around the room to one of his guys and asked, "Did we have anyone on that floor? Was it Wilson?" Wilson was the firm name of the subcontractor who was doing some of the flooring.

"Nope. They were working in the south wing on the third floor," was the response.

"I don't know. Why?" the superintendent asked.

Neil fished out his cell phone and found the photos he had just taken and handed it to the superintendent.

"Whoa. Where's this?" he asked.

"On the main floor in the corridor across from the alcove where the private elevator is located," Neil said.

"I walked through there late yesterday afternoon. It wasn't like this." He handed the phone to one of his guys. "Can you ask around and see what is going on?" By late, he meant 3:00 p.m.

He addressed Neil. "We'll talk to everyone and have this cleaned up this morning."

"The owner is supposed to be here around 10:00. I want that taken care of before then," Neil said.

"We'll have it cleaned up by then, but it will take a while to patch and replace the plaster."

"Well. Let's find out who made the mess, what they were trying to accomplish, and make sure they understand this is NOT acceptable," Neil said.

"You got it," the Super said.

"Okay. Let's get going," Neil said referring to the meeting minutes that served as both a record of progress and an agenda.

«»«»«»

The next day Neil was making his morning walk-through of the chateau when he came upon another mess. This time it was on the residential floor. Someone had gouged a nasty hole in the wall on the west side of the corridor. It was larger and, if possible, seemed messier than the one he had discovered the previous morning.

"Son of a bitch!" he said to himself in anger.

He pulled out his cell phone and snapped several photos and then found the number for the superintendent.

"Dave. It's Neil. Did you find out yesterday who made the mess on the main floor?"

"No. We asked around, but no one took responsibility," the superintendent said.

"Well, they have done it again. You should come see this. I'm on the residential floor in the corridor."

He ended the call and waited for the superintendent to join him.

The superintendent and a couple of his guys had been in the trailer. It didn't take them more than a few minutes to get there. They all stood around the hole and remarked on how strange it was. Who would do this? Why?

"I want to know who is doing this, and I want them off the job," Neil said. "This has got to stop."

"I agree," the Super said. "We'll find them."

While they were still standing there, Keith joined the group. Neil nodded and Keith nodded back.

"One of the guys in the trailer said I could find you here. What's going on?" Keith asked.

"This is Keith Johnsson. He is Mr. Johnsson's brother," Neil said as an introduction. On the project site, everyone referred to David as Mr. Johnsson. The stories and rumors about his death swirled beneath the surface of most conversations about the project's scope and progress. Everyone seemed to know where he had died and where he was found. There were a few ghost stories and sightings. It seemed inevitable.

Most of the guys remained silent. The superintendent stuck out his hand.

"Morning. I'm Nick. I'm the superintendent."

"Good morning," Keith replied shaking the superintendent's outstretched hand.

"We are just looking at some damage that needs to be repaired," Neil said. "So what's up?"

"I'm just back in town and I wanted to see how things were going on the vault. Can we take a look?" Keith asked.

"Of course. I'll walk you down," Neil said. "Could one of you guys loan him your hard hat?"

It was one of those rules on a job site that had to be observed. Everyone had to wear a hard hat and proper shoes.

«»«»«»

Late that afternoon, Neil decided to walk the building again to see if there was any more damage. He rather hoped he could find someone in the act of tearing into a wall somewhere, as being caught in the act might be the only way to prove which subcontractor was involved. He thought that it was likely that the plaster sub was at fault. Neil had rejected some of the sub's work and required them to tear it out and replace it at no cost to the owner. They had not been pleased with him. However, the plaster specifications were very clear about the level of finish that was required and the owner was not going to tolerate substandard work. Even if it had been in a stairwell.

As he walked through the building he didn't see anything amiss. It occurred to him that the vandals, whoever they were, may not have gotten busy until some time in the night. He didn't have any desire to spend the night walking through the building. There was 24 hour security on site, but the project was large enough that they could be evaded easily enough by someone familiar with the building.

He decided to drop by the security trailer before he left and talk to the guard on duty. Perhaps if the guard knew what to be on the watch for, they might be able to scare them off.

«»«»«»

The next morning Neil left his office early. Sometimes he could barely manage to get out the door and to a meeting, while other days he found himself ready earlier than he would have thought with no reason not to get going. This was one of those days.

As he headed up the hill toward the project site, it must have been barely 6:30 in the morning. The west side of the hill was still in shadow and a bit of morning fog lingered along the edge of the valley. The turn off from the Silverado Trail came abruptly if a driver wasn't watching for it, the intersection was framed by the overhanging limbs of mature oaks that created a leafy tunnel. There were no cars on the road so he swung a wide turn and didn't slow, nearly colliding with a cyclist coming down the hill in the opposite direction, emerging suddenly from the vomitory of flora.

He was startled by their near miss and turned his head just enough as they passed each other to get a glancing view of the face of an equally startled, and probably angry, cyclist. If he hadn't known better he might have thought the cyclist bore a striking resemblance to Shelley. But in the fog, and his surprise, he discounted the thought to that of wishful thinking. A young, trim woman on a bike, with a cycling helmet hiding her hair, could be a description that fit countless women.

He arrived at the gate and was waved through by one of the night guards. He pulled up close to the main trailer and headed over to the security trailer next door. When he entered the trailer the guard had his feet up on the desk. He wasn't asleep, but he wasn't exactly alert, either. Here, just as with most security services, the guards were required to check in at a number of locations both inside and around the exterior of the building throughout the night. They carried a small handheld device that recorded the time they visited each designated location. This system ensured that the guard didn't just sit in the trailer all night. So Neil was fairly sure that the guard had been through the building probably 3 or four times during the night.

"Morning," the startled guard blurted out as he sat bolt upright in his chair.

"Morning," Neil said calmly, telegraphing nothing to the guard. "Find anything unusual last night?" he asked.

"Nope. Deadly dull," was the reply.

Neil checked the sign-in sheet. No one had signed in or out since the previous evening.

"All right, I'll go take a look," Neil said. "When is your next circuit through the building?"

The guard looked at his watch. "I guess it could be now. I have one more before my shift is done."

They left the trailer together and entered the building.

It was cool and dark inside. There were several construction lights burning to keep the interior from being left in total darkness. But it wasn't bright by any means. As he had so many other times, he entered the chateau from the garage level.

"So what is your route?" Neil asked the guard.

"I usually start at the top and work my way down. There isn't a specific order. I just have to hit all the check-in stations."

He pointed to a small metallic disk the size of a large button that had been affixed in an obscure location. He took a small handheld device and held it near the disk until it beeped, before moving on.

Neil said little after that. He walked with the guard to the top floor, the staff quarters, where they made their way down the hall and into only two of the apartments. At the far end of the hall, they used the exit stairs to walk to the residential floor and repeat the process.

As they emerged from one of the guest rooms, Neil stopped and swore under his breath. Several fresh new holes had been gouged in the wall on both sides of the previous hole, which though it had been cleaned up, had not yet been repaired.

"So what the hell?" Neil said. "You didn't see this? You walk past this four times last night and this does not strike you as a problem?"

"It wasn't like this," the guard said defensively. "Really."

Neil looked at him incredulously.

"When was your last circuit before now?" he asked.

"About 3:30 or 4:00," he said. "I'm telling you it wasn't like this. I swear. You can come back to the trailer and check the computer logs. Every stop I make is logged in with a date and time. I can tell you to within about a minute when I walked past here last. And I swear to god it was not like this."

The damage was worse this time, both in extent and in the clumsiness of the demolition. A heavy, short handled sledge hammer laid near by. It appeared to have been used to do the work. It looked as though whoever had done the damage had been in a hurry and perhaps was more determined this time.

Neil walked over to the hammer and picked it up. It looked similar to a sledge hammer he owned. He looked at the heel of the wooden haft.

"Son of a bitch!" he roared, startling the guard who had knelt down to look inside one of the holes and quickly jumped to his feet.

"What?!" he shouted, grabbing the shaft of his flashlight ready to use it as a club for an immanent fight. "What is it?"

Neil looked at him in anger. "This is my *fucking* hammer!" he shouted with a heavy emphasis on the explicative. "Someone is using *my* fucking hammer to tear into the walls!"

The guard relaxed a little, loosening his grip on his flashlight.

"Wow," he said. "I thought it was something bad."

"It *IS* bad!" Neil shouted as he marched toward the main stairs. "It's *fucking* outrageous!" he said and disappeared from sight.

«◊»«◊»«◊»

Neil got in his car and sped down the long drive, nearly running one of the sub-contractors off the road. He was halfway down the hill before he realized that he didn't know why he was leaving or where he was going. He was just so mad that he stormed off with his sledge hammer bouncing on the front floor of the passenger side of his car.

He took out his cell phone and fumbled for his address book, glancing up and down between the road and the phone's screen. He found Sean's phone number and hit the call button.

"Detective Andrews," Sean said in his typical emotionless greeting.

"You will not *fucking* believe what I found this morning!" Neil roared into the phone. "Guess! Just *fucking* try to guess! You'll never guess!" Neil continued.

"Who is this?" Sean asked with a little annoyance.

"First someone breaks into MY place and steals MY stuff! Then they use it to try to frame me in some rich asshole's death! Then I get arrested by the *fucking* FBI for having a birthday for crying out loud! . . ."

"Neil? Is that you?" Sean asked, interrupting Neil.

". . . and now some asshole uses my own *fucking* sledge hammer to destroy my *fucking* project!" Neil was so angry he was practically spitting on his phone. He didn't normally swear, but he was so angry the only word his brain could consistently conjure was the f-bomb.

"It's weird," Sean said. "I was just about to call you. I am afraid I have some bad news."

"What?" Neil demanded in surprise. Sean's calm response brought Neil's tirade to a full stop.

"What bad news?" he asked warily.

"I'm not sure I should tell you given your present state of mind," Sean said.

Neil was quiet for a moment, his mind racing through possible bad news scenarios.

"What?" he finally said in a calm voice. "Go ahead and tell me. I can take it."

"All right," Sean said. "I got a call this morning from the fire department. Someone tried to torch your house."

"What?!" Neil exploded again. "Someone tried to burn my office?"

"No. Your house."

Neil was shocked. It was the last thing he needed at the moment. He had made a little progress on it as his cash flow had improved, spending enough to install custom windows, essentially weatherizing the shell. He had put the cost of the windows on a high limit credit card hoping to be able to pay it off quickly.

After several moments of silence, Sean asked, "Neil. Are you still there?"

"Yes," came the weary, defeated reply.

"I'll meet you up there in like 20 minutes, okay?"

"Fine," Neil said. His voice full of resignation. He could imagine the entire project laying in a smoldering ruin on top of his bridge. However, he doubted that the bridge had burned.

When Neil got to the entrance to his property, he found the gate wide open. The fire department had cut his chain in order to get onto the property to fight the fire and hadn't bothered to close the gate when they left.

He drove up the dirt road thinking he was going to see all his hard work reduced to a pile of twisted rebar and smoldering ash. Instead, he was pleasantly surprised to see the structure essentially intact. The new windows he had just installed looked to be a mixed loss. Some looked to be okay while the glazing in others was blown out - but the steel frames remained in place.

He parked and walked down to the house for a closer look. While he stood taking it all in Sean pulled up behind him.

"It's still for sale," Neil said.

"Maybe now I could afford it," Sean shot back.

"What time did the call come in?"

"I don't know. I only found out when I arrived at the station and read the morning report. I think it was logged in between 6:00 and 6:15."

They could see smoke damage and broken glazing from where they stood. The windows that Neil had installed were expensive. While he was not happy about this setback, it could have been much worse and wasn't as bad as what he had imagined before seeing it.

They walked down the path and onto the bridge. They were able to enter through the front door which had not been damaged by the fire, but had been destroyed by the fire crew. As they entered they were greeted by the acrid smell of things burned and then doused with water. The floor of the house was wet with the prints of boots and drug hoses marring the otherwise uniform polished concrete. Toward one side of the main space a pile of rubbish and construction debris had been gathered and appeared to have been ignited as the intended source of fuel. It had burned down into a melted mass of inflammable bits. Having been started near one of the main window walls, the tempered glazing had either broken out of the frames completely or had crazed. The heat of the fire had burned off the powder coated finish from the steel windows and had left the ceiling nearly black.

The California Building Code requires new residential construction to include fire sprinklers, however, they only work when they are completed and while Neil had installed the system, it wasn't operational.

They walked through the rest of the house and came to an area where it appeared someone had been squatting. There was a thin backpacker's pad, a sleeping bag, and a few of the barest essentials. They poked through the items, but gained little insight about who they might belong to or how long they might have been in-residence.

"When was the last time you were up here?" Sean asked.

"It's been a while. I've been so busy on the chateau that I haven't had time to do anything on this. And, since it's been more convenient, I have been sleeping at the office."

"When we spoke earlier, you were pretty pissed about something. What was going on?" Sean asked.

Neil had been so focused on this personal disaster that he had momentarily forgotten about the vandalism at the chateau.

"Someone's been using one of my sledge hammers to vandalize the chateau. It's not extensive, but it makes me crazy. We've been finding new damage each morning. The night shift security guards haven't seen or detected anything. So we don't really have any idea about who's behind it. Then this morning, I'm walking the project with the guard and I find my own friggin' sledge hammer had been used!"

Neil was winding himself up just regaling Sean with the details. Sean was silent and just listened.

"Was the damage extensive?" he asked.

"No. It just started happening. Luckily it's been confined to the main corridor on the main two floors," Neil said.

"What's on those floors?" Sean asked. It had been almost a year since he had been inside the chateau.

"It's the main floor and the residential floor," Neil responded.

"So why would someone trash those floors?" he asked.

"What?"

"Normally, there is a reason that people do stuff. It's possible it's random, but then I would have thought the damage would have been random, too."

"Hmm. I hadn't focused on a motivation beyond just assuming that someone wanted to cause trouble. When I found they had used my sledge hammer this morning, I assumed they either were toying with me or were trying to frame me or something."

"How'd they get your sledge hammer?"

"I don't know."

"Has it been missing?

"I don't know that either. I haven't used it in a long time."

"Was it one of the tools that was stolen?'

'Maybe."

"That's interesting. Let's say it's wasn't missing. Then it's been here the whole time, right? And if someone just took it, they would have had to take it from your storage container. Has it been broken into?"

"I don't know. I was so focused on the house I didn't notice anything else."

They walked back up the path to the level portion of the property where Neil's trailer was located. They headed over to his storage container and found it securely locked.

"Well, at least you learned your lesson about locking up your stuff."

"This is even more strange. At least if it had been broken into again, we would have known that the person squatting in my house was probably the same person that was doing the damage at the chateau. This suggests the sledge hammer has been floating around lord knows where for the last year or so and then just happens to show up at the chateau. What were you saying earlier? That there is a reason people do stuff?

"Yep. Another piece of the puzzle, perhaps."

«»«»«»

Keith's tour of the vault was satisfactory. The outer doors to the low security vault had been replaced entirely with a more robust set of doors. The exterior roll-up door had also been replaced as had all the electronic keypads. The door to the private entrance to the vault had been replaced with a new door. It probably could have been patched and repaired, but Keith didn't want anything but the best. So it was replaced with a newer and sturdier door. Originally, it had opened into a small vestibule that provided direct access to the vault. This had been modified with the introduction of a new heavy steel security grill. This new door required all the same security as the other doors and yet another layer of protection.

By now, the interior of the vault had been completed. The lighting and humidity controls had been installed and tested. All the shelving was in place and it was ready to receive the high value assets for which it had been designed.

Keith was satisfied.

As he left the chateau, Keith knew David would have loved to have seen his vision nearing completion. He was momentarily overcome with grief. David deserved to have enjoyed the fruits of his success. Instead, he had been murdered for a painting. For someone as wealthy as David it was the equivalent of pocket change. It was pathetic. Thinking about it made him burn with rage.

As he drove away from the property he was consumed with the desire to avenge his brother. He just needed the find the killer. He thought he had been close in Grand Cayman, only to lose the trail.

He hit the autodial on the steering wheel of his car. The sound system in his car broadcast four rings before David Wilder answered the call.

"Wilder," he said.

"Josh. It's Keith. Have they found her body?"

"No. And they won't," he said.

"What? Why do you say that?" Keith was surprised.

"Because we found the taxi driver that took her from Key West to Miami. She didn't stay in Key West. She grabbed a ride late the same night she supposedly drowned and got the hell out of there. She's smart. She knew her ruse of falling overboard would attract a lot of attention and she didn't wait around until it was focused on her."

Keith had thought that David's killer was dead. He wanted to get his pound of flesh and had been disappointed when Shelley had disappeared. He hadn't been sorry that she might have died, only that it might have happened as an accident. "Where was the justice in that?" he thought.

"So what else did you find out?" Keith asked.

"The boat driver didn't know much. She paid him well for the ride. That was all he cared about. He thinks she's dead. We didn't disabuse him of that perception. Anyway, the taxi driver took her to Miami. She claimed she was leaving an abusive fiancé. He also said he dropped her off in front of the Marriott Hotel in downtown Miami. We can't find any trace that she stayed there. I'm not surprised. That would have been too obvious. I suspect she caught another ride or two. Probably took public transportation and didn't sleep until she was well away from Miami."

"So what's next?"

"We keep looking. We were guessing she might have been involved before. Now we're sure. She's out there. She'll make a mistake and when she does, we'll find her. But it may take time. As I said. She's smart. The smart ones can cover their tracks pretty good."

Keith was sitting at a stoplight, one of the few in St. Helena. A cyclist crossed in front of him and they made momentary eye contact. His mind was intently focused on what Wilder was saying and nothing registered immediately except that the cyclist was a young woman. Attractive face. She looked at him, then turned away quickly and seemed to pedal off furiously.

Then with a bolt of recognition, he shouted, “Son of a bitch!”

Wilder was accustomed to Keith’s temper and his occasional outbursts so he took it in stride.

“Keith. Calm down. We are going to find her. You are just going to have to be patient.”

Keith was anything but patient. He floored the accelerator, turning the wheel hard. He shot out in front of an on-coming car and was greeted with a loud horn. His wheels were spinning leaving rubber and smoke from his high performance tires as he quickly accelerated. He owned an elite sports car for fun, but had never demanded such sudden acceleration. The engine and transmission burst into synchronized action quickly accelerating him from a dead stop to nearly 60 miles per hour. Heads turned at the initial squeal of his tires then from the throaty muscular vibrations of his engine bouncing off the quaint 19th century store fronts.

He could see the cyclist weaving in and out of traffic ahead of him, but very quickly Keith’s progress was slowed back down to the legal speed limit. The cyclist turned and disappeared down a side street.

Keith had not responded to Wilder’s gentle plea for calm, but Joshua had heard the squeal of the tires and the roar of the engines.

“What’s going on?” he asked.

“I’ll call you back,” Keith said and ended the call.

By the time he got to the road where the cyclist had turned, there was no one in sight. Keith punched the accelerator and his car leapt forward. He braked hard as he came to the end of the block and entered the next intersection. He quickly turned his head both ways and had rolled all the way through the intersection before his brain registered that he needed to turn left. He accelerated heavily as he cranked the steering wheel hard to the left. Again his car performed as advertised and burned U-shaped rubber marks onto the asphalt. He immediately spun the steering wheel hard to the right, never lifting his foot off the gas pedal. He shot down the road, again the cyclist had turned and was nowhere to be seen.

He guessed she must have turned in the second block and he instinctively turned right, away from the main drag through town. His hunch was correct and he could see the cyclist ahead of him several hundred yards down the road. He punched it.

St. Helena is only a few blocks deep in some places on the east side of Highway 128. The transition from residential neighborhoods to vineyards is abrupt. As he raced to catch up with the cyclist, she turned unexpectedly and headed into one of the vineyards. He approached the point of her turn at a high rate of speed and braked heavily. He could see the back of the cyclist as she disappeared between two rows of grapevines. He tapped the screen of his navigation system trying to bring up the map. It seemed to take forever. He zoomed in the map and located a street that crossed the valley about a mile to the south. He spun his car around and reversed course. He was determined to intercept the cyclist when she emerged from the vineyard on the other side.

In a small town like St. Helena, speeding is strongly discouraged. If you choose to speed on residential streets, you will inevitably attract unwanted attention. And if you speed on one of the several roads that cross the valley between Highway 128 and the Silverado Trail, your chances of getting a ticket are high.

Keith sped south on the residential street that paralleled the vineyard, waited impatiently for cross traffic to clear and then made a hard left turn followed by a rapid burst of acceleration. One of St. Helena's finest was there to record the impressive acceleration with a radar gun. His reflexes were not quite as impressive as Keith's, but his lights and siren were on in no time and he was on Keith's tail momentarily.

Because of his background, Keith never wanted to attract any attention from police of any stripe. He pulled over where he expected the cyclist to emerge and looked down between the rows of vines as the police officer pulled up behind him. The spaces between all the rows he could see were empty. No cyclist emerged. He sat stoically as he received his prize for winning the race. The other contestant was a no show.

«»«»«»

Neil went back to the chateau after visiting his burned out house with Sean. He had missed the morning meeting, but walked the project with the superintendent. They decided to not bother fixing the damage for the time being as they didn't know what was going on and it all seemed to be concentrated in one area.

Neil had a long and stern conversation with the contractor and the security company. Until the project was completed and handed over to Lydia the damage was on the GC. As such, Neil's annoyance wasn't about the cost. It was about the schedule. It was agreed that going forward a guard would be stationed on each floor after construction activities were completed for the day and then through the night. It was also agreed that as far as possible, the interior of the chateau would be illuminated from dusk until construction crews arrived in the morning. As a further precaution, Neil hired a local security company to partially activate the interior security camera system where it had been installed and was awaiting electrification.

These steps seemed like they should put an end to any further vandalism.

Later that evening, Neil finally made it back to his office. He unlocked the door and stepped into the darkness of the vestibule. The interior of the house was dimly lit from the street light on the corner of the street outside, but was mostly in heavy shadow. He knew his way to his desk in the dark, and headed there with a heavy roll of drawings under his arm.

He dropped the drawings on his side table with a heavy thud. He tossed his keys on his desk and slipped the strap of a leather carry-all bag from his shoulder letting it drop to the floor beside his desk. He eased down onto the chair in front of his desk and felt for computer mouse he knew was on his desk, giving it a little wiggle as his fingers came in contact with the familiar shape.

This brought his computer screen to life, bathing his face and upper torso in bright light that flickered through various colors as his computer's operating system woke itself up from its energy saving sleep mode.

He logged in and clicked an icon to bring up his e-mail. Out of the corner of his eye he detected motion and looked up to see the ghostly visage of none other than his old assistant moving slowly toward him. Her unexpected appearance startled him and he involuntarily blurted out a profanity under his breath as he raised his arms in an unneeded, but involuntary, defensive motion.

"What are you doing here?" he said in shock. His body tingled from adrenalin and the hair on the back of his neck stood up as his muscles tensed.

"Neil. I'm sorry. But I need your help. I think I'm in danger and you may be, too," she said with a low, but concerned tone in her voice.

"What? In danger? From whom?" he asked. He was as confused by her greeting as he was by her sudden appearance.

"It's complicated, but I don't know whom else I can trust. Could you turn your computer monitor off?" she asked.

"Why? What's this about?" he demanded.

"Please. Just do it," she said with urgency in her voice.

He pushed the power button on the side of the monitor and the screen went black and they were thrown back into deep shadow.

"Thanks," she said in relief. She backed away from his desk and sat on the nearby sofa. Neil stood and walked around his desk and sat on the other end of the sofa. As their eyes adjusted to the darkness, they were able to make out the profile of the other, but not much else.

"Okay. So what is going on," he asked gently. "You scared the crap out of me and I don't scare easily," he said.

"Sorry. I just didn't know where else to turn," she said.

"How did you get in here?" he asked.

"I hid a key outside a long time ago in case I got locked out," she said. "I guess I never mentioned it and you never found it. So when I looked for it earlier this evening, it was still there."

"How long have you been here?" he asked.

"Since just after dark. I didn't want to risk coming here while it was still light, in case someone was watching your office," she said.

"And why would anyone want to do that?" he asked.

There was a backpack on the floor next to where she sat. She felt for it and picked it up placing in on the sofa between them. He realized that she had been sitting in the dark waiting for him to return and that he had walked right past her.

She opened the bag and pulled out what, in the semi darkness, looked like a rectangular object about the size of one of his coffee table books.

"Because of this," she said. She held it out in his direction.

As he took it he knew immediately it was a painting on a canvas stretched over a wooden frame. But he was still not putting the puzzle pieces together in his head.

"It's a Michelangelo," she said.

"What?"

"It's one of David's paintings," she continued.

"Wait. What? How did you get this?" he asked, still not comprehending that Shelley, his friend and former lover Shelley, had come into possession of one of David's paintings.

"I took it," she said calmly. "And all the others, too."

"You? You were the one?" he paused. "Wait. You killed David? he asked, his voice rising in protest.

"I didn't say that. And I most certainly did not kill David," she said defensively, but softly. "But I did take the paintings that went missing from the vault."

Neil was shocked. He sat there with a priceless painting that he could not even see as waves of disbelief rolled through him in mounting anger.

"So you broke into the vault, stole the paintings, and then let me get arrested?" he said in a wounded voice more to himself than to her as he began to process what she had just told him.

"Oh my god," he said. "I don't believe it, but of course! That's why you left. It was getting too close to you. Amazing. I am such a stupid *fuck*." He started to get angry as the enormity of his ignorance and naïveté came into focus.

"And now you've come back for help? Are you out of your *fucking* mind?" he said angrily.

Shelley just sat there saying nothing. She knew Neil was going to be angry when she told him she was involved. She hadn't developed a plan on how to tell him or how to deal with his anger. She was just trying to stay alive and he was the only source of help she could think of.

"I'm sorry, Neil. You were never supposed to get caught up in this mess or to get hurt. That's why I left. If you give me a chance, I'll tell you everything."

"Do I want to know everything? I think you should leave. I think I should call the police. I should call Sean," he said standing.

Just then, there was a sharp and insistent wrapping on the door. They both re-acted with surprise. Shelley grabbed the painting and slid it under the sofa.

"Hide me," she said in a whispered but desperate voice.

"Where?" he whispered back. "You can't leave this room without being seen."

She moved quickly toward his desk and crouched down beneath it squeezing into the knee space.

Neil stood as if frozen. The banging on the door continued. He looked toward his desk and couldn't see anything, so he slowly moved toward his front door. He flipped on the porch light and the knocking stopped. He unlatched the door and opened it slowly it to find Keith Johnsson staring at him.

“You are home,” Keith said. “I wasn’t sure. He took Neil’s surprised expression as a sign of weariness. “I’m sorry. Did I wake you?”

“No. I mean, yes,” Neil said in a somewhat confused manner. He wasn’t much of an actor, but his total surprise worked to his advantage. “I might have been asleep,” he said. “Sorry. You want to come in?” he asked opening the door wider.

“Sure,” Keith said pushing past him.

The house was still dark.

“Let me get some light,” Neil said. He flipped a switch and the ceiling light in the foyer bathed them in a soft yellow light. It was an old brass fixture with a creamy off-white glass shade.

Keith looked around. He noticed a bike parked in the side office.

“Do you ride?” he asked Neil skeptically.

In the dark, Neil hadn’t noticed it was there. He knew immediately it was Shelley’s.

“No. It’s one of my employees. They leave it here sometimes,” he said lying. “Let’s go sit in here,” he said, moving into his office.

He flipped on another light as he moved ahead of Keith into the space. He walked behind his desk and pulled his desk chair around in front of the desk facing the sofa. He sat down gesturing for Keith to sit as well.

As Keith sat down, Neil’s eyes fell onto Shelley’s abandoned backpack sitting on the floor next to Keith. He leaned forward and pulled it slowly back toward the side of his desk. He hoped he had not drawn unwanted attention to the backpack by his action.

“Sorry. Let me get that out of the way. I have been so busy with the work on the project that I have let this place go. I’ll find the time to clean it one of these days,” he said with a sigh.

Keith just stared at him without emotion. Neil felt like Keith could see right through him and the desk and could see Shelley squeezed into a fetal position.

“I heard about the damage at the house,” Keith said finally.

“Yeah. It’s a problem,” Neil offered. “Did anyone tell you what we are doing?”

he asked.

"You mean the extra security and stuff?" Keith asked. "I heard. I think those are reasonable counter measures."

Neil nodded. "The contractor asked around and all his subs swear they know nothing about the damage."

Keith was silent. He had been on Shelley's tail. Lost the trail, but with Wilder's help knew she was still alive. After his aborted chase earlier in the afternoon, he was pretty sure she had returned to the valley. He didn't think it was a coincidence that she showed up and then there was damage in the house. That was too coincidental for him. He thought she must have been the one who was digging into the walls. But he didn't understand why. He just had an unformed hunch, as another felon might, that the vandalism had something to do with David's death and the eighth missing painting.

They sat in awkward silence for several long moments, neither one saying anything.

Finally, Neil broke the silence. "So, is there something I can do for you, Keith? I assume you came over for a reason."

"Have you seen Shelley lately?" Keith asked.

"What? No. I haven't," Neil lied. "Why?"

"Just curious," Keith said noncommittally.

"I don't understand why you would care even if I had," Neil said. "What are you thinking?"

Again, Keith was quiet. He was unsure how far to go in revealing his suspicions to Neil about Shelley. If she was involved, Neil might be involved. Even if Neil wasn't involved, he might blow it and tip her off and she would run again.

"I just thought I saw her riding her bike through town today. I tried to catch up to her to say 'hi', but was unable to get through the traffic."

Neil nodded. He was a bit confused, because to his knowledge they had never met.

"Did you know Shelley?" he asked.

"Not really," Keith said.

"Not really as in you didn't or not really as in you did?" Neil asked. "Had you two ever met?"

"No. But I know she was your assistant at the time David called you to work on his project. She disappeared after he died. She was with you when you were arrested. It's all just coincidental stuff, but sometimes things that seem coincidental aren't."

Neil leaned back in his chair and crossed is arms and drew a long breath and exhaled slowly. It could not get more weird than this, he thought. The project is vandalized, his house is set ablaze by an arsonist, Shelley shows up with a painting she stole, and the brother of the dead guy shows up having put two-and-two together, and Shelley is under his desk as they speak.

"Look. You came by once before asking about her. At the time, I didn't connect the dots. But I guess that was why. I have no idea about what happened to your brother or how it happened or who did it. Nothing. I will say I would be absolutely shocked if Shelley was involved in his murder. She was a decent person. I don't think she would ever hurt anyone for any reason."

Keith was not moved by Neil's testimonial. He knew what perhaps Neil did not. She had stolen or at least sold the paintings. She was involved at least that deep. But he thought it likely she had played an even larger role. Either way, he was determined to find out.

"You seem to be a nice person, Neil. I don't know if you had anything to do with David's death. I've been watching you trying to figure it out. So far, you seem clean. I hope for your sake that doesn't change. But your girlfriend, that is a different story. I think she was involved. I might even go so far as to say I know she was involved."

Keith paused.

"I intend to find her. And when I do, I will find out by any means necessary what she knows."

Neil considered what Keith was saying with a look of grave concern.

"You understand what I am saying?" Keith asked.

"Yeah. But I don't understand why you're telling me this. If you think she is in the valley and she stops by for old time sake to say 'hi', you expect me to call you or something so you can beat the crap out of her based on a hunch?" Neil asked. "I don't think so. If you think she is involved, you need to go to the police. Sean Andrews needs to know."

"Oh, please," Keith said sarcastically. "That guy isn't going to find her or anyone else."

"And you are?" Neil asked.

"Yes. I am. I will not rest until my brother is avenged. Even if it takes the rest of my life," Keith said.

"Here's what I'll promise you. If you're right and she is back in town and she stops by to say 'hi', I'll ask her if she was involved. If she says 'yes', I'll try to convince her to turn herself in. If she says she wasn't, then I'll tell her she needs to go talk to Sean and have him call you down to the station so you can question her there. Fair enough?"

Keith considered Neil's approach. It's what you would expect from a boy scout.

"Do what you want. I'm going to keep looking. For her sake, you better hope she comes to you before I find her," he said standing.

"I don't think I'll have any control over that," Neil said truthfully.

He walked Keith to the door and bid him good night. He watched him walk across the yard to his car and drive away before he turned to see how Shelley was doing. She had heard every word and had probably been extremely frightened.

"Just stay there," he said softly. I am going to putter around for a while and then turn down the lights as if I were going to bed. When it is dark in here, head for the basement. I'll meet you down there and you can tell me exactly what kind of mess you are in. Agreed?" he asked.

"Okay," came the hushed and tired response.

"And if you give me any crap, I may just call Sean anyway, for your own protection. Understood?" he said.

"Yes."

"All right."

«‹›»«‹›»«‹›»

"Eventually everything connects - people, ideas, objects. The quality of the connections is the key to quality per se."

-- Charles Eames

Chapter Nineteen

Neil had some things to do in addition to his normal bedtime ritual. He pushed his desk chair back around to the normal location and sat down to check his e-mail. He paid a couple of bills. Then shut his machine down. He turned off the lights in the front part of the house and checked the lock on the door. He then went to the back of the house and used the back bathroom off the kitchen. Then he brushed his teeth. While he did this Shelley quietly slipped from the cramped confines of the space under his desk and crawled on all fours to the doorway that led to the basement.

When Neil was done brushing his teeth, he walked quietly through the house listening for any strange sounds. He did not entirely trust Keith. Given his threatening tone and Shelley's earlier warning that they both might be in danger, he thought it prudent to go through the protracted charade of getting ready for bed, just in case someone was watching. As a final precaution, and it wasn't much of one he knew, he took a chair from the front office and jammed it under the door knob on the front door. It might slow someone down or make enough noise to give him time to call the police.

When he got to the basement, he found Shelley sitting in a corner, in the dark, still curled up. There was no point beating around the bush.

"You have to tell me everything from the beginning. Don't leave anything out and don't lie to me," he said. "I have had a long day. Not a good day, either. This is the last thing I needed. We didn't have time to talk about it earlier, but someone tried to burn my house down today. So as you might imagine, I am not pleased."

"I know," she said.

"You know what? That I am not pleased?"

"About your house, and that you are not pleased," she said.

"How do you know about my house?" he asked.

"I was staying there. When they torched it, I knew I had to come here and warn you," she said.

"Warn me of what specifically?" he asked.

"I don't know what they might do next. Just that you are in danger because of me."

"Who are they?" Neil demanded.

"I don't know. Whoever wants the last painting and thinks I have it."

"But you do have it," Neil said.

"But I didn't until today. This morning. It's why I had to come back. I've been getting threatening messages for the last couple of months. At first they were just annoying. Then they started to claim they knew where I was. And then recently, they started to say that if I didn't give them the painting they would hurt you. So I had to come back and try to find it," she said, her voice trailing off.

"So you were the one breaking into the walls at the chateau?" Neil said more as a statement than a question.

"Yeah."

Things were making a little sense, but not much.

"Goddamnit," he said with annoyance. "All right. Start at the beginning," Neil said.

"You know the beginning. I took the call from David Johnsson the day he called. I googled him while you two were talking. I didn't think much about the job at first, but then as you started to describe what a huge house it was and how rich he was, I got curious. So on one of my rides a day or so later, I was in the area and I thought I would ride by and see what all the fuss was about. It didn't look like much, but it was big."

"So this was before David died?" Neil asked.

"Yes," she said.

"You're sure?" he asked.

"Yes."

"How can you be sure?" Neil asked.

"Because I saw him in the chateau. Alive."

"Why didn't you tell me?" Neil demanded. "Why didn't you tell the police?"

"Because I stole the paintings. I couldn't tell them I saw him alive in the house. They would have busted me!"

"Wow. I can't believe it!" Neil said in anger and disappointment. "All that time you knew. You were complicit in the whole thing and you just played me."

"It's not like that, exactly," she said.

"No. I'm pretty sure with just what you've told me so far it was just like that. And taking me to that hotel for my birthday, and getting arrested, and then dumping me. I think I get it now," he said.

"Neil, . . ." she started.

"Don't. Just finish telling me what happened," he said, clearly wounded and annoyed.

There was a long silence before she continued.

"When I rode by, the gate was open. So I rode up the dirt road and hid my bike in some bushes on the south side of the building and slipped inside. It was late afternoon and getting dark, but not too creepy or anything. I walked through the main floor and imagined how amazing it would be when it was done. I had looked at the plans with you and kind of remembered where things were. The ceilings were so high and the spaces so large. It was clearly going to be something else, just like you said."

"I climbed some stairs and then as I emerged, I heard a noise. It kind of freaked me out, so I hung back. Then I heard someone run by and a loud cracking sound. I peeked around the corner where I was hiding and saw a man frantically looking around. He had an open case in one hand and something else in the other. He disappeared into one of the walls where there was a space between the wall . . . ," she said.

"You mean metal studs. Right?" Neil corrected her.

"Right. Anyway, he popped back out and ran further down the hall. Then as I was trying to decide what to do, someone else ran past. I didn't see who they were, but they were dressed in black. They seemed to be chasing him and he was trying to get away. Or at least that is what I think now. At the time, I was just surprised to see someone else and even more afraid."

"Then I heard the second person, a woman. I'm pretty sure it was a woman's voice, say, 'You know why I am here, David. Give me the painting.' Then David, I didn't realize it was David at the time, but then David said, 'I don't have them. They're in the vault.'"

"Then the woman said, 'Open the vault.' I couldn't hear much else, but they argued loudly. There was shouting and then I heard sort of a wail or a cry and then a moment or two later sort of a thud. That must have been when he fell."

Neil had been listening with his eyes closed. In the dark, as she spoke, he could see the interior of the chateau and knew by her description exactly where she had been hiding and where David had tried to hide something, and then where he had retreated to and ultimately fallen to his death.

"What happened next?" he asked.

"I don't know precisely. It was very quiet. I didn't know where the other person was. I was very scared they would come back toward me to use the stairs I had used, so I moved through the studs and then made a run for it down the stairs. But my bike was at the other end of the building. From there I went out through the main room, the big oval one, . . ." she said.

"The salon," Neil interjected.

". . . the salon, and outside. I ran to my bike and started to head down the main drive when I realized that I must have been seen. I heard a shout and then a car engine start. I was flying down the road and was aware that there was a car catching up to me very quickly. I knew a trail that cuts straight down the mountain and managed to make that turn before the car caught up to me. I nearly fell a couple of times, but I was so scared, I didn't dare slow down. When I got to the bottom of the hill I headed for town on the Silverado Trail. I probably should have just found some thick bushes and stayed hidden, but I was too panicked to think straight. I was peddling as hard as I could and thought maybe I'd made it when out of nowhere, I was nearly run down by a black SUV. There is a closed bridge up a ways that cuts across the valley, she said.

"You mean by Zinfandel," Neil asked trying to keep pace with her story in his mind.

"No, further up. I think it's Pratt or something like that. There was a small landslide and they barricaded the bridge with those big moveable concrete things. So I turned there and managed to squeeze my bike through. The SUV tried to run me down but crashed into the river instead. So I got away."

"Then what did you do?"

"I came here and took a shower and cleaned up."

"Was I here?"

"Yeah."

"What did I say?"

"You asked me how my ride was."

Neil shook his head in the dark. He couldn't believe it.

"Continue," he said.

"You had been puzzling over the vault and didn't know what it was. He said there were paintings in it and I knew he was dead. So I decided to go back up there and poke around. But I thought I might need some tools, so I broke into your storage shed and borrowed some of yours."

"Borrowed? You mean stole," he said.

"It seemed more like borrowing at the time, she countered, as if her interpretation made a difference somehow.

"Go on," he said.

"So I was very careful the next time I went up there to make sure no one was there. You probably don't remember, but I took a few days off. So I had time to keep an eye on the place and pre-position some tools where I could get them easily."

"So that's where my sledge hammer has been this whole time? Sitting in the woods on David's property?"

"Yeah."

"And then when you busted into the walls the last few days, that is where you got it?"

"Yeah."

"Unbelievable. Did you cut off his thumbs?"

"No. Trust me. I didn't do that."

"Then how did my bolt cutters get down into the elevator pit?" he demanded to know.

"You keep interrupting me. Let me tell you. So I had them with me, I didn't know what tools I needed. I thought maybe that would be enough. So I had them with me when I realized someone was back in the building. I freaked out and left them in my panic to get out."

"And"

"And whoever that was used them to cut off his thumbs."

"How did you find the other entrance to the vault?"

"It took me a while, but I eventually understood that David was trying to go somewhere to get away and that I should try to figure that out. Once I did, that's when I moved your welding gear onto the platform. The thumbs were there. I just took one of them with me when I left."

"So you cut through the door and just waltzed out with seven paintings worth millions?"

"It was more complicated than that, but yes. That is basically it."

"Unbelievable. Then you set up the sting with his ex-wife and boyfriend and get me arrested. Nice."

"Neil. I never meant to hurt you or involve you in this. Sitting here now, I wish I had never done any of it. But I can't go back. It's done. And now I have someone on my tail. They know who I am, but I don't know who they are. And now I have Keith after me. Not to mention the police and the FBI."

"You've made a huge mess. And for what? A few million bucks?"

"It didn't start out as some sort of huge heist. I just fell into it and followed along. But I knew the risks and didn't stop. I should have, but didn't."

"So now what?"

"I don't know. I just came to tell you that you were in danger and to be careful. I'll figure something out."

"You should go to the police or the FBI. You're going to do time, but that would be better than getting killed. That's what you should figure out and fast."

"I'll think about it."

"You don't have much time. I've hired staff. They'll be here in the morning. It's almost eleven. They usually show up at around eight. You can stay here until then. I'll call Sean and he can come over and then you would be under police protection."

"Let me think about it."

"All right. You can sleep down here. I'll be up on the sofa. What about the painting?"

"Could you put it in my backpack and bring it to me?"

"Sure. What's it worth?"

"I don't know. Maybe a $100 million," she said guessing.

"What? Oh my god. What have you gotten yourself into?"

"It's too late for that."

He retrieved the painting and delivered it to her before sacking out on the sofa.

In the morning, she was gone.

«»«»«»

Shelley's phone became a heavy burden with the receipt of increasingly frequent threats. It buzzed with a new threatening message almost hourly. While the threats themselves were annoying, they didn't relay any information about the sender. Was it one person or a syndicate? She couldn't tell. It made her estimation of the threat more problematic.

She didn't doubt that Neil would contact Sean Andrews at some point, but she didn't think he would make the call immediately. However, when he did make the call, she guessed that Sean would inform the FBI and they would descend en mass and her freedom of movement would be severely restricted.

She also knew Keith would be prowling around, but he couldn't be in more than one place at a time, whereas the FBI and local police could be in multiple places at once.

With Neil's house and office off the list of places to alternately stay or hide she didn't have many options. She had to stay somewhere as she devised a plan for extricating herself from the mess. She concluded the only place that every potential nemesis might visit, but not thoroughly explore was the chateau itself.

So after leaving Neil's office in the early hours of the morning, she headed once again back up the hill. This time, however, she approached the property from the north side, walking her bike through the woods.

She found a sufficiently thick clump of underbrush to hide her bike and then a nearby area where she could watch the goings on at the chateau from a concealed position a safe distance away. She had already gained a sense of the daily rhythm of construction - the times that the contractor and his subs showed up and when they left for the day. Contractors seemed to start early, she noticed, and knock off early.

As she watched the site she nibbled on one of the power bars in her backpack and thought about the forces arrayed on the field. It wasn't exactly a chess match, but it was similar. And she was down to one game piece on the board.

How could she trap the killer, with the painting, satisfy Keith so he would leave her alone, keep from being arrested, and not make it any worse on Neil than it had already become?

She thought she could accomplish one or maybe two of these things simultaneously, but not all of them.

«»«»«»

Shelley's phone buzzed again. It was another threatening message. She decided she had had enough and little to lose, so she finally rose to the bait.

"What do you want?"

"Don't insult me. You know what I want."

"No. I don't. Stop playing around. Tell me."

"That's rich. You're the one playing around."

"Tell me."

"Give it to me or your architect friend dies."

"I can't give you what I don't have."

"Oh, you have it."

"What?"

"The painting."

"The painting?"

"The one David Johnsson was hiding when he had his unfortunate fall. This is your last warning. The architect dies tomorrow."

"Wait. What are your conditions?"

"No conditions."

"How can I give it to you? Where? When?"

"Tonight. You and the painting. Alone."

"I'm not doing that. I don't trust you."

"Probably shouldn't. But I don't trust you either."

"I'll leave it where I found it. If you are so smart, you know where that is."

"I do. No tricks."

"No tricks. Then leave me alone. And Neil, too."

"I might. If there are no tricks."

"No tricks."

«»«»«»

She regretted having responded. Up until then, for all the months she had been getting messages, she had mostly ignored them. Now her response had moved the game clock forward and she still didn't have a plan.

She texted Neil.

"I need Keith's cell number."

It took him about ten minutes to notice the text and respond.

"Why?" He responded. He wished she had not texted or called him. Now he was on record as having been in contact with her.

"Things are looking dicey. Be careful. Call Sean."

"Already did."

She smiled at that. Was Neil predictable or what?

She texted Keith.

"Want to catch the killer?"

"Who is this?"

"You know. I can help."

"How do I know you are not the killer?"

"I was there. I saw what happened. But I didn't do it."

"But you stole David's art! You should pay."

"Why? You got it back didn't you? And the money paid wasn't yours. I'd say I did you a favor."

Keith hadn't thought of Shelley's involvement from this perspective. He had believed so completely that she killed David that he hadn't stopped to consider what she accomplished by scamming Georgia and her boyfriend. And he hadn't needed to get involved.

"Maybe you did. What do you want?"

"Help. I need you to leave the vault open tonight. The private entrance."

"Why?"

"Let's just say the person who caused David's fall will probably show up looking for a certain item that will be inside - if you leave the door ajar."

"Then what?"

"I haven't gotten that far yet."

"Some plan."

"You got something better?"

“No.”

“All right. Make sure vault is open. Security is down. No police or FBI.”

“I can do the first part.”

“You can’t be there either. This guy is dangerous.”

“So am I.”

“Stay away. He said no tricks or Neil is dead.”

“Nice.”

“He means to play rough if he does not get what he wants.”

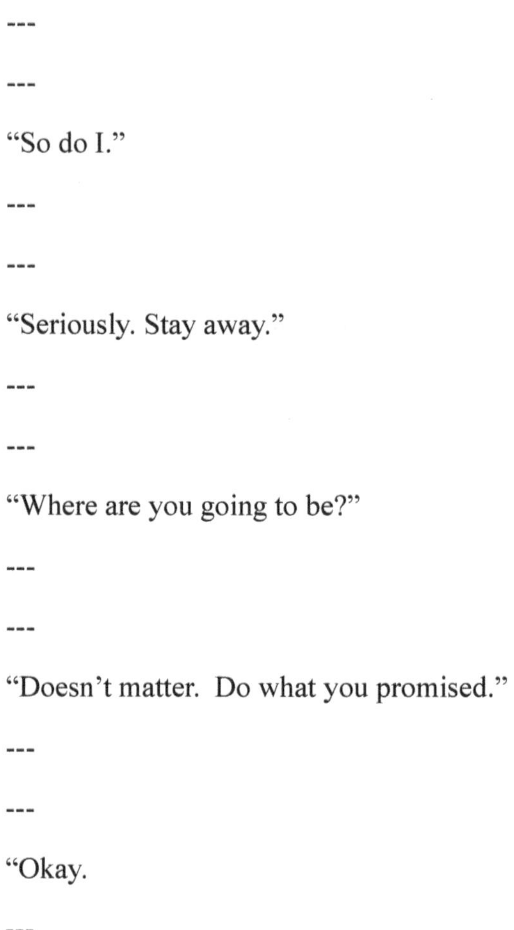

"So do I."

"Seriously. Stay away."

"Where are you going to be?"

"Doesn't matter. Do what you promised."

"Okay.

Keith reread the exchange several times then called the company providing the on-site security.

"Hey. This is Keith Johnsson. I heard about the extra security that the architect asked for. I spoke with Lydia. She doesn't want to pay for it."

The manager at the security company was disappointed, the ramp up in security had basically doubled the security level for the job and as night time security 24/7 garnered overtime pay, his markup was significant.

"All right. We'll go back to our normal patrol route. What about the cameras?"

"They can stay for the time being. I just don't want to pay for the O.T."

"You got it."

«»«»«»

Sean had taken Neil's call with no idea of how big a break in the case it was going to represent. He was in his office doing some paperwork when the call had come through and had nearly spilled his coffee as Neil had described his late night visitor and the contents of her backpack.

"Where is she now?" Sean had wanted to know.

"I don't know. She was gone when I got up."

"You should have called me!" he said.

"You're right. But it was late. I told her she had to turn herself in and she sounded like she would in the morning," Neil replied. "I didn't think she would disappear."

"Okay. But if she contacts you again, you have to let me know," he demanded.

When Neil called again, Sean had already contacted Marcus Little in New York. He said he would fly back out, but that he couldn't be there until late that night. But the call from Sean got the wheels rolling fast at the FBI.

"All she did was text?" Sean asked. "I need the number."

Neil gave it to Sean.

"And what did she say?"

"She just wanted Keith Johnsson's cell number. I texted it back to her."

"And when was this?"

"A couple of minutes ago," Neil replied. "Oh. And she said to call you and the FBI."

"Hmm," Sean mused into the phone. "Something must be about to go down. Call me immediately if she texts or calls you," Sean ordered.

"Of course," Neil replied.

Sean would have been disappointed to know that Shelley had turned that particular phone off and had removed the battery and SIM card - so there would be no tracing it or using STINGRAY or any other questionably legal means of triangulation to find her based on the location of that phone. The FBI didn't know this either and they pulled out all the stops to get a warrant to locate the phone. But it would all be for naught.

«»«»«»

Keith made a late afternoon visit to the job site after all the subs had gone home. He had gotten several calls from Sean. He hadn't answered the calls forcing Sean to leave messages demanding to know first if he had been contacted by Shelley and in a second call what was happening.

Keith just smiled. Like he was going to tell the police anything. "Fuck the police," he thought. They could do their own work. He knew more than they did and he wasn't going to lose his shot at being the first one to get a piece of his brother's killer.

"I'm just going to take a quick trip through to see how things are coming along," he told the security guard on duty.

By this point, everyone knew who Keith Johnsson was and he didn't need any ID or to sign-in. Since it was after hours and the chateau had passed the more dangerous phases of construction, the guard did not try to enforce the hard hat and safety vest work site rules. Besides, there was no one there except him to know.

Keith entered the chateau and headed to the private elevator. He pushed the call button and waited momentarily for the elevator to arrive. When the chateau was complete, this elevator would be programmed to require a security code in order to be operated. But it had only recently been powered up and had not yet received the final programming and security codes.

He went down a floor and arrived at the secure vestibule to the private entry to the vault. He approached the door and entered the temporary security code. He swung the heavy door open and entered the inner-vestibule where a second steel door had been installed. The second door was set into a stainless steel grate that looked very similar to what one might see in an old bank vault. You could see through it, but not pass through it without unlocking the door. He entered a code and used a key to open the door. He had picked up a short piece of metal stud on his way into the building. He used it to prop the inner door open and then left.

«»«»«»

"We are called to be architects of the future, not its victims."

-- R. Buckminster Fuller

Chapter Twenty

Shelley watched the house all day waiting for the construction crews to start leaving for the day. When she finally felt it was safe, she left her hiding place and slipped into the building unnoticed. Her plan was simple but risky. She intended to place the painting in the vault, wait for the unknown person to enter the vault and then to either shut the vault on them or to summon the police before they could get away. She wanted to be able to watch the vault, but not be seen. But this was a complicated and improbable goal. The only way to view who was attempting to access the vault was by seeing who was entering the elevator. Because the elevator stopped on multiple floors, she couldn't be sure where to wait and watch from a location where she could get away. She slipped through the building, oblivious to the security cameras recording her on the two floors where they were active.

Keith had retired to the security trailer and sat in one of the offices with the guard on duty watching the screens. He wished all the cameras had been powered up.

"You want me to call the police?" the guard asked.

"Not yet. I want to see what she is up to," he replied.

"You think she is the one who made the mess on those floors?"

"Probably," he said. "I need you to do me a favor."

"Okay. What?" the guard asked.

"I want you to drive my car back to Bowler's. Could you do that?" Keith asked.

"Sure, but I am not supposed to leave. I don't want to get fired," he said.

"Don't worry. You won't get fired," Keith said. He pulled out a money clip and peeled off several one-hundred dollar bills. He handed them to the guard.

"Just get a taxi and come back," Keith said. "There's no hurry. If you want to grab a burger or something go ahead. I have a feeling it is going to be a long night."

«»«»«»

After slipping quietly through the building, Shelley called the elevator to the top floor. She pressed the button for the floor with the private entrance to the vault. As she rode the elevator down her plan crystallized.

When the elevator doors opened, she pushed the 'hold' button to keep the elevator on the floor. She then stepped into the vestibule. She was apprehensive that Keith might be waiting for her, but had to take the chance. She pulled the vault door open slowly peering around it as it opened, making sure she did not leave her finger prints for Sean or the FBI to find. She was flooded with relief when she realized the inner-vestibule was unoccupied. She slipped through and found the inner door propped open just as Keith had left it. There was a light switch on the wall. She flipped the lights on and saw the recently completed inner vault gleaming with new paint, new metal shelving, and an epoxy painted floor. The vault was empty. She set her backpack down and opened the flap, carefully removing the painting from a plastic bag. She removed a protective layer of bubble wrap and a soft cotton cloth that covered the painting. She gently wiped the edges of the painting with the cloth, and set it on the closest shelf to the gate. That still put the painting about eight feet from the security grill.

She used the cloth to wipe any surface that she thought she might have touched before backing out of the vault and peered back in before finally shutting the gate. The locking mechanism barely made a sound as it secured the gate. Whomever came to retrieve the painting would be able to see it, but would not be able to retrieve it without considerable effort. She hoped that the conundrum would give her just enough time for her final maneuver.

Using her foot, she moved the piece of scrap metal to ensure that the vault door would not accidently shut. She then used her elbow to push the door until it contacted the metal stud.

She re-entered the elevator and peered at the ceiling, searching for the access panel to the top of the cab. She jumped and pushed it open. She pushed the button for the sub-basement then released the hold button. The elevator doors closed and the elevator quickly began to drop to the lowest level of the chateau. She quickly turned to the access hatch and jumped, grabbing the edges of the opening. She pulled herself up to a standing position, using the guardrail inside the cab to steady her feet. She poked her head into the darkness and with a final grunt, heaved herself up and then through the opening. The elevator came to a stop and the doors opened just as her feet disappeared through the hatch. She held her breath, but no one entered the elevator. The doors closed and the elevator began to move again. She quickly replaced the access cover, before reaching for her backpack.

"Oh shit," she groaned. She had forgotten to pick up her backpack. That meant it was still down in the vault's inner vestibule. Her mind raced. Should she try to get it? What was in it that could be linked to her - if her plan didn't work. She felt for her back-up phone. It was in the back pocket of her jeans. She had tossed the other phone and battery.

After the initial panic, she decided there was nothing in the backpack that could give her away, so it wasn't worth the risk of trying to retrieve it. She pulled out her phone and made sure it was powered down. She could not afford to have it make any noise, giving her location away.

Now all she had to do was wait. And that would not be easy. The top of an elevator is not designed for comfort. In fact it is not designed for anything other than access during periodic maintenance. There is a safety cable that is attached to a beam on the top of the cab. There is a fan mounted on the top of one of the panels to create negative pressure inside the cab, sucking out unwanted odors. There are typically lights mounted in the ceiling that project above the ceiling panels, but there is precious little space to sit or stand.

After Shelley's eyes adjusted to the darkness, she found the beam and sat down. She wrapped her arm around the safety cable and placed her feet on cross bars of the ceiling, and waited,

«»«»«»

Marcus Little and a team of FBI agents arrived in St. Helena after a direct flight from New York on a small FBI jet. It was early afternoon in New York when Sean called him. It took him an hour to get approval for the trip and another hour to secure the use of the aircraft. It was almost 6:00 p.m. before he and a few agents boarded the plane. They landed at a small private airport near St. Helena on the top of Howell Mountain at around 9:00 p.m. Pacific time.

An FBI van was waiting with a few additional agents. They deplaned, loaded their gear and headed to Sean's office.

Sean wasn't ready for what he had unleashed. He was sitting in his office reading e-mail when Marcus and his team descended on his small police station. He was expecting Marcus, but not the whole team.

Eight agents strolled in with cases full of communication gear, various portable computers, camera gear, the works.

"Hey Sean, where can we set up?" Marcus said as he stepped into Sean's office.

Sean could see the agents trailing in behind Marcus.

"Probably our conference room," he said. "It's at the end of the hall."

"Can we get some coffee going?" Marcus asked.

"Sure," Sean replied. "I'll get a new pot going unless you east coast types have to have Starbucks."

"We're not picky," Marcus said. "So what additional information do you have?"

"Nothing," Sean said.

"Nothing? What have you been doing all day?" Marcus groused.

"Well. I drove around for a while. I got coffee and a donut. Then I spotted lots of local residents and some tourists. But I didn't see any murderers or art thieves. Well, maybe I did. But they all looked like tourists."

"What about the architect? Anything new from him?" Marcus ignored Sean's not so subtle sarcastic push back.

"Not a peep."

"Let's call him," Marcus said enthusiastically.

"I don't think he is going to want to talk to you. You busted him the last time he spoke to you and he is still sore about it," Sean said.

Marcus just shrugged. "I can't always be right."

Sean reached for his phone and punched in Neil's number. The phone rang a couple of times before Neil answered.

"Hey Neil. Sean here. Just curious if you've heard anything?"

"No I haven't," he said.

"No texts?" Sean asked.

"Nothing. It's been quiet on that front all day."

"Okay. Thanks," Sean said ending the call.

Sean let Marcus know what Neil told him.

"I want to talk to him anyway," Marcus said.

"You know what time it is, right?" Sean asked. "I wouldn't be here if I hadn't known you were coming. Seems kind of late for a visit from the FBI."

"It's never too late for a visit from the FBI!" Marcus said.

«»«»«»

Shelley had been sitting in the darkness for what seemed like hours and was beginning to get cramps in her legs, when the elevator suddenly began to move. She was immediately flooded with adrenaline as surprise and fear set in. She had been committed to her plan when it was theoretical. Now that the critical moment had arrived, she felt nothing but panic.

The elevator dropped quickly and silently from beneath her. She guessed that after she had released the hold button that the elevator had ascended to the residential floor. But maybe it was the *piano noble* floor. As she dropped she guessed it was going all the way to the bottom. The elevator slowed and gently came to a stop. The doors opened. And one person entered the elevator.

She could see a little bit of the interior of the cab through a small hole where a fastener had been incorrectly installed and then removed. But it didn't reveal much beyond the movement of someone wearing black clothing and a black beanie cap.

The elevator lurched up again and then moved smoothly to the vault level and stopped. The elevator doors opened, and the occupant left the cab. Shelley knew she only had moments to put her plan in motion. She silently removed the access panel took a quick look down and then lowered her feet into the cab dropping to the floor.

She immediately barreled out of the cab, hitting the vault door with all her strength, slamming it shut. As it closed, she heard the rushing of the person inside as they realized the door was being shut. It was no use. The heavy door was closing and the momentum of the door and the force with which Shelley was pushing forced the door shut.

The fatal flaw in Shelley's plan presented itself immediately as she realized that the short piece of metal stud that she had used prop open the vault door, now kept it from shutting.

She looked around desperately for something to use to keep the door from opening. But the vestibule was completely clean and empty. She could feel the force the person inside was placing on the other side of the door. A steady and increasing force pushed against her own weight as the door began to open.

She pushed with all her might and just managed to push the door shut again. But she knew she could not hold the door shut indefinitely.

She bolted back inside the elevator, released the hold button and repeatedly pressed the button for the topmost floor. It seemed like forever as the elevator doors slowly closed. She just caught a glimpse of the vault door swinging open as the doors of the elevator finally closed.

There was a heavy thud on the doors as the elevator began to ascend. Then she heard an angry roar follow her up the shaft.

"I'll kill you!"

The elevator stopped on the top residential floor of the chateau and the doors opened again. She punched the hold open button and then depressed the fire call button creating a loud clanging sound that seemed to reverberate through the entire chateau. She bolted from the elevator and ran down the hall to the main stairway.

Keith, who had basically fallen asleep from boredom, sat up in his chair and stared at the screen as Shelley darted down the hall.

He launched out of the trailer and sprinted toward the front of the chateau, nearly colliding with Shelley as she hit the grand lobby and ran through the portico.

"What's going on?" he shouted.

"They're trapped in the elevator lobby at the private entrance to the vault."

She didn't slow down. She hit the doors and ran out of the chateau.

"Wait!" he shouted after her.

Shelley ignored the command, disappearing into the night.

Keith's moment of truth had arrived. The presumed killer had been handed to him on a platter. He wanted to finish this himself, but thought about what his brother would have wanted. David would have let the authorities handle it. He stood in the darkness of the portico and thought for a long moment before heading back to the trailer.

He pulled out his phone and dialed Sean.

"Hey. Are you busy?" he asked when Sean answered the phone.

"Kind of," Sean said. "I'm at Neil's with the FBI. They are grilling Neil again."

"Geez. Could you tell them their time would be better spent actually apprehending David's killer?"

"I don't think that is something I want to tell them," Sean said.

"Well then, why don't you tell them that while they have been badgering that poor architect, the real killer is stuck in a confined space at the chateau. Or is at the moment at any rate."

"What?!" Sean shouted into the phone. Everyone in the room turned to look at him.

"Tell them they might want to hurry. I can think of five or six ways I could escape if it was me. And if they get away, I am not going to be happy with the FBI!"

Sean ended the call and quickly announced that the killer was at the chateau. This caused mass pandemonium as eight FBI agents made a beeline for the door. Sean told Neil he would call him later if something important came of their hasty retreat.

On the way to the chateau, Sean called in an all units bulletin to both his department and to the county for anyone they could spare. He asked several units to head toward the winery on the east side of the hill, while everyone else poured through the front gate and up the rutted drive.

The small security trailer was immediately overrun with agents and police much to the surprise and bewilderment of the lone guard.

Sean posted officers at both entrances to the underground parking structure and at all the entrances to the chateau. Before long, a county sheriff helicopter was buzzing overhead. Two K-9 units arrived, and 4 news helicopters followed.

It took about 20 minutes for several heavily armed officers to be dispatched to the top floor, board the elevator and to descend, with weapons drawn, to the vault level. When the elevator doors opened, the vestibule was empty.

All they found was Shelley's backpack, which the K-9 units found very interesting. They also found a 500 year-old sketch of Michelangelo's David, sitting on a shelf in the inner vault. Right where David Johnsson would have wanted it.

«»«»«»

Sean, Marcus, and the assembled team of law enforcement officers began a methodical search of the chateau. Several officers searched the parking structure and barrel room. The officers at the winery split up with one using his vehicle to block the entry while two more entered the winery itself and searched every nook and cranny. They looked inside vats and tubs, crushers, and tanks until they were satisfied the space was empty. They scoured the office, toilet rooms, and storage spaces and found nothing. They slowly walked up the tunnel to the barrel room, using their flashlights to shine light where ever they thought a space was large enough for someone to hide.

At the end of the tunnel, in the barrel room they joined up with other officers and headed up stairs using all the stairways. They searched the length and breadth of the house, and found themselves at some point forgetting why they were there and simply marvelling at the nearly completed mansion. Not only was it immense, they agreed, it was palatial.

After searching every space, every closet, every attic pocket, they reassembled outside the security trailer and compared notes. "Nothing." They had drawn a blank.

Keith was still hanging around and beginning to have second thoughts about leaving the apprehension of the killer to the police and FBI.

Marcus wondered out loud if they had been played by Shelley. He didn't add that he might have been played by Keith and Shelley.

"What did she say again?" Marcus asked Keith.

"She said, 'The killer is trapped in the elevator lobby'," Keith responded.

"That was it?"

"That was it," Keith replied.

"This whole thing could have been a ruse to take the pressure off her. We're running around here like idiots and she has vanished," Marcus grumped.

"I'm not buying that," Keith said.

"And why not," Marcus demanded, his professional pride clearly offended.

"A couple of things. She gave up her ultimate bargaining chip by leaving the painting in the vault." Keith used his fingers to tick off his points. "She told me she was doing this because they were threatening the architect. They told her he would die tomorrow if she didn't produce the painting. She sat in there somewhere for several hours waiting for the killer to show up, knowing that the architect had called Detective Andrews and that you couldn't be too far behind him. And in my book, that took real guts."

Keith paused.

“I think there was someone in there with her. They may not have been as trapped as she thought. But they were in there,” he concluded.

“Well they’re gone now,” Marcus added. “And I am tired and have a bunch of reports to write in the morning. The FBI is departing.”

He signalled his team and they headed to their van and loaded up. Undoubtedly, they would be back in the morning.

“Keith. Is that painting safe enough for your liking?” Sean asked.

“Sure. I’ll shut the outer vault door and it will be more than secure,” he said.

Late that night after everything that could be was sorted out, Sean, as promised, called Neil.

“We came up short,” he said. “Either they got out of the building before we got there or they eluded us. So you need to be careful. This person or these people are probably dangerous.”

‘Hmm,” Neil grunted. “Too bad. Where’s Shelley?”

“Don’t know. Keith said he passed her running out as he was running in after the elevator alarm was tripped. No one has seen her since. Have you seen her or communicated with her?” Sean asked.

“No.” He knew the chateau at this point probably better than anyone. But Shelley knew her way around all the bike trails and byways of the Valley better than anyone he knew. She was probably miles away by now.

“I took Marcus through the building,” Sean said. He had a difficult time calling it a house and chateau was not a word in his vocabulary.

“Oh yeah? What did you think?” Neil asked. It had been some time since Sean had been inside and he was curious to know what he thought.

“It’s quite the place,” he said “I wouldn’t want to live there, really. But I could probably get used to it if I had to.”

“Well, you would need the billion dollars or so it would take to keep the place up. Then there would be the money for the property taxes, the grounds crew, the utilities, the house staff, the wine bills, and that is not even taking into account your dry cleaning or security expenses,” Neil said.

“I did see something that you should look into,” Sean said.

“Yeah? What?” Neil asked.

“I took the elevator down to the barrel room and when the doors opened, there was a tripping hazard. Like maybe an inch or two like the alignment is off. You might trip if you weren’t careful.”

‘Hmm,” Neil grunted again. “I was just on that elevator earlier today and didn’t notice it. Was the elevator too high or too low?”

“Too high,” Sean said.

Neil was quiet for a moment.

“Oh,” he said finally. “Where are you?”

“On my way home.”

“FBI and everyone gone as well?” he asked.

“Yeah. Why?” Sean wanted to know.

“I think you just found what you were looking for,” Neil said.

“What?” Sean was puzzled. “Oh . . . ,” he said his voice trailing off. “I guess no one looked there.”

“Right,” Neil said.

“Want to meet me there?” Sean asked.

“No,” Neil said. “I’ve had enough of that sort of thing.”

Sean turned around and dialed Marcus about Neil’s hunch. He agreed to gather a couple of agents and head back to the chateau as well. It was approaching the early morning east coast time and Marcus was tired. He had been up for 24 hours with only a brief nap on the plane, and that sort of sleep is never really useful. But he knew Neil was probably right.

It was approaching three in the morning when everyone had reassembled. One of the FBI agents was dispatched to lock out the elevator on an upper floor. Down in the barrel room, Sean, Marcus, and even Keith who had not left the site, gathered in front of the elevator doors.

The doors were pried open and a flashlight was handed to Marcus. He stuck his head into the dark shaft and pointed his flashlight down into the pit.

"I'll . . . be . . . damned," he said very slowly.

«»«»«»

"Call the coroner," he said. Then he handed the flashlight to Sean who peered down into the elevator pit. Keith was there leaning in as well to see what had drawn the puzzled response from Marcus. There laying on the floor was the crushed body of Jennifer Singh.

"Who is it?" Keith asked first, before Sean could say anything.

"It's the art dealer," Marcus said. "Jennifer Singh. When I think I have seen everything in this business and can't be surprised again, I am invariably surprised."

"Architecture arouses sentiments in man. The architect's task therefore, is to make those sentiments more precise."

-- Adolf Loos

Epilogue

Marcus Little spent a year to trying to resolve the questions posed by Jennifer Singh's death. He and his team developed a time-line of probable events that provided the broad outline of what may have happened. Even then, he was never able to fill in all the blanks and his time-line was partly fact and partly conjecture.

Sean Andrews' files contained information about a burned out SUV crashed into the Napa River that matched with Shelley Marston's story of being chased. Sean was also able to provide some information about David's Jag. It took a warrant and a thorough search of Jennifer Singh's New York apartment, including all of her electronic devices, to gather the various bits of information that established Jennifer's connection to David Johnsson.

Jennifer's apartment contained thirteen valuable paintings, along with a will, trust documents, and other paperwork from her late father, one Winston Tulles. A careful review of the all the documents found showed that the artwork had been purchased by an LLC controlled by her father, with David Johnsson as a silent partner. There were also letters from David to her father withdrawing from each of the LLC's, essentially leaving Winston in complete control of the LLC's and the paintings. Marcus' agents also found paperwork and communication between David and Winston for an additional six paintings that David had purchased that Winston had left to David upon his death. It appeared that the LLC's controlling these paintings had been joint purchases. But the most interesting and relevant paperwork involved the purchase of the work by Michaelangelo and communication between David and Winston at the time of Winston's death establishing that the painting, which had been a joint purchase, would be turned over to David.

It appeared that when her father died and she had inherited the pieces that were his alone, she had discovered that her father had spent nearly $40 million, in addition to the millions David had contributed, to purchase the Michelangelo piece. Thus began her fatal obsession with the eighth master that David had tried to place in his vault.

The documents included in her father's papers established that Blackbridge had brokered the sale of the painting to David and her father. And it seemed likely that her discovery of this motivated her to devise a plan steal it. Her plan ended up converging with events surrounding David's divorce from Georgia Calhoun Johnsson and Georgia's dependence upon and manipulation by Derek Storque.

What role Derek and Georgia may have played in David's death was not clear. Given Georgia's death, Marcus doubted he would ever know. In the meantime, Derek Storque had disappeared and was now on the FBI's list of most wanted fugitives.

Marcus could only surmise that Derek probably had been the person to break into the architect's office, stealing the plans to the Chateau. However, Georgia's purchase of the stolen paintings was perfectly clear. But whether it was Georgia or Derek or both he would never know.

He believed that Jennifer Singh had assembled a team to steal the painting by brute force. Instead, they realized that David was moving paintings into the vault in his partially completed estate. So rather than break into the vault, they decided to wait and try to intercept David as he moved the painting.

Based on interviews with the architect, Marcus believed Shelley Marston's representation that the person responsible for David's death agreed to meet her to receive the painting, but was instead trapped in the same location where David had fallen to his untimely death.

All in all, it was a strange case where the theft of a wealthy man's art resulted in his death and yet all the art found its way back, either to his collection or to its rightful owner.

In the end, Marcus Little and the FBI would continue to look for clues about where Shelley Marston might be hiding. The FBI is patient and in the end they almost always get their man, or in this case woman.

Lydia Mankovich and David's child settled into a rarified life of living in a French-inspired chateau in the Napa Valley.

Keith Johnsson continued to do what he did best which was to skirt the shadows. But in his spare time, he kept Joshua Wilder busy looking for Shelley. He had let go of his anger toward her and looked for her out of simple curiosity. He thought it would be better if he found her before the FBI did.

And the architect? He just struggled on. But he did get several calls a year after things settled down from potential clients who really did want to hire him to design their dream winery. He even managed to finish his own house. Although, he could never get Lydia to spend the night there, which suited him just fine, because even though he wasn't a huge fan of the style, he did have to admit, waking up in the master suite of the chateau beat his little place all to hell.

«»«»«»

"They say you're not a real architect until someone tears down one of your buildings. So far, I can account for all of mine."

-- JD Rutherford

About the author:

JD Rutherford is a pseudonym. That is all there is to say.

www.ingramcontent.com/pod-product-compliance
Lightning Source LLC
Chambersburg PA
CBHW020935310726
48980CB00007B/780/J